In the Rift

By Pam Uphoff

Iron Ax Press

Houston

The Miss Outer Space Pageant thought it would stir up audience interest to run their pageant on the furthest settled planet from Earth.

The New Territories, the broad region beyond the Pegasi Rift, are voting on a petition to join the United Countries and Planets.

The politics are vicious, and entangled with the widespread hijacking of ore shipments and even some piracy of passenger ships. The interested parties are closing in on the planet Autumn. Emissaries from other regions, politicians from opposing parties, corporate executives with mining and shipping interests, independent miners, established colonists, Aliens . . .

The Far Seeker is an older ship, relegated to the fringes of human territories, but with a long enough range to cross the Pegasi Rift. Stuffed to the bulkheads with passengers, including three of the Miss Outer Space contestants, their sponsors, their entourages, their wardrobes . . . and the plump seventeen year old sister of one of the beauty queens.

Jenny Poppenhusen is finding space travel rather boring.

That's about to change.

WINE OF THE GODS SERIES

Genetic engineering enabled psychic abilities in the test children. And the ability to control the machinery to open portals between parallel Earths. But prejudice turned into exile, and the escape of the most powerfully "magical."

OTHER NOVELS

Fancy Free
Artificial personalities are illegal. Destroyed whenever found.

The Lawyers of Mars
A spoof on lawyers--cold-blooded and scaly--that got a bit out of control

Time Loop
Saving the world . . . as often as it takes.

YA by ZOEY IVERS

The Barton Street Gym. A world without sleep, and a lot of unexpected consequences

Demi God A YA fantasy. When even the Gods are corrupt, how can a bunch of kids save a young prince?

Chapter One
The Fat Girl

Jenny Poppenhusen prowled the corridors of the station, trying not to gawk like a tourist.

Transfer Station Four of the Beta Pegasi system was basic and utilitarian, floating along at the edge of the gravity well where the interstellar jump ships could come and go without venturing into the small gravity waves and ripples of the inner system.

As a tourist attraction it was lacking in charm, although some of the residential areas had made efforts. But no amount of shrubbery in pots could hide the wall-to-wall spacecrete construction, the repetitive nature of the house fronts, or cover the stale odor of recycled air. And then there was the overhead . . . Ten meters up to the "sky blue" ceiling, broken with lights and openings to the decks above.

Occasional broad stairways led up and down between the station's twenty levels, but she doubted she could get seriously lost. No matter what, the station's spinning donut-shaped ring was only two hundred meters wide, and there was always a subtle balance change when you turned that let you know spinward from anti.

All things considered, the station was rather like a poorly

planned cross between a Suburban Mall and an Urban High Rise. With huge airtight doors ready to slam down in case of emergency.

It was well lit, with full spectrum lights that mimicked a twenty-four hour day. Jenny thought it was rather a shame they hadn't gone for twenty-six hours. An extra hour to get stuff done and an extra hour to sleep in, wonderful! They were two months out from Earth, in an artificial environment. Why not use some common sense?

Jenny blinked often and occasionally had to stare hard to focus. In her rather frequent moments of self-inspection, she realized she had rather overdone the teenage rebellion phase. It wasn't until her sister offered this trip and she realized what a problem glasses would be in zero gravity that she'd gone to the doctor to have her lenses reshaped. Another couple of weeks and this irritating itchiness and occasional slow focus should be gone.

Now, unfortunately, she was slow focusing on two men who were blocking her path. She'd wandered into a section undergoing renovation, apparently a bad idea. She didn't slow or show any alarm; best to get as close as possible before they started anything, if they were planning on starting something, because if the sounds behind her were any indication, she couldn't run.

She gave her vague 'publicly polite smile to a complete stranger you didn't want to meet' smile as she tried to sidestep the man on the right.

He grabbed her arm and pulled. She stepped compliantly toward him, maintaining her balance as she pivoted slightly, lifting her right knee and then snapping out her rather heavily shod foot. He saw it coming and turned to protect the obvious target. Her foot connected hard to the side of his knee. As his leg collapsed, she heaved him into the second man and something clattered to the floor.

A pistol.

She scooped it up and stepped back, thumbing off the obvious safety as she brought it up and fired. Silently. Despite the lack of shrieking stunner harmonics, the second attacker hit the floor limply.

She turned toward the others, but something about her movements must have telegraphed competence, because she was suddenly alone with the two men on the floor. She looked at the weapon, with obvious secondary welding plus an oversized power clip and realized what it must be, although she'd never seen one.

"Customized a stunner, did you?" She asked the man whimpering on the floor, as she studied the neatly welded but bulky additions.

"My knee. You broke my knee."

She nodded. "Sure did." She studied the stunner. "Regular stunners are legal where I come from, despite the problems, and I suppose they're the weapon of choice for habitats. And perfect for rapists when customized."

She eyed him thoughtfully. "Just jack up the frequency till the harmonics are out of human hearing range. Perfectly safe unless you've got a heart or breathing condition, isn't it? And point blank to the head one out of twenty or so healthy victims suffer permanently reduced cognitive function? I don't suppose you'd care if I got suddenly a bit stupid, but I care."

She wavered, pointing it at him, then shook her head and walked away. Not worth the Bad Karma, although she might garner plenty from the next woman to encounter these creeps.

She hesitated at the next 'non-organic trash' chute. Would there be any security checks getting on the next ship? And she didn't need a stunner at all, let alone an illegally altered one. With a sigh of regret, she pulled the high-rated power clip and dropped the stunner down the chute. She'd have to ditch the clip elsewhere, it wasn't the sort of thing to feed unsuspecting garbage compactors.

Maybe she should start taking some martial arts lessons when she got back to Earth. They wouldn't be as good as Dad's lessons had been, but it had been four years, and she'd forgotten a lot, not to mention getting fat and out of shape. Every time her mother had told her 'Jenny, you'd be so pretty if only you'd lose five pounds' she'd proceeded to stuff her face. 'Jenny, let's get your hair styled' was why it was in a

4

stringy, brownish ponytail down her back with a few stray broken strands getting in her face. 'Jenny, you'd look so good in these new fashions', hence the jeans and army surplus boots.

Yep, Jenny, you certain did a bang up job of teenage rebellion!

Around the curve she caught the babbling sounds of people in fair numbers and followed it back to a lived-in looking section. A quick glance at the locater numbers at the next staircase showed that she'd made the entire circuit of the station and was three decks below her starting point in the transient waiting area.

She spotted a hazardous waste disposal bin and fed it the power clip, then bracing herself, climbed back up to the passenger lounge, where the screw up in just about everyone's reservations was still being worked out. The first half of the trip had been smooth, but the transition to the next leg had turned into a major mess.

Several families with wiggly children were clustered around a vid. "Hi, welcome to this edition of 'Fanny Farmer of the High Frontier.'" Jenny noted that Fanny was the same nauseatingly perky brunette, attired in pink topped with her usual ruffled white apron, that Jenny used to watch for comic relief. Surely these colonists weren't going to . . . well maybe the twit made sense out here, but really the show was basically one big long advertisement for Xuny Appliances.

The kids were obviously not very impressed by it and were variously whining, running or fighting with siblings. The vid set was high end, producing programmed scents to match the show.

Jenny retreated from the odor of frying garlic, and wished briefly that she were in a position to emigrate, but if half the Wild West reputation of the New Territories was deserved, emigration was best done as part of a group or by buying into an existing colony. Which took money, currently a very scarce commodity in her life.

But maybe I'll keep my eyes open, once I'm on the other side of the Rift.

Beyond the vid lounge, the shipping companies' counters were six deep in pissed passengers. The air was even staler, with sweat and oily mechanical overtones. Jenny circled around the pack and spotted her sister and her entourage in the first class lounge. Ugh. Well, perhaps she could grab a book and retreat to a less populated area with fresher air. She wandered over to the lady who seemed to have been put in charge of the luggage.

"Hi Miss Pearson, have they gotten all our luggage unloaded?"

"Oh, yes, finally!" The thirty-something woman was immaculately dressed and made up, a beauty contestant in her youth she was still way beyond attractive. "They were amazingly rude when I insisted on checking that it was all in good shape."

"They're overworked, and not getting a bit of understanding or sympathy today, Miss Pearson." Jenny looked around. "Poor things, this must be a nightmare for them, putting up with several shiploads of bumped passengers."

The Pear sniffed. "Those diplomats should have used military transport, not suddenly commandeered passenger slots already bought and paid for by people already in transit. It was appallingly rude of them."

"I gather that a lot of the military ships are on the far side of the Rift, trying to impress the hicks." Jenny shrugged, stepping carefully into the pile of luggage to extricate her own small case. "Very poor planning all around." She extracted her reader and found an empty seat. Might as well just ignore the hubbub until someone worked out the mess. She certainly wasn't in charge of it.

***

Whoop-de-do! The wildly popular and famous (Ha! As if!) Nicole Peace, Miss Great Plains. Stuck on an industrial grade space station in the middle of nowhere like the rest of the mob.

Nicole's gleaming golden hair cascaded in a froth of curls over her expensively draped shoulders. And she knew that even the frown she was bestowing on the passenger lounge couldn't detract from her beauty.

Heaven knows I practice it enough in front of the mirror to be sure of that.

Like all women who live on their good looks, she could stand, sit, or recline for hours looking intelligent, alert and fascinated, mysterious and alluring, or simply blank, as needed by the situation.

This situation seemed to call for irritation, not because it could be changed, but because some show of anger might prevent a reoccurrence, and maybe even elicit a present or two. Not realizing that they were going to be abruptly dumped on the station rather than transferred straight to the next ship as they'd expected, she'd been caught wearing a casual jewel tone veil and wrap over a plain jumpsuit.

A more professional, intelligent look would have been better for standing around in public, or dealing with clerks. Anything but this soft, lounging look. Actually, something threatening, with lots of black leather and jingling chains, would have been perfect.

I'll have to remember to get an outfit like that.

She sent a jaundiced glance around the utilitarian ticketing and boarding area.

Hopefully we won't be here long enough to shop for one.

One of her assistants was fussing irritatingly around behind her. "I can't believe we've been bumped from the 'Queen of the Waves'. How could they do that?" Mrs.

In the Rift

Caruthers was a magician with makeup, absolutely brilliant, but not much help with this mess.

Nicole dumped a bit of her own frustration on the immaculate widow. "Michael assures me he had confirmed our reservations."

It wasn't as if she could vent her spleen on Michael, and in fact Nicole had better not say too much in front of anyone, especially someone Michael paid, and had in fact hired himself. Potential backstabbers, every one of them.

"I'm afraid that the government, in its wisdom, has decided to mess up the travel plans of thousands of voters rather than discommode some bureaucrats."

There, if Caruthers carried tales, it would not be of her criticizing Michael.

Michael Bornstein was not just rich, he was handsome as well. A rarity among the breed. Without him to pay the way, she'd either be stuck back in Oklahoma or traveling economy with only one or two attendants. She scanned the crowd and spotted him, tall and athletic in his charcoal suit and natural silk turtleneck.

The official Corporate Sponsors were tight with money this year, and had balked at anything but the basic travel expenses. When the contest organizers had had the brainstorm of actually holding the Miss Outer Space Contest actually out in outer space, specifically on the planet Autumn of the Eta Pegasi system, the travel costs of the contestants had suddenly skyrocketed.

The corporate sponsors had choked and barely coughed up the price of tickets. They had been delighted when her suddenly acquired 'friend' had decided to lavish her with a bit more pomp at his own expense, and had promptly elected him as their official representative.

Michael, meantime, was coming back with a scowl of his own on his handsome face. For him, she lit up and glowed hopefully.

"It's no good, Nicole, we've been bumped by a bunch of diplomats bound for that big conference on the New Territories petition. The only other ship leaving today is quite a bit smaller, although it does have the range to make Eta. Everyone's trying to get aboard, so the 'Far Seeker's' accommodations are stuffed. The company man has allotted each group two first class suites, everyone else will just have to make do in second class."

His exasperated sigh and glinting eye reaffirmed her earlier recognition that nothing more could be done. Well, any ship was better than having to stay in this . . . floating industrial park. The air smelled old and everything was faintly greasy, except where it was moldy.

"Mrs. Caruthers," Nicole turned to the matron. "I'll need you and Mrs. Daimler in First Class with me. Please sort out the luggage we'll need and make sure it is properly labeled and available."

In the Rift

Mrs. Caruthers looked simultaneously pleased and uncertain. "Shouldn't you keep your little sister near you?" she asked, rather tentatively. "She's only seventeen."

"The way she's let herself go? She'll fit in much better in Second Class. And, anyway, she's nearly eighteen." Nicole glanced across the crowded lounge toward the rotund figure slumping into a chair, looking like a reject from the Army of the Obese, before dismissing her from her thoughts.

Michael was still looking tense and it was much more important that he be happy, he was a new sponsor and she didn't know the limits of his patience.

She oozed over against him, but didn't take his hand. She'd learned quickly that he didn't like that. "That was so sweet of you to try, Michael," she cooed. "But we mustn't interfere with diplomacy. I'm sure the 'Far Seeker' will be fine. Perhaps, even more romantic." She lowered her eyelashes and deepened her voice just a bit, and was rewarded by the relaxation she could feel in the man's muscles.

Then she stiffened with an angry hiss, as she saw another woman entering the lounge. "What is Aria Dune doing here?" she asked between clenched teeth.

"She's one of the reasons there were only two first class suites available. Ethereal Savanna is another." Michael shrugged. "They were bumped off the 'Star Cruise II' last week."

"Last week?" Nicole shuddered to think of being stuck in this dump for a week.

God! It would be as bad as going home to Oklahoma.

"There aren't many ships outbound from here. The next station is too far for most ships' fuel capacity. As far as I know there are only six passenger ships on this route." Michael shrugged with masculine indifference. "Lots of freighters, of course, but nothing *we'd* take. I understand they've lost some ships, probably to accidents caused by poor maintenance, although the shipping companies tried to claim it was pirates."

Nicole shivered appreciatively. "Pirates!" she exclaimed, pretending to believe. Men just had to have danger around them to feel strong and masterful. "We aren't in any danger are we?" Oh, that nervous squeak came out perfectly! She was rewarded with a hug and a reassuring smile.

"None whatever. I doubt there are any pirates stupid enough to work such a lightly traveled route." His eyes widened at something he could see behind her.

Nicole turned to look and then frankly stared. The man had to be a bodyguard, wearing what was practically martial arts gear, all in black except for the brilliantly red sash. Two of her previous sponsors had had bodyguards, but nothing like this!

The man was taller than anyone else in the crowd by at least ten centimeters, with a deep bronze complexion. His shaved head had an angular jutting nose that seemed at odds with his asian eyes. He loomed over an ancient oriental gentleman, and the crowd parted to let them through. A rabbity young man followed in their wake, staggering under a load of luggage.

They walked up to the purser, who had been turning all others away from the entrance to the ships, but now scrambled to open the elevator door behind him. He bowed the three through with some grace, then closed the door behind them and entered something on his hand comp. Two people in some sort of uniform consulted with him, then started scanning the crowd. Were they picking specific people or groups to board next?

"Wow, who was that!" breathed Nicole.

"That was the former Chairman of the Red Dawn Revolutionary Council of China." Michael answered absently.

"What?" Nicole wrinkled her brow. "Oh, you meant the little chinaman."

Michael gave a snort of amusement. "I suppose you were looking at the bodyguard. Don't waste your time. I recognize the look, that must be one of the few remaining Red Guards left."

"You mean, one of those gene-engineered Supermen?" This time she squeaked without meaning to.

"Oh, good grief, Nicole," came a gruff voice at her elbow. "Even you can't believe that nonsense."

13

Nicole scowled down at her disgusting sister. "I suppose you've read all about them, Miss Too-Big-For-Her-Britches?"

"At least I know how to read," sneered the slightly shorter girl. "The guards are just big strong guys with post-hypnotic suggestion to make them obedient."

"I've heard that they were bred on purpose, from mixed race bastards that the Chinese considered subhuman," put in Michael, frowning thoughtfully at the ramp. "I'll go see if we can board now."

As he moved off, Nicole turned on her sister. "Really, Jenny, you'd better behave around Michael. And if you won't at least try to look decent, don't hang around me. Your hair looks awful, and how can you be seen in public in clothes like that!"

"Well, we Second Class types have no taste whatsoever, sister dear. By the time we get to Eta Pegasi, I'll probably have picked up some even worse habits." Jenny smirked up at her insolently. "Although I doubt I'll be running around in public in my jammies."

Nicole stiffened. "This is not." She stopped herself forcibly, and took a deep breath. "You are correct in that this is not street wear. Pity Astroliner didn't warn us we were about to get evicted. I'm glad to see you're finally getting some grasp of fashion sense."

Jenny raised an amused eyebrow and walked away. Really! Like she wasn't doing her sister a favor dragging her

14

out of that horrid school that had let her balloon out like this. Maybe after she'd seen a little more of the Galaxy she'd realize how important appearance was.

At the moment, a new group of unhappy people was advancing on the already abused ticketing clerks. Had this long delay been for the sake of that little chinaman? Were these his unhappy former shipmates? She wished them luck, but wasn't going to give up her space for them. She caught a gesture from Michael, who had captured one of the uniformed types, and strode over to join him, abandoning all luggage to the care of her staff. She was out of this backwater station!

Chapter Two
Into the Rift

Jenny Poppenhusen (fat chance she'd change her name to 'Peace') was delighted to get away from her sister. The tiny cabin was cleverly designed for livability. It was on the inside of the curving corridor, down a bit from the lifts and the lounge and bar. The beds folded up into plush recliners in the corners, with storage under them, two tiny shallow closets, long cupboards really, and a fold down sink.

Actual fresh smelling air blew out of vents over the recliner beds. The showers and toilets were down the hall. She tucked her bookpad and clothes under one recliner, setting the one real book she'd brought on the seat by way of staking a claim, hung her one good outfit in one of the cupboards and stuffed her case with her extra pair of shoes and everything else into the bottom of it, and set out to explore the ship.

The first thing she saw coming down the passage toward her was an ambulating coat rack. "Oh, Virginia, good! We need to find a place to hang Nicole's clothes!"

She looked at the coat engulfed woman in horror. "Miss Pearson? Why didn't you have all that put in cargo! Nicole doesn't need more than one coat while she's onboard!"

"Jenny, don't be silly! She can't wear the mink with light colors and anyway the ermine is her favorite."

A third voice came from beyond the coats. "And the Silver Fox goes so well with her eyes."

Jenny peered around the coats and spotted Mrs. Sandeman. She seemed to be carrying several very large plastic bags full of shoes. "Where are you going to put all of those?" she asked, with a sinking feeling, reluctantly giving ground as the fur coats threatened to engulf her. Time for a pre-emptive strike. "Let me call a steward, perhaps there are some cabinets..." Her voice trailed off as the women shook their heads in unison.

"We've used up every bit there is. Good heavens! Did you see how much luggage that Savannah woman brought with her! Flowers and balloons! I ask you! The captain came down to see what the problem was, she made such a fuss over not being able to bring the balloons on board!"

Miss Pearson tottered forward under the load of coats, as she talked. As she got to Jenny's cabin she pressed open the door. All hope Jenny might have had of a polite stranger for a roommate was dashed. She watched as her clothes were ruthlessly shoved aside to make room for one coat, a bag of shoes was crammed behind each recliner, and a third just shoved against the wall between. Yet more women showed up with hats, belts, cosmetics, irons and curlers.

She managed to rescue her good outfit, folding it into the

under-recliner bin and thumbprint locking it. At least that
way it would only have folds, not wrinkles and mink hair.
There were at least a dozen women running from room to
room looking for storage space. Jenny grabbed her book and
retreated to the second class lounge.

Two women were hanging out the doorway, watching the
herd of perfectly coiffed and made up matrons running about
with bundles of clothing and accessories. They were of an age
with Nicole's entourage, but there the resemblance stopped.
Their makeup was thickly applied and outrageously colored,
their clothes more suitable for younger women and quite
revealing.

As Jenny passed them, she held her breath against their
overpowering flowery perfume. Settling into a corner chair,
she eyed the women. *Could they be prostitutes?* She studied
them with a naïve joy only a teenager could feel.

And as only an ugly younger sister could, wondered if
this was what her older sister would be like in another ten
years. Their variously shocking pink, electric purple and
vivid green ensembles fairly shrieked against the tasteful
subdued browns and beiges of the lounge.

"Good heavens, Honey." The pink haired woman looked
over at her. "Those aren't your clothes, are they?"

Jenny shook her head as she instantly decided to
distance herself from Nicole. "There are three contestants for
the Miss Outer Space Contest up in first class. This is the

overflow of their luggage. Can you believe they've got that much stuff?"

"Oh!" Exclaimed the lavender-headed one. "I read as how they were a'gonna hold it on one of the new planets this year! How exciting!" She turned to the pink hair. "Kissy Poo, we've just gotta sneak a look!"

"Now, Misty," reproved Kissy Poo. "Let's not get into trouble. Let's just sorta wait until dinner time, then we can just kinda stroll by the fancy dining room and glance in."

"Three beauty queens, eh?" Jenny looked around to see a man half hidden in a corner chair. The tall, middle-aged man had just a trace of Scots in his voice. "Should make for a really picturesque voyage, eh?"

Another man entered the lounge, his head cranked back over his shoulder. "Good Grief! Who are those women? There's even more of them up in first class!"

"Oh, Frank! We're so glad you got on this ship!" exclaimed Kissy Poo. "There are three Beauty Queens on board. They've totally filled up first class and overflowed into second!"

"Beauty Queens! Well, that would explain the shoes! I think there's at least one ballroom full of fancy footwear on board." His black hair was slicked back from his face. Jenny decided he was either Italian or Mexican. Maybe he was the whores' pimp! She felt herself blushing just thinking the 'w' word. She regretfully decided she'd better not try to say it out loud.

"You should'a seen the fur coats," sighed Misty. "They were beautiful."

"I can't believe it," said Frank. "Here I am, one of a few men surrounded by a sea of women. I must be dreaming!" He looked mournfully at the colorful pair. "So why aren't any of these beautiful women flinging themselves into my arms?

"Ha! That's 'cause it's a nightmare, not a dream. You'll not get any sympathy here, Frank." Kissy Poo spoke and Misty nodded. "We've heard it all."

"This young lady," Misty paused. "Ah'm so sorry, Honey, we got to talking an' didn't even introduce ourselves. Ah'm Misty Goodwin and this is my bestest friend, Kissy Poo Tannenbaum."

"Hi," Jenny squeaked. "I'm Virginia Poppenhusen, call me Jenny. Pleased to meet you."

"And we're plenty pleased, too," avowed Misty. "As I was saying, Frank; this is Frank Monico, he was on the ship with us from Earth, Frank, this young lady is likely the only woman on board who's younger than you are." She turned back to Jenny. "And don't you go listening to his nonsense, he's not the manager of a casino, he was the assistant to the assistant manager of a casino, and we don't want to know what he did to get fired."

Kissy Poo nodded her tall pink puff of hair. "She a nice girl, Frank. You bettah behave."

21

For his part, Frank looked more horrified at the idea that he'd be interested in a drab fat girl, than subdued by the · lecture.

Jenny caught the glance of the first man, who spoke before she could ask. "I'm Abraham MacGregor, everyone calls me Mac; I run a small shipping company out of Beta Pegasi, and I'm on my way to Eta Pegasi for the diplomatic conference on admitting the New Territories to the Union."

He shrugged deprecatingly. "I'm not in the Conference, of course, I'm just a lobbyist. We are hoping to gain a concession for a midway space station." There was more red than grey in his hair, and none of the signs of rejuv that she could see. Which made him practically a youngster, these days.

"So more ships could get to the New Territories? Instead of everyone having to transfer to long range ships at Beta Pegasi?" asked Jenny. "It sounds like a near necessity for the Territories."

He nodded. "Exactly, and . . . " at this point the lounge was invaded by the group of matrons. There seemed to be a great deal more of them than Jenny recognized, and she quickly realized that all the contestants' entourages had overflowed first class. It wasn't really fair to call them matrons, as only a few of them were over the age of forty. But they were, one and all, devotees of the higher beauty culture and social graces. The verbal knives were out in force.

In the Rift

An elegant woman with an elaborate maze of woven silver-shot black hair smiled gently over at an equally elegant blonde. "I would never allow a girl under my tutorage to wear something like that in public! Really, Boudoir Chic in a Low Class space station."

The blonde returned a razor edge of perfect white teeth. "Epona, Dear! You must understand the need to appear cool and comfortable at all times. Your Miss Savannah's nubby wool was, umm, giving her a bit of a . . . glow. Although it could have been worse. Miss Peace's black bodysuit looked like a bruise with that blue memory wrap cape. It may compliment her blue eyes, but she'd better do something about the frown on her face, it will give her wrinkles in five years' time."

The various perfumes clashed in an olfactory battle. The sheer mass of esters seemed to be overwhelming the filtering mechanism of the ship's air system.

"Not that she'll still be competing then, she's nearly over the hill now," tossed in a third woman.

Jenny started looking for an escape route.

"Oh, really?" Miss Pearson's eyes flashed at the attack on her protégé. "Well, Miss Dune is a bit of a late starter. It must be so difficult, overcoming lack of experience at her age. That pleated gold corselet was a bit too elaborate, and over a skin sparkle bodysuit, much too provocative a style for day wear."

The women were gradually shifting, coalescing into three

23

groups, the staff and friends of the three contestants. Jenny was amused to see that the groups were roughly color coordinated.

Nicole's friends were in various shades of blue, not a clash to be seen. Jenny recognized some of Aria's supporters, beauty contest regulars, all in oranges, browns and metallics; by default the rainbow of intense jewel tones must be Ethereal Savanna's group from Alpha Centauri, all strangers to her.

No, not quite all, was Opal Lawson one of Aria's group? There appeared to be some poaching of staff going on. That wasn't going to improve the atmosphere a bit.

"Nonsense, she's not just anyone, lost in a crowd. She is Miss East Coast. Of course she stands out." Jenny recognized Kenisha Weatherbee, who had been Miss East Coast herself, ten years ago.

Good God! Did Nicole have me watching beauty contests ten years ago?

"Now, one expects a Miss Great Plains to be a bit more plebian . . . "

Jenny rolled her eyes, and slid through a side door into the tiny second class bar, with Mac and Frank close on her heels. Misty and Kissy Poo, followed wide eyed. "Ah'm sure I know what all those words mean, but how'd they make 'em sound so nasty?" whispered Misty.

Kissy Poo pursed her lips as she withdrew her head from

24

around the doorway. "I ain't never heard women so polite and so rude at the same time. Do you know some o'them ladies, Jenny?"

"Some of them were on the 'Moonlight Express' from Earth," she said. "And that Miss Pearson? The one with that frilly pale blue dress and all the silver and sapphire jewelry? She and half of Miss Great Plains' wardrobe are sharing my cabin."

"Oh dear," said Kissy Poo. "She looks like the sort that snores."

"SKRUUNCKS"

They all exchanged startled looks, then Mac and Frank leaned over the bar. "Please tell me that's not our pilot!" begged Frank.

The women all joined the gallery as another stentorian snore rose from behind the polished faux wood barrier. The man curled up on the inadequate floor space had pilot's wings on his dark blue uniform, but when Frank eeled over the bar and rolled him over, he sighed with relief. "He's the third pilot. Don't worry, they won't let him do any of the jumps or maneuvers."

"Will he be sober before his shift?" Mac wondered. "Should we talk to the Captain about this?"

Misty and Kissy Poo mixed exclamations of "No, no! What if they postpone the flight! Not another day on that horrid station!" "It was awful!". "And we're nearly out of money!"

Frank looked thoughtful. "Yeah, let's get out of here first. Then maybe we should call the ship's doctor? He can sober him up with a shot."

"Oh, those anti-alcohol shots are awful!" exclaimed Kissy Poo. "We should just let him sleep it off!"

The third pilot, Juan Zuniga according to the embroidery on his tunic, abruptly swapped snoring for snorting and flailing and pushed himself up to a sitting position. He gazed at his rapt audience with horror. "Oh, Jeeze," he moaned. He hauled himself to his feet and stared blearily around. "I must have tripped on something?" he suggested tentatively.

"Yes," said Mac. "And you'd better see the doctor and be sure you're fit for duty." His voice was firm and the glint in his eye seemed to promise that he would be checking.

"Uh, yeah, sure." Zuniga fumbled under the counter, and a section of fake walnut popped loose to let him reel out. "I'll go see the Doc. Yeah. Right now." He walked fairly steadily out the door and turned right toward the stairs and presumably down to the crews' section.

"I sure hope he's competent when he's sober, although he didn't seem all that drunk," said Frank.

The departure chime rang and they scattered back to their berths.

"Jenny, honey!" exclaimed Miss Pearson, holding the cabin door open for her. "Quick, now, come and strap in!"

In the Rift

"Relax Miss Pearson," Jenny sighed resignedly. "Microgravity is no big deal, we shouldn't be maneuvering or accelerating at more than one and a quarter gees."

"But Jenny! It will give you wrinkles! It makes your skin sag! And anyway, I think these docking maneuvers are dangerous."

"We're undocking, Miss Pearson. And the worst that happens is a few bumps if the clamps don't all release at the same time." Jenny opened her book and grimly settled down to concentrate on shutting out Miss Pearson's voice.

"But Jenny, you've never been off-world before! How can you understand the dangers out here on the frontier?"

Jenny, reflecting that the Pear had never been off-world before either, just murmured a vague reassurance, as the ship surged to one side and her ears and stomach suddenly floated. "There, see? We had a perfect separation. We'll be under acceleration and maneuvering into the first grav jump in seconds."

The Pear was pale, both hands covering her mouth.

Personally Jenny had found space travel a bit of a disappointment. With the advent of routine passenger service, the space companies had gone to extensive lengths to avoid distressing their new source of income. As a result, this trip had little of the flavor of earlier space flight. She hadn't been allowed to experiment with zero gravity movement or anything!

She wiggled her floating toes a bit and decided to flout the regulations. The Pear predictably shrieked when she unclipped her restraints. "Relax, I just want to see what it's like." Then the ship turned under her, and she grabbed the chair and got her feet down just as the acceleration began. And she did sag. It was like carrying a heavy load. Or being even fatter, perhaps.

She lumbered around the room, ignoring the Pear's moans, then cracked open the door. Piercing screams that had failed to penetrate the heavy door assailed her ears. But rather than a battlefield, she seemed to be facing a field day.

"I can still lift you," chortled a small figure, hoisting a screaming, slightly smaller figure off the ground.

"Me next! Me next!" a third figure capered around the others with a supreme disregard of the acceleration.

"No! No!" screeched a voice from one of two open doors. "You come back here this instant!"

"Obey your mother this instant!" bellowed another voice from the next room. "Adam! Put your brother down NOW!"

"Be careful!" screeched Mother.

"Now!" bellow.

"I didn't get my turn!"

Jenny closed the door on the happy family and stumped back to her recliner.

Chapter Three
Meet-N-Greet

Nicole said nothing until her stomach settled down from the jump. It wouldn't do to belch instead of speak. She could feel the rush of relaxation as her nerves stopped jangling in response to the harmonics of the transition. At least jumps were so short you barely had time to feel sick before they were over.

"This is much nicer than I had expected!" She made her voice appreciative as she gestured around the small room. "These suites are very well appointed." She did not mention that they were half the size of the suites on the ship from Earth nor voice her opinion of the color combinations. The pastel mauve and lavender clashed horribly with her best colors, but Rule Number One was always show your appreciation to your sponsor. Or you'll lose him.

But it is a pokey little excuse for a first class suite. Stuck in here for twenty-eight days! Ninety-eight jumps. God, this contest had better be worth it.

"Just a few weeks, then we'll see," Michael threw her a toothy unamused smile, "if the diplomats have also taken over our reserved hotel suites."

"What!" She was momentarily appalled. "They wouldn't!

The Hotel Pegasus is hosting the Pageant!" Her voice firmed. "They won't have."

"Good thought." Michael looked impressed, maybe he liked smart women? Should she change tactics? Maybe she'd start watching the news, just in case she needed to say something intelligent.

"Let's circulate and see who else is aboard." He led the way out.

Nicole snatched a quick glance at the mirror, checking that nothing had changed since she'd renewed her makeup five minutes earlier.

Wait till Aria and Ethereal see my new deconstructed look ivory silk suit.

She followed him down the ramp to the Lounge. Really, it felt so odd! He was the first sponsor she'd had that didn't want her draped all over him. Except in bed he hardly touched her. He paused to scan the lounge before entering, then steered her to a plump mahogany leather chair facing diagonally out into the room. She sank down gracefully, not leaning back; slumping was so unattractive.

Michael sat beside her, his eyes studying the first class passengers as they trickled into the lounge. FarCo had parceled out the few first class suites among all the groups aboard, so Nicole was gratified to see that her rivals also had only a few courtiers in attendance. Aria's sponsor was a grossly fat man, strutting about with his hand on Aria's shoulder as if to emphasize his ownership. To the detriment of her wing shoulder pads. She was seriously stuck on gold. It went well with her copper hair and asymmetric metallic accessories, but couldn't she vary it a bit?

Ethereal Savannah's scarlet flounces were for naught, her sponsor's attention was on everything but her. The appalling young musician seemed unable to keep his hands off anything, running them along the furniture, touching the pictures on the walls, hugging women, shaking hands with the few men around. Aria's fat man glared when the musician kissed Aria's hand. But the creep turned away and approached the old chinaman as he entered the room. The musician just sort of bounced off the big dark man who was suddenly between them. The bodyguard looked expressionlessly down at the weedy musician, who, displaying surprising common sense, backed quickly away and circled over to Nicole.

"Well, well, well, the last of the beautiful ladies on board. Miss Great Plains, is it? How inappropriate!" He ogled her cleavage. "I'm Paris, and I'm very glad to make your acquaintance."

His bodysuit was reasonable for the ambiance, black with just a hint of sparkle and his makeup a bare echo of his stage paint, but still . . .

"How do you do?" Nicole kept her hands in her lap and her voice cool. Paris grinned and perched impertinently on the arm of her chair to hug her or perhaps gain a better perspective for ogling. She chilled her gaze and said absolutely nothing. It was an expression she'd picked up from her mother. It worked as well on rude musicians as it had on her drunken stepfather. Which was to say, not at all. Fortunately Paris was distracted by the entry of the ship's officers.

Captain Portman was a pleasant middle-aged man, blond going gray and balding. The officer with him, the ship's doctor by his insignia, was tall and handsome, but with a certain hard edge, as if he'd lived an exciting life. Nicole admired his strong features, set off by distinguished silver wings brushed back into his brown hair.

Paris bounced off the chair arm and made a beeline for the officers.

"What a remarkably obnoxious young man. Pity he can't sing or play a musical instrument. I can forgive a true musician much." Michael was amused, not upset by Paris' attentions, good. Hmm, would he mind if she spoke to that handsome doctor? Maybe she shouldn't risk it. If she'd learned anything in twenty-one years, it was never offend the man with the money.

Michael didn't seem inclined to meet the captain, so she sat and watched as the rest of the first class passengers drifted in. There were lots of women, mostly here to assist the beauty contestants, plus a few boring old couples. Four ugly businessmen; at least their wives were well dressed, if in conservative styles and clashing reds. They moved as a group, splitting up occasionally, but always drifting back together. This new fad of looking old was weird. Supposed to get respect? Not in her circles. At the first sign of wrinkles, she was going straight to the nearest rejuve clinic.

She watched in fascination the Cinnab that entered. Dressed in a rather old fashioned tuxedo, he, it, whatever, didn't look at all human, thank goodness. The natural Cinnaban ability to camouflage themselves by taking on a few surface characteristics of their usual prey depended on their eating the prey. Vat grown or not, it was a bit unnerving to know an alien was eating human flesh. So she shouldn't mind his sickly pale greenish skin. Really.

And thank god he doesn't seem to be staying!

Surveying the room, she decided Michael and the doctor were the only worthwhile men on board. And perhaps the dark bodyguard. She snuck another peek. No, he was creepy, she decided. His little chinaman master stood aloof, with perhaps a hint of superiority in his expression. He was a bit creepy in his own way.

She'd definitely have to find a way to spend some time with that mouth wateringly handsome doctor!

The Cinnaban came back, no the clothes were different, this was a new one, also icky green. Like the first, he just spoke briefly to the Captain, then left.

Immaculately uniformed waiters were circulating with drinks and canapés. She graciously accepted white wine, for the form of it. She wasn't about to risk her makeup, not to mention the calories, but carrying it gave her something graceful to do with her hands and arms.

The drool-worthy doctor walked over and bowed over her hand. "Miss Peace, what a pleasure. I'm Doctor Bernard Zimmer." His eyes admired her.

"Usually these icebreakers are deathly boring." He nodded politely to Michael to include him in the conversation. "But this one is setting a new standard of excellence."

She gave him her best smile. "I always enjoy watching people." Her eyes drifted to yet another Cinnab walking down the ramp. "You seem to have a lot of Cinnabs on board."

"Only three, but they're even more anti-social among themselves than they are with humans. That's why they're coming down one at a time." He smiled down at her.

God he was handsome!

"Avoiding their competition."

Michael shifted restlessly, and she felt a moment's panic at the thought that she might have made him angry so quickly.

"Excuse me a moment, Nicole, I want to talk to someone." He rose abruptly and stalked off.

34

In the Rift

She gave a frozen smile to the doctor and stood up quickly, nearly spilling the wine.

The doctor supported her with a great deal more physical contact than necessary, and she automatically leaned into him, while scanning for Michael. He wasn't talking to anyone, he just walked around a bit, took another glass of wine from a waiter and circled back.

Oh god, he is angry.

"Careful, my dear, the movement of the ship isn't as steady as real gravity." The doctor wasn't showing any sign of wanting to let go of her, which under other circumstances she would have taken full advantage of. Now she was a bit exasperated to find she couldn't get around him without being rude.

"I probably ought to walk around a bit and find my sea legs, so to speak." She smiled more and shifted to put her hand on his arm and try to turn him so she could walk him out of this corner.

He finally obliged her by shifting enough that she could walk past him, but moved along beside her. "Would you like a tour of the ship?" What a smile the man had!

Michael had stopped and was talking to Ethereal. "Perhaps another day." Her own smile was frozen, now. "I'm a bit tired tonight." *She'd better not touch my sponsor. Damn, damn, damn.*

"Another time, then, perhaps." The doctor finally

accepted his dismissal, and Nicole moved in to deal with the poacher. Wait a bit, the doctor was ideal.

She turned back to him. "Have you met Miss Alpha Centauri?" As he began to shake his head, she gracefully tucked a hand back under his arm and ruthlessly towed him over. "Ethereal, have you met Doctor Zimmer?" She leaned on him for just a second, for maximum effect, then straightened and dropped her grip as Michael turned around.

Ethereal fairly drooled as she oozed over to offer her hand. "Oh, I can see I'm going to be very ill this trip." Her dark eyes gleamed a bit hungrily.

Nicole was surprised to see that the doctor seemed a bit less than enthusiastic; his opening comment left no doubt as to the cause. "Alpha Centauri? Are you from one of the pioneering families?"

What a polite way to ask if you are part chimpanzee! Nicole covered her glee firmly.

"Oh, no." Ethereal's smile was a bit edged. At least the doctor was polite enough not to study her hands or hairline, not that he'd see anything, of course. "We're a relatively new family, my grandparents immigrated. It's home, but in some ways we pure humans never seem to really fit in." She gave an elegant shrug, very effective in her strapless gown. "I suppose it will always be that way."

You protest too much and I know it. You're ashamed of

36

your other grandparents, aren't you, darling? Nicole squelched a brief flash of sympathy. *My step-father's pretty low rent and I wish Mom had sense enough to kick him out, but I don't lie about them. And I was never ashamed of Dad.*

Zimmer, however, was now beaming at Ethereal. *Bigot. Hell with him.*

She turned to find Michael picking up another glass tendered by a waiter. As Ethereal steered her captive away, Michael surveyed the room thoughtfully. "I think I've seen quite enough of our fellow passengers. Stay and visit if you wish, but I'm going to deal with some mail and relax before dinner."

That seemed a broad enough hint that he wanted some privacy, so she smiled to hide incipient panic and murmured, "I'll mix a bit more." Her smile was starting to hurt as she turned away.

"Miss Peace, I missed you earlier!" She looked up quickly to see the captain of the ship advancing on her.

"Captain Portman, what a pleasure." Not enough emphasis to be a gush, but her warmest smile.

"Well," he twinkled at her, "I suspect it is more of a pleasure for me than for you. Dirty trick Astroliner played on you. None of that nonsense with FarCo. I'm glad to say." He cleared his throat a bit. "I know how awkward it must be for you to have sent most of your party down to Second Class, and I thought we could do just a bit to cheer them up.

"I've convinced my chef to make a special effort, so we'll be putting out two dinners every night up here in First Class. Your friends can join you up here on a," he looked a bit embarrassed, "rotating basis."

He spread his hands apologetically. "I wish they could come every day, but we don't quite have room enough. Perhaps you could invite six of them to dinner each evening?"

Her smile widened, probably as genuine as it had been all day. "That would be marvelous, Captain." She twinkled at him. "Are you sure you're not one of the diplomats bound for the conference yourself?"

"Nothing of the sort I assure you," he beamed back. "Those amateurs should try a few years in my shoes if they really wanted to learn their trade."

Oh my, a sense of humor. How irresistible! Bet he's been married for two decades minimum.

"You sound like you like the company, have you been with them long?" Ah, the joy of small-talk with a nice man. Not a bad way to wind up a party. Putting her worries out of her mind, she decided it was time to relax and actually enjoy herself.

Chapter Four

A Romantic Cruise—Not!

Neil Perris, better known as Paris-the-rich-and-famous-crash-rock-star, braced himself when he saw the expression on Ethereal's face. *I knew this assignment was a bad idea. I knew it.*

"This is a dump and you are horribly embarrassing." At least Ethereal wasn't one to beat about the bush, he was about to be told exactly why she was upset. The red of her dress reflected in her eyes. At least he hoped it was a reflection.

"Look," Paris gritted his teeth. "You take the bedroom and I'll sleep out here, we'll just cruise along pretending we're friends until the contest is over, then go our separate ways in peace, hopefully you with a crown on your head." *No doubt about it, getting together with an old girlfriend was turning out to be a very, very bad idea.*

"You dumped me and talked with everyone but me."

"You said," Paris tried to consciously relax his jaw. "That you wanted me to leave you alone. If you didn't mean it, you shouldn't have said it. I have trouble with mind reading, in fact I can't do it at all." He took a deep breath and tried to relax the rest of his body. "Why don't I escort you down to the early dinner..."

"No." She glared. "The late dinner. Let's at least pretend to both be civilized and sophisticated. I'll be getting enough comments about being from Alpha without acting like a chimp from the sticks."

This looked like a good time to give a bit. "Late, sure, no problem. Umm, I'll just read out here until you've changed."

"Are you implying that you don't like this outfit?" Her eyes narrowed dangerously, and her hands flexed. Not a good sign. She, like most Alpha Centaurians, including himself, had a few ichimp genes. He had no wish to find out if hers involved the more-than-human strength and speed some people inherited.

Was there any way to be both honest and non-inflammatory? Was there a way to lie and quiet this down? No and no. Or maybe. "I've never yet seen you go out in public in the same outfit twice in a row."

She actually stopped and thought for a moment, tapping her long fingernails on the tiny table next to her until she noticed she was doing it and returned her elegant hand to the approved graceful position. "This dress is appropriate for an onboard icebreaker. It is not suitable for a hopefully elegant late dinner. You are absolutely correct that I am going to change." She smiled, showing a great deal of teeth. "Perhaps you would be so kind as to fetch my staff?" And not come back was unspoken, but understood.

40

In the Rift

"Delighted." He practically bolted out the door, dancing around the aforementioned staff that was assembled and armed and about to ring the door chime. "All yours, Ladies," he said. The elegant Epona Venture raised an amused eyebrow at him. Little Sallie Halfacre, the most ichimpish of the Alphan contingent, snickered a bit as he retreated. A couple of them looked sympathetic, and perhaps even envious. Ethereal was totally on edge over the contest, and was taking it out on everyone. He shrugged his shoulders and looked around for something useful to do.

Perhaps one of the people on the watch list was hanging around the lounge, or planting the bugs his electronic implants had claimed weren't there (except for the two he had left) and he could actually get some work in. All things considered, this trip had been a flop so far. He'd much rather have been back on Earth tracing illegal nanos. He had neither the training nor the experience for this political beat. If there was anything going on, he'd probably miss it. So far Bornstein hadn't done a thing.

A quick peek down the ramp showed that the lounge was undergoing a quick change into an elegant dining room, snowy linens, silver, crystal and the works. He might have guessed that on a ship this size large rooms would do double duty. Drat. Or not drat, there was an awkwardly shaped alcove beside the head of the elegant sweep of the ramp, probably left over from the last refurbishing that had installed the ramp. The alcove was furnished with two large overstuffed chairs, vaguely obscene abstract paintings, potted plants trying to hide the cargo elevator door and an internal commset and that should have . . . yes, the passenger list. He scrolled quickly through the list.

Oh, this last minute reservation screw up had just handed him an early Christmas present. Abraham MacGregor was onboard, he hadn't expected that at all. Second Class unfortunately, he'd have to find a good excuse to get down there. MacGregor was the second biggest shipper, trader and business facilitator in the New Territories, even if he was based across the Pegasus Rift in Beta. And on the same ship as Bornstein. Plenty of opportunities for some political, economic and possibly subversive wheeling and dealing there, yes indeed. And that was without even considering the presence of Chairman Wong; what the hell was the Red Enclave's interest in the New Territories' petition for full membership in the United Countries and Planets? They'd never yet made any move on anyplace outside the two hundred light year radius of the UCP compact, why now? Assuming that they needed an excuse other than the incredible mineral wealth of this region.

And just look at that, another familiar name. The Franklins! Were the rest of the Wall Street Gang here as well? Yep Guthrie, Hannibal, and Kempner. Well, well, well.

42

In the Rift

There had been a pack of older couples he hadn't met at the icebreaker; that might have been them. The New Territories were a small part of their operations, but they shipped product all over human settled space; they had a big stake in the outcome of this conference.

"I wonder what side they're on?" he murmured to himself as he scrolled back and forth through the list committing it to memory. He wished all over again that he had the talent or instincts needed for political espionage. Or at least the experience. This looked Really Interesting.

Hmm, no one from Mayde Company, the biggest commercial interest out here, but then, they had their own ships. If they had someone onboard to contact or watch the other players, it wasn't someone prominent enough to have been mentioned in his pre-mission orientation.

Goddawful load of women onboard, probably the staff and friends of the beauty queens for the most part, a few other people, have to scope them out, three families with kids, probably colonists. He straightened with a grimace. And all stuffed onto this dinky long distance ship. He kicked back in a big chair to think and didn't move, even through another jump, until summoned to escort a very elegant and slinky Ethereal down to the First Class Dining Room.

Her shimmering blue dress matched the shimmering blue of her eyes, striking in the deep tan of her stunningly beautiful face. Pity about the personality.

He kept his hands to himself, keeping the attentive lover routine limited to body language and expressions as they walked into the dining room. It was half empty, and the Maitre d' seated them at the Captain's Table, Oh God, right across the table from Aria Dune. He seated Ethereal with a flourish and, wishing heartily that he could flee, sat down beside her. Out of the corner of his eye, he saw Ethereal's entourage being seated at a lesser table.

Then Chairman Wong came in quietly, moving quite well for an old man, perhaps he worked out with his bodyguard. After a brief discussion with the Maitre d', he and his secretary were seated at a small side table. The big bodyguard stood between Wong and the rest of the room, eyes scanning and alert. The waiters were going to love going around him!

Yanking his attention back to Ethereal, he made a fuss over choosing wine and ordering from the rather limited menu, not that the food mattered to Ethereal. At least there was a tiny fresh salad, which she ate with no dressing. The remainder of her dinner she cut up and shifted around her plate. She ate two tiny bites of the chicken that had escaped the sauce. No bread or potatoes or buttered vegetables passed her lips. The wine she had chosen (very expensive) she used to occasionally wet her lips. She barely spoke until she had declined dessert and accepted a cup of coffee, black. Then the knives were drawn, as she and Aria exchanged smiles.

"Darling," Ethereal purred. "Don't you think you're overdoing the gold fetish? One might think you had your mind on money."

Paris had rather thought the gold and various tints of brass ornaments in combination with Aria's red hair had a rather attractive overall metallic flare like an animated statue, and kept his mouth firmly shut. Across the table, Obadiah Latham heaved a visible sigh and braced himself.

"Not at all, Ethereal." She nodded approvingly. "I'm glad to see you've lost the crimson flounces, you looked like a refugee from a samba band."

Ethereal's complexion didn't show much of a flush, but Paris fancied he could feel the heat from where he sat.

"Do you know, Aria, I almost didn't recognize you at the Transfer Station." Ethereal's smile was very thin. "I thought for a moment you were someone who . . . worked there." She touched her lips with her napkin. "You have to be so careful with the Whore look." She rose, and Paris leaped to escort her. Obadiah placed a hand over Aria's and she shut her mouth on whatever she had been about to say, glancing at her overaged, overweight sponsor with rueful amusement.

Huh, does she actually care what he thinks? Didn't think there was much of that around these contests.

The bodyguard watched them expressionlessly as they walked by, then went back to intimidating the waiters.

45

Paris trailed Ethereal out of the room and up the ramp, trying to think of something he could say to her about her behavior, but gave it up as a bad job. He really didn't want to wind up sleeping in that comfy chair in the lounge. This is going to be the assignment from Hell.

Maybe I'll get lucky and somebody will kill me.

Ethereal swept into the suite, and through to the bedroom. The door clicked shut behind her.

With a sigh, Paris eyed the small elegant couch in the tiny antechamber. "Damn." Ethereal opened the door and threw his luggage at him. "Double damn."

Chapter Five
Second Class

Jenny ducked out of the Second Class lounge. The half a dozen little kids on the passenger list were glued to something silly on the vid there.

The regular invitations to dinner in the First Class Dining room had resulted in the Second Class lounge being only half converted to tables. The kitchen above sent the food down a little lift at the back of the bar and the waiters carried them off to the tables as the diners cycled through in a very casual manner. Jenny had heard it referred to as 'little better than a cafeteria' by Mrs. Sandeman, but personally she preferred it to the snob scene upstairs. She slipped quickly through the door and up the stairs to the lowest of the three First Class decks.

The physical shape of the jump rings shaped the interstellar ships that used them. The two big superconducting magnetic rings, separated by a distance usually between a third and a half the diameter of the rings, according to a complicated formula, had earned the ships their early nickname of flying cheeseburgers. It was still apt.

"What are you doing?" a shrill voice piped up at her elbow. "Can I come too?" Adam Brown was also escaping the silly show, or perhaps just his mother.

"I'm just . . . " Jenny paused as a group of passengers approached, the ship's doctor leading the way with Ethereal Savannah clinging to his arm.

"In a ship this small," The ever-so-handsome-and-didn't-he-just-know-it Doctor Zimmer was apparently conducting a tour. "a ring of twelve cargo modules slot in between the jump rings and take up about one third the volume inside the jump area. They connect to the ship at the crew quarters level but access isn't possible during flight."

Heaven forbid the Beauties ever found out they could theoretically get access to the rest of their clothes.

"Inside the jump rings, most of the first level is taken up by the bridge, as well as all the computing, detection and communications equipment." Zimmer waved at the overhead. "The next two levels are the First Class accommodations. Then the kitchens and the First Class lounge and dining room, then the two levels of Second Class," He raised a supercilious eyebrow. Jenny took a quick survey. Perhaps half of his audience had won the First Class sweepstakes. Behind the doctor's back, twelve-year old Adam stuck his thumbs in his ears, wiggled his fingers and crossed his eyes. A sizable percentage of the impromptu tour group grinned in agreement. Zimmer stiffened, but didn't turn around. Did he think snobbishness would help his standing with the elegant Ethereal fluttering admiringly at his elbow?

Apparently. "There are four stairwells, fore and aft, and on either side of the ship, as well as the lifts in the center. Below the Second class levels are the crew quarters, and then the engineering section, with the hydrogen fuel for the four fusion engines taking up almost half of the ship's interior space."

"Where's life support?" asked one of the women from the beauty queens' menagerie. The Doctor smirked at the old vid term.

"Centralized atmospheric recycling systems are totally obsolete, and exist now only on hopelessly out-of-date ships, and modern video productions written by someone with no space experience whatsoever. Even space stations have multiple smaller air systems, now. We have atmospheric units dispursed all over the ship." He said. "That way there is a lot of redundancy and no worries about areas where stale air pools and causes problems."

Where people die, Jenny edited that privately. Keeping the crew alive had been the major stumbling block to space exploration, three centuries earlier. Now, of course, most ships had adopted, or rather adapted, Cinnaban technology. The alien civilization had millennia of experience in space, and had been quite happy to sell the fruits of that experience to the humans who had met them shortly after developing gravity wave technology themselves.

The psychological differences between the races had

produced mostly mutual bafflement; the Cinnaban total lack of governmental structure was a Libertarian Paradise, other than perhaps their tendency to eat their defeated rivals. From their perspective, humans were apparently like some bizarre cooperative social insect, with schizophrenic alternating pacifist and berserker tendencies. After a few violent altercations, both races had mutually agreed on a line of demarcation between where Cinnaban customs switched to Human government, and cooperated (as best Cinnabs could be said to cooperate) on matters of crime and trade. Jenny had never met one face to face, and was still hoping in vain for an opportunity to meet the three that were on board.

"I've been impressed with the air system's ability to handle odors." Jenny kept her face straight and didn't mention the Captain's request for moderation in perfume, circulated the second day of the trip.

"Oh, that's simple," The Doctor shrugged. "I've never understood why the practice isn't more widespread, despite the additional cost. Our systems simply bubble the air through water to remove impurities, then the water is distilled and recycled."

As the Doctor turned his attention back to Ethereal, Jenny nodded politely to him and wandered off on a slow private perambulation of the level, Adam trailing her. Sticking her nose into the kitchen, she found it in full dinner mode. The First Class dining room still had the late dinner to serve and the kitchen was busy. The head Chef, Georges by name, spotted her and waved them in. "Jenny, welcome, and your young friend as well. I cannot talk just now, busy busy, but taste these cookies. Will our Beauties eat these?"

The cookie melted in her mouth, an insubstantial essence of sweetness. She shook her head sadly, as Adam snagged a second. "You might try just one, in elegant solitude on a small plate, but I really doubt they'll eat them."

Georges was an interesting man, very well traveled, even if his accent tended to drift in and out of a Hollywood stereotype of "some sort of European." He'd been grateful for her explanation of why his food was being returned uneaten. Since the advent of nanotech weight control, dieting was a lost art. He was now serving low fat, low calorie 'petite servings' to the beauty queens and those of their entourages who had adopted their eating habits.

He shook his head in despair. "At least they now eat nearly half their dinners." He glanced mournfully back at his high tech empire. "I am ruined if it ever comes out that I have served plain broiled chicken breast." He glanced past her and scowled. "The salads are prepared, I have sent them over."

Jenny glanced behind. The horribly supercilious Maitre d', Phillip Descartes was nodding his head, even that slight action looking condescending. "Good. There will be eight of the special meals required." He looked pointedly down his nose at Jenny and Adam.

Jenny rolled her eyes at Georges, then grinned, and left them to their work. Adam trailed reluctantly along with just one wistful glance back at the cookie plate.

When she wandered back to Second Class, the two families with younger children were gone from the lounge, and Adam's mother fell on him and marched him off trailing words like "shower" and "bed". The various minions and friends of the beauty queens were starting to retreat as well. They would be getting up early to assist their charges' transformations into exquisite icons of feminine beauty. Nicole's three-hour morning routine was apparently the norm. Jenny had spotted all three of the 'sponsors representatives' having solitary coffee in the first class lounge the first morning, evicted from their cozy suites (politely no doubt, but firmly) to make room for the transformation.

Poor things. Nothing better to do with their money than this? Perhaps Latham had 'done it all' and retired, after what was rumored to be three rejuves, but Michael was still young and Paris even younger. Men. Suckers for a pretty woman.

As the women trailed out, Mrs. Pearson glanced worriedly back at Jenny, but Heidi poked her and whispered something in her ear. As the Pear turned away, Heidi winked at her and followed. They weren't all bad, even as wound up for this contest as Nicole had them.

In the Rift

With their exit, the lounge reverted to a quiet, almost masculine ambiance, accentuated by Mac and Frank grabbing a table in the corner and pulling out cards and cash.

"Poker?" she asked.

"Like to join us?" Frank grinned up at her.

"Don't do it!" Mac told her. "This shark will clean you out."

"I don't have any money, no further cleaning possible." Jenny informed them, glumly. "The only thing worse than being poor is being a poor minor." She brightened. "But the New Territories don't have those ridiculous work rules, do they? Maybe I can get a job on Autumn."

Mac looked at her indulgently. "Honey, the New Territories are so oversupplied with single men that I suspect you'll be getting marriage proposals before you leave the space port."

Jenny snorted. "I'm not that desperate! Oh, no!" she frowned a bit. "I'd rather have a job than a husband anyway. Better hours, and much better pay."

"There are a lot of rich miners and farmers." Mac said.

"Then I'd be no better than my . . . than those beauty queens, living on their rich sponsors. I'd probably find myself stuck with someone I don't like, and no way out of it." Jenny pointed out. "Maybe I should ask Misty and Kissy Poo for pointers?"

Frank and Mac winced. "Just kidding," she assured

them. Observing Misty and Kissy Poo had enlarged her knowledge of human nature enormously. She really couldn't imagine saying things like that to any man, let alone a complete stranger! From a strictly practical angle, she had to admire their teamwork and coordination. They had a list of who was where, and usually tackled men that were rooming together so one of them could drift off to the man's suite for privacy, while the other lured her vic-umm, customer to their room. Occasionally one of them would spend an unusual amount of time charming a man at the bar while the other entertained 'at home'. They tended to return to the hunt shockingly quickly. It was very disillusioning to a teenager who had believed in romantic all night liaisons. And while she had tactfully not noticed the bruises Kissy Poo had tried to conceal one morning, she had also noted who had been subsequently shunned by both women.

Several of the first class passengers wandered in, two men Jenny didn't know and Paris, Ethereal's musician boyfriend. Somehow his youth and enthusiasm made it harder to put him in the 'I only sleep with him for his money' category. Mac greeted the other men as old friends and introduced them around. "The Wall Street Gang, or a quarter of it, anyway. Jenny, this is what happens when four New York sisters chose their husbands for utility and compatibility. Peter Franklin and Quincy Guthrie."

"And good looks, Mac," put in the silver haired Quincy.

"You left out that they wanted real live studs."

"I ship stuff for their clients' regularly." Mac continued. "I suppose you're lobbying also? How did you rate first class? I got stuck back here!"

"This trip you lucked out," Peter grinned at him. "You wouldn't believe the verbal knife fights up there." He turned to Paris. "Not meaning to be offensive, but why on Earth did you tangle yourself up with that woman?"

Paris laughed. "Actually, we're old friends, even if she is totally stressed out over this contest. And if you ever saw the packs of teenager girls, and pre-teens, that throw themselves at me, you'd see the advantage of having just one single solitary drop dead gorgeous girlfriend to, umm, limit the expectations of some of the fans."

"Throwing themselves at you?" Guthrie looked amused.

"Literally. Honest, I've been chased from the stage more than once. I have to hire security, above and beyond what the stage owners provide." He turned to Jenny. "You look like one of the most sensible teens I've seen in years."

"Well," she apologized. "That's because I don't like that caterwauling and gyrating you call music. Sorry."

He just grinned. "My secret is out. Caterwauling, with showmanship, it is. I, like the Beauty Queens above, get by one sheer raw good looks."

She looked at him dubiously, a little taller than average but thin with wavy dark hair; without makeup he looked more like an underfed marathon runner than a stage artist.

"Ouch. She didn't fall for that either!" Paris grabbed a chair and sat down. "Quick, deal them out. It must be my night to be lucky at cards."

Jenny curled up in a comfortable chair with her book, the background sounds of laughter and masculine voices drowning out the alien environment of the spaceship, almost like Dad and his buddies having an all-night poker game. Not enough cussing, though. Or smells-like-a-dead-camel cigar smoke.

During one break in the game, Paris wandered over and looked at her book. "Developmental Stages of Artificial Intelligences. Good God, the things young women read these days!" He wandered off shaking his head.

Mac grinned. "You're going to scare off all the young men if you keep reading things like that."

Jenny grinned back. "That why I put this dust jacket over the latest romantic trash story."

Paris wandered back, and with a careful finger, pulled the book forward enough to see the print. "Quasi-randomly generated electron pathways in artificial crystals? Romantic trash has changed since I was young."

He staggered back theatrically, making a cross with his fingers. The men laughed and Paris turned back toward them but hesitated. "What's wrong with, umm, electron pathways in natural crystals?" he asked.

In the Rift

"They're too random, and the crystals tend to be more flawed. The only really good ones are the big rubies they mine out here somewhere. They've got a tiny fraction of their aluminum replaced with gold and some of them handle electric currents in an almost analogue fashion. They're the new Hot Item for true artificial intelligence."

Mac nodded. "Mayde Company owns the system they're found in, their subsidiary, Corundum Computers, is making a killing marketing the finished product. I think they sell the rejects to be recrystallized."

"The recrystallized rubies don't perform as well, although they're miles ahead of non-crystal comps." Jenny told him.

Paris shook his head, and returned to cards, muttering about abuse of gemstones and Jenny returned to the mathematical explanation for the superiority of quasi-randomly generated electron pathways. She was already more than half way through the college courses she'd brought along for the trip, she'd test out of them when they got back to Earth and have a good two semesters of credit in the bag. All she had to do then was stretch the scholarship money to cover the rest.

Chapter Six
Desperate Dancing

Nicole tried hard not to pout. She had been so looking forward to this dance; her dropped point skirt was flared to swing gracefully on the turns, its multi-blue tones just right for her eyes, the tauntingly low bodice—wasted, apparently. One dance from Michael, and he'd considered his social duty done. She'd either have to skip dancing for the rest of the evening, or risk his anger and rejection if he became jealous. Which would be an utter disaster, especially out here. Perhaps she could dance once each with a number of men? Unfortunately, Michael was talking with Dr. Zimmer. Perhaps . . .

"What's this? Have you been abandoned?" Oh lord, the horrible little Paris! "Come and dance with me." Like most of the men, he was conservatively arrayed in a black suit. His, however, had sparkles, and of course he was wearing makeup, apparently his standard off-stage mask. At least it was subtle, not gaudy. He still looked masculine.

Was this better than nothing? Nicole saw the suppressed fury in Ethereal's face and immediately turned on her best smile, and dropped her voice to its husky best. "I'd love to dance." The horrid man twinkled, obviously quite aware of her reason for accepting. Nasty piece of work! She'd be doing Ethereal a favor to take him away.

"So are you looking forward to the New Territories? Grand tour and all that?" he asked, spinning her expertly.

"I expect to be too busy to see much," she spoke honestly, and un-encouragingly. Drat! He even danced well.

"I thought Bornstein was from Autumn?" Paris guided her lightly around the lumbering Latham and delicate Aria. "Isn't he showing you the sights?"

"Perhaps after the contest, although frankly I hope to be very busy after my triumph there." *Michael is from the New Territories? He's never said anything! Perhaps he wants to surprise me with his local knowledge?* She'd play dumb and not spoil his fun.

"Confident, are you?" Paris was laughing at her. "Tell me though, do all beauty contest hopefuls travel with six staff and six friends?"

"Oh, no." Nicole said, opening innocent eyes at him. "I've only got four staff, so I brought eight friends."

Paris started laughing so hard it broke his rhythm. Unfortunately they had swung back near Ethereal, who leaped into the breach. "I see you don't mention your fat little sister, but then, I've heard she doesn't admit being related to you either."

Nicole smiled sweetly. "Jenny's at that independent age. She imagines she doesn't need anyone." She shrugged her shoulders (an elegant gesture, she had practiced it repeatedly before the mirror). "As smart as she is, she may be correct."

"Oh, yes." Ethereal smirked. "I understand you got all the beauty, she got all the brains. Are you quite certain you have the same father?"

Does she think I'm so insecure I'll be anything but amused by insults to my parents?

"Darling," Nicole gave her her best patronizing smile. "You can do better than that." She scanned Ethereal up and down, as if that remark was more about the multi-colored halter gown. As well it might be. She should fire her wardrobe designer, or is that why she hired Opal? She barely suppressed a snicker as a thought hit her. *Or has Aria introduced a saboteur into the Enemy camp?*

Ethereal stiffened, not very effectively in the soft curves of the gown, and Paris winced.

Nicole glanced over at Michael; not a good idea to upset him by arguing publicly. But even worse, he was totally unaware of her. Better change that. Tasteless provincial rivals could go hang. She smiled meltingly at Paris, "Excuse me, thank you for the dance," and withdrew.

Just for a moment she wished she were just anyone, like the couples she'd privately nicknamed the four ugly businessmen. They were dancing and talking, laughing, no verbal sniping, friends. The husbands and wives so comfortable with each other. She'd overheard mention of children and grandchildren. When she was that age, would she be as happy? Not that she'd let her hair go gray like that . . .

"Michael! Dancing is more fun than talking." She sort of slunk up against him, but stopped when she felt him stiffen. "Dr. Zimmer, I believe I'm going to have to be jealous, he enjoys your company more than mine."

"Not all of us are brave enough to venture out into the gauntlet." Dr. Zimmer leered politely at her. "The diverse dancing styles in evidence makes it a veritable battle zone out there."

He was so dashing! She wondered how long he'd been in the service. She could picture him hunting down pirates, commanding fleets . . . but of course, he was a doctor. His place would have been to save the wounded after battle.

Michael was indifferent to the byplay, looking over her head.

"Captain Portman, a pleasure." Michael sounded brusque. "Nicole, you've met the Captain, haven't you? I suspect he'd love to dance with you."

And apparently he did, but Nicole wondered why Michael had as good as dismissed her. She smiled at the Captain, around a cold pit of fear in her stomach.

I have to win this contest. I can't keep on living off men who don't care about me. I have to win.

Chapter Seven
Small Stakes Poker

Tonight it was the fathers rounding up their respective reluctant children and carrying/herding them toward their cabins. Their wives, and the beauty queen contingent, were all off at some ladies-only get together organized by some of the older women passengers. Jenny figured they hadn't realized what they were getting into, and had ducked.

With a concealed sigh of relief, she snapped the vid display off. Silence descended suddenly, and the usual poker players quickly transferred from the bar to their usual table in the lounge.

"I refuse to believe that's a real person." Frank muttered. "It's not possible for anyone to be that perky. Got to be an AI."

Jenny grinned in sympathy while shaking her head. "You could make an AI with that, um, non-logical blather or salesmanship, but it would be awfully unstable. It's not a good idea to teach an AI to lie. I wouldn't rule out a plain old-fashioned acting program, though."

"No one likes an overeducated kid showing up her betters." Paris put in primly. "So what are you planning on doing on Autumn?"

Jenny eyed Paris with bemusement. He couldn't possibly be seeking her out deliberately, could he? The only boys who'd ever done that were the idiots that thought she'd be so desperate she'd put out for anyone. Or the stepfather, of course, once his drinking was totally out of control, and once her prettier sister had fled, but after-school activities, barricaded bedroom doors, thirty pounds of fat, and a scholarship to a boarding prep school had more or less fixed that problem. So what did this one want?

"I haven't a clue, I just jumped at the chance to go." She dragged her mind back to the question. "I guess I should check the comp for a guide book, or something."

"I've got one I'll loan you, honey," Kissy volunteered. She and Misty were having a night off, pretty much necessitated by a stern warning from the Captain. The large number of women on board had resulted in slim pickings for the 'working girls', reducing them to trolling among the crew, and attracting the Captain's wrath.

"I thought Bornstein was from there?" Paris looked around at Mac. "Do you work with him?"

"I've shipped stuff to him." Mac admitted. "Enough that I recognize the name. I don't know if he's a native, never met him before. Well, technically I still haven't, but this is the first time I've seen him."

Jenny studied Paris curiously. "Heaven knows the Beauties research each other and gossip to high heaven, but I hadn't realized the sponsors' reps did it too." Paris actually blushed. "I wouldn't have thought the competition was as tough on your end of things." Mac was snickering, so she continued. "Anyway, I only met him a few times before this trip, and while he's a step up from Nicki's last sponsor, he's hardly an object of fascination to me."

"Nicki?" asked Mac, splitting a frown between her and Paris.

"Ugh. My deepest, darkest secret." Jenny told him. "Nicole Peace, AKA Miss Great Plains, is my sister."

"Oh, my," was Misty's only comment.

"Ah, I had wondered what you were doing on this ship." Mac looked sheepish. "Sorry, but you're so out of place here."

Jenny sniffed. "You just say that because I won't play poker with you."

"Ha! I'll stake you to the tune of five dollars," said Paris. "I'll bet you I win it back in less than an hour."

"But if I lose that bet, I won't be in any shape to repay you." Jenny sensibly pointed out.

"Serve me right for corrupting a minor," he said.

An hour later he surveyed the pile of chips in front of her. "Who taught you how to play?" he asked in disbelief.

"My Dad." She grinned. "And his buddies, when they needed an extra." She put on her best innocent face. "Space Marines mostly, although they did rope in and fleece the occasional silver-suited sun god."

"Was he an officer?" asked Mac.

"Nope, he worked for a living." The men all grinned at the ancient joke. "Master sergeant."

"Er, retired?" Paris asked hesitantly, obviously suspecting the answer.

She shook her head. "Dead. Stupid training accident on the Moon." She shuffled. "Five card draw."

She won a total of seventy-five dollars. Sightseeing on Autumn was looking up.

Chapter Eight
Hijacked!

Nicole was both amused and impressed by the Captain's ability to smooth feathers ruffled by demotion to Second Class. By serving two dinners in First Class, early and 'romantically late', he had cycled all the insulted matrons through a flattering fancy dinner. Not that the food wasn't the same as was served in Second, but the silverware and china sparkled, the snowy linen was crisp, and the service was faultless under the stern eye of the Maitre d'. Well, the fresh green salad from the onboard hydroponics unit wouldn't be served in Second, nor the fancy dessert.

She was nearly dreaming about these tiny luscious desserts, but she couldn't depend on nanos to keep her slim. They were manufactured to be mild, slow acting, and programmed for fat and fluid levels far in excess of what she could allow herself. No desserts. Period.

She also rather doubted that the Second Class dinners included the better wines available up here.

Which were totally wasted on some people. Jenny was sipping hers, trying to look sophisticated, and pretending that she liked it. At least she hadn't done anything so gauche as ask for a soda. Nicole wished she would stop ogling the other passengers. Fourteen days into the voyage, this was the second time Jenny'd been invited to the first class dinner. Wearing the same 'nice' outfit both times. At least the business-like camel over black was unobtrusive. In Jenny's case, dull was much to be preferred over flashy. Her friends had been up here more often, of course, and Barbara had been here every day. Nicole owed her so much for her constant support all through her career, she felt awful dumping her in Second Class.

Some of the actual First Class passengers preferred this early dinner. Much to Nicole's (hidden) irritation that included Michael Bornstein and several of the most boring passengers. A few amusing moments had been afforded by Chairman Wong, who ought to have been exotic and romantic but was merely a picky old man with an obsequious flunky, the appropriately named Mr. Write, hovering over him and actually tasting his food. The dark bodyguard had stopped blocking the waiters and now stood back against the wall, scanning everything and looking at no one. The three Cinnaban passengers hadn't socialized at all, apparently they ate privately, from their own food supplies. Some Cinnabs enjoyed playing with the effects of Terran food on their metabolism, but all the ones onboard seemed to be conservative.

At least she didn't have any competition at dinner. Both Aria and Ethereal and their entourages ate late. According to the gossip, there had been some very snooty comments made and every night was a covert wardrobe competition. She got blow by blow accounts the next morning from whichever of her friends had been present.

The early dinner really was better, there wasn't a man at the table that wasn't sneaking glances her way.

"Excuse me, Nicole," Michael sounded puzzled. He was turned away from her, looking at something she couldn't see. He rose and strode past the foot of the table and out the side corridor. She only heard the noise because she was looking after him, and concentrating in that direction. A thud. Had he run into something, tripped? He fell backwards into the dining room, nearly everyone turning to gape at him.

The man who came out of the corridor was one of the attentive servers.

With a gun.

Even staring at the man she barely saw the faint purple flicks of light of the laser gun, but jumped at the crash as the Chinese bodyguard hit the center table in mid-leap. She had a glimpse of three burning embers lined diagonally across his chest before he rolled off the table and out of sight. Chairman Wong was scuttling away towards the corridor at the head of the room, but collapsed in a heap. More burning embers.

No noise. Nicole stood, half out of her seat, frozen in silence, shocked that violent death could come so quietly. For a moment all she could hear was the faint click of the trigger being pulled and the almost subliminal whine of the capacitor's quick recharge.

Then the painful high-pitched shriek of stunners started.

The room leaped abruptly back into motion and sound with an explosion of human screams and three-dozen panicked people trying to flee. Or fight. She caught a glimpse of Captain Portman grabbing a knife, as Jenny tugged her, and screamed "Run!" There was a burst of screams from the Captain's direction, she started to look, saw blood everywhere and turned away. There were other gunmen as well. And no place to run.

"Freeze! Freeze!" One of the gunmen was yelling. "All you women! Over there! In that corner! All the men, over there!"

All the waiters were in on it, Nicole realized, as even those without guns shoved them in the desired direction. They piled into the corner in a panicked sheep-like confusion of women.

"Hijacking," Jenny said in a stunned voice, barely audibly from behind her. "We're being hijacked."

Nicole counted in shock. There were bodies all over the room. The Captain, the Third Officer, the two elderly couples, the Chinese trio. One of the waiters, apparently the main source of the blood.

So it hadn't been totally one-sided.

70

In the Rift

Barbara. Oh god, Barbara was just lying there. Was she dead? She couldn't tell stunned from dead, and she shuddered, averting her eyes from the bodies to the nearly as bad view of the formerly polite waiters, well armed.

"All right, listen up and no one else gets hurt! You men! You behave until your ransom is paid, we'll release you with all your body parts attached. Try something foolish, we start hacking."

The Maître d' had been so cool and superior! He didn't even look like the same man now, a wild sense of his power gleaming in his smile. "You women. You are valuable. Behave and you'll stay that way."

"What, what do you mean, valuable?" Jenny's voice squeaked from within the packed women.

"There a lot of lonely men that will pay a king's ransom for a wife. In just a few months you'll all be married to rich miners. Or whatever."

Whatever. Nicole felt faint. In the stunned silence in the room, she could faintly hear more screaming echoing up from the other areas of the ship.

Chapter Nine
Risky Rescue

Lagging behind the other women as they crowded the wall away from the pile of bodies and hurried to the passenger lift lobby, Jenny checked the hijackers. More of them were with the men's group than the women's, and they were all excited and not methodical at all. None of them were looking at her and she stepped softly back into the alcove that contained the large cargo lift to the airlock.

The doors of the elevator were open, more bodies lay within. None of the hijackers came looking for her and she scanned the heap of bodies for familiar faces, and clung to the knowledge that neither Mac nor Frank were anywhere among them as an antidote to nausea. Drying red brown blood, off-color pale dead faces, with livid bruises. Smell of feces, urine, blood and burned meat. Hyperventilating wasn't helping. She wrapped her arms around herself to stop them shaking.

Herman Brown was dead. She wondered if the kids knew, or worse, had seen him killed. The boys at least weren't here, in this hideous collection the hijackers were probably going to jettison. Was there a market for boys? She was queasily afraid there was. All three Cinnabs lay here, and several crewmen, but not many. Here was Chairman Wong, even more shrunken and still faithfully attended by his flunkey and his bodyguard.

She listened carefully as just around the corner the women were parceled out, some being sent up, others down. Still no one looking for her. Hearing nothing at all, she stepped cautiously out, trying not to touch any of the dead men.

The bodyguard's hand twitched.

She froze, staring at the hand. Had it been her imagination? She eyed his scorched torso and saw the slight rise and fall of breath.

She peeked around the corner. The hijackers had apparently gone with the other women in the passenger lifts; she was temporarily alone, temporarily free; should she hide? In a ship where she couldn't open locked doors? Hadn't a clue how to fly? She stared down at the man at her feet; the staircase was right there and her room was down one level and around a curve. Hiding wouldn't do any good, but here, on the other hand, was an opportunity to do something, however small. If this man lived, he would be an asset.

"God, I hope I don't kill you!" She hovered, then decided to not pull on his arms, it might do further damage in his chest. Grabbing his feet, she dragged him to the stairway. "God! I wish you were lighter." Cracking the stair door, she listened, then looked. Empty. Now she had no choice but to take his arms, lifting his head and shoulders down the stairs, letting the rest of him drag, his boots thumping alarmingly on each tread. She dragged him quickly down in a terror of discovery. At her level, she cautiously tried the door. This time her luck had run out.

The corridor was packed with terrified passengers. Several blood-splashed women were simultaneously and chaotically telling the rest what had happened in the first class lounge and being told what had happened here.

Jenny slipped out of the stairwell and shut the door behind her. Standing on her tiptoes, she looked for Nicole. Mrs. Daimler was one of the hysterics; Mrs. Caruthers was trying to comfort her. Miss Pearson was missing, as was Mrs. Sandeman. The women from the first class dining room had been sorted by some logic known only to the hijackers, Nicole was nowhere to be seen, was she back in her own cabin? Women both familiar and not had apparently been brought down here. The Browns weren't visible.

Jenny scanned the mob of women. All the youngest and prettiest were missing. Up in first class for special treatment, no doubt. She wondered if being in second class meant she was safe from rape, but decided it was probably the other way around. The most valuable women were safe. Down here the hijackers could do as they pleased with the dregs. By some muffled sobs coming from several huddles of women, they might already have done so.

She spotted Kissy Poo and Misty, peeking out of their half-opened door and worked her way over to them.

Misty grabbed her. "Oh, honey! Are you all right?" and dragged her into the crowded room.

"Mac! And Frank, good God, I thought they were killing all the men." Jenny patted them to reassure herself of their reality.

"We were taking Juan back to his bunk, he was drunk again." Mac said, nodding toward what appeared to be dirty laundry sticking out from behind one bed.

"When we heard screaming, we shoved him in here, and then Kissy said we'd better stay hidden too." Frank added.

"She's right. They killed all the men except a few they thought could come up with a sizable ransom. They even killed Chairman Wong." She hesitated, then plunged in.

"The bodyguard was shot, but he's still alive." She grimaced. "Or he was a few minutes ago. I've got him in the stairwell, I was going to hide him in my room, but." She waved at the door and the crowd.

"Leave him there for a bit," Mac advised. "We can't do anything until the corridors are clear." He looked a bit grim at that.

"If they lock us all in, I can fiddle the locks." Frank said. "Then we'll move him."

"If they search the rooms, they'll find you, and him."

76

In the Rift

"They ran a fast search already." Mac threw a strained smile at her. "My back's never going to be the same again, fitting behind there," He glanced at the recliner bed. "But the utilities run the other side of this wall." He jabbed a finger at the back of the cabin. "If we can get a panel off, we'll be able to hide in-between the walls."

Misty had kept one ear to the door and now waved them silent.

An unfamiliar male voice was speaking. ". . . each go to your own rooms and stay there. If you haven't got a room, find one. We will be bringing rations around for you."

The women were scampering back to their rooms. Jenny nodded to the others and slipped out and headed for hers. The lock was warped and darkened; apparently she didn't have to worry about being locked in.

"The boss says we can have any women who wander around. So come on out if you want." The smirking man was wearing a ship's uniform with engineer's insignia.

An inside job. I hope Juan wasn't in on it! And we'd better keep him hidden. He's a pilot, he could get us home. She snorted a bit at the thought. *Yeah, when this coffee klatch retakes the ship!*

She left her door open two inches and watched until the hijacker turned and entered the lift. She slid the door open further, down the hall Kissy's door opened as well. She nodded the all clear to Mac. From their vantage they couldn't see the lift. Mac pointed to her, and made an exaggerated peering look. She nodded, and stepped out for a clear view of the lift lobby.

In the corner of her vision she saw Mac and Frank dash to the stair door, listen, and open it. They were right back out, staggering under the weight of the bodyguard. She stepped back and opened the door wide for them to hustle him through. They dropped him unceremoniously on her recliner, then with a squeeze of her shoulder, were gone.

She slid the door shut, frowning at the scorched lock. There was no way to brace it; perhaps she could wedge it with something? After committing gross abuse of a book, she turned back to her new roommate.

The man was still breathing. She twisted her hands together, feeling helpless. The three charred holes diagonally across the man's chest were nearly invisible in the quilted black jacket. Had the jacket saved him? It was thick and stiff, was there such a thing as laser resistant cloth?

She untied the thick red sash and carefully peeled the jacket open. He wore no shirt underneath. The three holes were oozing blood around slightly charred edges. Not *very* laser resistant. They were way beyond the first-aid she'd learned, but at least there was no sign of an internal steam explosion. The rifles must have been set on the briefest possible pulse, to maximize the number of shots for the charge they could carry.

In the Rift

"Shock." She spoke out loud, trying to think. "Keep him warm, lots of liquids."

It seemed pretty feeble, but she dug out Miss Pearson's blanket and tucked it around him, then got out Nicole's ermine coat and spread it over him as well. Was there internal bleeding with laser wounds? She supposed it depended on the location of the injury. This man had certainly had his lungs damaged, but the shots must have been at an angle to miss his heart. And all those big veins and arteries around it as well. She bit her lip, wondering if she should look to see if the lasers had gone all the way through.

And what am I going to do differently if they have? All I've done is keep him from being dumped out the airlock. The rest is up to him.

There was a pitifully tiny cup by the sink, but she couldn't try getting him to drink unless he woke up. As if he heard her mental commands, his eyes blinked open.

"Can you hear me?" Jenny whispered. Somehow that blank dull stare inhibited her voice. *Does he understand English?* After a long moment though, the eyes turned in her direction and focused. "You need to drink this water. You've bled a lot and need liquids."

"The Chairman . . ." The voice was raspy and faint, but English. So he could understand her.

Jenny winced and shook her head. "They killed him."

The dullness slipped suddenly into despair. "I didn't save him. I wasn't good enough."

She raised the head of the recliner bed and tipped the glass to wet his lips. "Then you'll need strength to avenge him."

His eyes narrowed, and he drank.

Chapter Ten
Not Locked Up

Nicole was back in her own suite, but with new roommates. Barbara Pearson had been dragged in unconscious, and now was moaning over her headache. Paula Sandeman had walked in on her own two feet, but she kept babbling, and what about Michael? She hadn't seen him beyond a glimpse of his unconscious body being pitched into another room. He was rich enough to be worth ransoming. Would he ransom her as well? Could he? The chief hijacker hadn't sounded like he was interested in trying. Were all these rumored lonely men so rich?

With the door open a crack, she could see Dr. Zimmer being escorted from cabin to cabin under guard. As he left the cabin Michael had been thrown into and approached hers, she drew back, sitting down and trying to look cowed and submissive. It didn't take much acting.

When the door slid open, the Doctor hurried in, looking like he was trying to avoid contact with the hijacker. To Nicole's relief the hijacker stayed out, and closed the door behind the Doctor. He slumped with weariness, his eyes looked hopeless.

"Are you ladies all right?" His voice was raspy and

sounded as tired as he looked.

"All right!" Barbara burst into tears. Again. Nicole almost wished for her to be stunned again. Almost. Anything that remotely suggested a dead body wasn't actually very desirable, just now.

"We're okay, so far. Barbara had a horrible headache from the stun, but it's gone." Nicole glanced worriedly at her, then back to the doctor. "How about you? You look awful!"

"I've lost a lot of friends today, umm," He looked vaguely at his bare wrist. "I suppose it's yesterday, now."

"What about Michael?" Nicole asked.

"Concussion, doubt there will be any complications, but I'll check on him tomorrow."

Nicole nodded gratefully.

"I'll be heading down to second class next, any messages you want me to take?"

Paula looked up from comforting Barbara. "Do you know if everyone's alive, down there? And why did they move some of us up here?"

"You're the most valuable. Some combination of age and looks, I guess." Zimmer patted her shoulder. "They want us alive. They won't kill us unless we do something really stupid."

"Tell Jenny I'm fine," Nicole wavered, but had to ask. "How much of the crew is still alive? Is there any hope..." Her voice trailed off at the expression on his face.

In the Rift

"They only killed a few of the crew, the others they seem to think either the company will ransom or they can be . . . persuaded . . . to join pirate crews." He sagged. "A lot of the hijackers were members of the crew. A couple of engineering assistants, the third Commo Officer, and virtually all of the dining and janitorial staff. Except the chef and a couple of young women. They think they'll get a high price for Chef Georges at auction. And all the women crewmembers, they're more valuable as women than techs."

Nicole gulped. "What about you?"

"Apparently there are whole planets with hundreds or even thousands of people, miners or farmers, I guess, without any actual doctors. The hijacker chief, you know that snooty Maitre d'? Thinks that people like that will be pooling their money to bid on me. They think I'm worth millions!" Zimmer's voice rose in tone, and he gulped visibly to get a hold of himself. He fumbled out some small packets. "For headaches, and to help you sleep. If, if there's nothing, else?" At the shakes of their heads, he fled.

***

Jenny breathed a sigh of relief as the panel finally yielded to her pocket tool and fell in her lap. She folded the multitool and pocketed it, wondering where she could hide it in case of a search.

The man was watching her with his dark eyes, noting

everything but saying nothing. If he weren't so badly wounded, she'd probably be frightened of him, rather than for him. She poked her head behind the panel. "I think you can fit, but it's not going to be comfortable. If it looks like they're going to leave us alone, you'd be better off out here." She looked worriedly at his unhealthy color and limpness. "There's three other guys hiding in there somewhere, they're friends." His eyes jerked suddenly toward the door. It was open a crack, so she could hear when anything happened. It was so well insulated, she doubted she would hear the hijackers killing her neighbors one by one with it closed. And now, the faint sounds of the elevator doors, and cabin doors sliding. Putting the panel down quietly, she pried the book wedge out of the door frame and opened it a bit more to peek out. Doctor Zimmer, under the gun of one of the hijackers, was entering the first cabin. She drew back and shoved the door all the way closed.

"They've brought the doctor," she started, then froze as she turned. How had he gotten up? How had he gotten so close without her hearing him?

"Good." His eyes gleamed, in defiance of the slight wheeze in his voice. "I will kill them."

"No," she said firmly. "There are two of them. The one with the laser rifle looked like he was staying at the lift. You need to wait. You need to hide." The gleam in his eyes started fading to despair, and he swayed, weakness catching up to him. "There will be an opportunity to get all of them. This is not the time."

She propped him up as he started to fold, guiding him to the bulkhead. Without a word, he squeezed in, and slumped. She stuffed the blanket in with him, pressed the panel into place, and started the corner screw. She didn't dare take the time to put them all in, finding her working on them would be much worse than the thin likelihood of their noticing the missing screws. The leftover screws she shoved under the bed cushion, she rehung the fur coat. Where to hide the tool? Was the doctor examining the passengers? Were they being searched? She stuck it into the toe of a shoe, deep in the bag of shoes as she shifted it in front of the loose panel. She was frantically looking for anything she'd left out that might be compromising when the door opened and Doctor Zimmer stumbled through, as if pushed. The door slid shut on the hijacker.

"You look awful!" Jenny was aghast. Mister Nasty Doctor had gotten his comeuppance, with interest. "Have you seen Nicole? Umm, Miss Peace, I mean?"

"Oh, yes." The doctor collapsed onto the recliner. "She's fine. Are you all right?"

"I'm okay, just scared," Jenny admitted. "Did you see a Barbara Pearson, she was shot and I couldn't tell . . . "

"Just stunned, she's fine now. She and someone else, Paula, I think, are in Nicole's cabin up in First Class. They haven't been . . . harmed."

"Oh good." She slumped in relief. "Did they really mean what they said, about selling us?"

"Yes." He rubbed his face. "They mean it. They won't kill you unless they have to, so don't get any silly ideas! It sounds," he hesitated, "like the men that will be bidding are just regular men, that have gotten desperate for a wife and don't have any other way to get one. They don't, don't mean to harm you." His voice trailed off at her look of disgust. "Well, if you're all right, I'll go see the next people." He sighed. "I think Mrs. Brown is going to need tranks. It won't be the nice guys bidding on her boys." He slunk out.

Jenny peeked at the guards as he left. One on the doctor, one at the lift. They didn't appear to be searching the rooms. She left the door open a crack again but didn't wedge it, catching the sound of Mrs. Brown's voice before that door shut. She shuddered a bit, and settled down to watch and wait.

After the doctor had been to all the rooms, his caretaker herded him onto the lift. The other man remained, and was shortly joined by five other men, who started searching the rooms. Some of them stayed in some of the rooms overlong, and Jenny heard sobbing as they left. As they approached her room, she let the door slip closed, and backed up as far as she could. The two men gave a cursory look around, opened the cupboards and drawers, but just kicked the bags of shoes and handbags stuffed in the corners.

"Don't touch the fat girl. She's probably a virgin and will be worth tons." The waiter . . . pirate. . . in the corridor glanced in. The other two looked her up and down, but shrugged and left. Sated already. She huddled in the corner and didn't dare open her door for a full hour. When she did, the deck was deathly silent. There was no one in sight, so she slipped down to the lounge. Also empty. Back in her room, she dug out the multitool and unscrewed the panel again.

The bodyguard eased carefully out, scooting away from the opening. Mac followed him out, standing up stiffly as Frank crawled out behind him. Juan stuck his head out, but ventured no further.

"Are you all right?" Mac looked at her anxiously.

"I'm fine, god knows about some of the other women, though."

The bodyguard slumped on the floor, Frank sat beside him, very nearly in a fetal position. "I'm not sure," Frank gulped, "but that I'd rather be killed than have to listen to that again."

"It's all quiet out there now, and the lounge is empty. Should I try to get a panel off there, as well?" Jenny stuck to practicalities, and stifled her imagination. She worriedly got the bodyguard another cup of water, and covered him up, although he looked no worse than he had before. "There ought to be more room, around the dumbwaiter and the plumbing. Or if they're done searching, maybe you don't need to hide."

Mac hesitated, but shook his head. "I think we'd better be overly cautious for now." He looked at the slumped bodyguard. "Maybe your new friend had better stay here, until he's better."

"OK. I'll be right back."

"I'll go," volunteered Mac, but Jenny shook her head.

"If they catch you, you're dead. I'm a valuable virgin, they won't even rape me."

"Let me get you something to use for a screwdriver," Mac stopped as she produced her multitool. "Resourceful woman! We'll keep our ears peeled. Scream if you need us, I always wanted to die a hero!"

Half an hour later, the three were hidden in the larger spaces behind the wet bar and the showers, the threads of the screws that held the panels half stripped, so they could get out at will, and she was alone again with the bodyguard. The wet bar had provided a packet of hot cocoa mix, hot water and decently sized mugs. He looked much better for the hot drink, and she tried to talk to him.

"What is your name?"

He sighed. "It was a joke from an old American comic book. They called me Captain Midnight. I'm much darker than the others. I was better than them at languages, but worse at everything else." His eyes closed. "I'm a failure as a bodyguard, they should never have sent me, but Master Wong wanted a translator that everyone would ignore."

"Cap," Jenny hesitated, unsure of how to proceed. "They targeted you, specifically. You were the first one they shot, because they knew you were the most dangerous. The best bodyguard in the Universe couldn't have survived. They were after you first and foremost, not Mr. Wong. They shot all the men they didn't want to try to ransom. Mr. Wong was one of them."

"But I did survive. There should have been something . . . I fainted." He cried, tears coming now. In his weakness he could only curl up on the bed and weep.

"You were shot three times," Jenny frantically patted his shoulder, then grabbed the fur coat and covered him, for what good that would do. "You can barely stand up."

"I wasn't dead, so I should have been able to do something!"

Unable to give comfort, she sat helplessly beside him, until he slept.

Chapter Eleven
Gathering Information

Nicole took the three plates from Stephanie. "They've drafted you as waitress?"

"Yes," Stephanie nearly whispered. "I was terrified when they told us to come out, but they haven't hurt any of us yet." She glanced fearfully over her shoulder and scurried back toward the lift.

Nicole carried the plates to her roommates. "Keep up your strength, and all that nonsense," she told them. Between terror, nerves and boredom they eventually picked the plates clean. With the queen-sized bed in the larger room and the recliners here in the tiny antechamber, there would have been plenty of room, if any of them had been able to sleep.

To Paula's vocal and Barbara's expressive horror, she kept the door of the corridor open a few inches to keep track of what was happening. Paris had eventually stuck his head out of the room Michael was in, he'd nodded cautiously to her, and thereafter his door had also been open a few inches. As the other passengers' curiosity slowly overcame their fear, doors up and down the hall were opened. Even her roommates eventually joined her in watching.

"Ethereal and Aria are alive, and most of their staffs as well," Nicole told them. "Stephanie and two of Ethereal's friends are next door with her."

Michael eventually peeked out of his door, but when she would have gone to him had shaken his head firmly.

"I can't see many cabin doors, but as far as I can tell there aren't very many men." Nicole pulled her head in and let Paula look out.

"Probably they were the richest men." Barbara dithered behind her. "And didn't Dr. Zimmer say something about some of the crew?"

"Yes, but they'll be locked in their quarters, not up here!" Even violent death couldn't shake Paula's sense of propriety.

Nicole wondered how the hijackers had decided who was rich enough to ransom and who was too much trouble and easier to shoot.

"Why did they send Jenny down to second class?" *I should have left her at home. But I wanted to show off, show her I could travel to the stars, and take her along if I felt like it. I wanted to lord it over the smart girl that sneered at me for selling my body.* "What are they doing down there?"

"We haven't heard any screams," Paula tried to comfort her. "Anyway, Jenny's fat and plain, they won't bother with her, they'll rape the pretty girls."

"Paula!" Barbara was scandalized. "Don't say things like that! I haven't seen Debby, Gail or Heidi up here!"

92

In the Rift

And then there are the friends I invited along. At least Barbara and Paula are getting paid for this. God! I wish Michael had been a skinflint. I've dragged thirteen people into this mess!

***

"Thanks, Stephanie." Paris took the quivering tray, the poor kid was scared silly, and with good reason. She scuttled off without a word. "Here, Bornstein, they're feeding us, so they haven't changed their minds about killing us." Paris handed off one of the plates and sat down carefully on the other recliner, trying, probably with limited success, to continue to sound like an idiot pop musician. His head felt like it was going to explode. He'd met toughs that bragged about how many times they'd been stunned. Mind boggling. At least as far as he could tell he was still thinking all right, even if it did hurt. Hell of a way to treat a valuable commodity, but much better than the alternative.

He turned his attention to his tray. The food had obviously been zapped straight from frozen to overdone, but he shoveled it in anyway. *This is not the time to imitate Ethereal.*

Bornstein just grunted, and after pushing the food around a bit, ate it all, then buried his nose back in someone's bookpad. Since he'd regained consciousness, Bornstein had been totally uncommunicative. Paris had at first wondered if Bornstein had been stunned on top of the obvious blow to the head, but then decided that he simply didn't want to communicate. Even when Doctor Zimmer had been brought around, he'd just glared and growled 'I'm fine' when the doctor tried to look at his eyes.

Paris shoved both plates out the door, and kept it open a crack to watch. Far from being locked in, the electronic locks had all been shorted out. It gave him an amazingly insecure feeling.

Bornstein came over once and opened the door wide enough to stick his head out. He shook his head at someone, probably Nicole next door who'd been watching the hallway since she'd been shoved in there last night. He himself had been caught flat-footed, sitting in his usual chair at the ramp head avoiding Ethereal's pre-dinner ritual. He remembered someone approaching him, and looking up into a stunner barrel. He'd woken up in this suite, which he rather thought had been Chairman Wong's. Nicole Peace and two of her staff were next door, Ethereal and two of her staff beyond them, poor Stephanie had been shoved in with them and was too scared to shift in with Nicole. Either that or Nicole was worse than Ethereal...

After about half an hour the hijackers came back, and sent two of the girls around to collect plates. When Paris tried to venture out and help, their laser rifles had zeroed in on him until he closed the door. "Don't be an idiot," was

In the Rift

Bornstein's only comment, nearly doubling the number of words he'd spoken since the hijacking.

When he stuck his head out again, there were no hijackers in sight. Paris decided it was time to get to work. *Hijackings weren't part of my assignment, but it appears that this one will be my job.*

The door to the port stairs was right outside the suite door, but it was shut and refused to budge for buttons or force. He scooted quickly down the hall to his and Ethereal's suite and slid through the door. Like his, the lock had been shorted out.

"It's me!" he hissed, in response to the screams. "Relax, are you all okay?" He scanned them worriedly, but they looked frightened, not abused. He slid the door almost closed. Hopefully he'd hear anything happening out there.

They were all nodding, so he asked, "What did you see? What happened?"

"I was getting dressed when the lock popped. I was going to yell at you," admitted Ethereal. "but it wasn't you. It was one of the waiters and he had a rifle and the way he looked at me! I was scared," her voice got very small.

"You two were in here too?" he asked Vela and Julianne. They nodded and he looked at Stephanie questioningly.

"I got off the lift, I was going to see if Nicole was here or at dinner, and there were a bunch of the cabin attendants waiting, with guns. They just grabbed me and shoved me in here and said to not come out." She gulped. "They didn't need to say what would happen, it was just the way they looked at us, like, would we please give them an excuse."

"They searched through everything," Ethereal spoke through gritted teeth. "And groped me. Then they went away."

"Okay, you gals just sit tight, they probably want money and won't hurt you. Just don't attract attention if you can help it." He slipped out and over to Nicole Peace's suite.

She frowned at him, through the crack she'd been watching through, and opened the door reluctantly. "What do you want?" She sounded surly. He hadn't met the two women with her, and nodded vaguely.

"I'm trying to find out what happened." He told her. "Where were you? What did you see?"

"Good grief, how can you be nosy at a time like this?"

"I'm trying to find out how many hijackers there are and so forth, it can't hurt."

She sniffed, but let him in and started talking. "We were eating dinner, and Michael saw something odd and got up and walked down that side hall, you know the one to the little door at the umm, stern?"

He nodded encouragingly.

"I heard a thud and then," her voice started getting shrill. "These men came out of there, and started shooting. They killed that chink bodyguard and then the Captain and the third officer and those old people and they were yelling at us and splitting us up. There was blood everywhere, I think the Captain got someone with a knife." She sniffled.

"I hope they stunned him, instead of killing him." She was shivering and he grabbed a blanket and slung it around her.

"They said they were going to sell us." Her voice was high and tight. "They said the men they hadn't killed were rich enough to be ransomed, but all us women were going to be sold." Her eyes brimmed suddenly with tears.

"They took Jenny away, I don't know what they've done to her."

"They probably just locked her up in her cabin." He tried to reassure her, but his own stomach was starting to rebel.

That nice kid! And the other children back there!

He thought about the suite he had been shoved in. "What about Chairman Wong?"

"They killed him too, and that little guy that translated for him. I'm pretty sure of that. They used stunners too, but I saw the, the b, burning holes." She stopped, gulping.

"Oh, hell." He sat down beside her and hugged her, as much for his sake as hers.

We are in very very deep shit and I didn't come prepared and I'm not the big hero type anyway! I'm the guy who stays in the background collecting information, for Ivan's sake! I have some low-level surveillance gear—which will do me no good whatsoever. No weapons, nothing that can be made into a weapon. Why was I complaining about political spying? Now I'm really out of my league.

"Did they say anything about where we might be headed?"

She just shook her head.

He looked at the other women, questioningly, but they both shook their heads.

"We were eating and then that man crashed onto the Captain's Table, and everyone started screaming." Paula blinked back tears. "The guns were so quiet, I didn't realize they were shooting, at first, then those horrible stunners."

She put her hands to her ears as if in remembered pain. "Everyone started screaming and, and, they shoved us around and pushed us in here."

He studied them briefly, they were younger than most of the beauty queens' staff, early thirties instead of the more common late thirties or forties. *More valuable, so they're up here in First Class.* He wondered what sort of hell Second Class might have turned into, then quickly shut down his imagination. Some things he didn't need to know, just now.

"Okay, sit tight and keep a low profile. I'm going to see if anyone else knows anything." He peeked out the door, looked around and headed for Aria's suite.

She, like Ethereal, had apparently been caught in the middle of dinner preparations, with her staff. The five of them seemed to be all right, Aria having been reassured as to Latham's survival.

"The doctor said he was sharing a suite with him upstairs. He said that you and Michael Bornstein are the only men on this floor, the rest are up on the first deck, or locked into the crew quarters."

"Are there many men?" Paris was surprised. "It seems like they killed so many."

"Those four men that are married to the four sisters? They're up there and some of the crew, I think the Doctor said the Captain, two pilots and some engineers. Oh, and the Chef. He was the only non-hijacker on the entire service staff, according to the doctor."

"The Captain's alive then?" Paris received nods.

"I heard that they killed every man in Second Class."

Paris thought about the poker players and the fathers of the kids, the kids... and prayed for that to be wrong.

He heard the click of boot heels out in the corridor and scooted back to the door. He could see the doors closing up and down the curve, and slid Aria's door down to a tiny crack. He could only see a bulk pass by, but by the syncopated footsteps the bulk was composed of two men. As the steps faded, he eased the door back open.

"OK, I'm going to keep checking on everyone else, keep your heads down,"

He slipped out and cautiously around the curve.

Frowning, he skirted the ramp down to the lounge and hugged the back wall of his favorite alcove. The starboard side had yet another locked stairway access, this one across the ring corridor from the small niche with the passenger elevators. Access was now blocked by a table and two chairs, currently empty. Guard post. He eyed the stairway, but approaching footfalls made him retreat back past all the suites he'd already checked to the far side of Chairman Wong's suite to check the other suites on this floor. They were all stuffed with women, friends and staff of the beauty queens. Several of the women had been down in Second Class when the hijacking started.

"They shot all the men, they shot those kids' fathers right in front of them." The thin brunette was one of Aria's group, still shivering and shocky. Marcie Some-thing-or-other.

"They hauled us up here." Opal was one of Ethereal's hired help, a dressmaker and aspiring designer. "I was very, very glad to get away from that bald one, there was, he was." She stopped and gulped. "I don't think, the way they were talking about us, that they're being left alone down there."

"They sorted us out, and sent the pretty ones up here." The brunette sniffed back tears. "That horrible bald one was saying we were too valuable to play with."

Opal hugged her reassuringly, at the same time she nodded to Paris. "Marcie's right, they sounded like they want us unharmed, and," she blinked back tears. "I guess they have enough women that they can, can," she gulped. "Down in second class. Epona and Ruby are down there, I think. I don't know about any of the others."

Paris gave them the list of women he knew were on this level, the short list far from reassuring.

Gulping a bit himself, he left. He couldn't hear footsteps, but something was going on further around the curve. He eyed the door to the last suite. It was solidly shut, no one peeking from that one. Dithering a bit, he finally snuck far enough around to see the bare edge of a man sitting down. A chair creaked, a man laughed and then the unmistakable sound of cards being shuffled. He was back at the guard post. No chance of getting to that last suite, and however much he'd like to talk to any of the flight crew who had survived, and find out what had happened on the bridge, it wasn't going to be possible.

Retracing his steps, he paused at Nicole's door long enough to pass on the news about the Captain's survival, but didn't enter.

Prowling forward, he again found the furthest suite under the eyes of the card playing guards. Whoever was in there wasn't going to be interviewed any time soon. When he got back to 'his' cabin, he was grateful for Bornstein's silence. He felt very ill and knew he desperately needed to think of what to do, when all he really wanted to do was shut his brain down.

He tried to correlate what he'd heard into something useful. How many people worked in the kitchen, the wait staff, the service people? A dozen, perhaps. And the hijackers obviously had a flight crew, so how much of the regular crew had been in on this hijacking? Maybe nothing at all had happened on the bridge. A grim thought.

Did knowing how many hijackers there were make a difference? They had lasers and stunners. He hadn't even remembered to get his toiletries bag from Ethereal's cabin. Right. He wasn't even armed with his nail clippers. He flopped onto the bed and pulled a pillow over his still aching head. Tomorrow he'd start a headcount of hijackers and weapons.

***

"Dinner, such as it is." Jenny announced, as the door opened.

The women inside exhaled their held breaths as one. "Do you have any news?" One of them asked.

"I haven't heard anything from first class," which must be where these women were from, she didn't recognize any of them. "Were you traveling with anyone?"

"Our husbands." There were four of them crammed into the tiny cabin, and probably without a change of their own clothes.

Jenny gulped nervously. "Were you with them, when the

102

hijackers struck?" She hoped she wasn't going to have to give them any bad news.

"Yes, don't look so apprehensive, dear." One of them actually patted her shoulder. "They said we were good ransom prospects. They split us up so we'd behave, or so they said."

"I think they just felt mean. We're too old for them to even want to rape." They were all four in perhaps their late fifties, all with silver hair, all tiny thin women. Like a bunch of clones. As if she could read her mind, one of them grinned suddenly. "Don't worry about telling us apart, we're sisters. We all answer to all our names."

"I'll pass on any news," she assured them, handing out four ration bars. "I need to go deliver the rest of these."

"Certainly, dear."

The next room, which she had to open herself, contained two women huddled in a corner, watching the door like . . . like women who'd been raped and knew it wasn't over.

"Mrs. Daimler? Mrs. Caruthers? It's me. It's safe for now." Jenny found herself whispering, and cleared her throat. "Irene? Corella?"

With a sigh of relief, Corella Caruthers straightened. "Jenny, dear, sorry, we weren't expecting . . . your sort of company. Are you all right?"

"Yeah, they haven't bothered me." Jenny looked worriedly at the two women. Irene Daimler had slumped back against the wall, looking too tired to even eat.

Corella glanced worriedly at the other woman, but smiled wryly at Jenny. "Good, you youngsters don't have enough experience to put this in perspective. I just kept telling myself that at least I wouldn't have to go through divorce proceedings to get rid of them."

Jenny boggled a bit, unsure if she was joking or serious.

Corella shrugged, and actually managed a bit of a twinkle. "I keep remembering all my counseling after my last disastrous foray into matrimony. It lasted three weeks, the last mostly spent in the hospital. I'm trying to pass on all I can from the rape survivors groups I joined, but it's a bit difficult when you know they can come back anytime they want to."

Jenny nodded her comprehension. "Assertiveness and situational awareness and avoidance won't get you too far just now." At the older woman's surprised look she added. "We all get classes in stuff like that in high school, along with sex education, child care and how to handle credit. Not that any of it really sticks, you know? Here are some ration bars, they just tossed them off the elevator and left." She gave two to Corella. "I need to take the rest around to everyone."

Corella patted her on the shoulder. "Yes. We'll be all right."

The three families were the worst. All the fathers had been killed, all in front of their wives and kids. Most of the

104

kids were still terrified and huddling behind the recliners and their mothers as if they could hide. The oldest, Adam Brown, was angry. His mother looked frightened, but also grimly determined. She still had a lot left to lose.

There were three crew women on their floor. "That Descartes didn't want them to start fighting over the only women in the crew's quarters, well, the hijackers quarters, now. There's another engineer, my boss, that they didn't kill, and two pilots that are locked up somewhere. I suppose they think the men will be salable, or maybe corruptible. To them, we're just women." The engineer was a chunky, healthy looking blonde.

One of the other women, a skinny blonde, sighed. "We're maid service, not a chance the company would pay to get us back." The redhead glumly agreed.

"It sounds like it would take a great deal of money to outbid their clients, and it's not just women," Jenny told her. "Doctor Zimmer and the Chef are alive. I think they're up in first class."

The engineer snorted. "Poor Georges is probably mortified, and Zimmer thinks it's his just due."

"Actually, Zimmer's in a complete funk. Looks awful. Pity," Jenny said. "That he's not as dashing and dangerous as he looks."

"Ha, fat chance. All he's good for is charming the female passengers. Yeah, I noticed he'd been taken down a peg or three. Bet it doesn't last long. I'm Ursula Parker, by the way."

"Jenny Poppenhusen. You're an engineer?" the woman nodded. "Excellent, all we need to do is kill twenty or so pirates, and we can cruise home."

Parker frowned. "Fat chance, kid, I said engineer, not pilot. Sit tight and wait. The fleet will come looking for us."

"I suppose so," said Jenny, dubiously. "Of course we won't be overdue for another fifteen days, which will rather widen the search area." She bit her lip. "Did you actually count them, or anything?"

Parker frowned at her. "The hijackers? They seemed to be the service staff, so there are eighteen at least."

"Plus whoever's flying the ship, unless they were pretending to be waiters." She hesitated. "How many of the crew are recently hired, do you have any idea?"

"All of us." The engineer scowled. "They just shifted the 'Far Seeker' to this run and I think only the Captain and the Doctor are old hands."

"And you said 'Descartes' is he that Maitre d'? Former Maitre d'"

The redhead nodded. "Phillip Descartes. I thought he was so handsome! Ha! I guess Mother was right when she said I had appalling tastes in men."

The skinny blonde was frowning. "He hired me, he said they needed more women on the staff, to put the lady passengers at ease, he said. I guess he was just loading the ship with as many women as possible."

Jenny thought about that for a moment. "Yes, this ship has a lot of women onboard. I think that must have been deliberate, I wonder how that was arranged?" She was still thinking about that as she left.

The beauty queen cliques had apparently declared an armistice. A cluster of them at the far side of the hall from her cabin had taken in their compatriots evicted from first class. Heidi Schmidt and Tia McPeters had shoehorned a girl from Ethereal's group into their room, and several women she didn't know were in Stephanie and Debby's cabin. Looking at them, even after the last twenty-four hours they'd survived, Jenny couldn't see why they were considered of lesser value. Well, sure, Heidi's healthy freckled face and Tia's long one were no rivals to Nicole's beauty, but they were both pretty and very shapely, well, thin.

"Dinner," she announced, handing out the bars. "I'm Jenny, Nicole's sister." She introduced herself randomly to the women peeking out of various rooms.

"Sallie Halfacre." The girl with Heidi reciprocated. She was clearly young—rejuve never got skin quite back to its youthful bloom—and Jenny suddenly realized that her short stiff red hair was probably an indication of ichimp ancestry. She eyed the rest of Ethereal's companions curiously. One elegant woman had long black hair with silver streaks in it that had to be cosmetic. Nature wasn't usually so dramatic, even though this woman had the slightly softer relaxed looking skin of a rejuve. She didn't look Alphan. Her hands were a bit shaky, like, Jenny eyed Tia and Heidi again. Pale and trembling, behind a good facade. Oh. All the rape victims, pretty and young or not, had been shoved down here. Handy for the pirates when they got hungry again or just keeping them from panicking the first class group? Hopefully the latter.

Debby and Gail were also putting up a good front. Hell, they all were. They were mostly city girls, but overprotected, not street smart. Their lax, by her own father's standards, upbringing had probably included lots of casual sex, or at least an accepting attitude about it, but not a whole lot of street smarts or unpleasantness. Jenny handed out ration bars, and made a mental note to try and get Corella to come around to this side for some group counseling. Or survivor tips, or something.

She left Misty and Kissy for last. "Are you guys okay?" she asked, after assuring them of Mac, Frank and Juan's safe concealment.

Kissy wrinkled her nose. "Yuck. I've . . . associated . . . with worse customers than these, but the potential for violence just sort hovers around and . . . spoils the ambience."

Misty snorted. "Don't worry about us honey, we've been there, done that, and then turned around and done it again."

108

In the Rift

She didn't look very happy, for all her verbal unconcern. "But Kissy's right about the violence. They've been getting almost as much of a thrill killing as raping, and that's scary. You be very careful."

"So far so good, for me at least." She dug into the crate she was carrying. "Do you want extras? They just tossed out a whole box. I'm going to keep extras myself, and there's plenty to slip to the guys."

"Sure, just in case." Kissy hesitated. "That man . . . "

"He's getting better, so hopefully we'll have some serious muscle on our side, if an opportunity presents itself."

Back in her cabin, Captain Midnight wolfed down two bars and drank about a gallon of water, before stretching out on a recliner to sleep.

Chapter Twelve
Coming and Going

It was three days before she dared venture out to visit Michael in the cabin he shared with Paris. Paris had been the first of the prisoners to venture out. Nicki had noted jealously that he had quickly checked on Ethereal and her group, and in fact with everyone on the floor, even coming to see her. If she hadn't been so anxious for news about Michael, she wouldn't have let him in.

All he'd really wanted was a good gossip though. 'What happened in the dining room?' indeed! Well, answering the nosy pest's questions had been better than sitting and worrying.

Seeing Michael again was good, too. Especially since he wasn't too worried. "All these hijackers care about is money, so don't get hysterical about their threats." He glared at Paris who at least had the decency to pretend he wasn't listening. "There is no slavery in the New Territories. They are making these threats because they get their jollies frightening women. Once they have everyone totally frightened, they'll send out ransom demands, rake in the cash and drop us somewhere inconvenient."

"Oh," she breathed. "that sounds much better." *And very*

logical. Slavery in this day and age, how ridiculous.

"What about passengers that can't afford to pay?" a new thought struck her. Michael would pay for her, and probably Jenny, but what about her staff and friends? They were all nearly as poor as she was.

"They'll keep making threats until FarCo, the company that owns the ship, pays them something to get their passengers back. FarCo would lose too much business if they just abandoned passengers."

"Oh, good, that makes sense." Nicole ignored the skeptical look on Paris's face. "I feel so much better talking to you. Barbara and Paula take everything the hijackers say as truth, and get hysterical." She snuggled up just a bit closer to Michael, and he responded with a hug. But she could feel the underlying tenseness in his muscles and started worrying about whether he was just trying to calm her down and didn't really believe what he'd said.

Stop it! Michael has money, and that can fix any problem.

Paris was still staring at the ceiling, pretending not to listen, but he'd talked to everybody . . .

"Paris, have you found out who's still alive?" Nicole braced herself. "I haven't seen most of my friends up here."

"Some of them are up on the upper floor of First Class, the rest are down in Second." Paris said. "They didn't kill any of the young women, or even the old ones that have money.

112

In the Rift

There's four sisters, you must have noticed them? They all look alike? They're down in Second Class, and their husbands are up here. There were a few older couples down in Second, they killed both the men and women. And all the rest of the men in Second Class, too." He blew out a breath. "I guess they figured anyone down there didn't have enough money to be worth ransoming." He shot Michael a frown. "Or perhaps they figured the men would cause more trouble than they were worth, and just kept the women."

"Right." Even Nicole could see a few logical holes, but she wasn't about to explore them. She was here for comfort and company, not disaster scenarios.

"Bornstein, you're pretty familiar with the New Territories, what . . . "

"Oh, shut up, you twit, you're not the hero that will save us all, welcome to the real world. Now go away and stop alarming Nicole."

Paris scowled, but scouted the corridor, then left.

"Thank you, Michael. I'm so glad you're here." She leaned into his shoulder and wondering why they had so much freedom to roam. Not that she minded being able to visit Michael, but it seemed odd that Paris could, hmm, spy on the prisoners? "Michael, could Paris be a, a, inside agent? Watching us?"

He snorted, stifling laughter. "Him?" He snickered and cleared his throat. "I really don't think so, although . . . "

He trailed off thoughtfully and Nicole sat quietly, not interrupting. "I think I will keep an eye on him." He nuzzled into her neck. "And you tell me everything he does or says."

***

Jenny stuck her head out and surveyed the dim corridor. Why the hijackers had turned down the lights was anybody's guess. *Psychology? Make us think it's night and we'll sleep? Make it creepy and we'll stay huddled in our cabins? If so, it's working pretty well, most of the women scuttle out to the lavatories and back to their rooms as quickly as possible.*

It certainly isn't to keep them under surveillance, they either didn't have cams on the hallways, or didn't monitor them. The first time Mac, Frank, Juan and Cap came out from behind the bulkheads the hijackers would have been down on us like a horde of locusts.

The hijackers patrolled periodically, at random times, and while they'd threatened the few women they'd caught out of their rooms, after the first rampage through Second Class they'd left the women alone. Was it bad for hijacker morale to rape while on duty? She snorted a little at the thought, but whatever the reason, hoped it would last.

Tonight, there was no one in sight, so she headed for the lounge, keeping her eyes open. Misty and Kissy had evidently been watching also, they popped out and followed her

114

silently. Cap was following her too, but she often didn't see him, and certainly never heard him. As had become ingrained habit, she searched the lounge before signaling the men to come out, and tonight found an eavesdropper.

"Adam! What are you doing here?" The scrawny twelve-year-old looked embarrassed as he crawled reluctantly out from under the wet bar sink.

"I wanted to find out what you are up to." He glared at her. "If you're going to kill some pirates, I want to help. I'm going to kill that man that shot my Dad." He stopped as his voice started quivering.

"Just now we're gathering information and trying to figure out what to do." Jenny told him. "We are so split up that we can't use our superior numbers to our advantage. In fact, by threatening the prisoners on one level they can control the rest of us. We may not be able to do anything until we get to wherever they are taking us, and we can act as one big group."

"Jenny, you shouldn't say things like that, he's just a little boy!" Misty exclaimed. "You just leave everything to us, honey, and it'll be okay."

Adam gave her a look of contempt, and Jenny shook her head. "Adam is old enough to understand that we are in a very dangerous situation, and that we may have to wait until we see a situation where we have at least some chance of winning."

She looked at him seriously. "Adam, I do have some secrets that may help us later, but I can't tell you now. I would like you to bring me any information you have, tell me anything you hear the pirates say, even if it doesn't seem helpful." She thought for a minute.

"Do you by any chance have a pocket knife? Or your Dad's? Or any little tools?"

He nodded a bit uncertainly.

"Look around for anything like that, and find a place to hide them where a quick search by the pirates won't find them, but you can grab them quickly if we get taken out of here." He looked a bit happier, probably because she hadn't wanted him to give them to her.

"Go back now, is your Mom awake?" He shook his head. "Good. Quietly look for tools or anything that might be used as a weapon. Put it, hmm, see if you can jam it up under the sink in your room, something like that. OK?"

He nodded and slid out.

"Jenny, was that a good idea?" Misty was still worried.

"Yes." The voice from the floor made all three women start. "It gets him thinking about the situation instead of thinking about trying to kill hijackers. And collecting things that might be useful." Mac grunted, squeezing out of the hole.

They had rigged the panels here so the men could open and close them from the inside, but they couldn't see out to check for watchers.

"I'll be right back!" Mac made a beeline out to the hall and in the direction of the lav, quickly followed by Frank and Juan.

"Maybe we ought to start coming a bit earlier," giggled Kissy, jumping as Cap slid out of the shadows. "I wish I could move that quiet!" she said, strolling out to where she could see any women who might also be lavatory bound.

The men returned quickly and grabbed ration bars. "Did anything happen today?" Jenny looked around. "To anyone?"

They all shook their heads, and Mac spoke for them all. "Nothing. And back there we can hear anything loud. It's been almost a week and we're still underway and jumping regularly. I didn't think anyplace but Eta Pegasi was within reach?" He looked at Juan.

Juan was shaking his head in disagreement. "Regulations make us carry big reserves of fuel, we could actually get much further if we needed to. And this one gee acceleration, it's only partly for matching velocities with our destination, it also runs the generators and charges the capacitors for jumps of course, but mostly it's for the passenger's comfort. If we dropped everything but power generation, we could get even further."

"We just couldn't dock when we got there?" asked Frank.

"Depends, but even so, someone could bring us fuel, so we could match velocities." Juan hesitated. "Assuming we'd gotten somewhere that they have fueling equipment and a ship to run us down."

"Now." Jenny was trying to remember things read too long ago. "I know stars are very thin here, but there are some, the Pegasus Rift is just a, a romantic sounding name the media came up with. Are there any failed colonies or mining operations that could have been abandoned? And left equipment out here?"

Mac was shaking his head. "That's why the New Territories are so hot. There are a lot of new stars, third and fourth generation, very metal rich, and so are their halos. The planets with any active geologic processes to concentrate ores have been mind bogglingly rich. This is where all those new crystals they use for AI's are mined, and transuranics, stuff that's so rare other places."

He shook his head. "Any mining equipment that made it this far, and there wasn't much because the stars are more than a bit sparse out here, was grabbed and moved to one of the new finds. I don't think we can be headed for anything inside the rift, but despite the New Territories reputation, shit like this wouldn't be tolerated on any of the closer worlds. Even the most distant planets . . . there are a few that have pretty bad reputations, but we'd have to refuel to get to any of them."

"Could we be meeting another ship?" Cap asked.

"That's what I'm afraid of. Ship-to-ship rendezvous are

118

difficult, but there are enough stars in the rift, they could meet near one of them." admitted Mac. "Once the women are off the 'Far Seeker' they'll be almost impossible to trace."

"If worst comes to worst," Jenny told them soberly. "You should stay with the ship and try to make port, somewhere. Anywhere. Then at least the authorities will know that we're alive to be looked for."

Cap's hands clenched, as Frank hissed in dismay. "I hope it doesn't come to that!"

Jenny looked at them with exasperation. "Don't do something heroic and pointless. Getting yourselves killed leaves us worse off. Remember that!"

Mac snorted. "That's what men are for, Jenny." He shook his head at her glare. "You're right, but it makes me feel like a coward. What a mess. I wasn't looking forward to smarming up to a pack of politicians over the annexation; now it sounds like heaven."

Chapter Thirteen
Sightseeing

Paris waited until the guards had passed from sight on their usual round, then slid quietly out the door and down the ramp, and spotting no guards on this level, tried the door of the kitchen. A knife, or ice pick, tools . . . too late, he heard something behind him and started to turn, freezing at the jab in his ribs.

"You are getting to be a real pain." Paris looked cautiously over his shoulder, directly into the teeth and bad breath of 'the bald one,' as the passengers called him. "I wonder if your fans would pay as much for the rest of you if we sent them your prick?" he snickered. "Or is that all that they are interested in?"

"Probably." Paris answered. "You might want to start with fingers or ears. Or nose. I've always hated my nose."

"Glad to know that." The hard object retreated from his ribs as the man swung him around.

He tried to throw himself back as he saw the gun butt coming but wasn't fast enough. His face exploded in pain, then a second blow behind his ear knocked him flat and woozy. A couple of kicks to the ribs, not very hard, Baldy knew he was valuable and was just playing with him a bit.

Paris stifled his fury and any response that would escalate the force behind the kicks. Today is not the day to start the rebellion. When he was grabbed and dragged back to his feet he tried to stand, to walk, to not hit his head as he was shoved . . . into something soft. Ah, his favorite chair in the alcove at the head of the ramp.

Footsteps faded as he cautiously felt his nose. Broken, but not out of alignment, and of course bleeding like mad. Lump behind the ear. Better than a stunner, theoretically at least. He could hear voices from around the corner. Baldy giving orders to the guards? After a vain search of his pockets, he shucked off his shirt and tried to find a way to staunch the bleeding with minimal pain. He sat for the better part of an hour, doing nothing more than sitting still with his shirt plastered to his nose and thinking.

Why the hell hadn't he been thrown into 'his' room? That wasn't a good thought at all. Because if the hijackers didn't want to disturb Bornstein's snuggle with Nicole, that implied a whole lot about Bornstein that he was going to have to find solid, stand up in court, type proof of. After he escaped and captured the rest of the hijackers, of course.

I had all those classes in self-defense. What happened to them? I'm much stronger than I look. I might have been able to take that goon's gun away from him. But then what do I do? Imitate a holovid hero, marching through the ship shooting bad guys right and left (never running out of power), single-handedly rescuing an entire ship full of gorgeous women? He almost smiled at the image. *Only the ship full of gorgeous women is real.*

I guess I should have taken classes in counter-hijacking. Have to check if any are available when I get home. He nearly grinned, picturing the expression on his boss's face if asked for such a class. *Although, if he couldn't find one for me, he'd make me organize one. I expect the _fleet_ has classes like that.*

At the sounds from below, he pulled the shirt away from his nose with a wince, and leaned over the railing to listen. Unfortunately the steps and voices were coming nearer. Baldy glared up the ramp at him and he backtracked hastily toward Ethereal's suite.

"Oh, no you don't, pretty boy." Baldy's voice stopped him. "Back in with the other jerk. You people are wandering around a bit too much. Time and past to lock you in."

Paris hustled down two doors, getting a helpful shove from Baldy as he opened the door. Nicole's glare switched to fear instantly as she saw the hijacker behind him. At least she was dressed. Bornstein started forward, but stopped at a look from Baldy.

"Save any sugar for me, sweety?" Baldy leered, grabbing her and pulling her out the door. "Get back where you belong."

Bornstein glared at the closing door, then at him. "What

123

did you do, you idiot?"

"Took a look around." Paris squeezed into the miniature bathroom and examined his nose in the mirror. "Yeach." At least it had stopped bleeding. He ran a sink full of cold water, and dunked his face, and then the bloody shirt.

"So what did you see?" Bornstein asked.

"Baldy." He admitted glumly, dabbing at the blood. However swollen, his nose looked reasonably straight. He put his head down as a wave of vertigo swamped him, another grav jump. The water in the basin started sloshing and he hastily flipped the drain open, and grabbed a handhold as the ship maneuvered. "I think we may have just arrived at our destination."

Chapter Fourteen
Pirate Station

"How long have these hijackers been active?" Mac sounded shocked, and Jenny floated over to see what he was looking at. He had an exterior camera shot showing on the vidscreen of the second class lounge. With the passengers hiding in their rooms, and the hijackers hopefully busy with the approach maneuvers, Mac and Frank were taking the risk of leaving their hiding place.

"A space station?" said Frank. "Surely this bunch of pirates can't have their own space station!"

"Geeze!" Mac sounded breathless, staring over her shoulder. "It isn't even finished!"

The station, designed as the standard wheel shape, was barely visible in the starlight. But even in the faint light Jenny could see seams; there was no overcoat of spacecrete, no paint and few lights. The queasy feeling in her stomach had nothing to do with zero g, as she wondered silently how airtight that wreck could be.

"What's all that stuff attached to the hub?" asked Frank.

Jenny could see the tangled profusion of tanks and pipes and structural beams protruding from the far side of the hub. It wasn't rotating with the station.

"Fuel separator, by God!" whispered Mac. "They're mining asteroids or comets for fuel."

"They can't have built it from scratch, can they?" Jenny asked. "They'd have to have space refineries, foundries and, and, a lot more stuff than this," she frowned. "A whole industrial setup. And if they had that, why would they be hijackers?"

"I know what this is!" Mac hissed. "Fifty damn years ago the first station for Beta Pegasi, the whole construction fleet, big freighters with the pieces, tugs and everything, disappeared en route."

"I read about that!" said Jenny. "It was, like, the Bermuda Triangle of space, but they wrote it off as a major jump miscalculation. It's why fleets don't jump in formation anymore, and every ship does their own calculations independently."

"Yep. That's the one." He blew out a long breath. "I wonder what they did with the construction crew, when they were done?"

"Did you have to bring that up?" asked Frank. "How are we going to get off?"

"Maybe you shouldn't?" asked Jenny. "Hide until the hijackers are all off, then take the ship and run for Beta Pegasi. You've got Juan. We'd be safe on the station, until you could get back with rescuers."

"No. You wouldn't," said Mac. "They'd hold you hostage

if the station were attacked, and kill you if they thought they were losing."

"Could be." Jenny shrugged. "But I think I'd rather risk that, than get auctioned off to the highest bidder. If it comes to something like that, I'll try to see if there is any way we could take and hold a part of the station."

"What? You and the beauty queens and those, those . . . beauticians of theirs?" Mac shook his head doubtfully. "Maybe if your Captain Midnight keeps improving and can get onto the station . . . I hope to hell we can think of something better!"

Still watching the vidscreen, Jenny complained. "I don't see any light shadows on the station, where's its primary? It does have to be in orbit around something doesn't it?"

Juan finally gave in to curiosity and joined them. "It must be, otherwise, without a gravity well to break up the gravity waves it would be almost impossible to jump close enough to go the rest of the way on fusion jets. Plus, there wouldn't be any ice to mine."

"What's that?" Jenny asked. "Down there, see, is that a planet?" It was a patch of darkness, circular, with a hint of texture and an absence of background stars.

"Maybe, hard to judge the size without instruments." Mac looked at Juan. "Would a free floating planet be large enough to find, gravitationally?"

Juan chewed a fingernail. "Maybe, if you knew where it

was. But the zone of small grav waves around it would be tiny. And they wouldn't be very small grav waves, either." He added. "You know, it would be quick and easy to approach and leave . . . it might be ideal."

"I wonder how they found it in the first place?" Jenny wondered.

"Pure luck, I suspect," said Juan, and glancing toward the control room. "Bad luck, from our point of view."

Then they heard the faint whine of the lifts, Mac hastily killed the vid screen and they scattered to their cabins and hiding places.

***

The grinning line of pirates handed the women off like so much luggage, passing them from one to the next, grabbing wherever they wished. They had mag boots and stuck to the floor; the women floundered helplessly in zero G. Nicole twisted away from one man who seemed to think she could be towed around by her breast, only to be grabbed by the hair and fondled. Her attempt to kick was laughed at, and the next man tugged her away and shoved her into the elevator. Which moved with an unnerving sway and vibration. The shocked and traumatized score of women clung to each other, and the things they'd brought from the ship, with little conversation. Even the shivering sobbing brunette kept one eye on the pirate operating the elevator.

128

In the Rift

Vela or something like that. One of Ethereal's friends, she'd refused to leave her room when ordered. Nicole shivered, remembering what she'd heard coming from that suite. At least it hadn't lasted long.

As the elevator descended they sank to the floor. As shaky as Nicole felt, it was hard to say whether the apparent gravity was normal or not.

"Welcome to Paradise, Ladies." The grinning man pulled the nearest woman against him and thrust his hips at her, laughing as she pulled away and fled. Nicole joined the rest in a concerted rush out the door.

Paradise was . . . spartan, to say the least. The two hundred meter wide tube curved up in either direction, disappearing into darkness in one direction, in the other, the sporadic lighting illuminated the bare bones of the station's construction. A rusting, echoing ruin was plainly revealed to their gaze.. The section containing the elevator shaft was joined to two more sections, curving appreciably as they were welded into more. The floor was a metal grid, with piping and wires dimly visible below. If there had been landscaping in the empty boxes scattered around, the three open tanks of water would have been pools, or perhaps fountains. The area might have been planned as a park in a residential area or some such. A very much unrealized potential. Without softening décor, or apparently much maintenance, they were sterile and lifeless, almost ominous in the dim lights. Squinting at the overhead, Nicole could see that only about a quarter of the lights were operating, almost randomly scattering well lit areas and dim corners, darkening ominously to the left. The overhead rectangles of plex were dark, there was no natural light. It was brighter to the right, where a vertical mesh barrier blocked travel. The other side looked as barren and empty as this side. Several bleak boxy rooms were finished, relatively speaking, in rough spacecrete, spaced along the curved wall of the space station tube before her.

"Is there anything to eat around here?"

Nicole jerked around on her sister. "Trust you to think of your stomach!" She glared at the fat girl. "Even these pirates don't want to rape you, so why should you be worried?"

Jenny scowled back. "I'm worried about you. We're all in shock and a hot drink would help loads, just now." She stalked over to the nearest of the crude rooms and started rummaging around, opening the boxes stacked inside. Nicole rubbed her temples.

A hot drink would be wonderful. Maybe there were advantages to having a hungry fat person around.

She trailed Jenny into the, well, her mother should forgive her calling this anything so civilized as a kitchen. It was stuffed with plastic crates, and had a spacecrete shelf along one side at countertop height. Jenny was already fiddling with a spigot that was spitting water into a pan she

130

held under it.

Jenny pointed across the cramped, box filled space. "Is that a hot plate? See if it will work."

It was plugged into a horribly dangerous looking jury rigged outlet just screwed onto the metal grid above the counter. Nicole prodded the button for the highest setting, and to her surprise was rewarded with a red light and a faint wash of heat across the hands she held out over it. "It's on."

"Great," Jenny sloshed across with the pan full of water. "Let's open these boxes and see if there's anything to put in it." She was popping the seals on the first crate as she spoke. "Eww! Instant Entrées. Those have got to be the worst tasting things!"

"When did you ever eat something like this?" Nicole couldn't help but be amused. "That expensive boarding school you attended never served dehydrated meals!"

"Hiking, Nicole. You know, walking up mountains and all that stuff. They were really hot on hiking."

"Well, maybe you should have taken fewer of these things and walked faster. I can't believe Mother didn't just have the doctor deal with your weight. It's not like you're ugly or anything."

"I refused the meds. It was my kind of teenage rebellion, not to mention a good way of dealing with the stepfather. You were lucky you were old enough to leave home. I was stuck there. Even after I won the scholarship and talked

131

Mother into sending me to the Academy, I still had to go home for holidays." Jenny wrinkled her nose. "In retrospect, I should have waited until he was falling down drunk, then beat the crap out of him."

Nicole was floored. "He said he only wanted me." Her voice sounded small, somehow. "So I ran off with Edward, his parents were rich, he helped me get into the first contests. I didn't think, I didn't . . . " her voice gave out altogether.

"There wasn't anything you could have done. He was a drunken nasty pervert who married Mother because she had two young daughters. Not that he was ever after me like he was with you. He had to get pretty drunk before he started trying to paw me. We both coped as best we could." Jenny smiled wryly. "Not that I wouldn't be delighted, just now, to only have to deal with one perv, instead of forty."

Nicole smiled back. "Yeah." She dragged her mind out of the past. "So, how do you fix these things?" She poked dubiously at the packs in the crate.

Jenny, rooting through another crate, pulled out a box. "Tea first, then we can try for a stew."

***

Paris was trying to ignore his throbbing nose and sleep when the hijackers finally returned. He turned up the lights at the first sounds at the door, and unbuckled himself, hanging onto the edge of the bed in zero g. He'd felt the jolt as they'd docked, to a ship he presumed, they were twenty-five jumps from where they'd been hijacked, and who knew how far off course. Could they have crossed the Rift to another system, or had they met a ship in the rift? No, they hadn't gone far enough for that. They were still in the Rift, somewhere.

The hijackers ignored him and gestured Bornstein out, closing the door behind them. Were they switching to another ship? He floated uncertainly. Were they transferring some of their prisoners, or all of them? What did they want with Bornstein? If it weren't already hurting, he'd bang his head on the wall in pure frustration.

He stewed for another three hours, then the door rattled as they returned. They gestured him out. He had two escorts, one of whom he'd never seen before.

Not good. They're multiplying.

The former waiter grabbed him and held him as the new one searched him. Satisfied, they dragged him into the lift, which carried them all the way to the upper airlock, which stood open to an unmistakable station hub. To call it basic and utilitarian was to flatter it. He looked around with growing apprehension. It was rusting, for christsake.

Where the bloody hell are we?

The hijackers hauled him past one of the four structural shafts and into a very utilitarian elevator. The station spin staggered him sideways and he gratefully grounded his feet as the lift sank, rattling and jolting unevenly. By they the time it had crept down to the rim, his hair was standing on end.

Can this thing take one gee? Am I about to find out it can't? Am I more afraid of a rickety elevator than two armed pirates?

The lift heaved.

Yes.

Fortunately it stopped, and the door slid almost smoothly open. He scrambled thankfully out and gaped around.

At least down here there's enough spacecrete sprayed around to cover any rust. Inexpertly applied 'crete, with gaps and thick spots, no texturing or paint, mind you.

His escort shoved him into a filthy office and pointed to a chair in front of a vidcam.

Across the desk from him, the former Maitre d' looked him over with a pained expression. "What will your fans say when they see you like this?" His tone was more irritated than flippant, as he shrugged. "Record a message to whomever you most trust to send money fast, keep it brief."

Paris frowned at the vidcam. "My agent, I guess. Marty Monkenstein, New Savannah, Alpha Centauri."

The hijackers stirred behind him. "Damn monkey," one of them muttered.

134

In the Rift

"As long as he can send ten million dollars, unmarked UPC bills, yes large ones will be fine. We'll add the shipping instructions ourselves." The Maitre d' smiled and cued on the vidcam.

"Uh, Marty?" Paris touched his nose carefully, then his ear. "As you probably know by now, I've got a big problem. Please access my accounts and rustle up ten million bucks." As he opened his mouth to continue, the active light on the camera blinked out. "Hey, What about, umm, Ethereal and the other ladies, I've got more money than these hicks out here . . ." He trailed off as the man started laughing.

"Fat lot you know. There are miners out here that have hundreds of millions of dollars. And nothing to spend it on, and no one to share their lonely beds. You men, if I had my way, you'd all be dead. Ransoming you is a bad idea, very risky. Stupid." He scowled, then straightened, his face slipping back to the emotionless and severe snobbery of the Maitre d'. "Please show Mr. Paris to his accommodations." He pointed to a roll of fabric against the wall. "Your bed and a change of clothing, sir."

He kept count as they walked, of men and weapons. The standard safety wall between station sections was tight, all doors sealed. The small door level with the deck had a guard in front of it, and something taped to the wall beside it. Audio pickup perhaps? The guard turned and blocked Paris's view to tap a code into the pad beside the door. He listened carefully. Sixteen taps. Shit he was going to have to try to figure out a sixteen character code with a guard and an electronic ear on the other side?

He stepped through the door and studied the cage he was in. Expanded metal mesh, the sort of thing that ought to be reinforcement for a layer of 'crete was underfoot and walled off the entire width and height of the station torus, apparently keeping the men separate from the women.

Why? If they don't want their 'goods' damaged, they ought to have treated them a bit more gently themselves.

A couple of rooms were walled off with the same poor quality spray job as the pirates' section had boasted. Ditto over on the girls' side.

The men were watching the door warily, and visibly relaxed when it closed behind him. The Captain, the first mate and the chief engineer were in a position that hinted they were considering attacking. He took a quick survey. The Wall Street gang was plastered against the mesh, talking quietly, sort of almost touching the spouses both sides must have worried about for so long. Bornstein and Latham, Dr. Zimmer and the Chef, three other crewmen. Yi! Were these the only survivors? Fifteen men total. Not much of a fighting force; he'd counted twenty men on the other side all armed and no doubt an incomplete count. Was he the last one the pirates had moved? He could feel his tired brain shutting down and all he could think was that the air was stale and a bit too humid and either his nose was hallucinating or someone had cooked something. His stomach rumbled. Later.

He looked back at the door. It locked with a standard six by six alpha numeric pad, numbers first, two larger buttons, enter and reset, below. Sixteen characters? He spread the fingers of both hands around the edge of the pad and started to punch in "pirates of the rift" with his thumbs. Fat chance, but the tiny circuits in his finger tips detected the faint tingle of a weak current with every button pushed, and yip! a stronger tingle in the upper left with the third button. So. Rejecting the entry? Or had he detected an automatic check after three buttons? That made his job harder, or rather, more tedious, than if the program checked every entry, but doable, given enough time. He hit the 'a', no tingle. Oh, nice! He reset, another tingle. Hmm. Have to try all random combinations to check for a different response. For now, what were the popular vids, vid and music stars? Apart from himself. He started punching in every one he could think of.

The mesh thrummed and the noise echoed faintly as some of his fellow prisoners walked over. The large space ate sounds, while the hard surfaces bounced it around, the background noise was almost like an irregular surf.

What had that Martre 'd said? "You men, if I had my way, you'd all be dead. Ransoming you is a bad idea, very risky. Stupid." *He is not the boss.* Paris casually moved his hands into a normal typing position, without looking around.

"Do you really think that will do any good?" Bornstein peered over his shoulder. "New Texas Frontier? What on Earth is that?"

Latham snorted. "A very horrible vid. I took a nephew of mine to see it for his birthday. He loved it." He looked dubiously at the lock pad. "Surely they use something more random than that?"

"The alternative is to do nothing," Paris voice trailed off, and he turned away from the lock. "I suppose all of you also recorded messages?"

"Yes, I recorded withdrawal instructions to a New Territories Bank." Bornstein smiled toothily. "If they come in and shoot me someday, you'll know what will happen to you when your banks pay up."

"Then we'll hope they haul you away, and leave us in ignorance of whether they actually released you or not." Latham wandered back toward the dividing mesh, where an anxious Aria stood.

Captain Portman ran a weary hand through his thin hair. "I recorded a message to the company, about how much to send to ransom Ernie and myself." He nodded at the first mate. "It seems they have plans for the rest of my crew, and are planning on keeping the ship." He turned away, grim faced. Ernie Givens hissed a bit, and walked away as well.

Paris spotted Ethereal and raised a hand. She nodded

dispiritedly and didn't even come over. The women all seemed to be drawing together for the night, and Paris, rubbing his temples, decided to see if sleep would help clear his head.

Chapter Fifteen
Do-It-Yourself Prison Improvements

The exhausted women slumped everywhere. There were no beds, and only the blankets they had brought from the ship on the hijackers' orders. The four sisters slept across the mesh barrier from their husbands. The men had been shoved through the far door one at a time, hours after the women had been brought down. Michael had told of recording ransom instructions.

Jenny, fighting off lassitude, decided it was not just the stress of the situation that had nearly everyone asleep. It was the air. Through a fast developing headache, she took a quick census. Fifty-seven women and children. On the far side of the mesh wall, the fifteen men deemed ransomable, or perhaps useful, in the case of the surviving crewmen, slumped unmoving. A station this size should routinely handle thousands. Just how poorly was the atmospheric machinery working? Surely the pirates wouldn't risk their valuable prisoners. Maybe it was just poor air circulation. She frowned up at the soaring curve of the overhead. No fans.

Drifting over to the nearest vent she held her hand over it. Nothing. No air movement at all. But the one in the kitchen had been blowing. She walked back to it, yes, a steady slight breeze. So were there two separate systems, for redundancy, or were some of the vents closed off, she frowned down at the metal mesh floor, somewhere down there?

Asking the hijackers for help was the last option, not the first. With dragging feet, she started searching for controls. Nothing. They couldn't even turn the lights on and off. But tucked away beyond the first lavatory and hidden by one of the apparently randomly placed empty metal troughs, she found a rectangular hole with a lip, and a piece of mesh fitted over it, no ladder. On inspection, it proved to be held shut with nothing more than four hooks from the other side. Her multi tool quickly popped them loose. The mesh deck was more than halfway down the cross section of the tube, so it was not too much further down to the bottom, but would be difficult to get back up without a ladder, although the wall was rough, and well off vertical, she might be able to climb it or . . . she dragged back to the kitchen and emptied three plastic crates, and dragged them to the hole. No one stirred enough to even ask what she was doing. The largest crate wouldn't fit. Oh well. She shoved the two small ones in, wincing as the noise rattled and echoed, then climbed over and hung to search out toeholds on the rough slanted wall then climbed down until the wall became more of a steeply slanted floor that made her doubt the efficacy of the boxes.

In the Rift

In the dim light filtering through the floor mesh above she
could see pipes running along the bottom of the curve, did
they run the complete circumference of the station? One was
cold to the touch, probably water, she decided. The two
largest sounded hollow when she knocked. One had a faint
vibration. Parallel air systems, one turned off? The other
pipes were smaller. Power? Communications? What about
sewage? Peering through the darkness underneath the
kitchen, she could trace smaller pipes to the lav facilities,
larger diameter pipes there went straight to a sealed box,
from whence pipes went to the ponds. Ick! Hmm, all the
metal troughs had lines draining into the treatment system
also. Perhaps they were meant to have plants in them?
Something that needed drainage, in any case. If the pirates
had built this place, why hadn't they either finished it or not
bothered at all with things like that? Her fertile imagination
unfortunately immediately conjured up a captured
construction crew desperately prolonging the construction
and their execution on its completion.

She shuddered and walked on. The dim light coming
through the metal mesh overhead and the growing hush
raised the hackles on her neck. She walked as quietly as she
could, just a slight crackle from the dust underfoot. Just out
of sight of the kitchen plumbing, she found an air intake and
fan system for the working air ducts, then the same, but still
and quiet for the parallel system. A red light shone on one

side of the box below the intake. Unscrewing two screws allowed the side to swing open. It was just like a copier at school, a tiny window scrolling the words 'Empty carbon before restarting' 'replace filter before restarting'.

It must remove carbon dioxide, split it electronically or something, perhaps.

Pulling, sliding and scowling at various drawers and cupboards led to the discovery of both a filter and a bin full of black powder.

"Looks like carbon to me," she muttered. "But what do I do with it?"

It was in a bag like an old-fashioned vacuum, ha, yes and there were empty bags in the 'supplies' drawer. No new filters, however. She carried the bag a few steps and placed it carefully where she wouldn't kick it accidentally. The fine powder looked messy, if not dangerous. The filter . . . taking it away from the intake, she knocked it on the deck a few times, raising a bit of dust, but nothing like the amount of dust an AC filter collected in Oklahoma.

The taps raised echoes, but no alarm.

The air is very bad. Surely the pirates know that?

She replaced the filter, put a new bag in the carbon dump and pushed the restart button. She leaped back at the screech of unlubricated bearings, but the noise quickly subsided.

Jenny bit her lip indecisively. Should she go check on the

prisoners? No, not yet. She turned away and started walking. She passed another water treatment system, with pipes leading to and from a section of solid flooring. Another lav perhaps?

The women had all just huddled together, and even she hadn't explored.

How far could she get? She counted her steps, casting frequent glances backwards. Was this station a standard eight kilometer torus? If so she had probably come nearly a quarter of the way around. And she wasn't going to get any further.

The barrier looked like an airtight wall, the only door a small dogged and locked hatch. The alphabetical lock pad had a dim light behind it. She tried a few combinations, but neither the ABC's nor hijackers or pirates worked. Stepping back she tried to peer upward through the mesh. The airtight wall seemed to continue up there as well.

Scrambling up the slanted sides, she found the bottom corner of a large door in it. In a civilized station it would be open all the time, closed only in an emergency, or a loss of pressure drill. Of course, in a civilized station there'd be about twenty levels of floors with emergency airseals ready to drop between and along them. On this wreck, it was probably a good idea to have the big quarter doors closed full time.

I just wish I were the one in control of them, rather than those rapists.

Unfortunately she couldn't see anyway to jam the doors shut. *Not that slow starvation is a goal to seek either.*

Another pair of carbon exchangers, filters and fans marked the end of the pipe runs. Apparently this section handled its own air and water treatment. She examined the filter boxes, and dumped and relined both carbon bins, before heading back. Her headache was gone, and she felt much more energetic. She passed the kitchen again, and kept going, creeping quietly under the men who were starting to stir above, until another airtight wall blocked her path. The two air purification boxes were both out, but she left them. No need to let the men above her know about her egress. No sign of the hijackers. If they could seal the doors and elevators could they keep the hijackers out?

"Only until the food ran out." She muttered, as she braced a teetering crate on a rough seam and scrambled up the rough wall and heaved herself through the hole. She shifted the mesh cover back on as quietly as she could, and bent the wires hooks back into place. Perhaps an inventory would be a good idea. First, though, she'd check the airtight doors up here.

***

Paris sloshed his shirt around in the cold water and considered his situation. He hadn't been able to do a damned thing on the ship and now they were on a space station with

146

even more hijackers, and so far all he had done was sleep. He wondered uneasily if that had something to do with the air, and if so whether it had been deliberate or accidental. What's worse? Sadistic torturers getting their jollies turning down the oxy level until they overdo it, or a sporadically working air system that could quit at any moment? At least his head was clear this 'morning'.

Captain Portman poked around at the primitive set-up, a permanent scowl on his face. "I'd deck the man that called this plumbing."

Paris wrung out the shirt and hung it precariously by a button through the metal mesh. The hijackers had collected a change of clothes for each of the men, but the laundry facilities being what they were (nonexistent) he figured that he could wear the trousers for a while longer, and shrugged into his other shirt.

"I'm more worried about the air, myself,' he admitted.

Portman nodded. "I think they adjusted it last night, the humidity is down and the oxygen levels up. I suppose they didn't want to kill us right off, but it's not very reassuring, that the air could get that bad in the first place, is it?"

Paris froze, finger on buttons, as the rough scritch of the door sliding open attracted everyone's attention. A trio of pirates stepped through, covering them all with their lasers. Chef Georges stepped in, shuffling away from the man behind him who surveyed the prisoners, then pointed.

"Bornstein. Out."

For a moment Bornstein seemed likely to refuse, then scowled and stiffly stepped between guards and out the door, the pirates retreating after him.

"They cannot possibly have gotten a reply yet," Captain Portman growled, then raised his voice to the chef. "What did they want?"

"Breakfast." Georges was looking speculatively at the kitchen. "Perhaps . . . "

"Yes, please." The Captain sighed, muttering. "Not that I can command anything."

Paris finished buttoning his shirt, wondering a bit at the unexpected consideration about clothes, and then decided that it had probably been a matter of checking for weapons or whatnot, no doubt one reason none of them had been locked in his own suite, although he could have gotten anything he needed during the voyage.

It was very odd, how they hadn't been locked in their cabins onboard. It had made it easier to distribute food, but the sporadic patrols hadn't kept them from wandering pretty much at will.

Was Phillips Descartes' hijacker boss, if he existed at all, disguising himself as one of the prisoners? Had the lax security been for this theoretical quisling's convenience? Did it even count as poor security? He sure hadn't accomplished anything.

In the Rift

This was supposed to have been an easy assignment. Hang around with the other sponsors' reps. Listen and report everything. He had no weapons to conceal, and his few electronic gizmos were not designed for this sort of action, although with patience they'd enable him to work out the key code for the doors.

Apart from that he had nothing but his brain, and that didn't seem to be working very well. How do you defeat a couple of dozen bad guys, armed with nothing but a horde of beauty queen wannabes?

Bornstein. He'd been told to especially keep an eye on Bornstein. Nobody'd said anything about pirate connections, but . . . the door gritted open again, and this time only Bornstein came through. The door sealed behind him.

Portman stalked over, and Paris followed on his heels.

"What was that about?" the Captain asked.

"Had to redo the ransom tape." Bornstein looked irritated. "Pack of incompetents. Instead of worrying about their killing us on purpose, I think I'll concentrate on worrying about them killing us accidentally."

Portman actually barked a laugh at that.

Paris turned away. *True or false? How often would the pirates communicate with an insider? Why were they even bothering with the charade . . . unless maybe we really are going to be released after they were ransomed. Hold that thought! There is hope.* He glanced over at the women's side.

Some of us may get out of this.

He walked over, opposite Ethereal, who frowned, but came over.

"How are you?" he asked, knowing better than to start by asking about anyone else.

She gazed pointedly around. "Just fine." Her voice was as sarcastic as he'd expected, but to his surprise, she softened as she look back at the rest of the women. "Compared to some people."

Ethereal becoming empathetic? He sensibly kept a sarcastic comment of his own, something about the end of the world, to himself.

"How bad are they?"

Ethereal sighed and closed her eyes. "Epona was gang raped. And Ruby. They left Sallie alone, so now she feels guilty. I suppose they didn't like her looks. Katherine . . . they really beat her. She's still very . . . I think she must have at least broken ribs, and possibly her collar bone."

Her eyes swept past him. "She says Doctor Zimmer strapped her up, and they left her alone after that, so hopefully she's healing. A bunch of the other groups' people were hurt too. Apparently they formed up a group on the ship, some of the women had had bad experiences before . . . rape, and, well, that Caruthers woman had had an abusive husband and has been passing on what she learned in counseling to the rest.

150

In the Rift

It's not of much help while we're still . . . " Ethereal had tears running down her face and was trembling a bit. Paris put a hand against the mesh, unable to even hug her to try and share the pain. "I listened in last night, figured I'd need the advice sooner or later."

She wiped her tears and turned away from him, walking away stiff shouldered.

Sooner or later. If we can't escape.

What a joke, he had nothing, nothing, that he could see that might even start, let alone succeed in getting them out of here. He'd never even heard of anything like this, let alone dealt with it.

He frowned at the thought. Most piracy was of freighters, for their cargo. Usually the crews were left alive, encouraging surrender rather than fight-to-the-death. But lots of ships disappeared as well.

Were those the ones whose crews were killed? How organized are these pirates? Clearly large enough and with enough contacts, moles or bribe money to get their people all onto the same ship.

Why would a large, successful pirate organization pull such an attention-getting crime right now? Surely this hijacking would show how badly the New Territories needed policing? Or did they think that showing up the Fleet would have the opposite effect?

He was jerked out of his thoughts by the smell of

151

cooking. Biscuits, or something similar. Cinnamony. God he hoped it was on their side this time. Last night he'd chewed on a ration bar. He'd been about ready to try cooking himself.

Sticking his head inside the kitchen, he found that Georges was going to save his fellow captives from that fate.

Looking around, he saw Bornstein walking over to the mesh barrier to talk with Nicole, and Jenny was walking over to join them. The more the merrier. Maybe the women would kick start his protective instincts and get his brain going.

Chapter Sixteen
Death of a Pirate

Nicole leaned against the metal mesh, getting as close to Michael as she could. "I was so frightened when they came and took you away."

"Their cheap recorder ate my ransom note." He shrugged.

"Jenny's got a bunch of the women organized for the cooking and cleaning duties. Just having something to do has helped them a lot." She wished they had more privacy, the Captain, the doctor and that nasty Paris were coming over, and Jenny was hovering.

"That's good." He lifted his head and surveyed the approaching people. "We've got a Master Chef having vapors." He hesitated. "That's not really fair, he's pulled himself together. I just hope those hijackers leave us alone. They've got enough on their platter as it is. I overheard them talking. They think someone was hidden on the ship, the man they had on board was found with a broken neck. They're organizing a search of the ship."

"Isn't that a bit of locking the door after the horse has gotten out?" asked Jenny.

"You think someone would leave the ship?" returned

Michael. "Why?"

"For family." She waved at the women's side. "For a crew," She pointed at the uniformed men. "Or revenge." She paused as a sudden thought struck her. "Weren't there three Cinnabs onboard? Could one of them have survived?"

"I heard they shot them all." Paris broke in. "They have that healing trance though, don't they?"

Nicole was wide eyed. "And camouflage! Remember the camouflage reaction they have. Could they have eaten one of the hijackers?" She gulped at the thought.

The doctor looked nauseous, not that he hadn't been looking pretty sick since the hijacking.

"They could be walking around in plain sight!" Jenny was grinning. "Just grabbing any hijacker they catch alone." She bounced a bit on her heels. "I'll never harp on their weird cannibal society again."

"Hell," said Paris. "If there's one eating these pirates, I'll go snack down with him." Nicole scowled at him. He looked like hell without makeup and a swollen nose. She couldn't even work up any sympathy; he'd no doubt deserved to get punched.

"We're just speculating, here," Michael warned. "We don't actually know that's what is going on." He stood abruptly as the small airdoor behind him slid open wide enough to admit two men at a time. The six hijackers carried their laser rifles and fanned out, covering the men. The seventh man, the former Maitre d' from the ship, appeared to be counting.

"Ha!" whispered Jenny. "They're checking that no one's escaped. I'll bet they've lost another man, probably on the station."

Nicole shushed her, watching as Michael approached the leader slowly, hands open and spread peaceably. She couldn't hear what was said, but the hijacker grabbed Michael by the shirt and pulled him up to his face to hiss something, then shoved him to the floor, and walked out, taking his men with him. The door slid jerkily shut.

Michael picked himself up and brushed himself off, in a pointless reflex of fastidiousness, as he walked back. "They've lost another man, as you said, on the station this time. You may be right about the Cinnab."

Jenny grinned. "That's great news." She sobered suddenly. "I forgot to ask, earlier. When you were over there, did you hear anything about two women? They aren't here, and I saw them after the hijacking."

Michael wrinkled his nose. "They've kept a couple of prostitutes that were on the ship over there for, well, so none of you get hurt."

"Really, Jenny, you pick the strangest friends!" Nicole exclaimed. Behind Michael, Paris made an exaggerated shocked face.

"Oh, they were nice. And funny. I hope they don't hurt

them." She looked anxiously at Michael. "They have value, too, don't they?"

Paris nodded agreement, looking worried. He'd spent enough time down in Second Class that he knew Misty and Kissy. "It's probably just that their value can't be lowered through, umm, use."

"Ick!" Nicole didn't even want to think about it.

"How many hijackers are there? Could you get a count, Michael?" Jenny asked, but her glance at him included the other men. Nicole scowled at her. *Why can't she go bother someone else? She acts like she's organizing a war.*

Captain Portman answered. "There were thirty-four crew members. Fourteen directly associated with operating the ship, the flight crew, plus Doctor Zimmer, and nineteen on the steward's staff, cooking, cleaning, serving and so on. All that group except the chef and a couple of maids," he nodded toward the knot of women behind her. "Were in on this. The third commo officer and two of the engineering assistants are with the hijackers. So there are only nineteen of them." He grinned briefly. "Seventeen, now." His face fell. "But there may have been some men left here, with the station. Practically everything's automatic," He looked around dubiously. "But it's prudent to leave some people on station."

"I snuck a peek as we came into dock," admitted Jenny. "There were two other ships docked here. They must have crews. These guys may also go out and take ships as pirates."

In the Rift

"Did they just hijack us like this because of all the women on board?" asked Nicole.

"Hey, what am I, chopped liver?" Paris put in, indignantly.

"Probably," answered Michael, probably not to Paris. "The ship must have been too tempting to pass up."

Jenny was frowning. "How did they know far enough ahead of time that we'd all get diverted from the different flights we were on? Did they cause it, or just learn about it?"

Nicole gritted her teeth as Michael leaned back and regarded Jenny with respect. Dammit, he never looked at her like that. Even Paris looked interested.

"I think they must have," Michael said slowly. "How else could they have infiltrated the right crew? They must have agents at Beta Pegasi Station that cancelled the reservations of the female heavy groups and switched them to the Far Seeker. If . . . when we get out of this . . . "

"We have to get out of here!" Nicole's voice was both louder and shriller than she had intended. She burst into tears, and her sister had the only shoulder available to cry on. Michael got up and walked uncomfortably away. "Why did this have to happen?" she sobbed. "Everything was going so well!"

"It's okay, Nickie, we'll be fine. Remember we heard about the Joint Fleet maneuvers before we left Earth, there'll be that whole huge fleet looking for us as soon as the Far

Seeker's overdue at Eta Pegasi. This hijacking will really be newsworthy, the government won't dare drop it."

"But not in time!" Nicole pushed away from Jenny. "Not in time! Where will they take us? What about this auction thing? They can't go to every little halfway livable planet and search for us!"

"Then we'll have to be really tough. C'mon Nickie, it's time to forget the step-pervert and start remembering our real father. C'mon, you must remember him better than I do, I was fourteen when he died. What would Dad do?"

Jenny's words were like magic. She could see Dad in her mind, trim and confident in his uniform, nearly touch him. And certainly hear him. 'Stop crying and get even. Don't let them score another goal.' This wasn't soccer, and Dad wasn't coaching, but she wiped her nose and straightened anyway. "Dad would have cleaned house on these pathetic low lifes." She gulped. "Thanks, Jenny. Okay, we've got to look out for each other, and get away from them whenever and however we can."

Chapter Seventeen
Midnight Tour

Jenny woke abruptly when she was poked. After her first sick jolt and twitch, she relaxed, and tried to look around unobtrusively. She was on the outskirts of the huddle of women, none of whom seemed to be moving.

"We must talk." The bare thread of a masculine whisper. *Captain Midnight.*

Most of the women were sleeping in a section between the kitchen and lav where a higher than average number of lights were burned out, which combined with the solid walls of kitchen and lav to give a tiny feeling of privacy. The children were nested in the middle, with their mothers around them, the rest of them had just sort of accreted to the edges. She pointed silently past the lav, then got up and put on her shoes. She, like all the women, was sleeping fully clothed. It wasn't a very trustworthy privacy. She saw absolutely no sign of the big man. How . . . as she looked down to avoid stepping on her neighbors, she caught a brief flicker of movement below the floor. Of course. Bundling up her blanket, she walked softly past the lavs, to the hole. Cap had already seen it, the cover lifted silently from beneath and she helped ease it down on her blanket with no betraying clangs. As she started to slide gingerly through the hole, she was grasped and lowered silently. Apparently he was feeling much better. He turned away silently and moved quickly to the far end. The hatch in the airtight wall was open, but it was even darker in there than here. She stepped in, feeling the invisible deck right where it should be. The hatch shut, eliminating the last dim light.

"There is no one in this section at all." Cap spoke from behind her. "Nor the next one. They are all in the quarter beyond. Come, I will show you." A dim light sprung up, barely enough to show the floor, and moved with eerie silence away from her. She followed as quietly as she could, past dead air intakes, the slight crunching of gritty dust underfoot loud in the utter silence. She'd swear that she was making twice as much noise as Cap. It was as hard as following her dad through the woods, hunting. *Wish we'd had more time for that!* The light hit the column of the station spoke. This one had no door; she stepped in and gazed up into the darkness.

"I can break the latch of the door at the top of this shaft, if it will do any good." His voice was right next to her ear. She hadn't heard a thing. "But I cannot open the airlock doors. I got out with no problem, they left the airlocks open wide while taking some supplies out of the ship, but now I cannot get back into the ship."

A hatch in another airtight wall yielded to Cap in
160

seconds, and they walked on through another dark, silent quarter of the station, this one with an odd faint smell. "They throw their garbage in here, and store the extra food, and things they've stolen, but don't use." His teeth gleamed in the faint light. "It took them a long time to search it, especially with the cat occasionally making noise."

"The cat? They have a pet cat on the station?"

"It seems to avoid them. Perhaps it came on one of the ships, or perhaps they brought it to control vermin. I have not seen a single rodent here."

"Most stations are very careful about all kinds of plants, fungi and animals." She glanced around. "I hadn't thought about it, but this place is just begging for . . . well, maybe there's nothing for anything to eat." She sniffed dubiously.

Garbage. Ick. Poor cat, I hope they're feeding it.

The next hatch let a bright gleam of light and a hum of background sounds through as Cap opened it slowly, listening.

As her eyes adjusted, Jenny realized that this section was even dimmer than her own. The floor above was solid except for a few rough-edged holes. She climbed up the sloping wall and examined the nearest. The edge looked like ordinary spacecrete, an amalgam of the ubiquitous dust that coated most asteroids and airless moons either mixed with plastic and spray foamed on interior surfaces or semi-melted and heat applied to exterior surfaces. The light above was bright, and Jenny retreated as a wave of laughter rolled through the hole. Listening carefully, she decided she was hearing a card game.

She wandered through the section, listening at the holes in the spacecrete, trying to garner any information that might be useful. Unfortunately none of the hijackers seemed inclined to speak out loud about their future plans. In fact they were speculating on the chances of 'the chief' letting them keep any of the ladies. The consensus was that he wouldn't. But that didn't keep the possibly drunken men from arguing over which women they'd keep if allowed. With a nauseous gulp she kept going, listening, trying to see what was above. There were two access ways, both covered, and both, Cap whispered, now easily opened.

After several hours things quieted down. Apparently even hijackers slept. Cap motioned Jenny back the way they'd come. She pointed ahead, but received a firm headshake. She followed him back through the hatch, and as she stood waiting for her eyes to adjust, he explained.

"The barrier on the other side has microphones wired to it. They listen through the wall, so be very careful what you say."

She nodded, invisibly. "When I was talking with Nicole and Michael, I wondered if that might be the case, and when Michael said that a man had been killed on the ship, I speculated about one of the Cinnabs having survived.

Hopefully they're all keeping an eye on each other and won't look so hard for you."

"That must be why they've started walking around in groups of four." A faint gleam from his feral smile. "That was a very good idea. They are easier to avoid when they are in groups, rather than spread out."

"I'm surprised you could hide," Jenny said. "There's not much . . . well, I guess there's a lot of stuff in their dump."

His teeth gleamed again. "I spent most of yesterday sleeping high above your kitchen, above even the lights. They only searched the bottom of your section, and didn't even notice that the mesh over the access was loose. They probably spent most of their time searching the dump." He started walking again. "They are not very good."

"Do you know how many of them there are? I wondered if the other ships had crews?"

He rattled off his information like a report. "There are thirty-one hijackers on the station right now. Apparently a ship left shortly after we arrived, they said it was taking the ransom demands to be transmitted to the authorities at Beta Pegasi. They have mentioned other ships that are out somewhere now, but expected soon. The two ships still here are small cargo ships they have captured and not yet sold. They seem to be expecting another ship that will be bringing back new ID's for the ships, something about salvage."

"Ah, just like cars, back home. All you need to do is find

the same type ship being junked, buy it cheap and switch all the numbers with the stolen ship, and viola, you sell the 'repaired and reconditioned' ship. And you use a false name in case someone figures it out and investigates."

Cap sighed. "I only know about languages, and guarding, but not very well."

She hesitated, uncertain if he would accept her sympathy.

"I won't fail again." He stepped away and walked on, opening the airtight door to the prisoner's section slowly and carefully. "The code for the doors is 'Your Royal Majesty'; that has worked on every lock I have tried, down here. Be careful who you pass that on to."

Jenny nodded and slipped through, trying not to lag on feet that were getting more than a bit sore. She must have walked fifteen kilometers tonight, more, the way she'd wandered back and forth in the pirates' quarter. Cap boosted her up through the access hole, and fastened the hooks on the mesh cover from below.

Through the mesh, in the poor light, he looked like no more than her imagination, or a shadow. With a sigh, she took her blanket back to the huddle of women and collapsed gratefully for what remained of the night.

"That Philip Descartes, may he rot in Hell, said 'fix enough for forty, the leftovers won't go to waste'. There were maybe thirty of them, and those poor ladies they are keeping over there. They did not eat a bite between them."

Nicole sniffed. They were prostitutes, the only difference was they weren't being paid. Why act like they were innocent virgins? She shifted slightly. Everyone was sitting in two uneven semicircles while Chef Georges talked. Sitting both gracefully and comfortably on the cold rough metal mesh was apparently impossible. Especially in a thin bodysuit. Jenny looked like hell, sitting cross-legged in her jeans.

I wish I had jeans. And some really ugly clothes, in case

. . .

She stopped that train of thought quickly. She fidgeted with the scarf she wore wrapped around her shoulders, twitching it into attractive drapes. I need to keep looking good. Michael must not have any reason to not ransom me, to not try and find me.

"They have the best of cooking equipment, just ripped out of ships and shoved into a corner. Three little hydroponic units like we had on the Far Seeker. I do not like to think what happened to the people that were on those ships." He threw his arms out, barely missing Paris. "They are not here. Not any longer."

Captain Portman looked grim. "Dead or sold. I suppose some of the crew may have decided that being a pirate was better than being dead." He looked around at the surviving crewmen. The cute first mate was scowling at the others too, who were looking a bit hunted. Nicole shuddered. It was all too easy to see them saving themselves.

I'd save myself. The wash of shame she felt at the thought didn't change it. *Not a bit.*

Jenny jumped in with a question. "That Descartes, he was the Maitre d'?" Georges nodded and Jenny continued. "He's the boss?" Nod. "Were they all armed?"

"Most of them had side arms. Some laser pistols and some stunners. Some few of them carried rifles, the ones escorting me, watching me while I cooked. I saw some in one of the rooms over there." Georges scowled. "I keep my eyes open, but always there is someone to watch me and I cannot get to one."

"What does it look like over there, how are the walls arranged? Where do they sleep?" Jenny finally stopped for answers. Paris was looking at her oddly, so was Michael for that matter. Nicole couldn't see why they were answering her.

Probably just being polite to the bossy ugly duckling,

166

but really!

"It is much like this over there," Georges started. "But they have the spacecrete. Three recyclers and water conditioners in every quarter, and the three public lavs, as usual in this type station, eh? They used to build them all the same. They put up walls and made rooms along both walls, but just in the middle by the elevator."

"It's pretty filthy over there," put in Paris. "I hated to sit down in a chair to be recorded."

Nasty little fop.

Georges nodded emphatically. "Much though I would love to make them all sick, I think it is a bad idea, and wash everything before I cook." He scowled again. "I could do it on purpose, if you like." He looked to Jenny as he said it, then belatedly over at Captain Portman.

"I think you're right, for now." Jenny answered. *Did she think she was the leader of the prisoners or something!* "And forget trying to get a weapon, for now. They would miss it and search." She pondered briefly. "If any of us hear anything that might mean time is getting short, then you should look to pick up a gun, and poison the food."

Paris was nodding, but Michael was scowling, thank goodness someone had some sense around here.

"You'll get us all killed." Doctor Zimmer was slumped off to one side, apparently sunk into serious depression. So much for his dashing looks, it was all show and no gumption

167

there.

"It beats waiting around for my Fairy Godmother!" Jenny snapped.

Ha, don't like someone not treating you like God, eh? Nicole thought smugly.

"Now, Georges, if possible, try to talk to Misty and Kissy."

Michael's lip curled his opinion of the names. But Georges was listening to Jenny.

"Ask them to listen and pass on through you anything they hear."

Georges looked doubtful.

"It will give them a purpose, something to think about other than the situation they are in."

"Ah, like brave spies, two Mata Haris!" Georges perked up a bit at that contortion of the truth. Even Nicole had to admit it sounded better that way.

Portman snorted a bit. "Go ahead, Georges, it can't hurt. But no guns until I tell you to try for one. Let them get into a routine and get sloppy."

"All of you guys came down through their quarter of the station, did anyone see anything noteworthy?" Jenny was jumping back into her girl detective role. They were all shaking their heads uncertainly.

"What about 'The Far Seeker'" Jenny asked. "Does it have enough fuel to make it back to Beta Pegasi or on to

Eta?"

The crew members all straightened up at that. "I think," the senior pilot Barry Corvallis scratched his eyebrow thoughtfully, "that we've probably got enough to get to either, or at least close enough that someone would find us. We might have to ration the hydrogen for charging the capacitors for the jumps instead of trying to match velocities or keep up one G of acceleration for comfort, but we had a big enough reserve that even though we're way off course, we ought to be able to make it into the main shipping route and a good way toward either Beta Pegasi or Eta."

The other three crewmembers were nodding agreement, looking happier at the prospect that if they escaped, they could make port.

"Good point, young lady." Portman was nodding like another convert. "We need to think in terms of getting back to the ship." He frowned around the gloomy station. "I suppose that's one reason to keep us separated. We can't all rush them at once, and if we men could get through that door," he nodded back at the wall, "they could come around or through the hub and take you ladies as hostages."

"It may come to that," Jenny said. "Whatever the risk, take any opening, because one chance is all we might get." Jenny and Portman locked eyes and nodded, like a pair of vid heroes.

Chapter Nineteen
Plumbing

Jenny dodged the splash the youngest of the Brown kids had aimed at his older brother, but turned back curiously. "How deep is that water, David?" The rim of the tank was about half a meter above the deck. She tried to think what it looked like from below, it had hung down about a meter, perhaps?

"I don't know," David replied glumly. "Mom says it's too cold to swim in."

Jenny stuck her hand in. "Brr, I'll say!" Shaking her hand dry, she circled the tank. The bulge where the pipes entered was slight, but the seams and a screw seemed to indicate some sort of access. The screw yielded to her multitool and the cover slid off. The controls were very basic, a simple on/off and an up/down arrow pad. On resulted in a bubbling and finally a small fountaining at one end. The up and down didn't seem to affect it. She nudged it up, just in case it was a temperature control.

"That's very pretty, Jenny," Ethereal had her arms wrapped around herself. "But it's sort of giving off a cold mist."

"Sorry," Jenny turned the fountain off, to the vocal

disappointment of the seven kids that had been drawn to the splashing water. She put her hand back into the tank and could feel the flow from the pipe. It was warm, or at any rate warmer than the water in the tank. "I may have turned up the heat though. We'll have to see."

Adam quickly crowded by his brothers and stuck his hand in to feel. "Yeah, it's warm. Mom!" They turned pleading eyes as one and ganged up on the target.

"We'll have to see how warm it gets," she said firmly. "And then see what to wear. You only have one change of clothes each."

The four girls were all younger, Irene Denver's daughter Rena was seven and her sister six, Jackie's two were six and four. They hung back a bit longer, but Rena finally ventured out to test the water. She yipped at its chill bite and retreated back behind her Mom.

Jenny checked the other two tanks as well, adjusting their temperature settings. The water in them smelled clean, and after some hesitation she tasted it. It tasted like distilled water, absolutely chemical and mineral free. She wondered if the kids swimming in it was going to imperil their water supply, and after a moment turned the temp in the last tank all the way down. Better safe than sorry.

She wandered back to the kitchen.

They had quickly gotten in the habit of leaving a pot of water on the hot plate and she made herself some tea, while thinking about dinner. They had all fallen into a routine ruled by their watches. They had no control over the lights, they shone all the time, spottily. The three mothers had enforced bedtimes by their watches and everyone else had accepted that with a bit of relief. There was something so normal about bedtime. And arguments over same. Jenny regretted not having her bookpad along, but Aria had remembered some old classics, then Opal had told stories, Jenny had even surprised herself with a fairly good version of Lord of the Rings. Even the little girls had liked it, although one of the older women had dryly commented later that she had not remembered the female characters being quite so prominent, not to mention feisty.

So dinner was seven PM, and since Brooke and Taylor had made something vaguely resembling chicken ala king yesterday, today she'd try beef something or other. Rummaging through spices and dried veggies and, hmm corn meal. They'd found a frying pan, could she manage tortillas? Only one way to find out...

***

Apparently I am not the only one to underestimate chubby teenage girls. Paris thought indignantly as he watched Jenny nonchalantly pull a tool out of her pocket and start up the fountain. *Where did she get that? Hadn't they searched the women? They could have almost anything over there. He was sitting here doing nothing, coming up with no ideas whatsoever, and the fat chick was practically running the show. Even Portman was listening to her. So far the most constructive thing he'd managed was to count how many alphanumerics it took to unlock the lock of the airdoor. Sixteen, for christ sake!* He'd been working at it systematically all week, to no avail and damn slow progress. The circuit detectors under the skin of his fingers didn't seem to be able to tell a right choice from a wrong one. Or maybe he hadn't found any right ones yet, at least, he hoped he hadn't found the right first three keys combo yet. If he had, he hadn't detected it. But the implants had detected circuits on several spots around the door, and found bugs in the lav and the kitchen.

He watched as Jenny turned the fountain off and walked off to the next tank, pottered a bit, then walked on around the curve. When she came back she went to the kitchen and started cooking. *If we get out of this alive, maybe I'd better recruit her. She has Georges organizing the pros into a spy ring, and apparently is taking up plumbing repair and cooking for sidelines. Maybe I ought to marry her. Maybe hard work stimulated the brain?* He walked over to the so-called kitchen.

"Georges, you need any help in here?" He noticed the chef's bristled jowls and scratched his own chin, frowning at the gritty feel. Had it been two months since his last

174

electroshave . . . yep. Damn. Not even any old-fashioned razors around, of course. "We're going to be a hairy lot pretty soon, aren't we?"

The chef grimaced. "I have not attempted a beard since . . . well, perhaps two weeks when I was sixteen. My only consolation is that I could not possibly do a worse job of it now."

"No kidding." He looked around the makeshift kitchen. "Do you need help?"

"For only a dozen people it is easy, if not satisfactory." His brown eyes twinkled for a moment. "There is however, the matter of professional pride. I need to know what those women are cooking so that I can do better." He sniffed deeply, and frowned. "I do not recognize the smell. Find out and I will show you how to make it."

"It's probably unrecognizable because of the poor quality ingredients." He sniffed deeply. "It smells good, whatever it is. I'll go ask." Paris stifled a grin. *At last, proper spy work!* He leaned against the mesh until Sallie came over, eyebrows raised inquiringly.

"What are you guys cooking tonight?" He dived straight in. "I think Chef Georges is hoping for a challenge."

She grinned. "Does Georges even know what a tortilla is? Jenny and Nicole are making a pile. I suppose the end results will be a rough approximation of enchiladas or tacos or something like that."

"Uh oh. The Guys' Chef is going to have his work cut out for him." He sniffed. "Oh yes, fresh off the grill tortillas. That smells wonderful." He walked off drooling, hoping Georges was up to the challenge.

Chapter Twenty
Midnight Meeting

"Shi Wei Zhang is the oldest of us. He is over four hundred now, he is the only one of the original guanjun still alive. He and the others kept the leaders alive through the sack of Beijing, got them out of the city, and safe in the mountains, where a few loyal vassals held on. There were only thirty-two guanjun; the next step of the experiment, to use the improved genes on pure Chinese of excellent abilities, was never carried out. We mixed breeds were never meant to be anything but the preliminary experiment, the alpha test I believe you call it, to find all the mistakes."

Jenny sat beside Cap in the dim light of his flash. Asking about his past had opened a floodgate.

"They lost the gene engineering knowledge in the rebellion; the scientists were killed, burned with the institute. For years the Government-in-Exile lived almost primitively. The Guards were allowed to take wives, then. The leaders knew that they would need the Guards, that they needed fresh blood.

"Their sons served them well, but their daughters were barren. Some of the granddaughters were fertile, however, and they intermarried until the Masters regained scientists and could see who had which of the improved genes. Then those of us who had only a few of the new genes were no longer wanted for breeding. They tested us, and I failed, and was not allowed to marry when I reached adulthood. Nor did I do anything but routine guard duty for years.

"Mostly I studied languages. It was what I did best. Finally that came to the Masters' notice, and I would have audience room guard duty whenever a foreign delegation came to speak with them. When they spoke among themselves, I would hear, remember and report. And so, finally, Master Wong took me with him, so that I might hear everything at the conference, and tell him." He sat back, leaning against the wall.

"I thought there weren't very many Red Guards left?"

"There are three types of Red Guards, now. By what the West calls Red Guards, the genetically altered caste, only Shi Wei Zhang, the Servant, has all the improved genes, although some of the young ones now may have most." He shrugged. "I have not paid much attention, I just know that I didn't have enough to qualify for the breeding program."

He thought for a long moment. "That sounds so cold now. At the time I felt like a worthless failure, good for nothing. There are three thousand regular guards, but most are hired, not descendants of the Guanjun, the Champions. There are perhaps five hundred of us who have some of the new genes but not the ones they felt were critical, or not

178

enough of them; we serve in the regular guard units. Perhaps two hundred have large numbers of the genes. They are all in the elite guards. One of them should have accompanied Master Wong."

Jenny studied him carefully, then asked. "How old are you?"

"Eighty-one. The gene for long life seems to be one that I have."

"Were genes for fast healing part of the changes? I think you have them." Jenny pondered. "You weren't allowed to marry? But you had girlfriends didn't you? You couldn't just study for eighty-one years, could you?" Appalling thought, however much she hungered for knowledge herself.

Well, he's old enough to be my grandfather, so he probably doesn't care anymore.

"There were pleasure girls, but they did not care about me, nor did I care about them." He was silent for a long moment. "The Servant said that the love on the vids I watched to hear the languages of the West was a fantasy of the decadent West, that you were all unhappy because you chased a dream that didn't exist."

"Sometimes it is just a dream, I think." At eighteen she felt horribly naïve, speaking of something she'd never experienced. "But I think I'd rather try and fail, than to never have that dream." She threw her mind into the past. "I think my parents caught that dream. Mother was always so happy

179

when Dad came home. He was a Space Marine. He was away a lot. And then he was killed in a stupid training accident." Jenny sighed in memory. "Mother tried to recapture the dream. She married again, and it was awful. Nickie, my older sister, left immediately, ran away with a rich man. I was just a bit too young, so I whined until I got sent to boarding school. I felt guilty about abandoning Mom to that man, but she could have thrown him out. She should have, the first time he got drunk and hit her."

"Your mother, she could choose to . . . throw him out?"

"Yes. It was her house, she and my father had bought it together. If the house had been his, she still could have left him. Just taken Nicole and me and left." She hesitated. "It's a bit more complicated than that. The laws should have protected her, but she didn't call the police, didn't try to escape. He'd sober up and be ever so sorry, and she'd believe that it would never happen again." She thought over what he'd said, and how. "Yes, to throw him out or keep him was her choice. I think she chose unwisely, but it was her choice."

"We had no choice. Man or woman. Even the pleasure girls." He thought for a moment. "Especially the pleasure girls, they did not like me, because I am so obviously not pure of blood, but they could not refuse. In the end I found less shame in my hand."

Jenny blushed furiously in the dim light. *And then again, I'm eighteen, so what do I know about an eighty-*

years-old's libido?

"In my country there are prostitutes, and they are usually too poor and desperate to refuse a customer. It is not just your culture that forces people into roles they do not like. Anything we do costs money, and our choices are constrained by considerations of money. It sounds like you don't even have the choice of trying to work your way out of it, though." She stood up awkwardly. "I think I'd better get some sleep."

Chapter Twenty-One
The Haunted Space Station

Nicole avoided the splashing children as she headed for the showers. The ominous tanks of water had transformed into the children's main playground, entertaining them as it used up their abundant energy.

"Wait up, Nicole." Stephanie was hustling after her. Nicole waited. It felt safer to always be with someone. Heidi and two other women grabbed clothes and trailed after them.

She envied the kids their ability to laugh and play. She hadn't dared strip down to her underwear to swim with them, like a few of the others had, but just watching them was good therapy. The adults, in their own way, had manufactured as much normalcy as possible. They rotated through kitchen duties in groups, each one trying to recreate recipes and outdo the last group.

Nicole hung up her change of clothes. Such a pity she'd been too scared to think to bring a bit more. At least she'd been among the lucky ones with access to her own clothes when the hijackers told them to pack a change of clothes and a blanket.

Stephanie hung her clothes beside Nicole's. "Thank goodness Jenny got those women in my cabin to bring lots of extras. I'd hate to be stuck without even a change of undies."

Nicole scowled to herself. *Who's Jenny to order people around? She is only seventeen,* Nicole frowned, *no, she's eighteen. Jenny's birthday slipped by a few days ago and I hadn't even thought of it. Whatever the Brat's age, when she makes suggestions, or asks questions, people answer. And everyone is so happy that she's taken charge. Jenny organized the women in second class, and they'd brought stuff for those that were separated from their own clothes, and had found other stuff for themselves in case the women in first class didn't return the favor, which they mostly hadn't. Even the men seem to hang back and let her take the lead.*

Stephanie visibly gritted her teeth as she turned on the water. "The only thing worse than cold water showers would be no showers at all." She leaped in and got wet as quickly as possible, then turned the water off. "I think," she muttered through chattering teeth.

Heidi and Tia thumped in carrying a plastic box half full of warm water from the pool between them.

"I'm sure." Heidi said. "It's strictly sponge baths for me." Nicole didn't comment on her partial undressing and hasty washing and redressing. Heidi had been down in the second class rape territory. She wasn't as shaky as some of the women, but getting naked was something a number of the women weren't able to make themselves do, yet.

184

In the Rift

Nicole cringed as she rotated quickly under the cold water, turning the water off to soap down. And that was another thing, she thought, it's just not natural for a teenager to think about bringing things like soap and shampoo when she was a prisoner, going to an unknown fate. She'd even brought her damn toothbrush!

After she'd warmed up in her clean clothes, and washed her dirty clothes and hung them up to dry, she felt mellow enough to think kindly about Jenny. Maybe smart people just naturally took refuge in thinking, when there was a problem. And glancing back at the showers, she wondered if Jenny could think of a way to warm up that water as well. One week of cold showers was enough.

Stephanie ran her fingers through her hair. "I can't believe I didn't bring a hairbrush."

Nicole nodded, pulling Jenny's stiff one through her hair. "I don't know about you, but I'd kill for some makeup. I don't know what Michael must think."

Stephanie shook her head firmly, accepting the brush from her. "I don't want to look good. I don't want those hijackers to even look at me. That Maitre d', Phillip Descartes? He makes me feel dirty every time he looks at me."

"It's Baldy that scares me," admitted Nicole. "He's not just bad, he's abnormal. Irene and Corella said he just watched and laughed and, and, made suggestions when the hijackers were raping women down in Second Class."

"Don't talk about it." Tia was pale, hustling back into her clothes. Heidi hovered solicitously, but helplessly, and followed her out quickly with an apologetic wave.

Stephanie sighed. "See? They're more afraid of him than the ones that actually." She broke off with a shudder. Nicole nodded agreement. A lot of the women were very subdued, and were sleeping a lot, but very poorly judging by their looks. Corella's support sessions didn't seem to help much. Heidi and Tia were still jumpy. They were not alone in that. Jenny, thank god, had been spared rape. Zimmer had told Nicole that the pirates figured she was a valuable virgin and were under orders to not touch her.

Valuable.

A sudden change in the tenor of the background noise snapped her head around, and she edged over to look out the door just as the first of the hijackers entered.

"Out." He jerked her past him, his eyes and gun scanning the rather dim space.

She hustled out, the others on her heels. The rest of the women and children were pressed up against the mesh wall, being carefully counted. Beyond them, she could see that the male prisoners were being rounded up and counted as well.

The hijackers . . . Nicole eyed them warily. They looked more hunted than hunting, braggadocio in their every move, and then a quick glance over the shoulder. The slight sweating. Baldy was in charge, and he looked angry.

Nicole pressed in next to Jenny. "I think they must have lost another person."

The nearest hijacker glared at her.

"I think this station's haunted," Jenny whispered back, a bit louder. "The ghosts are picking these guys off, one by one."

"Shut up!" the hijacker hissed, stalking over to get in Jenny's face. "Just shut up." He walked off, his shoulders hunched. Jenny's lips twitched in a suppressed smile.

The hijackers who had spread out to search retreated back to the group watching the prisoners. Nicole could see them shaking their heads as they reported back to Baldy. Well, of course they hadn't found anything, they would have shot it if they had. Baldy followed two others back beyond the lav, apparently something had been found, but they returned promptly, Baldy shaking his head this time. " . . . leave it . . . " trailed back to her ears.

"What did they find?" she whispered to Jenny. Good grief, like Jenny would know?

"There's an access way to below, but it's locked."

Good grief, she did know.

"You mean they could get up here?" She thought about that for a second. "I guess it doesn't matter, when they can come down the elevator or through the door any time, does it?"

"No. And even if we could get it open it doesn't do us any good, the doors down there are probably locked as well." Jenny looked over her shoulder. "Looks like they're done with the men."

Nicole glanced over in time to see Descartes on the far side lead his men off, taking the chef with them. Over here Baldy waved his people off and they all walked off through the far door, staying together as a group, with a few of them darting off to recheck the far lavs, then quickly re-joining the mob.

"They're well and truly spooked," Jenny said, looking satisfied.

"But is that good for us?" Paris asked from behind them on the other side of the mesh.

"The enemy of my enemy is my friend." Nicole failed to remember who she was quoting. "I'll take the scariest ghost in the world over any of these creeps, thank you very much."

Michael snorted. "I don't relish the thought of finding myself alone on this station with a hungry Cinnab. At least I know the hijackers won't eat me."

"I wonder what shape the bodies are in?" Jenny asked, glancing around at the men. "Has anyone heard?"

"Georges may have, he's the only one with regular contact."

"Does that mean the bodies are being found, or not?" Jenny was frowning.

188

In the Rift

"Well, they can't just disappear!" Nicole shuddered. "Unless they are being eaten."

"Or shoved out an airlock," Michael said, frowning. "How far would a body go? Wouldn't it just sort of sit there?"

"Depends on if the lock was popped when there was still air in it, I suppose," Jenny speculated. "But even so a body wouldn't go far, would it?"

One of the crew, Nicole thought his name was Barry, put in, "This station isn't very well stabilized, it precesses and so forth, a body would eventually get bumped enough to drift off and away. If it had enough vee to not get hit by the wheel as it wobbled, it would drift away even sooner."

"Ick." Nicole abruptly didn't want to talk about dead bodies anymore. Unfortunately she was the only one.

"How many men have they lost so far?" Jenny was apparently counting in her head, and answered herself. "The one on the ship and the one the first day. So this is only the third, unless there've been some we didn't hear about."

They all twitched in unison as the door behind the men opened, but it was open just long enough for Georges to be shoved through.

He looked a bit wild eyed and hustled over to them. "Four of them, all patrolling together have been found dead, with not a drop of blood spilled." He continued, his words rushing together. "They are very upset, yelling and shoving each other, Descartes has stunned two of the others and they searched them, stripped them and even stabbed them a bit to be sure they were not Cinnabs." He grinned gleefully. "They are all arguing about who to stun next, and how to test for being human." His face fell abruptly. "They hustled me out, they didn't want dinner any more, they were going to stun and check Misty and Kissy I think." He scowled and cracked his knuckles. "They had better not hurt them."

Nicole suppressed hysterics, although whether over the thought of defending the honor of prostitutes or the thought of a vengeful chef, she wasn't sure.

That was the last of the information they got, but speculation ran on for hours. Some of the people on both sides drifted off; as time passed, they were breaking up into cliques, the rape victims keeping more to themselves. Nicole wondered if it would get worse, if instead of supporting each other they'd begin to resent the women who had gotten off lightly. Even Jenny was sometimes remote, sleeping off away from everyone else, not really part of any group.

Did something happen, and I'm not noticing? She's so in the middle of everything during the day.

Nicole eyed her little sister uncertainly. She seemed to be the most confidant, active person here. Nicole leaned wearily on the mesh and wished Michael was leaning from the other side.

I'm alone too. We're all alone, individually and as a group.

190

Chapter Twenty-Two
The Cat

"The Dump" was aptly named. It contained the cargo and stripped out equipment of what Jenny was afraid was probably dozens of ships.

At the end closest to the quarter the pirates lived in, shelves carefully displayed jewelry and high end electronics. Industrial-looking lasers, lacking power sources, unfortunately, mining equipment, perhaps? Huh. Some actual small earthmoving equipment. Eyeing a baby bulldozer, she decided that it could have fit in the elevator. Barely. She thought wistfully of driving a bulldozer through the pirates . . . but it had electric motors and the power gauges didn't even quiver when she tried them.

Then there were stacks of lesser value items.

Then piles. Large heaps. Mases. Towering, unstable-looking piles. Mountains of jumbled . . . Jenny looked closely and finally decided she was looking at all the plumbing and wiring that had not gotten installed in the stolen space station. At the far end, a smelly heap of ordinary refuse demonstrated the pirates disinclination for washing dishes, and, Jenny suspected, lack of technical personnel with space station maintenance experience. Or maybe just a lack of recycling equipment. Most of it looked like paper or plas wrap of one sort or another. It could have been worse.

Cap had let her through the small airdoor in the wall between quarters. The egress from the lower level in this section was blocked by a collapse of fabric. The small handlight Cap had handed her showed an avalanche of bolts of exotic brocades and brilliant silks. They felt stiff and dry beneath her fingers. How long had they been piled here? Did they predate minifacs that could produce cloth, or, she fingered a brocade, was this beyond anything but a specialty factory?

She started at movement high in the mountainous jumble to her left, clicking off the light and shifting as silently as she could away from her previous position.

"It is the cat." Cap, unheard as usual, breathed in her ear. "It finds me and tracks me easily. I think it makes noise on purpose, it seems to find startling me amusing, but it stays away when the pirates enter. Fortunately."

Jenny contemplated the difficulties of hiding with a meowing cat winding around one's ankles and agreed.

Jenny clicked the light back on and moved on to a tangled mound of wiring. "I could make a hell of a cattle prod, but I don't think it would be a wise idea."

"No, you'd need to step up the voltage to induce a loss of consciousness, and even so you'd have to be within a few feet of the target and fast enough to get all of them present." Cap picked up a thin section of pipe and stretched forward in a slow motion sword thrust. "I do not think it would be practical."

Jenny nodded reluctantly; there wasn't anyplace handy to hide even a small one, but she picked up a small coil of wire anyway. Could be useful, and could be tucked under some boxes.

Better than absolutely nothing, which is what I'm starting with. She hefted a short section of pipe. It looked just like all the exposed piping in the lavs; she could hide it where it was within reach.

There were real weapons, too. Both stunners and lasers. But no power chips. She gazed wistfully at them.

I should have kept that illegal stunner I captured on the Beta Pegasi station.

She contemplated briefly how different the aftermath of the hijacking might have been . . . no. The hijackers had searched the cabins. They would have been very interested in someone with an illegal weapon. Very. *Pity, though, that I didn't keep the power chip. Of course, I would have left it on the Far Seeker, so it wouldn't do me a bit of good anyway.*

A grating noise and flash of light ended her speculation. The lights above flickered to life, flooding the quarter, leaving her in plain sight. She leaped out of the central aisle and Cap thrust her deep into a crevasse in the fabric mountain. She felt suffocated in the soft but tight space, but tromped the incipient claustrophobia hard, staying motionless. The bolts of fabric formed rectangular projections outlined against the exterior brightness. Cap had not followed her in, was he hiding elsewhere, or stalking the pirates?

Noise penetrated into her cocoon, but muffled and distorted. Was that footsteps? Many footsteps? Voices calling back and forth. Sudden yelling and running? Had they seen Cap? She caught a whiff of smoke, chemical and sharp. Had they shot something?

Footsteps and a silhouette running past her soft crevasse. And finally an understandable voice. " . . . damn cat this time!" Relief gripped her. They were chasing the cat that had startled her earlier. More running. More smoke. More shooting? Lasers were soundless, she had no idea if they were being fired or not.

A blur flashed into her hiding place, snarled and reversed out without a pause. The fabric at the opening nearly exploded, flaming debris flying. She flinched back and felt the mountain slipping.

Oh. Shit.

To be crushed or to be seen.

She grabbed a bolt of fabric with her left hand, fumbling with her piece of pipe, holding it over her head, trying to keep some space open around her, but to stay covered . . . The mountain slid away and left her crouched waist deep in fabric, staring straight at a startled pirate.

His laser swung away as he started grinning. "Hey!" He lunged for her, as she kicked herself free from the heaps of unstable, slithering material, tangled and slowed as if in some hideous nightmare. "Away" involved too many obstructions. Keeping the pipe low and a bit behind her, she swung her bolt of fabric feebly at him. He swatted it out of her hand and grabbed her wrist. She hung back only long enough to trigger a hard pull. She went with the pressure, staggered out onto even flooring, and kicked the man's knee as hard as she could, twisting out of his grasp.

He yelled and swung the laser rifle, she threw up her left arm to block it and swung the pipe as hard as she could at his head. He ducked, taking most of the force out of the blow, backpedaling.

Don't let him get far enough away to shoot!

She lunged and grabbed, tripped him and went down herself. Shoved an elbow in his face, so his yell was inarticulate. He shoved her off, rolled over and got his hands and knees under himself, and collapsed. Cap stepped over the body, and extended a hand to help her up.

Silence.

A slight rattle pulled her gaze to a pile of boxes. A taupe and black striped shape glared at them through yellow eyes and then vanished.

"It's such a small cat," Cap commented.

"When did size ever matter with cats?" Jenny scanned the horizon of detritus but caught no sight of the animal. "Anyway, out here in space it's probably an F-cat from Alpha; they handle travel and motion better than real cats. The Alphans do, well, they used to do, lots of genetic engineering. If that's what that is, it or its ancestors, were totally engineered, mixing genes from cats, dogs, rats, ferrets, bats and whatever else they had handy. God only knows why. Partly for the practice, I suppose. They had to undo a lot of bad engineering on themselves."

Cap glanced dubiously at the cat's last perch. "Rats?" He shrugged. "We need to display our latest victims for maximum impact. Bring his laser." He picked up the pirate effortlessly. Jenny gulped a bit at the indented back of the man's head, and scooped up the rifle.

He did that with his bare hands? All I could do was inconvenience him with a pipe!

They passed two other bodies on the way to the door to the pirate's living quarters. Cap arranged the bodies in a neat row, arms crossed over their weapons, where they would have to be stepped on or moved to get through the door. Jenny patted them down, refusing to cringe from dead bodies. *I've seen a lot of those, lately. Many more and I won't hardly notice at all.* She gleefully pocketed an extra power chip she felt she could safely abscond with . . . no. With three more dead comrades, the pirates ought to search

196

very thoroughly. She looked around, wondering if they should turn off the lights.

As if reading her mind, Cap said, "The switch for the light is on their side of the door."

As they passed the firearms display, she looked longingly at a laser rifle in the back stack, and hid the power chip near it. What the pirates ought to do, and what they would actually exert themselves to do, might be different enough that they would miss it. Maybe after the pirates had searched again, she could bring it and hide it . . . somewhere. She dug through the side of the collapsed fabric mountain, and found her light and hid it among stacked electronic goods. She looked worriedly at Cap. "Where can you hide, this time?"

He flashed his teeth at her. "Before they find the bodies, I'll be in their quarters, high above their heads." He pointed upwards. "There are doors up above, where there should be other floors. But it is easier to travel below, and climb." He led the way back through the empty quarter to the door to the prisoners' quarter, carefully slid the small door open and slipped through. She followed, closing it behind her.

"Go ahead, speak to anyone you see. I'll get myself through the hole."

Jenny walked openly back to the sleeping women, detouring to tuck her pipe in amongst the plumbing of the lav and check the kitchen for midnight snackers. As she lay down, she thought she saw a black shape moving in the shadows, but heard nothing.

She slept poorly, dreaming of Cap metamorphosing into a black cat that stalked her.

The next day started early, with another search by frightened pirates. Too frightened to do more than threaten, with half their attention scanning for danger.

Chapter Twenty-Three
Failure

Paris curled up in what he hoped was a convincing semblance of sleep a scant meter to the side of the door. Both captors and captives had drifted back into their routines after three days with no further alarms. Chef Georges would be returned to them shortly. Many of the women were also settling into their usual sleeping spots. The Wall Street Gang, as Mac had called them, were setting up camp, the sisters on one side of the mesh, their husbands on the other. Portman and Givens were walking over, they'd taken to hovering around the door, and one of these times they'd rush it, he just knew it.

He could see Jenny pacing, no doubt also wanting news from Georges when he finally showed up. The click of the lock release sounded loud in the quiet, everyone watched the door slide, relaxing just a hair to see Georges with a single guard. As usual, the escort shoved him through the door, but this time followed him through to survey the area. It was Baldy today. Good. Baldy was a sadist and liked to push them. He eyed Portman and Givens, but they were too far away to constitute a threat. His gaze fell on Paris, so close to the door, and he slid the door shut behind him, as he stepped up and kicked. Paris yelped and flinched back, sitting up and scooting away, but not far, oh no, not far.

Satisfied with that reaction, Baldy ran his eyes over the silent group and sneered his contempt. "Not a one of you with any backbone." Portman glared back but remained still. Baldy turned away, and started punching the code into the pad beside the door. Starting near the bottom right corner, then the left side line, left corner, low center a double letter. Baldy shifted and Paris dropped his eyes. *I'm no threat, I'm not looking.* He glanced up to catch three quick taps in the lower right corner, then the door slid open and Baldy was gone.

He lay there a moment, committing what he'd seen to memory. He'd missed a lot, but if it were a word or phrase, it could be enough. Even if it were random it would be a good start. But it wasn't random. Baldy hadn't used any of the number keys at the top. When Paris was sure of his recall, he peeled himself off the deck and walked over to hear Georges reporting to Jenny.

"They are bored." He sounded worried. "They are talking about you women." He stopped, not that he really needed to elaborate. "Descartes tells them to keep their hands off. So far, they listen to him." Most of the women exchanged worried glances. Someone at the back of the crowd ran off toward the lav, Katherine Nesby, he thought, from the glimpse of dark brown hair. Several women hurried after

200

her, he was glad to say. It was so easy in stressed circumstances to blame, to argue instead of support each other. Perhaps if the pirates continued to mostly leave them alone, the fragile peace would hold.

Paris leaned into Portman's side. The Captain turned and glared at him. "Time to get a gun," he barely breathed, shushing him. "Tell Georges, very, very quietly, not in the kitchen or lav, or near the wall, while I go make a bit of noise."

He grabbed the first man handy, Doctor Zimmer, and led him over by the door.

Zimmer jerked his arm out of Paris's clutch. "What do you want now?" he sounded grouchy.

"Look, you know all of the crew's names, right? Let's try them all on this lock."

"You are so stupid!" the doctor exploded. "There is nothing that we can do. Get that through your head. You'll be okay and the rest of us are just screwed." His voice was rising, more than a little hysterical.

"Look," Paris tried to think of something sensible to say, he had more noise than he'd planned on. "We have to keep trying..."

"No we don't!" Zimmer snarled, and stalked away. Portman was walking away from Georges, who was standing by Bornstein. Paris winced, hoping like hell that if Bornstein was a political subversive it didn't go so far as associating with pirates. He leaned wearily back against the door.

It popped open under his hands, and his pratfall was quickly transformed into a high speed collision with the floor as Baldy's entry kick connected with his kidneys. He caught two more kicks before he rolled out of the way of the rest of the pirates.

His inadvertent spoiling of Baldy's grand entrance had given Portman the opening he had wanted. Unfortunately this time Baldy wasn't alone.

Portman's punch as he rushed the pirate was probably intended to push the pirate back through the door. But Baldy blocked the punch and added the Captain's momentum to the power of a swinging rifle hilt. Paris heard the agonized grunt as the air was forced out of the Captain's lungs, then a boot hit Paris in the ribs and he concentrated on his own problems, which involved getting out of the way of the next kick. Still on the ground, he twisted and stuck a foot out and tripped a man coming through the door, then jerked away and shoved himself to his feet. He jumped a pirate from the back, arms around his head and neck and wrenched hard, collapsing with the man as he was hit from the back in turn.

He had a confused ground level view of all the prisoners piling into the fight and tried to locate the door. They had to keep the door open. Had to. He threw himself in that direction, and was tackled around the knees. He twisted to reach for his attacker when the shriek of stunner fire started.

202

In the Rift

He kicked desperately, frantically, but another pirate grabbed his arm and twisted it behind his back. He arched his back and tensed to bring his superior strength to bear—but it was already too late. Trembling with useless adrenalin, he watched helplessly as the last of the prisoners were subdued.

Phillip Descartes stepped daintily through the door and surveyed the scene. Paris saw that he was carrying a laser rifle, and twisted his head around to look for casualties. Four limp prisoners, hopefully only stunned. Two limp hijackers, hopefully dead. Obediah was clutching his leg, but there was no blood showing. Captain Portman was cursing under a pile of hijackers, apparently not too badly injured.

Descartes strolled over to the mesh wall where the women were standing silently. There was a faint ripple of movement as they drew away from him. "I'm tempted to just let you watch while we rape your wives and girlfriends." He frowned suddenly, reaching out to push the mesh, revealing a foot long section of cut mesh. Paris froze. *Jenny's tool! She had been cutting through to join the fight!*

Descartes swung around. "Search them, one of them has some sort of cutting tool."

When they don't find it here, they'll search the women. This is going to get even uglier.

With three hijackers to every prisoner, the search was over quickly. Paris watched as something was removed from

203

Georges' pocket, and handed to Descartes. "Well, well, Georges, I hadn't realized you were the type to take home company property. We'll have to keep a closer eye on you."

Paris closed his eyes in a brief prayer of thanks. *Better Georges than Jenny. He was sure Georges would agree.*

A boot to his abused ribs brought Paris's attention back into closer proximity. Baldy glared down at him. "I want to kill this one. He tripped me coming in and he killed Breaker."

Descartes sniffed. "Too valuable. Pick another." He walked back to the pile of still squirming bodies concealing most of Captain Portman. "Do you know, I think Our Gallant Captain is just too much trouble for the money we're likely to collect."

Baldy grinned. "Yeah. And the little mama's boy Lootenant was right behind him, jumping me."

Descartes waved negligently. "Feel free to express your displeasure." He offered the laser rifle like a bottle of fine wine at dinner.

Paris heard a rustle from the women's side. Helen Brown was hustling her boys away from the barrier, the other mothers quickly following her lead.

The pile of hijackers shed live bodies until only two men held the Captain pinned down. Baldy kicked him a bit, then walked over to the also pinned Givens, for another kick.

"I'll flip a coin. Heads, good old Jolly Captain Portman,

tails, Lieutenant Brown Nose." He pulled out a coin and flipped it. Ping, ping, tinkle. It fell through the grating. "Damn, gonna have to kill you both now."

He adjusted the laser rifle power level a bit, then dropped the muzzle casually as he walked up to the Captain. He put his left foot on the Captain's chest and leaned on it a bit. "I really, really enjoy doing this you know?" Studying the Captain's face carefully, he pointed the rifle to his right and pulled the trigger.

Paris flinched as an explosion of steam and blood erupted under the Captain's trouser leg, ripping through the cloth, trying to block out the screaming, wishing he could block out the screaming. He screwed his eyes shut, then forced them open again.

The smell of blood and charred meat turned his stomach. Baldy was still savoring the Captain's pain.

"Oh deary me! Did I have my rifle set for the long pulse! How awful!" As the Captain controlled himself down to whimpers, Baldy pushed off, and stalked over to Lieutenant Givens.

"You're a wimp, hardly worth killing, but hey, I just feel like it today." He didn't even look where he aimed, the muzzle was nearly in contact with Given's stomach anyway. The steam explosion was much worse, this time. The Lieutenant's shirt ripped as the steam propelled his intestines out through the hole, which ripped and fresh blood spurted where the explosion had torn blood vessels, large ones, pumping out the Lieutenant's life in minutes. Mercifully few, as he whimpered and his hands clawed briefly at the deck, then stilled.

Baldy grinned back at the Captain. "Let's see how long it takes *you* to die." He walked off, looking sated. Descartes jerked his head and the hijackers disengaged from their prisoners. They picked up their own dead and withdrew. The door sealed them into silence.

Paris peeled himself off the floor, feeling all the blows he'd been oblivious to during the fight. "Zimmer?" He looked around for the doctor. "Anything you can do?"

"With what?" he snapped. "I don't have any medical supplies at all here, you know." Nonetheless, he knelt briefly at Given's head, fingers searching for a pulse. He grunted back to his feet without comment and stared down at the Captain. "All I can do is wrap it up, Captain." Portman nodded, fingers locked to the mesh floor, his breath jerky and fast, face pasty with shock.

Paris looked around, mentally surveying the group. Two of the crew and one of the Wall Street gang were stunned. Another Wall Streeter, Ronald Hannibal, was clutching his shoulder. "Doc, look at this next." *Finally, something you might be able to fix.* "Peter, Quincey, rip up a blanket for bandages. Bornstein, help me with this." Paris picked up a blanket at random and walked over to the Lieutenant's body.

206

In the Rift

His right wrist sent a warning every time he moved it, but they got the body rolled reasonably tidily, and moved it to the wall by the door. Paris hoped sincerely that the pirates would come back and dispose of it. Soon.

A pained gasp brought his attention back to Zimmer. Ron was moving his shoulder gingerly. "Straightforward dislocation, keep a sling on it, it should be fine." Zimmer looked better for one success and accepted the strips of blankets from Peter, but as he turned back to the Captain, his face fell. Paris shuddered. *Unless the hijackers give us access to the Far Seeker's sick bay, or at least some antibiotics, there's not a chance.*

Laser injuries ran the gamut from nicely cauterized burns to hideously destructive steam explosions, depending mostly on the burst time. A short burst did much less damage than a longer one, on a wet target like a body. Of course the longer bursts took more energy and thus fewer shots per power clip. The Captain's injury, mostly to the outer side of the leg, had little bleeding, but much tissue damage. Paris gulped and turned to help roll the unconscious men onto blankets, wincing every time he used his right hand. The wrist was swelling like a balloon.

He was sitting wearily against the mesh wall when the door opened again. He didn't even move. The hijackers were armed to the teeth, and grim. The leader counted them, frowned at the blanket roll of the Lieutenant and peeled it back far enough to see the Lieutenant's head. Then they backed out and left.

"Why are they counting?"

Paris flinched at the voice behind him and turned.

"Sorry." Jenny was just the other side of the mesh. He hadn't even heard her come.

"Maybe the Cinnab has struck again?" he said wistfully. "I wish I believed that. Probably they're just checking that no one snuck out during the fight."

The sudden sound of voices and feet thrumming on the mesh floor preceded the hijackers' appearance around the curve of the section behind the women. Again they did a headcount, and quick search of kitchen and lavs. They stomped off around the bend and silence fell again. Jenny walked after them, and came back to report that they had gone.

Eventually, Paris got up enough energy to get Zimmer to strap his wrist, the stunned men groaned their way back to consciousness, and in a defeated stupor he dozed off and on, listening to Captain Portman moan, and then dreaming over and over the fruitless deadly fight.

Chapter Twenty-Four
Regrouping

Sometime, early or late he hadn't a clue, Paris awoke when he was poked.

Jenny was crouched on the other side. "Hold out your hand." He could barely hear her, but held out his hand and caught something she slipped through the mesh. A capsule. Ten more, two types. "I think the orange are antibiotics, the grey and yellow painkillers." She got up and walked quietly away.

Paris stared at the pills. *Is Jenny in contact with the Cinnab? If so, why does she always talk about the Cinnab killing the pirates?*

Because there isn't one. All the talk of a Cinnab is a red herring.

Whatever is going on, Jenny has inside information. His mind shied away at the thought that she could be cultivating one of the pirates, seducing, using or being used by a pirate. He stared at the handful of pills. How to account for having them?

He got to his feet and walked quietly into the kitchen. They had glanced through most of the crates, but not in detail. He dumped out the one with all the littlest packages, condiments mainly, spreading them around. There were several clear bags with little salt and pepper servings in them. He dumped one and put the pills in the bag.

"What are you doing?" The querulous voice behind him belonged to Bornstein.

Paris held up the bag of pills. "I just remembered seeing this. I don't know what they are."

Bornstein snatched them. "Anything to shut up the whimpering," he snapped, stalking out of the kitchen.

Paris scrambled up in time to see him shake the doctor awake.

"Do you know what these are? Can we give them to Portman?"

The doctor rubbed his eyes and frowned at the pills. "Antibiotics." He angled a capsule into the light and squinted at it. "I think this one might be a pain killer..." He smiled ruefully. "I seem to have misplaced my reference pad."

Paris backtracked to get a glass of water, and helped prop up the Captain so he could swallow the pills. Whatever they were, they were powerful. The Captain was asleep in moments.

Where did Jenny get those pills? From whom?

With a weary sigh, he sought his nightmares as a relief from reality.

***

In the Rift

Jenny leaned on the mesh, concealing her deep apprehension. What might have been their only chance to overpower the hijackers had come to nothing. *I should have had most of a hole cut through some place inconspicuous as soon as we got here.*

Georges had just returned, and thank god, when the hijackers had finally decided they needed his cooking and came for him, they'd taken the body of Lieutenant Givens as well. It had been a very bad three days.

"Kissy says they are very frightened. Two more died while we were fighting in here." Georges looked worried. "They are certain that Misty and Kissy are human, but they have started locking them up and do not talk so much to them, any more."

"I can't think what could be happening to them. They must have lost at least ten men by now," Jenny said, frowning artistically. "It's so very strange." *This could get dicey. At some point Cap will either be seen, or the hijackers will snap and start shooting everyone. I'd better talk it over with him.*

"Gotta be a Cinnab, like you said before, Jenny," Terry commented. The engineer looked like he'd aged several years in the last week. All the surviving crewmen did. Ensign Parker had cried herself to sleep for several nights running.

"Oh, I like the ghost theory, myself," Paris quipped.

Jenny smiled, happy to see even a brief flash of the

211

musician's humor. The Captain was still hanging on, between the painkillers and the antibiotics. She wasn't at all sure Cap could get any more, or how the pirates would react to Paris 'finding' more. He'd been very clever, but he wouldn't be able to do it again. She looked over at the corner where Portman lay. The pills could only do so much. The wound needed to be cleaned, needed engineered stem cells to rebuild destroyed tissue, needed modern nanotech medicine, needed all the things they took for granted. As it was, he wasn't healing, just dying more slowly.

The horrors of the last . . . Jenny frowned, had it been a month since the hijacking? She glanced at the calendar on her watch. No, not quite. "The Far Seeker is now a week and a half overdue at Eta Pegasi," she said aloud.

"The Joint Fleet was at Eta. They should be out searching for us." Terry didn't sound very hopeful.

If they do find us though, we're in worse trouble than ever. Sitting ducks for the hijackers. We can't keep them out. Can we get someplace we can barricade?

They needed control of the elevator, and the codes for the airlocks. Or even just the airlocks. They were desperate enough that they could all climb up the next section's elevator shaft. She frowned at some of the ultra-thin women. *Maybe. Getting the Captain up would be difficult. No rope. Ask Cap. There's bound to be rope in the Dump.*

The Captain would have the code for the ship's airlock.
212

In the Rift

But what about the station? Would there be another airlock? I'll ask Cap.

Georges headed for the kitchen, to cook the prisoners' dinner, or as he muttered, attempt to turn what Paris had started into something fit to eat.

"Hey," Paris whispered, rather loudly, "what are you guys fixing tonight? Go spy for me?"

Jenny grinned, and several of the others smiled too. *Keep up the façade of normalcy for as long as possible.*

Chapter Twenty-Five
Pirate Ship

Paris stood carefully flexing his right wrist, listening as Jenny once again debriefed Georges.

"There is another ship, it came sometime today," Georges started without preamble. "The men, they are like visitors, they are not members of the hijacker's gang, they do not take orders from Descartes." He waved his arms. "They talked about attacking a ship that turned out to be a fleet decoy. They had to run and have only narrowly escaped, I think. They have much energy, and much anger." He waved toward the airtight wall. "In there it is the armed camp and a shaky truce, I believe."

"Pity we couldn't count on them shooting each other." Captain Portman's voice was still weak, but loud enough to carry. He had shown steady improvement the last few days and Paris was beginning to think he might actually live. Of course, he'd just taken the last antibiotic . . .

Michael shook his head. "We couldn't count on the relatively benign treatment the hijackers have shown us. These pirates might have other ideas."

"For some very odd definition of benign, the hijackers are only benign for now, and only if we do absolutely nothing to set them off. Again." said Paris. "I for one am not all that sure they'll let us go after they get our ransom money. To say nothing of their plans for the women."

"Why did they come here?" Jenny asked. "Is this a refueling depot or fencing operation for any and all pirates out there?"

Georges nodded vigorously at that. "They said they would be fueled and leaving in the morning. They had no cargo to unload, but it sounded like that was unusual."

"Cripes," muttered Paris. "I thought the New Territories were a Wild West type of Frontier. This is sounding more like urban decay, or Chicago during Prohibition."

"Probably in the morning they will want breakfast," added Georges. "I will try to discover more." He frowned worriedly. "The girls may find out more." He waved in vague apology. "I can steal no guns, they watch me now and search me always before I return."

Paris thought about Misty and Kissy dealing with a shipload of angry men, and hoped they were able to report in the morning. As the group broke up, he settled back where he could watch Jenny.

She wandered about a bit, took her time, checking the kitchen and lingering in the lav until all the others were abed, then faded into the darkness beyond the lav. Unlike most nights she returned almost immediately. What was she up to? Once she had settled down for the night, he got up and went to study the lock pad. He'd done it so much no one paid any attention to him anymore. Bornstein had been hovering lately, but not tonight. Time to get serious.

So, the key started in the right bottom corner. S, T, Y or Z. Then the left side. C, I or O, he bet, then a U. That had definitely been the corner button. He positioned his hands carefully and tried SIU. His right third fingertip implants gave a tiny zing, hopefully the sign of the lock program rejecting the combination, not just checking it. If he was just picking up the current generated by checking . . . he hit the reset button. SCU. No. SOU. No. TIU. No. TOU. No. TCU. No. YIU. No. YOU. He froze. For the first time, no faint tingle from his sensors at the third entry. And a word. Oh yes. Now a double letter near the center. E, F, K, L, Q or R. R would make it 'your'. He tapped it twice. Still no tingle. Good. Unfortunately that brought him to the part he hadn't seen. But Baldy had ended with three quick taps in the lower right corner. S, T, Y or Z again. And sty was a common ending, so, what filled in the gap? Your R, eight blanks, sty? Piece of cake for a crossword puzzle fanatic. Biting his lip he carefully typed O, Y, A, L, M, A, J, E, S, and T, so mesmerized by the lack of tingle in his fingers he nearly typed the final Y. He hit the reset button, turned away and wrapped himself in his blanket with careful, controlled motions. *I am not going to laugh, scream or caper about. I am going to sit down and try and figure out what to do next.*

Chapter Twenty-Six
Half Is Better Than None

"OK, Ladies." Baldy grinned, and Nicole tried not to run and hide in the corner like most of the women had. "Today you get to go back to the ship long enough to grab some more clothes."

"I wonder why they care," Jenny whispered suspiciously from just behind her.

"So, we're going to split you up into four groups, and one group at a time, escort you up and back." He ran sneering eyes over the group, stopping at the Wall Street Gang. "So, how about age before beauty? And all those kids, get them up here." After a moment when no one moved, he added, "We can come and get you, if you'd prefer." The other two men behind him started grinning.

That shifted the women. Mrs. Brown moved first. "Come on boys, let's go get clean clothes." The other two families drifted uneasily after them. The hijacker made a chopping motion with his hand. "And you lot. Now" he added as the women flinched back. The four sisters, Opal and Paula shuffled reluctantly past him and into the elevator. The door closed jerkily on them.

"Now, let's just see if we can do this next run a bit

faster." He looked them over, then made another chopping motion. "You, no, all of you." He scowled at Stephanie Correy as she tried to slide back behind the group that was more or less hiding behind Nicole and Jenny. Stephanie scuttled back to the first group. "You'll go next." He scowled again. "Then you lot split up, you get over there." He gestured half of them off to the left, Jenny drifted off with them. "You'll go last."

The women barely whispered, mostly waiting in uneasy silence as the minutes dragged on, then the elevator finally came vibrating down the shaft again, and disgorged women and children carrying pillowcases lumpy from the clothes stuffed inside. Baldy leaned inside the elevator. "Next time send Chad back down with the empty elevator, this is taking forever." Then he waved Stephanie's group in. ###

This time the elevator returned empty, and Nicole led the way onboard. 'Chad' looked them over, but kept his hands to himself as he sent the elevator on up. As their weight started dropping, the women started grabbing the side bars of the car. Chad had mag shoes and stuck to the floor, smirking at their incompetence and helplessness. When they stopped they were all nearly floating. Then he made them wait, while an impatient man tried to organize the second group that was still flailing around in zero G, then gave up and stuffed all the women into a side passage. The air stank of vomit. Nicole disciplined her stomach to iron hard steadiness.

220

In the Rift

I've had boyfriends that made me feel worse than this. I refuse to lose it in front of these goons.

Nicole could see more of the hub than she had noticed when she'd been here before. There were four elevator shafts, or rather the elevators were located inside the main structural spokes of the station, which extended above them and joined in a cross. The faint weight she felt mean that they were rotating, but from her perspective it looked like the ends of the cylindrical chamber were moving.

Passages led off in various directions from the one she was being prodded toward, most of them dark and forbidding. Two were lit up. The other group of women had come out of one lit passage, and were being sent down the other. Was the 'The Far Seeker' down the first passage perhaps?

One of the hijackers at the second passage was yelling ". . . and stay here until the other group is out of the Hub, move back further, damn it," at Stephanie's group.

Is the other ship down that corridor? Why are they shoving everyone back?

Her stomach nearly rebelled, and it wasn't the smell.

What are they doing? Playing with us?

As the last of that group was corralled, Nicole's group clumsily bumped their way into the nearer passage, and the 'Far Seeker' was indeed at the end of it. Swimming up the stairwell to First Class, she quickly grabbed her most modest undies and pants and shirts, and a sweater, stuffing them into a pillowcase, tooth and hair brush, but no makeup, then left quickly. Revisiting the cold empty ship was not a welcome change of scene. She needed to find Stephanie and her group, make sure they were all right.

But before she left the ship, more women came, the fourth group. Apparently the hijackers had given up on keeping them separate. Or is the confusion on purpose?

Jenny came flying in with considerable speed. "Nicole! The second group hasn't come back!"

"What?"

I knew there was something wrong! I knew it.

She scrambled back down the stairs to the lounge and the vid screen, trying to figure out the directions, as she led the way, wasn't there an outside cam that they could look around with . . . Yes. "They shoved them into, I think it must have been that one, maybe I'm turned around, though, there's nothing there."

"Turn the cam." Jenny's voice was grim, and Nicole randomly moved the cam. "See those lights? A ship is leaving." They watched as the lights dwindled. "They must be on board." Jenny leaped across the room, graceful despite her girth in zero G. "The other two ships are still there. Nicole," Jenny called back to her, "tell everyone to try to stay on board, some of us may be able to get away."

"What?" Nicole barged after her, losing ground rapidly

as Jenny swung down two levels and into the second class lounge and started banging on the wall beside the wet bar. "Mac, Frank, quick! About half the passengers are on board, a quarter have just been taken off in another ship, this is the best chance . . . "

To Nicole's shock, the wall panel came loose, and a man, three men emerged. "We can go, I think, but what about the rest?"

"We'll have to leave that for the authorities, this looks like the only chance to get some of us out of here." Jenny sounded authoritative and sure.

"OK, we'll head for the control room and engineering."

"I'll get the airlock sealed," said Jenny. "Nicole, go find Ensign Parker." Apparently she looked blank. "The lady in the ship's uniform, for Christ sake! She's an engineer. Go!" Jenny swung out again, and Nicole, after a moment's indecision, turned the other way.

***

"Get back in the ship!" Jenny grabbed Mrs. Pearson and pulled her back. "Go hide in your cabin." She grabbed another woman, shoving her also. Damn, she was too late, some of them were out of the ship already. "Get back in the ship!" she yelled, and there was the little engineering ensign, halfway across the hub, turning to see what the fuss was about. Jenny flew across to her. "Get back to engineering,

Juan Zuniga is piloting, get as many people out of here as you can! Get the airlock closed!" Jenny shoved off her, propelling the engineer toward the ship's lock, and herself, unfortunately, toward the two hijackers starting to take alarm and move in. Jenny took a deep breath, and started trying to remember her karate lessons. *Won't work in zero G, unless . . .* When the first man grabbed her and pulled, she grabbed back and pulled, too. The top of her head met his nose with painful force.

"Oww!" He shoved her to arm's length, but kept hold, little spherical globs of blood scattering as he turned his head. She saw the other man heading for the airlock and twisted to snap a kick that just barely grazed his shoulder. It did have the effect of spoiling his aim toward the lock, and twirling him around. She curled back up and started kicking the man holding her. The second man came in suddenly from the rear, and there was an arm around her neck and she couldn't breathe, and as her vision tunneled down all she could see was the first hijacker's eyes widening in terror. Then she was spinning around through the air, sucking in deep breaths. She barely got her hands up in time to protect her head as she hit the wall. A muffled crunch drew her eyes, Cap was already releasing the limp hijacker, and the other one also floated, his head at an odd angle. In the sudden silence, the thump and bang of the ship's separation was loud. She looked wistfully at the airlock.

In the Rift

"At least Nicole got away."

***

Nicole blundered down the stair shaft in what she thought was the general direction of the crew's quarters, and came face to face with a startled hijacker. Some zen combination of recent gymnastics and older karate lessons from her father took over and she grabbed the center stair rail and vaulted into a kick that hit him in the throat even as he started to reach for her. And then he was grabbing his throat and blood was spraying from his mouth as he gaped like a fish and choked, trying to breathe.

"Damn," said an admiring voice from behind her. "You are really something. C'mon." The petite engineer shoved the hijacker out of the way, and pulled her along. "I've got to get the engines started, if we really do have a pilot."

Nicole looked back at the hijacker. Was he dying? "Got one, Dad," she whispered.

Parker checked momentarily at the sight of the harried man hovering indecisively over the controls. He glanced up. "Thank God! A real engineer." He backed away from the control panel. "Relax, I'm a passenger, two of us and Juan Zuniga have been hiding out in the utility spaces. They're up in Control."

Parker nodded, and started punching buttons, and then reached for the comm. "Control, engines are prepping.

Maneuvering jets are okay for separation."

Her shoulders relaxed when a voice replied. "Roger. Separation in ten."

Nicole felt the slight jolt as the ship separated, then, as the ensign tapped controls, drifted across the room as the ship moved under her. "We've escaped," she whispered, not quite believing it.

"At least we've started." The man was frowning. "It all depends on how quickly they raise the alarm. There's another ship out there."

A different voice came over the comm, which was apparently on all the time. "They're moving away, opposite the direction we came from. If possible we'll just lay doggo until . . . there. They just jumped. Now we can go the other way. Juan's been studying the automatic jump log, he can get us back to either Beta Pegasi or we can go on to Eta, it's about the same distance."

"Eta," Parker was definite. "The Joint Fleet will be there because of the conference."

"Eta it is." The voice on the comm sounded cheered. "I really want to see these guys on the other end of the gun."

"Main engines ready." Parker put in.

"Main Engines to half thrust." The first voice commanded. Nicole sank to the deck as thrust built up quickly.

The second voice chimed in. "Is Jenny back with you

guys? I thought she'd be up here?"

Parker shook her head. "She's still back on the station, the hijackers grabbed her, and I had to close the lock before they started shooting."

"What!" Nicole staggered, feeling faint for the first time. "I can't leave without Jenny."

"You already have. Now we have to get help as soon as possible."

***

One of the other of the four elevator doors was open. Drifting over, Jenny saw the shaft was empty. Rungs ran up one side, receding into the darkness.

Cap pushed the dead hijackers down an unlit passageway. "Their communications here are very bad. I don't think they know anyone got away."

"Good. There's another ship out there somewhere, that might be armed." She bit her lip worriedly. "I didn't think of that when I sent everyone off." She peered out an airlock porthole, but all she could see was the inside of the airlock with the equally small porthole opposite reflecting light back at her. "Do you think they'll search the station again, or assume that everyone got away on the ship?"

"They'll be certain they got away." He smiled down at her. "But they may still search. They don't understand heroes, but they do understand revenge."

Jenny could feel herself blushing, and cleared her throat. "Do you think we could get everyone else into one of the other ships? There were only three men down there . . . " She broke off abruptly as the rattle of one of the poorly maintained lifts started.

"In here." Cap led her into the open elevator shaft; with so little gravity she held on by one hand and nearly floated. Cap pulled the doors shut manually and put his eye to the crack, she joined him in time to see the two dozen hijackers crammed into the lift explode out with laser guns at the ready. They checked the docks and even at this distance Jenny could hear the curses echoing indecipherably up from the airlocks. She noted with interest that none of them attempted any sort of pursuit with the two other ships. Not armed? Fueled? Maybe not even spaceworthy! They didn't check the elevator shaft either, which was just as well. The line of light shining through the crack was irregular, as if some considerable force had been applied.

"In a hurry, were you?" she asked.

He nodded. "I located the motors and where to pry for best results weeks ago. As soon as they started taking everyone up the elevator, I thought an opportunity might be manufactured. They have always been very lax in their supervision of you women. They don't think you are at all capable." He grinned. "Fools."

Jenny thought about the beauty queens and their

228

entourages and bit her lip.

The pirates were now yelling at each other, their voices echoing around the chamber and unintelligible.

Cap oozed back from the doors and motioned to her to follow him downward. It was easy at first, just a matter of not getting up too much speed as the apparent gravity increased. The ladder was on the trailing side of the station's spin, so they tended to drift against it and not away, but the last bit had her puffing a bit to keep up Cap's pace. He didn't speak until they were down and cautiously through the door at the bottom.

"They will start searching soon, although they must know the women are gone. We need to hide."

"Perhaps I could sneak back into the women's group, or would hiding be better?"

He hesitated. "Go back with the women, I think. I can move and hide much easier by myself."

Jenny nodded, and headed for the airtight door.

Cap escorted her most of the way, but dropped quietly back as she slid up to the lav and peered around the corner. The shrunken group huddled now around their belongings, glancing nervously toward the closed elevator doors. Adam, the oldest of the boys, was the first to spot her, and she waved him over, as the other women noticed as well. "What's happening, have all the hijackers left?"

"Yeah, one of 'em came down and yelled at this bunch

and they yelled back, and they all took off. What are you doing? Hiding?" God bless nasty little boys.

"Yes." As the other women drifted over, she raised her voice a bit. "Didn't any of the other groups come back?"

"No, only us." Mrs. Brown was looking a bit wild eyed.

"What happened up there?" Jenny asked, trying for a baffled look.

"We were back before the others went, we didn't see anything odd."

"There was that other ship!" Opal said. "They had the airlock open, we could see straight through to it, just like the 'Far Seeker' and there were people in there, them, I mean, the pirates."

Jenny let the women babble on, adding nothing herself, afraid she'd give something away. Looking over toward the men's side she saw them watching anxiously, and walked over, wondering what she could say.

Chapter Twenty-Seven
Secrets and Uncertainty

What the hell is going on? Paris wondered frantically. *Opportunity or further disaster?* The entire male contingent was plastered to the mesh barrier. The first group of women and children had gone up to the ship and come back with more clothes. And then the second group had gone up, and the third, and the fourth . . . and they hadn't come back.

Finally a man had come down the elevator, and called the rest of the hijackers away. And still the women were gone.

Except for Jenny. She could claim to have been hiding all she wanted, but she had definitely gone up with the last group, he was sure of it. She'd gone up the elevator, and walked back in from the far end of the women's section. She must have the keycode for the airdoors. She had to have come in that way.

He thought it over again. *Had she gone up with the last group? Maybe I'm mistaken, that would make more sense. I won't be able to ask her a thing, the hijackers have this place bugged. Maybe she could have hit on the code to the doors? I've seen her sneak off in the middle of the night often enough.*

She can't be one of them. She can't. It just isn't possible. It would explain so much. He rubbed his aching head, and watched her walking over. Saw her reserve, and how much she was not saying. *Oh, Shit!*

"Do any of you know what's going on?" She aimed the comment vaguely toward Dr. Zimmer while scanning the group. Was she looking for Bornstein?

Zimmer shook his head. "While they were organizing you, they came and got Bornstein, said his ransom should be ready, and they'd take him along, just in case."

Paris put in, "They must have put him on the other ship Georges says came in yesterday."

"So." She glanced back at the women and children. "That other ship might have pulled out with Michael? I wonder if they could have taken everyone else, as well?"

You're not worried enough about your sister, what do you know?

"Or did they leave in the Far Seeker?"

Are you trying to add a bit of confusion? Christ! IS the Farseeker gone?

"If they were going to take that many, why not all of us?"

"They split you up quite deliberately into four groups." Captain Portman was leaning heavily on one of his pilots, but refusing to stay in bed. He was sweating; Paris hoped it was from pain and exertion, not infection. "Did they take three ships out of here?"

232

In the Rift

Jenny looked surprised at that suggestion. "There were those two other ships, weren't there? I assumed they had taken the Farseeker, but perhaps not."

"They were very angry men," the chef put in. "They ate apart from the others, and there was," he waved his hands vaguely, "aura. Bad feelings. Last night they were angry."

"I think you're right about the anger," said Obadiah Latham. "They made me redo most of the instructions to my bank, I think something went wrong with the first ransom attempt." He looked over his shoulder. "How about you?"

"Oh, yes," Paris hunched his shoulders. "They had me put in all the horrible things they were going to do to me." He shrugged. "First I'd heard of them, and frankly, I could have done without. Maybe Bornstein's ransom worked because he's from Eta, he didn't have to deal with Earth-based banks."

Then the elevator rattled down again.

***

The women shifted toward it eagerly, but shrank back as a dozen of the hijackers spilled out, weapons at the ready. From the back of the elevator, they dragged Misty and Kissy, tossing them in the direction of the others, then they spread out, searching, kicking over boxes of food, and pounding down around the curve. They had powerful flashlights that illuminated the piping through the mesh. They prowled angrily to glare at the men, but their small section was clearly unable to conceal over forty women.

This time they pried off the cover to the lower level and dropped down to inspect closer. A black puff and desperate coughing marked a pirate kicking over one of the carbon bags. The micro fine powder floated up through the floor in a cloud, and Jenny pulled her t-shirt up over her nose.

The gasping hijackers pulled themselves back up through the hole and with their laser rifles roughly welded it closed. The carbon flickered in the air, snapping and burning like tiny fireworks. Whatever form the carbon was in, it fortunately wasn't very flammable.

As the hijackers scrambled cursing and coughing back into the elevator, she hurried over to where Misty and Kissy stood in mutual support. Literally. They looked like they'd both collapse if they let go of each other. Jenny gulped at the still developing bruises and swellings on their faces, and obviously their faces hadn't been the only targets of the maddened brutes. The black powder settling out of the air caught in their tear tracks and bloody streaks.

Jenny was afraid to touch them. "Come and sit down? Or lay down? We've found a tiny little first aid kit." Helplessly, she led them over to the kitchen, snatching abandoned blankets along the way to cushion the crates the women slumped on.

She got one pan heating water while she carefully

dabbed at their faces until they asked her to stop.

"We just need to hold still and let everything settle down, honey," Misty told her. "I can't figure what set them off like that."

Jenny bit her lip, then started carefully, "I thought they'd taken a bunch of us off to sell, but they're so mad that all I can think is that either they escaped, or there's been a falling out, and some of the hijackers took off with the best loot." She looked from one woman to the other. "That's probably the most likely, after all, how could anyone escape without a pilot?"

Their eyes widened, and their lips curled up just a bit as they looked at each other, and said nothing.

Chapter Twenty-Eight
Midnight Chat

"When they kept us back from the other passengers, we knew we were in for it." Misty was still doing most of the talking. The entire right side of Kissy's face was bruised and swollen. She had eaten only very soft food, very slowly and carefully, leaving Jenny worrying about broken jaws or teeth. The dim backwash of Cap's flashlight hid most of the damage.

Jenny hadn't counted on meeting Cap tonight, but she was hugely grateful for his massive dangerous presence. It felt so strange to feel safe in the presence of such a man. As a civilized person she ought to be attracted to the rich successful Michael Bornstein type, or, being eighteen, she supposed she should have a crush on Paris. Fat chance. She'd had a good solid lesson in the advantages of having a trained killer on her side.

Pity he's so old. Not that he looks that old, but he . . . feels like someone with eighty years of life behind him. And anyway, he's a linguistic scholar, not a, well, yes, he is also a trained killer. And a damn good thing, under the circumstances.

"It wasn't so bad at first, then that new bunch came in

and they was just wild." Kissy nodded agreement, tears starting in her eyes again. "I think something must'a gone wrong for them an' they was taken' it out on us." Misty stretched painfully. When Jenny had gotten up in the middle of the 'night' to see if Cap might be at the airtight door, they had been wide awake and had followed her. They had startled badly when Cap materialized silently from the shadows. Cap, on the other hand, had taken their presence in stride and had ushered them through the small side door. Jenny had kept between them, for their nerves' sake.

"They said," Kissy's voice was faint and slurred, "that they were headed for the outback and would take a sample along. Thought they meant us."

"The outback." Jenny sighed. "I wonder if that's an actual place or if it just means far away? They split us into four groups, they said, to go back to the ship for clean clothes. I don't know why they did it that way, did they think it would be easier than dragging sixteen of us out of here kicking and screaming?

"The second group sort of disappeared, so I rousted out Mac and Frank and told them it was time to make a break for it. They headed for the control and engine rooms, while I went to make sure the third group of us didn't leave and the fourth group all got on board, and to close the airlock." She grinned wryly. "Somehow I was on the wrong side of it, though."

238

In the Rift

"You jumped the hijackers that could have stopped them, and given the alarm," Cap put in. "You got half of the women away."

Misty and Kissy stared at her.

Jenny shrugged. "And they were in the process of killing me when Cap got them. Anyhow," she tried to get the days straight. "It took us what, twenty days to get here?" Jenny asked. "So if they get back to Beta Pegasi and there is someone, something armed, a police or Joint Fleet ship, actually there and they come immediately, it will still be close to forty days before we can expect rescue. Minimum."

Kissy just curled up a bit tighter. Misty moaned. "Forty days. We ain't going to survive."

"Yes we will." Jenny thought quickly. "First, I've already said something over by the men's section; they've got it wired and can hear everything."

Both the women nodded.

"So I said something to try to tip the hijackers into thinking that it's their fellows that took the women. That way they won't be thinking the Fleet might show up." She hesitated. "So they won't just shoot us, or rush the work on the two other ships. So we'll still be here when the fleet arrives."

"To be used as hostages." Misty hadn't any doubts about that.

"Could we barricade ourselves in there?" Jenny looked

around dubiously. "Or here?" Probably not a good idea, the water system was empty, although it was mercifully clear of the black powder.

"What we need is a way to communicate with a Space Navy ship, if, when they get here. A comm or a two-way radio, something. Then when the Fleet shows up, we can barricade ourselves in, and tell the marines where to hit the bad guys, that we're not hostages and have airtight doors between us and them."

"That, that would be great, but they can open the doors. We can't, well, couldn't." Misty eyed Captain Midnight. "Can you scramble the door codes? Or break the locks?"

He frowned. "I think so. I will experiment, and also try to find a comm I can steal. Something small, that you can hide."

Kissy climbed painfully to her feet. "Ah'm going to try an' sleep now. Ah feel a lot betta knowing you're around." She glared at him through her unswollen eye. "You take good care of this little girl, y'hear?"

He touched Jenny gently on the shoulder. "I will." He pushed the door open a crack, looked, then opened it wider.

Jenny stood up when Misty followed her, but hesitated. "Are you all right, Cap? I haven't thought to bring you food, or anything."

"I steal their food, I am well." He loomed down at her. "I fear for you, I am too far away to help you, if they come."

Breathless, she stammered. "You came, when I needed

you." Her pulse was pounding and she was nearly panicked by conflicting emotions.

But he stepped away and looked back at the door. "If I can change the code for the doors, I will make them 'Jenny Poppenhusen'. But not for perhaps forty days." He faded silently away, disappearing into the shadows. With a gulp, she turned away and squeezed through the door, closing it and activating the lock.

Chapter Twenty-Nine
Thirty-two and Counting

Jenny slept late, then hustled into the kitchen, but Mrs. Brown was already at work. "I guess with only, only, umm, how many of us are left?"

"Nineteen, dear. I can get breakfast this morning, why don't you see if the men have found anything out?" It was hard to tell if she was genuinely at ease, or putting up an iron front on sheer will power. Jenny would have bet on the will power, she'd seen her own mother acting entirely normal the morning after being beaten by her drunkard husband.

Georges was still away, fixing breakfast for the hijackers. So there wouldn't be any fresh news yet. Zimmer wandered over to talk to her, Paris trailing after.

"I've been thinking about what must have happened," Jenny started.

"Dear child," the doctor said wearily, "what's the point of talking it to death?"

"We're still in this, and maybe this will help us." Jenny glared at him. "Buck up, will you? If they've had a falling out, and it sure sounds to me like some of them took off with the prime loot, that means there are fewer of them here."

"Prime loot!" Paris started snickering. "What a

description!"

"Well, look at what's left." Jenny retorted. "A bunch of kids, the oldest of the women except Opal, Paula and the fat chick. And you guys. You've got to know that ransoming is higher risk than selling women. They say half of the men out here are here because they're wanted criminals elsewhere."

"Well," sniffed Paris. "You know my fans would cough up the dough even if I weren't already rich."

"And maybe have the police or the Space Marines or the Joint Fleet tracing it." Jenny took a deep breath. "Look, just tell Georges to count pirates today, see how many have split. Okay? Ask him to check especially if their boss is still here. If there really is a Cinnab running around loose, Descartes would be the ideal person for it to have taken."

Pity he wasn't one of the ones Cap killed yesterday.

"Crumb! You really do think there's a falling out among thieves, don't you?" Paris studied her, and she reminded herself that he was actually quite bright, somewhere under the pop music idol exterior, which was getting a bit thin, since the fight. "Do you have any information?"

"Just an overactive imagination, probably." Keeping the pirates' microphones in mind, she spoke clearly. "But they're gone, and only the pirates had pilots. They didn't even need to take Barry or Carl. This lot may have been left holding the bag."

"I can't take this. You carry on like there's something you

can do!" Doctor Zimmer threw up his hands and walked away.

Jenny bit her lip, then decided to take a chance. Gesturing Paris nearer, she pointed at the door, and put her finger to her lips. Put a hand to her ear as if to listen, then pointed to the door. He nodded. Paris definitely got the message.

She turned to the wall and started to write 'your royal majesty' in the thin film of black dust.

Paris, wide-eyed, threw up his hand to stop her. *He knows it already. Did he actually manage to figure it out?* She felt a half panicky wave of suspicion as his glance flickered from the wall to the door. He bounced a bit, biting his lip as he thought. He looked frustrated, unable to ask her anything. Not angry, alarmed or belligerent in any way.

He's got to be okay. He's a Superstar with tons of money.

She wiped down the wall. "Remember, ask Georges to count pirates." He frowned after her in frustration as she walked away.

Chapter Thirty
It's On!

The women were just settling down to sleep, and Jenny was waiting quietly before wandering off to find Cap, when the rattle from the elevator shaft had them all up and bunching together like sheep hearing the wolves howl. It was the usual group of six, but this time Descartes himself followed them off.

"Well, Ladies, we've had a bit of trouble and are greatly in need of some TLC." His eyes measured Kissy and Misty, dismissed them. "I think we'll have something fresh and new." As he strolled smirking toward them, they moved as one, flattening back against the wall, then splitting up, starting to scatter as they ran out of room. "You'll do nicely." He hooked Paula's arm and pulled her out of the clump of women all trying to hide behind each other. Paula shrieked. "No, no, no . . . " He shoved her into the arms of the gunmen as he turned back and focused on Opal. She turned to run, but he grabbed her long trailing hair. Panting in panic, she stumbled back to the pirates. "And, I think, the fat girl." Descartes grinned as Jenny back pedaled, and stalked after her.

Jenny tried to jumpstart her frozen brain as she backed

away. *Where is Cap? Should I go with this group to their quarters, can I accomplish anything there? Is it possible to start a battle now and win? It's too soon! We can't hold them off until the Fleet gets here!*

The grinning pirates were following along and she was peripherally aware that they were giving their chief advice, laughing and betting.

She saw just the faintest twitch of movement in the shadows behind her to the right, and backed further, more quickly, past that dark patch. Descartes followed, trailing his cheering section. And the shadows now behind them reached out and engulfed one of them quickly and almost silently. As the first pirate collapsed to the deck, the nearest turned and was grabbed in turn. He got out the start of a shout, enough for his companions to turn. One died instantly, a kick nearly taking off his head.

Descartes whipped around, drawing a pistol with blinding speed and Jenny pounced, trying for one arm around his neck, the other grabbing his gun arm. At first touch, he reacted faster than she could believe but her flailing grab knocked the gun from his hand. He shoved loose from her inexpert grip, as his gun clattered to the deck. He didn't stop to pick it up, but sprinted for the elevator, quickly outdistancing the only other pirate still on his feet. Cap dropped the man he held and leaped after them. He brought down the one pirate, but that gave Descartes enough time to reach the elevator and start up. Cap slammed into the doors and tried to pull them apart, but it was too late.

Jenny grabbed the four nearest laser rifles and raced to the mesh wall separating them from the men. "Stand back." She snapped, tucking the three extra rifles awkwardly into the crook of her left arm to bring the fourth to bear. Seeing the weapons in her hands they scrambled out of the way.

Safety is already off, switch to continuous fire, check the background. Jenny cut a neat two meter wide hole through the mesh.

Paris was already tapping a code on the lockpad. Cap took one of the rifles from her and was sliding through the hole before the cut section hit the deck.

Paris hauled the door open and Cap was through it and into the Pirates' quarter.

Jenny stepped through the hole she'd made, handing a rifle to the eager Terry. Paris snatched one practically out of Zimmer's hands as the doctor reached for it, and bolted after Cap.

She followed, clinging grimly to her own weapon. Switch back to single shot, hold fire until clear of the others, but the pirates had been unprepared for this, drinking and playing cards and waiting for their fellows to return with the women.

No comms? And Descartes has to take a rickety elevator up to the hub, and then take another down here. We beat him here!

Cap took nearly half of them out with a single continuous burst; Paris and Terry picked off a few more with more controlled fire. Jenny shot a man who popped out of a doorway behind them. Stepping carefully over bodies, she made her way past them to the elevator and waited. Standing back out of grab range.

"Should we take some prisoners?" She raised her voice over the clamor. The next man that came face to face with Cap received the butt of his rifle to his face.

"If you wish," he replied.

The elevator doors sprang open and Descartes nearly fell out, his mouth open to command his men, and froze.

"You want to surrender, or shall I just kill you now?" For a second she thought he was going to jump her, but his eyes flicked behind her, to Cap probably, and he stayed in place. His hands rose jerkily and he stood frozen while a last few shots and thuds followed the quick search of the pirates' quarters. He stared blankly through her, and she had the uncomfortable feeling that he was thinking very fast. Paris emerged from one room with a roll of wire and pliers, and set to work immobilizing Descartes. The other survivors among the hijackers were three that had surrendered quickly enough to avoid Cap's lethal tendencies and two who were passed out drunk.

"Well," Paris stood up and nudged the still silent Descartes. "I've got to say that was a bit unexpected."

250

In the Rift

"Damn good job." Mrs. Brown surveyed the scene with grim pleasure, a rifle in her hands. Cheryl Franklin and Laurie Guthrie were behind her, with the last rifle and Descartes' pistol. Most of the rest of the passengers were trailing in behind them.

Some of them were eyeing Cap worriedly. Zimmer grabbed the rifle from Cheryl and started to raise it, but Jenny was there and shoved it down.

"This is Cap Midnight." Jenny told them. "He was Mr. Wong's bodyguard."

"Do you know," Paris asked, "what happened yesterday, or whenever that was, when so many people disappeared?"

"Yes." Jenny organized her thoughts. "The second group of women that went up were taken away by the pirate ship that came in the day before. Several others of the passengers and crew of the 'Far Seeker' survived by hiding in the utility spaces, including one of the pilots. When the pirates took that second group of women off in another ship, I figured it was time to do something, or they'd just take us off to sell a few at a time. Nearly half the passengers were up there, so they grabbed the opportunity and took off."

"Why didn't you go? If you know so much about it?" Zimmer sounded more resentful than relieved.

"I got into an altercation with two of the pirates when I tried to get everyone onboard from the hub and the airlock closed. I wound up on the wrong side of the lock."

251

"So help is on the way?" asked Paris.

"Yeah, but it will take a while. It's twenty days or so back to Beta Pegasi, and then they may not find the Fleet in residence. So I don't know how long it will be before someone shows up," Jenny said.

"In that case," said Mrs. Brown, "let's clean this mess up and take inventory. We may have a long wait." She looked around with satisfaction. "This bunch of trash I will be delighted to throw out."

"First, we should check out the rest of the station, and those two ships." Jenny said. She eyed Paris, he was unexpectedly competent. "Cap? Check the station. Paris, go with Barry, Carl and Terry to check the ships."

Jiminy! They were all taking her orders!

"Dr. Zimmer, will you check that these things are really dead? Then we'll start sending them up the elevator and dumping them out an airlock." She walked over to Descartes. "What's the airlock code? Tell, or we'll let your deceased friends here share your living quarters for the next forty days or so."

Still showing little expression, Descartes told her where to find the list of airlock numbers and locking codes.

Adam walked among the hijackers, turning them over until he found Baldy, and nodded in satisfaction. He went back to his mother, who'd been watching him worriedly, and his brothers and spoke to them.

252

In the Rift

As they searched, they opened all the airtight doors and then they spread out. No one wanted to sleep in the prison quarter, and the pirates' quarter was a smelly mess, with, as Opal said, a bad aura, even after the bodies were disposed of.

Even Georges refused to cook in the kitchen there, with, as he said, the equipment ripped from a dozen murdered ships. But they did have a picnic style feast in the next quarter after they'd hunted through the stacks, disposed of the actual garbage, and unearthed some furniture and more cooking equipment. The quarter must have been used as the hijackers' storeroom and garbage dump for decades according to some of the dated supplies.

Captain Portman rested comfortably, on painkillers and antibiotics, his leg wound cleaned and covered with nanos. Further treatment, rebuilding the destroyed tissues, would have to wait until they got to a real hospital, but Zimmer was confident that he would live.

Two more hijackers had been found onboard one of the ships. Without the lethal Cap present, they had been captured alive, and were now locked into the men's side. The mesh from the hole Jenny'd cut was wired and locked in place; the airdoor lockpads had been reprogrammed rather unexpectedly by Paris, who was pleased to show her how easy it was, once the door was open.

The former prisoners slowly wound down and collapsed into a grateful sleep. The kids were again clumped in a central nest with their mothers on the perimeter, the Wall Street gang was back together, but somehow the 'men's barracks' remained beyond them, and the single women, reduced to five now, were on the far side of the children. The men organized a night watchmen's relay, and Jenny left them to it, asleep as soon as she hit the blankets.

***

Paris prowled through the dim space station, grinning. He still felt a bit stunned at the sudden turnaround. Not only did they have control, but a ship had left two days ago and would, eventually, bring rescuers. He passed the open airtight door into the prison quarter. Voices were echoing down from the far end and he approached cautiously. The prisoners were facing Captain Midnight, throwing a chaotic combination of threats, bribes and curses through the mesh barrier. Cap glanced over his shoulder at Paris, then returned to silent contemplation of the former hijackers. After a long while, he turned and walked away.

"They appear reasonably healthy and mentally normal, if not highly intelligent." He said. "What can cause a man to have so little regard for others that he becomes a predator of his own species?"

Paris blinked in surprise. "That question has been around for as long as man. I've never heard a satisfactory answer that covers even a majority of cases.

254

In the Rift

"I suppose that all the explanations: poverty, drugs, broken families, lack of a father figure, lack of proper socialization, lack of discipline, prejudice, genetics... are all correct and all occur in combinations and alone and sometimes corrupt men's honor." He shrugged. "I don't know, I can only try and stop it when I see it."

He snorted. "Although perhaps for best results, I should just stand aside and let Jenny deal with it. She was awesome."

"She saved me on the ship." The big dark man in his black gi nearly faded out of sight even from a few feet away. "She saw that I was breathing and, in a moment when the hijackers weren't looking, dragged me away and hid me."

"Where those," he jerked his head back toward the prisoners, "kill without remorse, thinking only of themselves, she saves without thinking about the possible consequences to herself." And under his breath, almost to himself. "I will be more like her, and less like them."

Paris felt goose bumps springing up on his arms. "I suppose your background is very different from most in the West." He kept his tone neutral.

I've listened to too many tall tales with the Red Guards as the boogiemen. Kill without remorse indeed, that was some rampage we just saw today—not that I'm going to complain!

"Perhaps." The man was silent for a long moment. "The

goals of my rearing may have been different, but I was raised by parents that loved me and instilled discipline and a rigorous education. I was trained to kill, but not to hate. In fact, until the hijacking I had never killed or in fact, actually fought in earnest."

"Did you travel often with Chairman Wong?"

"Never before," Paris could see the flash of his eyes as he glanced his way, but that was apparently all the information he was going to give out.

They walked silently through the warehouse section, passing the sleeping bodies without disturbing them, and on into the pirates' quarter, now silent and empty. It had easily three times the light tubes of the other sections. "I can hardly stand this section." Paris said, looking around at the remains of the pirates' last party, and Cap nodded.

"It was always filthy and noisy, even when no one was awake there was music, or snoring. I was tempted to come in and see how many I could kill before they raised the alarm." He glanced around. "It worked much better this way, with more people armed."

He smiled, the first time Paris had seen it. "Especially Jenny. I should have known that she would not be helpless."

"I think that she might have been in over her head today, without you."

Cap looked doubtful, but nodded.

They stood still for a long moment, listening. There was

no sound above the whisper of the air system. Cap nodded in satisfaction, and moved on. Paris followed, trying, and failing, to move as quietly.

As they walked, he tried to marshal his thoughts and get back to his job, which was to study the political players of the New Territories. *OK, Perris, you've got a lot of your big players, or the remains of their groups here. So study them.*

What we have here is the Wall Street Gang, Jenny and Paula who are loosely associated with Bornstein, Obadiah Latham, a representative of the Red Enclave, a few colonists, a few spacers and a few strays.

Back in the warehouse, Cap waved him toward the aisle down one side, and headed for the other.

The three mothers didn't seem political at all, he probably could ignore them.

Obadiah Latham hadn't paid much attention to anything but Aria on the ship, and Opal was a friend of Aria's, even though she was along as part of Ethereal's paid staff, and hadn't there been furious accusations of poaching just flying around.

He boggled a bit, at his mental return to Beauty Queen backstabbing politics. How things had changed. How fast would they return to normal, now?

He'd talk to Opal, see if she knew anything about Latham's politics from previous years. Latham's business was mostly Earth-based, and what wasn't, was in Earth's orbital construction zone. He hadn't been known to express an opinion about the petition. But he really couldn't be ignored.

What about the strays?

The pros? At first glance they might be a good messenger service. Paris shuddered. Not an idea that could survive long after actually meeting them. If they were involved, they were absolutely not major players, nor would anyone give them any possibly damaging information. Still, observing who they contacted when they finally got to Autumn might be worthwhile.

The crew? Descartes' treatment of Captain Portman ought to rule out any possibility of collusion. Barry, Carl and Terry seemed to care for nothing but the mechanics of their beloved jump ships. Was that why they hadn't been killed? Someone figured they could be corrupted, threatened or bribed to crew pirate ships?

And what about Georges? He had regularly gone back and forth to the hijackers quarter, but interstellar politics? Mind boggling, but he really couldn't be ignored.

Doctor Zimmer, now there was a possibility. He'd met and talked to everyone on the ship, First and Second Class alike. In fact, now that he thought about it, Zimmer could have been a messenger between Bornstein and MacGregor. He chewed that one over distastefully, he'd liked Mac, enjoyed the poker games.

In the Rift

At the end of the piles, he angled back toward the center of the tube and was joined by a black shadow. "Cap? Who were the other survivors on the ship?"

"Juan Zuniga, the third pilot, and two passengers, friends of Jenny's, named Abraham MacGregor and Frank Monico."

"I see." *And does that mean the hijacking had something to do with politics? Mac survived and Bornstein's gone off with pirates. I do not like the smell of this at all.*

Okay, where was I? Zimmer. Right, and he's here where I can question him. Subtly. Along with Latham and Georges. He glanced at Cap. *Without telling anyone who might decide to kill them.*

And what about the Red Enclave? Was this man just a bodyguard? His command of English is excellent, no accent beyond an occasional lapse into very correct grammar. Paris cast his mind back to the ship.

The nervous Mr. Wright, a native of San Francisco, had translated for both of them, hadn't he? And Cap had given no indication that he understood anything said to him. At the conference he would have heard and understood anything said in his presence. I'll bet he's got very good hearing. If the New Territories didn't join the Union, how would their relationship to the Union and thus the Enclave change? Could this be a way that the Enclave could expand into space without having to join the Union?

Paris grumpily realized that he needed to talk to one of the bureau's political experts about all of this. *I need to go back to observing, reporting, and tracing illegal drug and nano use among the Pretty People of Hollywood. I don't know this political stuff. Not to mention hijacking and piracy. If they'd realized what I was getting into, I'd at least have had my head stuffed with the right kind of data and the faces on the wanted list!*

In the empty quarter, Cap stopped at the elevator shaft and leaned through the open doorway to peer upward. Joining him, Paris saw nothing, including an elevator.

"I'm going to check the Hub and the ships," Cap told him. "Keep patrolling down here." He started climbing the ladder on the side of the shaft as if it were easy. Having climbed a few vertical ladders himself, Paris was glad to refrain. He stepped back and walked on toward the prison quarter.

"In fact," he whispered to himself, "I seem to be taking orders from an eighteen-year-old girl and the rep from the only non-Union, non-Joint Understanding signatory country in Human space. My boss is going to have something to say about this."

An eighteen-year-old girl. Yeah. What about Jenny? He grinned helplessly. *She is definitely not with the hijackers and pirates, either that or her quarterly review is going to be really bad.*

260

In the Rift

So, did that mean Bornstein was likewise not connected? No, what had Jenny said? "I've only met him a few times and while he's a step up from Nicole's last sponsor . . . " So he's fairly new.

Before or after Nicole won the Miss Great Plains Crown, I wonder? Did he first find the girl and try to skew the contest, or wait till the contest was over and seduce the winner?

Paris flinched a bit at the memory of his own actions. "Hi, Ethereal, remember me?" And if one of the other women had won the Miss Alpha Centauri Crown, his next words would have been "Why don't you introduce me to the winner?" But with his recording company as the main corporate sponsor, it had been so easy, so non-contrived, for him to be the representative. He sighed.

At least Ethereal is off on the Far Seeker, and out of danger.

How about Paula? Not a very bright woman, paid staff, had Nicole known her, or had Bornstein hired her? Gossip and find out. Maybe.

The prisoners were still locked up, and he turned and walked back. If the station was eight kilometers around . . . he must have walked nearly twenty kilometers just tonight.

He took a deep breath. *And someone is cooking!* He glanced at his watch, yes it was morning already, and he could make someone else take over.

Chapter Thirty-One
Freedom! To . . . Worry

"Even without the three hydroponics units, there is so much stored food, we could live out here for years." Dr. Zimmer looked much better for having had a safe night's sleep. Actually, they all did. "They've also got all the medical supplies stripped from who knows how many ships, so we're set there." He nodded toward Captain Portman, sitting propped up on his pallet.

Barry Corvallis nodded. "The two ships here are functional, but the comps have been completely wiped and reformatted. Until we're desperate, I don't think we should try leaving. There's no navigational information on how to get anywhere, or even figure out where we are."

"Is either ship armed?" asked Paris.

"No, they're just small cargo ships, Cinnab manufacture. Their type is common as dirt, making short hops all over the New Territories. The pirates were in the process of removing all their ID numbers and substituting new ones, presumably from wrecks they'd bought legally." Barry hesitated. "What would we do with ship mounted weapons anyway?"

"Protect ourselves if the next ship to come in is a pirate." Paris answered. "We know that there's at least one pirate ship out there, there may well be more."

That unpalatable thought sat heavily on them for a long moment.

"What do we do if they come back?" Opal hesitantly fielded the thought for all of them.

"Could we trick them into docking?" Jenny wondered. "We've got nine captives, to talk to them on the comm."

Peter Franklin spoke up. "I'll take a look at their comm. If they've recorded any of their conversations, we'll know the customary contact routine, and how to answer without alarming them."

Jenny nodded agreement, or perhaps it was permission. Somehow the events of yesterday had resulted in people looking to her for guidance. Maybe Captain Portman should take over . . . but a quick glance his way showed that he'd succumbed to the painkillers again and was asleep.

"We'd better have a twenty-four hour watch on the comm, as well as a patrol walking around, in case we've missed any pirates inside here." She hesitated, was she really in charge? If so, it was time to delegate.

"Peter, you organize the comm watch; Cap, the patrol. Georges, you're in charge of anything having to do with food." She bit her lip. What else? "I know enough about the air system here to change the carbon bags, does anyone know more?" Silence.

"Well, that's mine, then. And Barry, the ships are yours.

In the Rift

Check them over, get them as ready to go as you can, just in case we don't have the option of waiting here. Doctor Zimmer? You're still the doctor." She grinned at his glower.

Irene spoke up then. "About all I'm good at is cooking, cleaning and minding kids. Georges is a better cook than I'll ever be, so I'll stick to my other specialties." She glanced over her shoulder at the pirates' quarter. "Starting with a major spring cleaning and redecoration." They all laughed a bit at that, and when Jenny stood up, apparently took it as official dismissal.

They were busy all day, happier than they'd been for weeks. While Irene conscripted 'volunteers' and stripped the pirates' quarters to the wall and washed everything, Jenny buried herself in all the air units, emptying carbon dumps and, having searched the built-in comp for them, reading the instructions and then washing filters. She was under the pirates' quarter, trying to find instructions for the water treatment system maintenance, when Cap found her.

"Peter has five people to man the comm, and I have five to patrol, but everyone seems to have been drafted to clean today. Irene has finished the pirates' quarter and has started on the dump."

"I escaped," Jenny looked ruefully down at her dirty, damp clothes. "Then I wound up cleaning filters anyway."

He nodded. "Reporting to you is my escape."

Jenny tried to imagine anyone telling this man to start

scrubbing, and failed utterly. "How did I get put in charge?"

"You keep telling people what to do. Sometimes it just works like that." He was silent a moment. "The pirates probably deliberately killed any of the crew that had any leadership ability. Ordinarily the Captain, the doctor or Barry should have been in charge, but Portman is injured, the doctor is pathetic and Barry just doesn't try. Dr. Zimmer seems to have recovered now that the danger is less, but I do not think he can be relied on, if there is a battle. I do not want him to have a gun, the way he looked at the prisoners, I think he would kill them."

"What about Paris?" she asked. "He's much more than he lets on."

"I think he's an undercover policeman."

She blinked. "You're kidding."

"No. Now that he has stopped acting like a musical idiot, it shows. He is working hard to hide it, but it shows." He shrugged. "I have not asked him."

She nodded and bit her lip. "The slightest rumor would have gotten him killed. If we get out of this he'll just go back to making that awful music, I suppose, and never let on."

"I like his music."

She started laughing silently. "Finally! I've found something about you that is not perfect! You have no taste in music."

"Finally! I have found something you are wrong about."

266

In the Rift

He smiled and walked away.

Right. Bad taste counts.

Paris, a cop. That's . . . useful.

Chapter Thirty-Two
Playing House

By the next day, they had made the station as much theirs as thirty-three people could make a space designed for a population of thousands. The pirates quarter was stripped clean; stark and sterile, it didn't look like the same place. The dump quarter was in the process of being transformed.

The crates, empty and full, were being stacked into walls. Georges had moved some cooking equipment, and they had found tables among the loot for a dining room. The Wall Streeters had large bedrooms with crate furniture and real mattresses, the families had complete suites, and the singles their own rooms. The accumulated piles of loot were being sorted through, some used but most of it just left for an odd combination of warehouse and playground for the kids. Unfortunately the quarter had no plumbing installed, so they built their little nests close to the door to the Pirate Quarter; all the plumbing and water treatment there seemed to be working.

The actual garbage, plastic containers and paper wrappers mostly, Jenny had claimed. She rather suspected their relatively clean condition was due to the cat, not the pirates. She was going to try cutting, chopping and crushing it into the planters of the prison quarter. Not what anyone would call soil, but possibly a texturizer for the carbon and the waste sludge from the air and water treatment units that would eventually have to be emptied. Only trial and error would show if it could grow plants.

But before she tried that she needed to install some of the boxes and boxes of light tubes she'd found, and do a bit of rewiring so people could turn their lights off and on. She suspected the large crates of electrical supplies had been part of the original cargo of small parts for the space station. Certainly there was enough to have wired and lit multiple levels of the entire station.

Fortunately space station wiring was designed to be altered, replaced and changed. Her wiring was probably not to professional standards, but by the end of the second day everyone had a ceiling level light – with a switch – in their rooms and the public areas were well lit with switches for variable light levels.

"Playing house" they called it, as they all dumped months of anxiety. They even had a pet.

The first meal they'd fixed, the cat had strolled nonchalantly out of nowhere and lounged regally above the reach of the children until Kissy had taken the hint and served it some chopped rehydrated meat. Paris, the only actual Alphan in the group was quite certain of its Alphan origins. "Look at the paws, how long the toes are. Anyhow, F-cats handle travel much better than real cats, they're about all you find off Earth." It, she, rather, had studied Cap intently, and actually rubbed against his leg before disappearing.

"There's gratitude for you." Kissy huffed.

"It's a cat." Paris grinned.

Cap looked embarrassed and admitted to having slipped the cat food occasionally over the last month.

Jenny was just as glad to be ignored, but the children were disappointed. As the cat had managed to avoid armed pirates, she supposed it could avoid kids. At least it didn't seem inclined to bite or scratch.

Her own room was rather bare, perhaps tomorrow she'd have enough time to join the treasure hunt for colorful odds and ends to personalize it. The olive green pad on the floor was probably a shipping wrap, but made an adequate if bland rug. The open ends of the crates that made up her walls were empty, so far. The bed, even if it was only more shipping wrap on top of boxes, was definitely a step up from the floor.

The two hundred meter wide tube of the station torus, even stuffed with decades of loot, seemed empty, soaring over their heads into darkness. Jenny was the furthest of the single women, with only the long stretch of the 'warehouse' beyond her. At least it didn't echo, the irregular stacks and piles ate sound and produced a hush worthy of a church.

She did hear the soft footsteps though, and turned with a frown. The man's silhouette showed briefly as he came through the door.

"What can I do for you, Doctor Zimmer?" she asked quietly.

"I thought you might like some company tonight." He was close in the dark. She stepped away, putting her hand on the light switch.

"No. Go away, doctor." She made her voice firm with an effort to keep a wave of anger out of it.

"You should stay away from that creature, he's not normal, you know." He was close again.

Who? Cap? Do you imagine I'm in love with him?

She flicked the lights on, and he flinched at the sudden light.

"Doctor. Go. Now." She chilled her voice, and to her surprise it worked.

He backed to the door, but as he turned, he threw over his shoulder, "It's for your own good, you know. He's a homicidal maniac; say the wrong thing and he'll kill you."

She listened to his steps retreat, then turned off the light and stepped to the door to watch him stomp all the way across the night dimmed commons. She heard nothing, but just felt the looming presence behind her, and sighed with relief.

"He's right, you know. I felt very much like a homicidal

272

maniac, just now. May I kill him?" His voice was actually light, as close to amused as she'd heard him; hopefully he didn't mean it.

"No, we may need a doctor, before this is over."

He laughed almost soundlessly. "You are a child. Very competent, but terrifyingly young."

"Yeah. Dammit."

***

". . . And then Ethereal was selected as one of the early arrivals, for the New Territories tour, so we booked passage on the . . ." Paris looked blank and turned to Opal. "What was the name of that ship?"

She actually giggled, startling herself. "'The Percival Excelsior'. It was a huge ship and had very nice accommodations, despite the name."

Paula sighed wistfully. "We came in on the 'Moonlight Express'; it was nice too. We were supposed to transfer straight over to the 'Queen of the Waves', and I can tell you it was quite a shock to find ourselves and our luggage parked on the dock scrambling for a berth. 'The Far Seeker' was a big step down. I was surprised Michael didn't wait for one of the larger ships, but then Beta Pegasi wasn't exactly posh either." Her brow crinkled a bit. "I think my standards for shock and posh have altered a bit. Pity we didn't wait for another ship."

Opal smiled wryly. "We all wish we'd waited for another ship, but the next ship was booked solid also." She'd sorted through the piles of fabric and was doing something with a brilliant sparkly blue fabric.

Paris nodded. *Another lead to follow, who had put all the beautiful young women on the ship with the cabin crew thoroughly infiltrated by hijackers?*

He caught Zimmer's eye and invited him to join with a nod toward an empty chair. "Hey, Doc, we're insulting your ship. What did you think of the 'Far Seeker'?"

"Paris," Zimmer gave him a dry look, then inclined his head graciously to Opal and Paula. "Ladies. I would be delighted to join you in disparaging that ship. At one time she was as good as they got, but as the planetary systems filled in she moved further and further out to where her long range made her profitable.

"But frankly? She was old and while her engines and jump rings were kept up to date, the passenger facilities were cramped. Just not up to modern standards." He scowled. "If I hadn't owed the company director a massive favor, I'd never have joined the crew."

"It was a bit cramped in Second Class," Paula noted. "Michael, of course had purchased First Class passage for all of us on board the 'Queen'. We were all taken a bit aback at what we wound up with."

"Oh, my dear, you have my entire sympathy. Second

Class was no better than a dormitory!" Zimmer gave an exaggerated shudder.

"First Class was a bit small, but well appointed," Opal said. "Whoever the fashion designers were, they made good use of the space available."

"Oh yes, she had a complete interior renovation a year ago. FarCo put her on a special fast shuttle directly from Earth to Tau Ceti. That was a rather nice run, full of business executives, although of course there were always tourists in Second Class."

Zimmer sighed. "When the New Territories Conference was arranged, FarCo switched us over to this run.

"The first two runs we were stuffed with, umm, not even bureaucrats, their low level staff actually, doing the groundwork for the conference. Then, instead of getting the important politicians, we wound up getting the people who were bounced by the politicians. Not," he hastened to add. "That you ladies weren't a big improvement!"

Note to self: check the history of the steward's staff, Paris told himself. *Did they come from the Tau Ceti run or did FarCo hire all new people?*

Paula smiled at him. "That's very gallant of you, Doctor, but I suspect that carrying the Secretary of State and so forth would be a real feather in any ship's cap."

"Well, actually he probably had a military ship at his disposal, but some of the lesser dignitaries might have been fascinating to talk to."

Paris turned as clanking started up in Georges' makeshift kitchen. Misty and Kissy were helping him again, self-appointed hunters and gatherers of canned and dried necessities. He squinted at his watch. "Bit early for dinner."

"Oh," explained Opal. "It's all this dried food, it has to soak forever to be edible, and so you might as well add something special to the marinade, and perhaps get some vegetables started and," she sat up straight, squinting at the kitchen. "Have they found a bread maker? Oh, that sounds so wonderful! Fresh bread!"

Like some form of magic, the newly discovered device drew half the women over to exclaim about it. Paris exchanged shrugs with Zimmer, then leaned closer "Tell, me, what's really worse, a ship full of government flunkeys, or a ship full of women?"

Zimmer snorted amusement. "The level of intellect may be higher with the flunkeys, but their interests are so narrow as to preclude normal conversation. I'll take decorative and dumb anytime."

"How's the Captain?" Paris asked, belatedly.

"Well enough." Zimmer shrugged. "This belated treatment is better than nothing. but the shock and pain of the original injury followed by a week of minimal treatment . . . has sapped his reserves. I'm ensuring he gets a lot of sleep, so he can heal as much as possible. The infection is gone, the pain is under control, and the nanos are laying skin over everything.

"He needs a rehab hospital to deal with the large muscle damage, but he's not going to die," Zimmer nodded toward Jenny, who nodded politely back as she passed by, hands full of wire spools and more light fixtures, "unless our Heroine muffs the next episode."

Paris smirked. "Next episode! However, if you're looking for intelligence, there it is."

"And she'd be reasonably decorative if she'd lose weight," Zimmer said. "Pity she has so little self-respect, you have to wonder about people that do things like that to themselves."

Paris blinked in surprise. "Nothing there a few nano rounds wouldn't take care of. It's the women like these beauty queens that worry me. Horribly malnourished, and completely focused on winning at all costs. Have you seen the statistics on their life expectancies and future health problems?"

"Oh, yes, the anorexic look has just as many medical and psychological complications as the opposite." The doctor shook his head. "It's the excessive use of anti-fat cell nanos that's the big problem now. The fat cells aren't just reduced in size, you know."

Paris did, but let him lecture on.

"The actual cells are destroyed, and often so fast that the kidneys are damaged eliminating the wastes. And if too many are destroyed, the body's fat ratio falls well below optimum levels and can never recover. When the body manufactures fat, it has no place to store it and that's very bad for the arteries. So then these women overuse artery cleaning nano's and suffer aneurysms and strokes.

"On top, of course, of the infertility problems. Do you realize that fertility on Earth and the old colonies has fallen so far below the replacement level that there's talk about encouraging immigration back toward Earth? Unbelievable."

"And, then out here on the fringes, there's a bad male to female ratio problem," Paris pointed out. "I guess most of the population growth must be in the outer parts of zone one and two, and the inner part of three and four."

"Mostly." The doctor shrugged. "These things come and go. Sometimes it's popular and high status to have children, and sometimes it's not. I personally think that sooner or later the government will have to start using replicator technology to maintain population."

"Someone's got to raise the kids," Paris pointed out, recalling his conversation with Cap. "Otherwise you're just raising a crop of sociopaths."

Zimmer sniffed. "Parents barely raise their own kids anymore, anyway."

Paris grinned helplessly, and quavered in falsetto, "Back in my day, Moms were Moms and Dads were Dads! Back in the good old days!" He snickered. "Totally ridiculous, the

278

more things change, the more they stay the same. And one of the things that stays the same is that the more government tells people how to raise their kids, the worse they turn out. God help us if they take over the job wholesale."

"Ha! You've got that right," Latham said, pulling a chair over. "And there's no need in this case. Fast population growth is disastrous. Slow and steady does it. Look how much the human race has spread out since we discovered Grav technology. We've got over two thousand settled worlds in less than three hundred years. A period of consolidation wouldn't be a bad idea."

"What do you think about the New Territories petition?" Paris asked him.

"It seems premature, there's only two planets with over a million population; most of the other so-called settled planets are just mining claims. The population of the entire region can't exceed, what, seven or eight million people? I grew up in a city larger than that," Latham said. "On the other hand, I've recently noticed that it's become a haven for criminal activities, and that has got to stop."

Zimmer snorted. "I find it hard to believe the petition was even submitted properly. From what I've heard most of the planetary censuses were inflated, except where they were made up out of whole cloth. They've got over a hundred planets spread over an area nearly equal to the entire Zone four, and they got signatures and population counts in six months? The people I've met from out there are there to get rich and or get away from Earth. I refuse to believe that they are asking to join up and be taxed."

"Now there I think you're wrong," Latham jumped in. "They all know that the prices their metals bring are depressed by the taxes the buyers pay when they bring it into Zone four. It just flat won't make any difference. What will change is the number of shipments that disappear en route."

Zimmer scowled. "If the UCP is already getting money from the New Territories, they should already be patrolling."

"Under the Joint Understanding Treaty with the Cinnabs, the Fleet cannot patrol outside of the designated zone, the two hundred light year radius around Earth. Just the small amount of escort duties to Eta and the patrols along the rim of the rift are pushing it," Latham argued. "The Cinnabs are not happy with the situation. If we annex, we'll also have to amend the JUT."

"Will they just include the New Territories, or try to enlarge the radius all around?" Paris wondered.

"Well, they can't do it all around," Latham answered, "or we'd be running into the Cinnab jurisdiction. But they could flatten the sphere there, and expand it everywhere else. Might as well, while we're at it, and avoid this sort of mess happening all over again."

"Speaking of which," Zimmer added, "A lot of humans are less than comfortable with aliens with . . . peculiar . . .

dietary habits infiltrating the military. Maybe they can amend that as well."

The three spacers wandered in, probably drawn by the odors starting to waft from the kitchen areas. The women had dispersed, but not come back to join them.

Barry Corvallis spoke to Zimmer. "Ah, the Cannabs are only in the Joint Fleet, not the Marines or anything, and they're pretty thin even there, they just don't handle chains of command well and rarely fit in at all. I heard that there's a grand total of less than three hundred actually serving."

"Cannabs?" Paris wrinkled his nose. "As in cannibals? I hadn't heard that, um, nickname."

The spacers shrugged in group embarrassment. "It's not very peecee, but spacers use it all the time. It's actually about the only pun I've ever heard one of the Cannabs catch." Barry squirmed a bit. "They don't have much of a sense of humor, except for the ones that grow up around humans."

Cap wandered in and grabbed a chair from another table and started listening in, and the Wall Street Gang drifted their way.

"How do you know that many, if there are so few in the Joint Fleet?" asked Paris, genuinely curious. He'd met very few himself in the course of his career. Cinnabs didn't 'get' music, and thought romance was silly and human sex nauseating; they avoided Hollywood with a passion.

Corvallis looked surprised. "They're all over, with their

little one person ships. They trade and transport and explore all over. Most of the new planets sold are either first or second hand Cannab claims."

"Those creatures are out here?" Zimmer looked aghast. "Out here in human territory?"

"Yeah, just like we're all over their territory." Barry smirked. "Don't like 'em, Doc? What the partition says is everything on this side is human admin, everything on that side is Cinnab admin. There's no travel or business limits, Cinnabs can live here, but they're under our laws, Humans can live there, but they're under Cinnab laws."

"Cinnabs don't have any laws," snapped the doctor.

"Kinda like the New Territories, that way," Terry said. "Guess they feel right at home."

Chapter Thirty-Three
Sand and Gravel

"Why am I singing happily while cutting up garbage?" Jenny asked herself out loud. She was far enough around the curve of the Prison quarter to be out of sight and hearing of the new inmates.

"Because you are happy?"

Damn, how could he move so quietly in this echo chamber?

"Actually, I'm kind of smelly."

"That's what happens when you play with garbage." He looked a bit dubiously at her bin of shredded paper and plastic. "Plants will grow in that?"

"I'll be emptying the traps on the water treatment boxes and mixing the sludge in. I'd be happier if I had some sand to add to it all," she told him. "I'm not sure how these scraps will work for aeration and keeping it from compacting and so on."

"Sludge? That sounds even worse than garbage. I will try to find you some sand." He sounded quite firm and determined.

She grinned back at him. "I really don't think you'll find any, short of going out asteroid hunting. That's where they get the dust for spacecrete." She frowned, looking around. "Mac talked about building a halfway station between Beta and Eta Pegasi. This is not too far off the ideal position. I wonder if you can claim a space station as salvage? It was stolen, not wrecked. I haven't a clue what the laws about this would be."

"You want to stay here?" he asked.

"I . . . I don't know. I don't know that I would be allowed to, actually. I'm still a minor, for some legal categories. I don't know if an eighteen-year-old can claim salvage rights." Jenny realized that this was the first time she'd actually seriously thought about her future for weeks. "Maybe we could all form a salvage company? That might work. I'll check with everyone this evening."

Cap was frowning around the curved passage. "I had not thought about owning . . . anything. It's not allowed."

"Are you going to go back?" Jenny's stomach knotted itself. *They treat you like a servant. Out here you are a hero. A man with a future full of possibilities.*

"I must report . . . I won't stay there." He sounded surprised. "I will go get your sand for you, now." He walked away, silently, of course.

***

Paris had joined the asteroid hunt on the spur of the moment, a feeling perhaps, that an adult should be present . .

In the Rift

. The smaller of the two freighters they'd captured along with the station was performing flawlessly, but everyone's high spirits had evaporated.

A quarter of the lidar returns had been artificial alloys.

Adding trial-and-error to distant lessons in remote sensors, Paris was able to frame the nearest of those artificial returns as Carl shifted the freighter cautiously closer. Paris centered the screen on the oval and zoomed in. A ship.

"It looks like a freighter." Cap identified. "Earth design. All the cargo pods are gone."

"We should board her and check . . ." Carl's voice trailed off as the slow rotation of the big freighter brought her living quarters into sight. Holed and open to the vacuum.

"How did they move her here?" Cap spoke over Paris's shoulder.

"That was either luck or a damn good shot." Barry, in the navigator's seat, tore his eyes from Paris's screen to his own controls.

Terry's voice came over the comm from engineering. "The jump rings aren't touched, and see the exit hole? It was angled to miss the fuel tanks and straight between the two leading jets. A man in a suit could still fly her. Probably."

"Don't get any closer, in case it's trapped," said Paris. "I'll note the position and orbit, for the authorities, if they ever get here."

Carl turned abruptly back to the lidar, and brought up

the position of the nearest objects with natural characteristics. "This one looks like gravel and ice," he said, nodding as Barry sent the course changes. "There will be lots of sand and dust sized particles as well. It's small enough to fit into one of the cargo pods, too, we won't have to break it."

Perfect or not, Paris understood their desire to get back to the station with its lights and warmth and proof that the pirates were history. Carl matched velocity like the old pro he was and Cap assisted Terry in remotely opening the outer cargo hatch and talking Carl into maneuvering the ship around it.

Paris trailed along, hanging back and not interfering as Terry called instructions for maneuvers Paris could barely feel as he hovered in zero G. He definitely felt the asteroid thud into the aft wall of the cargo pod.

Terry winced. "It's generally a good idea to strap cargo down." He peered through the viewport, and keyed the outer door closed. "But it's sort of fallen apart, so I guess we'll just leave it."

Unnerved by the casual treatment, not to mention the impact that had shaken the entire ship, Paris retreated to the cockpit. "I really thought loading cargo and so forth was a bit more of a controlled situation."

"Only in the movies, although we really prefer to minimize the momentum differences." Barry and Carl exchanged grins, their sense of adventure apparently restored by Paris's nervousness. "We'll maneuver real slow and careful on the way back. Promise."

Despite the grins, the trip back was indeed slow and careful. Docked again, the crew fussed with the cargo pod, while Cap and Paris cycled the airlock.

Jenny's voice greeted them. "I can't believe you did that. Are you going to take everything I say literally?"

Cap just grinned happily. "You wanted sand. Barry wanted to see how the ship was running. So we went asteroid hunting." He sobered a bit. "We found more than asteroids. There's a ship's graveyard out there, everything the pirates captured and couldn't resell they just pushed out of the way."

Carl's voice preceded him into the lock. "There were at least nine lidar returns that were refined metal or ceramics. It was harder to find a rock." He looked grim. "We didn't explore any of the ships. We just grabbed a chunk of gravel and left."

Terry, with Barry right behind him, joined them. "We think it's gravel. We just matched velocity, opened the cargo door and slipped around it. It's only about six tons."

"Six tons?" she asked weakly. "How are we going to move it?"

"We're heating it up, judging by its lidar return it's mostly gravel to dust size particles held together by ice. It should be a heap of wet gravel and mud by tomorrow."

"Wet?" Jenny bit her lip. "We don't have much extra

water, I wonder if we can keep that as well."

"I could start moving it now while it's still frozen," Cap volunteered.

"No way." Barry looked shocked. "It's probably got lots of methane and ammonia ice too, you know. In fact, with no sun out here, there's no telling what sort of ice it's got. I've got the hold set to vent gases at low pressure. We might save half the water, I suppose, it'll stay solid to a higher temp, but the whole thing's got to defrost and fall apart or we'll be bringing too much methane into the station." He gave Jenny a reproving look. "You've got to be especially careful about what you put in your atmosphere, when you don't have very much of it."

"Yes, that's true," Jenny admitted meekly. "Now that you mention it, I think I'd better look for any equipment the pirates had for analyzing the air. The only thing I've seen so far is the automatic air system boxes, and I haven't a clue just how complex their analysis routines are." She smiled wryly. "Something new to learn, first thing in the morning. But first . . .

"We've been talking, while you were gone. Since we captured this station, we figure it's ours. The Wall Street gang is trying to remember the legal code for space salvage, and they'll draw up papers for incorporating a salvage company. Everybody here gets equal shares."

The three spacers swapped looks. "The ships," said

Barry. "These two and all those out there as well. We should claim them all."

"We should keep them." Carl sounded wistful. Was owning a ship the dream of most pilots?

"No reason why not, I suppose." Jenny smiled. "Ask the Wall Streeters, they'll know." She looked back through the airlock. "Six tons? Maybe I'd better do some more homework on planting and so forth, really quick."

Paris leaned over to Cap. "You're the one that's going to end up moving that six tons, you know."

"Yes." He grinned. "I'm looking forward to it."

Jenny stared dubiously around at the makeshift control room. The pirates had stuffed a wide variety of equipment into one of the rough rooms they'd built, probably looted from multiple ships. Despite the ramshackle look, it was all apparently quite functional. At least, Peter Franklin thought so.

"The station's detection gear is more than adequate, and in fact might lead one to believe that they were paranoid about being attacked," Peter explained, giving the guided tour to the others.

"Pity the paranoia didn't extend to external weapons," said Jenny.

"Apparently it did at one time," Cap put in. "There are rocket tubes added to the hub, but they are empty."

"Why no lasers?" Jenny asked, then answered herself. "They didn't have the power, did they?"

"Nope." Peter nodded. "Solar power panels operate pretty poorly on starlight. A station like this should have a reactor."

"We ought to take a look at those tubes," Quincy put in. "I'd like to see if they were ever used, there may have been battles between outlaw groups here once." He waved a generally inclusive hand around the room. "This whole set-up boggles me every time I try to think of the implications."

Cap prowled over to eye the radio. "If the station is as old as it seems it must be, then there have been organized groups of hijackers and pirates for at least fifty years."

"Longer than that. That's when the station construction fleet went missing," Jenny pointed out. "By then they must have already been organized enough to see a need for an off-planet base."

"This must have been the fueling stop and fence for ships from both sides of the Rift." Peter grimaced. "I suppose they sell manufactured goods pirated near Earth in the New Territories openly, and then rough ingots and so forth from the New Territories to established manufacturers on the other side."

Quincy leaned over to wipe the radar screen. "Some of the early trading companies may have been quite happy to have a cheap cargo every now and then. It was too damn hard to check. It still is. That's one of the main reasons for the conference on Autumn.

"Politicians can pontificate all they want to about taxes and representation, but what will really help people is police investigation of stolen goods and confiscation from the receivers. Put the pirates out of business and trade will take off."

292

In the Rift

"You sound very frustrated," Jenny prodded a bit. "Have you lost much stuff?"

"Regularly. Piracy is a bane to shipping all through zones three and four. We always knew they were fencing the cargos in the New Territories, but we couldn't figure out how they were crossing the Rift. We knew they had to be refueling somewhere close to the gap on both sides, but hadn't imagined there was an actual central station. The pirates don't even have to go all the way."

Paris scratched his chin. "Where are we, anyway? I thought the Rift was an area of very few stars? Haven't they been searched?"

The Captain answered, "The Rift's about fifty light-years wide, it's not really much of a gap, on a galactic scale. Beta Pegasi to Eta Pegasi is the smallest distance across between two settled systems, and they're thirty-five light-years apart." Portman winced and shifted his position in the chair. "But they weren't coming or going from either. I was in the Fleet then, and believe me, we were looking.

"The star density is low here, but it's a huge area. Every star has been visited, repeatedly. But this station might as well be invisible, the gravity well is so small that it could only be found by sheer accident or by having the coordinates. If anyone did stumble over the planet, there's rubble all over out there. The station is actually between two asteroid belts. Very thin ones, mind you, and close in, rotating around a

Jupiter-sized planet, rather than a star."

Barry added, "Its orbit is at an angle to most of the closer asteroids, it's got the same inclination as a slightly thicker belt further out that gives good cover from anything coming in on the ecliptic. All this equipment," he waved at the comm room, "must make it easy for them to see anything coming and shut down what little EM noise it makes. Ships that didn't know its orbit would probably never find it. And this," he leaned over and tapped a screen showing a schematic with the system centered in a vast gridded emptiness, "is a grav wave monitor. They can detect ships jumping toward the system probably a quarter of a light-year out, and go silent."

"Well, well." Paris fell silent. Jenny wondered what thoughts were going through his possibly policeman's mind.

"We need to study all the recorded conversations." Jenny's mind was scouting ahead. "We need to be able to trick any pirates into docking and coming on board. We need more information from the captives we have, what the docking procedures are, who met the pirates, and so forth." She chewed a nervous fingernail. "So, how do we do that?"

***

Paris hovered, wondering if trickery would be enough. This could get ugly.

Quincy asked all the questions. "Identify this man."

Sneer. "What are you, a lawyer or something? I don't

have to answer you." Descartes leaned back, but stiff, not as at ease as he was trying to appear.

Cap growled something under his breath in Chinese, his hands flexed like he was thinking about someone's neck, and Paris hastily made calming motions with his hands and smiled placatingly and nervously. Descartes saw him several times a day, utterly silent and looming.

Hell, Descartes had seen him killed. Not double checking that all his victims were really dead was his first mistake. But then with a pile of bodies and prisoners to watch . . . understandable. And it wouldn't have mattered, except for Jenny snatching an opportunity.

"Keep him away from me!"

"Or what?" Quincy looked amused. "You'll sue?"

But all they got was more sneers, interspersed with insults and claims of ignorance. Even a bit of manhandling from Cap got them nothing. Descartes kept an eye on Cap, and seemed genuinely uneasy about him; he barely bothered to notice the rest of them. *Phobia about Red Guards? Or confidence that we're too civilized to be a threat?*

Paris finally gave up. "Lock him in that end room. Let's work over one of the men who was stationed here."

The next prisoner they escorted in was sweating, looking around. "Where's Descartes?"

Cap loomed, and cracked his knuckles suggestively.

"I don't believe you killed him." The attempted firm

confidence was spoiled by a waver toward the end.

"Kill him? Oh, no." Paris let the tiniest possible waver enter his own voice. "He's, umm, just fine." He swallowed. "We just locked him up again."

"Stop it, Paris. You can't pretend it didn't happen." Quincy switched his gaze to the pirate. "Cap's not a nice guy, like the rest of us. You were too drunk to remember, I suppose." He smiled coldly, not looking much like a nice guy.

"He's one of those Chinese Red Guards you've heard about. He killed five people with his bare hands, before he got a gun and killed the rest of your fellow criminals. Maybe you should talk with your friends who saw the mess he left."

The hijacker gulped a bit. Obviously he had already heard all about it. The men captured on one of the freighters had been marched through the pirates' quarter on their way to the prison section. So they had seen the full complement of dead bodies. Reluctantly his eyes drifted to the picture Quincy still held.

"That's John Masco, he's the comm op on the 'Dagger'."

"How odd." Quincy looked puzzled. "In the recording he answered to George."

Cap grunted and growled "He . . . lie?" like a stereotyped caveman. He leaned forward, his hands coming up to an obvious martial arts position. "I . . . kill?"

"George Mason on the 'Razor'," the hijacker squeaked.

Paris stepped in front of Cap, holding his hands out in

front of him. "Stop," he said as clearly as possible. Cap frowned at that, then subsided, staring sullenly from under his brows.

"And this?" Quincy asked, holding out the next pic.

"Captain Reynolds of the 'Gypsy'."

Every once in a while, Cap would lean forward, or shift or pace, or flex his hands . . . it was contagious. Paris had to repress an urge to talk like Humphrey Bogart.

Barry, Carl and Terry listened for information about the ships, inserting an occasional question. Cap and Paris escorted the prisoners from the lockup one at a time, Cap just rough enough that they realized how strong he really was, Paris nervous and placating, warning the prisoners not to misbehave as he cringed under Cap's glower.

It took all day, but in the end they had extended the scraps of knowledge they had gleaned from the comm recordings into something that might save them.

Chapter Thirty-Five
Gardening

Cap studied the rotating barrel for a long moment, then looked questioningly at Jenny.

"It grinds off the sharp edges; out there, there's no erosion to smooth off impact melted and splashed razor edges," she said. "Untreated space dust is kind of tough on the plant roots. At least that's what I read. I only run it for about an hour for each load, I hope that's enough."

"What about seeds?" he asked, poking at the contents of the half-filled metal box she was fooling with.

"There were lots of them for the mini-hydroponics the ships use for fresh greens. I'll start with something easy, like squash or tomatoes." She looked dubiously at the planter. "It doesn't look much like soil, does it?"

He dug his fingers into it with some difficulty. "I think soil is supposed to be fluffier than this."

"Yeah. It's so fine grained, it just packs down solid. I think I'm going to have to use all the chopped up paper and plastic anyway. Plus add gravel." She looked around at all the empty planters. "I guess I should try several different things and see what works. As soon as I'm done with the soil, I've got to do something about the light. The light tubes are labeled full spectrum, so I should just need more of them."

"If the ceiling was reflective, or at least white, it would help," Cap said. "I'll see what I can find."

"You're right." She looked around. "I suppose I should have started in the pirates' quarter, it's been coated. But it didn't have these planters. This quarter was apparently planned to have lots of landscaping. Probably it was supposed to be the residential area." With a shrug, she changed the subject. "What does the fuel situation look like?"

"The storage tanks are full, and both ships are topped off." He eyed her worriedly. "The spacers want to take the other ship out and try it. I thought I'd go with them, we're going to try to identify all those alloy and ceramic lidar returns we got while we were collecting your sand."

"May I recommend leaving one pilot here with the other ship, in case something goes wrong with the one you're on?" Jenny frowned at him. "Be careful with those derelicts, the hijackers might have mined them or something."

"We thought we'd just get close enough to read their identification numbers." Cap smiled. "I won't do anything too dangerous."

"Something tells me we may have a definition problem here. Too dangerous."

Chapter Thirty-Six
Pirate Ship

The screen before them chimed softly and an arrow popped up on the schematic. They all held their breaths as Peter and Barry leaned over it and stared. "Just one ship," muttered Barry.

"So far," amended Peter.

"The Joint Fleet patrols in threes," said Barry. "Unless they're coordinating their jumps, this is probably a pirate."

"I don't think they're coming in from Eta or Beta Pegasi," Portman growled. "Unless I'm totally wrong about our position."

"When should we comm them?" asked Jenny.

"Not until they comm us," Portman said. "That's the procedure that they have always followed. And judging from the time lags on the recordings, they won't do that until they're much closer, probably three jumps, although I don't know the local wave size here."

"Remember, there's no star, the grav waves are still very large, one more jump may do it. I think they try to stick to low powered transmissions, to minimize detection if there's another ship in-system." agreed Barry. "So it will be about six hours before they hail us, and another five before they dock."

***

"And if they ask where the regular comm operator is, he's sick, you think the Chef you kidnapped tried to poison everyone. Tell them nobody's died yet, even the chef, although his days are numbered. Got that?" Jenny glared at the hijacker, who just sneered back.

"It won't work, if you surrender, they probably won't kill all of you."

"Keep in mind that you are on this station too. If it's holed, you're going to die right along with us." *Damn! The leadership thingy isn't working with this creep. Time to turn the job over to someone else.*

With the doctor trailing along behind, Ron and Peter shoved him into the comm room.

"Cap, could you explain just what is going to happen to this gentleman if he doesn't cooperate?" she asked.

Cap apparently decided action was better than words. He reached out and snagged the man by the waistband of his pants and ripped, as the pants sagged to the floor, he shoved the hijacker into the station chair and sitting down on the floor with his back to the console, reached out and grasped the man's testicles. "If you are uncertain about what to say, this would be a good time to ask." He looked the man straight in the eye as he squeezed.

In the Rift

"No, no!" he gasped faintly. "I know what to say. You don't have to . . . do anything."

"Good." Paris leaned in from the side. "Now pay attention to this recording." Peter hit the button and the pirates' casual hail replayed. "Tell us about these guys."

"That's D'alembert's ship, he comes by regularly with small stuff and trades for fuel and food and odds and ends. He's one of the one's Descartes' was probably going to use to transport some more of the women. He'd pay plenty and take 'em off somewhere." Half the hijacker's attention was on Cap. He was holding very still, pressed as far back in the seat as he could go, and his words came very fast.

"Right. Now let's make a recording to send back; tell him you've got a great deal for him." Instructed Paris. "But be careful you don't give anything away." He tapped a piece of paper in front of the man. "Something along these lines, put some emotion in it, just like a vid star."

The hijacker nodded carefully, read the note and touched the record pad.

"Hey, Eddie, good to see you again! Wait till you see what we've got for you!" The hijacker sounded stiff and unconvincing to Jenny's ear. "Phillip says you got to see this to believe, and he'll talk to you when you get here." He gulped, glanced at the pickup, then back to the paper. "Actually we had a bit of a problem with our food, and he's sick as a dog along with most everyone else. This fancy chef we took tried to poison us all. At least that's what I think, the chef claims it's the filthy kitchen, so we haven't killed him yet." He shifted nervously, glancing down at Cap then back to the script. "I don't think he's worth what Phillip says, myself. I'll wait for your reply." He clicked off the recorder, sweating. Cap released him and he yanked his trousers up quickly.

They'd analyzed the comm recordings and questioned the prisoners as a cross check. Jenny's eyes slid to the lists of ships that the captured hijackers had told them about. If their coerced information was any good, D'alembert's 'Crazy Lady' had a crew of sixteen, and were experts at armed boarding. The comm officer was Eddie Sooner. So far so good.

They played the recording back. Stiff.

"That won't fool anyone," Paris said in disgust.

"Do it again." Cap stared at the pirate, but this time didn't touch him. In the end it took four recordings before they were satisfied.

"Still pretty stiff, but probably as good as we're going to get." Portman hesitated. "We need to send a reply soon."

"Sounds OK," said Paris. "I think we should send it."

Receiving nods all around, Peter touched the controls to burst send the recording. It would be at least a ten-minute wait for a reply. Jenny chewed her lip nervously. This part was fairly easy, they could preview everything the hijacker said before it was sent. As the ship closed in, and they started talking in real-time, it would get riskier.

"Okay, now let's get the other guy to put something in, so things look a bit more normal." Peter said. "Most of the old recordings had people putting in comments over the shoulder and so forth."

"I think a couple of you guys had better go get him," said Jenny. "I don't seem to intimidate very well." Ron and Peter nodded and headed off. They were back just in time for the reply from the pirate.

"Geeze, Marco, we were just at Eta and they're getting worried about the 'Far Seeker' with three of the Miss Outer Space contestants on board. That wasn't one of y'alls jobs, was it?" Eddie looked eager. "You haven't got a bunch of women do you?"

Another man abruptly loomed over his shoulder, older and ugly as sin. "Even Bouncer wouldn't do something that public, would he?" He sounded pissed, and Eddie lost his smile, cringing just a bit. "Answer," the second man snapped. The message ended with him reaching toward the controls.

"That was an interesting reaction." Paris was frowning. "This guy, is that D'alembert?" The two hijackers nodded reluctantly.

"He didn't seem to like the publicity the 'Far Seeker' hijacking is going to bring." He pulled on his lip pensively. "Bouncer, eh?" He eyed the hijackers. "I think just a short message, this time. "Something along the lines of 'the boss thought it was a good idea.' Then send it. I want to hear the reply before we get too detailed in our responses."

Cap showed his teeth to the first hijacker, Marco, but didn't touch him. Marco swallowed nervously, and pushed the record button. "The boss thought it was a good idea." Click. Peter nodded approvingly, and pushed the send button.

The reply came back a bit sooner, this time. "Jesus wept! You can't pull crap like that in front of politicians when there are newsies around. I might as well head for the farthest frontier and haul ore for the next two years, the way the Fleet will be all over any small ships after this. Tell that idiot this may be the last time I deal with him." Click. They waited in silence as the plot showed the ship moving in. There was no more contact from them until they were close in; "Dock three, I assume?" snapped D'alembert's voice. "Yes, Sir." Marco's reply was even briefer, and perhaps just a bit high pitched. Then Zimmer, Peter, Jenny and Ron were shoving the hijacker back into the lockup, while Cap, Peter and Paris headed for the hub.

The standard operating procedure was that a few, three or four, of the station crew would lock the docking ring and start refueling operations. The officers would eventually come out, to negotiate for any goods they needed or an exchange of cargo. Fat Obadiah, with his thin hair combed in greasy strings across his head, resembled one of the hijacker's crew who occasionally did docking chores. Tall scrawny Steve and muscular Quincy had been dyed and made up as best they could to resemble two other members of the 'regular' crew that attended to refueling. *If they just looked normal enough . . . if the pirates would just float right past them and into the elevator . . . if . . .* Jenny hated ifs and hoped they weren't all about to die. *Why the Hell couldn't there have been a great big dark Asian hijacker? Having Cap right there . . . was wistful thinking. Five armed men would be waiting in darkened passages for the first pirates to come off the ship. Or for the sounds of disaster from Obie, Steve and Quincy.*

Jenny, Peter and Ron hustled around to the dump quarter elevator, Dr. Zimmer dragging reluctantly behind. Jenny would have been just as glad to have him out of the way, he was not an asset in a fight. *He'll be needed for the aftermath though. This is not likely to be the one-sided battle we had before. I hope our tricks work.*

Chapter Thirty-Seven
The Trap Is Sprung!

"Let us go first, Jenny." Peter was firm and Ron nodded. Jenny reluctantly nodded back. The doors at the top were reprogrammed to open manually only, and the arrival indicator was deactivated. When the elevator stopped, they would just wait and listen...no, they could hear the yelling already. Something had already gone wrong.

"Everybody down," Peter whispered. Jenny grabbed the rail, clenched her toes to turn on the magnetic toe tips of her appropriated boots, and held herself down against the floor. Peter and Ron had their laser rifles ready, and manually pulled one door open a few inches to look.

The hub was a chaotic melee. The pirates must have come out in force. Peter and Ron eased out and around the elevator, aiming toward, Jenny estimated, the passage up to Dock three. The pirates there were shooting into the melee with little caution that Jenny could see. They quickly spotted the new danger, and Peter flinched back, grabbing his arm and ducking behind the shaft.

Jenny watched the slow revolution of the hub with quickening alarm. "We'd better get out of here before they can shoot straight in," she told Zimmer. "Come on." She slid quickly around the shaft. Ron and Peter were nowhere in sight. Peeking around the edges, she could see that someone (Cap?) had Captain D'alembert pinned down and was keeping him away from dock three. She hoped the pirates had enough loyalty to him that they wouldn't leave without him. Perhaps he had the command codes and they couldn't go without him? If she could see him, she could shoot him, but, perhaps it was best to leave him pinned down while they tried to take the ship. If their Captain was killed, the pirates might just back out and start shooting holes in the station. Zimmer was peering over her head, and cursing under his breath.

He slid back a bit and drew his pistol. She hoped he knew how to use it, and was turning back to the battle when it connected with her skull.

***

He hit me! Was the first thought that made it through her head. The second was that she wasn't on the station. She squinted painfully at the lights and realized that she was lying on the deck of a ship.

Turning her head cautiously, she saw she had apparently been dropped and abandoned outside an airlock, in a passage that led forward to the control room, clearly visible, and back into a corridor of closed doors and stairs down, probably to engineering and cargo compartments . . . cargo.

310

In the Rift

The hijackers they'd captured and questioned had given them details about the pirates that regularly refueled and traded with them. D'alembert's 'Crazy Lady' was the one with one of the external cargo pods replaced with the fusion pumped gas laser, wasn't it?

No one in the control room was watching her.

They were under heavy acceleration, she felt like a whale, and her knees screamed as she slid backwards quietly, carefully, no sudden movements, not letting her boot toes hit the floor with a betraying click, and down the stairs. The ship had the standard Cinnab layout, two levels, each with a circular corridor. Equipment on the inside, cargo pods or crew quarters on the outside, four stairways between. Jenny had always thought that stairs rather than ladders were a waste of space, but now, under acceleration, she saw their utility.

The first cargo pod was wide open, they must have been prepared to unload. She looked in: loot, boxed and strapped down. The next pod was also open. More cargo. She labored forward, away from the more likely to be manned engineering room, and across to the port side. The lead pod door was locked. The rear pod was open and contained more boxes.

She remembered the lessons in changing door codes . . . pulled out the multitool, and looked at the edge of the rear pod door. Looked about the same. Jenny removed the cover

311

to the lock pad and pulled out the controller. She pushed the test button. It flashed a sequence of four numbers and clicked as the latch flipped.

The same numbers opened the forward pod. *Thank you, Paris.*

Jenny knew next to nothing about large lasers, but had spent the last month handling laser rifles, and she knew a power source when she saw one. Not to mention the 'Warning: Do not operate without...!" signs. She unplugged, opened, closed everything she could see. And ah, ha! A pressure relief valve, which she jammed open. And then she heard the hasty crashing as someone rushed down the stairs.

She bolted out and thudded down the corridor, around a corner, another locked door yielded to the same combination, she locked it behind her . . . the fuel room, by god. "I think I'm going to get religion," she murmured. The huge pressurized fullerene tanks of hydrogen for the fusion drive, the liquid nitrogen to cool the superconducting jump rings.

First things first. Turning back to the door, she listened carefully, then opened it. It was the work of a few moments to take out the lock pad and reset it to a new number.

She locked herself in and started closing valves. She shut off the liquid nitrogen first. No need to let them jump too many times. She frowned at the array of pipes, but couldn't see any way to drain the rings or heat them, but eventually

they would warm on their own and stop working. She
wondered a bit uneasily just how long that would be.

And then the hydrogen. The electronic valves were
controlled from engineering, but there were manual valve
backups. Stiff manual valves. She started hauling on them,
closing the first one down as a wave of nausea hit her. She
collapsed, holding her head and no, it was not a hemorrhage,
it was a jump.

Damn, damn! Cap has two ships, can they track her?

Cap would try, but in reality Joint Fleet chases through
multiple jumps were rare tales of talent and luck, however
often they occurred in vids. The little cargo ships they had
couldn't keep up with this larger ship under fusion drive,
they had to be pulling nearly three G's and the greater the
distance between ships, the more divergent their position
after the grav jump was likely to be. She strained at the
second valve and it slowly gave and turned. She had to fight
it all the way, but as she walked over to the third tank she
thought the acceleration had dropped.

She hauled on the wheel, then braced her feet and
heaved. Nothing. She trotted desperately over to the valve on
the last tank, and her first heave dumped her to the deck as it
spun easily. She shut it, then looked for a lever for the third
valve.

Nothing! Not a tool kit, nothing!

She went back to the valve and settled grimly down to . . .

313

damn! She concentrated on controlling her stomach through another jump.

They must be cutting the limits as closely as they can, they shouldn't have been able to jump so soon.

She wondered with a sinking feeling whether Cap had a chance of finding her. The valve gave with a thin screech, but barely moved. She heaved again. She had no idea which tank the engines were fueled from, or if they were all used at the same time, or what. But, screech, this valve was going to have to, screech, be closed, because the thrust might feel a bit light, but they were still, screech, accelerating.

And maybe, if she could just close, screech, this valve they would have to stay here long enough for, screech, Cap to catch up. With a final screech the valve stuck with a feeling of finality, and the thrust dropped to a whisper and disappeared. Done.

Her thudding heart sent her blood in a rush to her head, and she clung to the wheel until the feeling that her head was going to explode returned to normal zero G queasiness.

She looked at the door. There wasn't anything more she could do, and there was no place to hide. She frowned at the door, was that spot . . . glowing? She retreated; the vicinity of the door looked a bit unhealthy . . . and were they using a welder or laser rifles? If they had laser rifles on continuous fire . . . she drew an imaginary line from the door to the nearest tank. Oh. Shit. She got behind the furthest tank,

314

quickly. Not that it was likely to do her any good, if a tank was breached . . .

Keeping her head out far enough to see the door, she watched as the hot patch shifted and moved in a slow arc around the locking mechanism. Bright flashes sparked briefly as the composites of the door burned through, but the pirates were being careful and not firing through the holes. They obviously understood the risks to the hydrogen tanks. She watched helplessly as they finished the arc and ducked back out of sight as they shoved the hot door open.

They must have floated in silently, the first sound she heard was the protesting squeak of a valve opening.

"Come out with your hands showing and we won't kill you." She recognized the angry voice of Captain D'alembert.

Should she? Why not, there wasn't any place to conceal herself for more than a few moments. As she started to move, the ship jolted.

In the torrent of cursing that followed, the only phrase she picked out was "being boarded!" The thumps and bangs of fast Zero G movement followed the cursing out of the chamber. Jenny peeked out. There was one man remaining, and he was still opening valves.

She took aim for him and pushed off. Not hard enough. And missed. Twisting, she barely managed to graze his head.

He started, then grinned as air friction stalled her forward motion. "I'll deal with you in a minute, Honey. And then D'alembert will finish you off slowly."

Words her only weapon, she sneered back. "He's as good as dead. We held back on the station to prevent you just backing off and wrecking it, but now we don't need to play soft."

There were faint high pitched echoes echoing in through the open door. "Hear those screams?" Jenny asked, "Those are your friends dying."

"Shut up. More likely it's your friends dying." He shoved off for the next valve, careful not to disturb her motionlessness.

Jenny shucked her jacket and tried flapping it. It didn't seem to do anything but spin her. Not an improvement.

"All right, let's see if you've still got hostage value." Her spin was partially arrested by a painful grip on her hair, as the pirate hauled her out of the fuel room.

She grabbed the door, and was rewarded by a thump to the head.

"Don't try it," the man advised. Dizzied, she didn't resist being towed up the stairs, but at the sight of a looming dark shape, got her foot against the wall and shoved her captor out into the open. She didn't actually see what happened, but the grip on her hair disappeared and she was shoved in the direction of the airlock. Taking the hint, she grabbed rails and swung through, into the familiar cargo ship. She stopped there and looked back, hesitated, then headed for the control room.

"Hi, Carl, need help? They've got their fuel turned back on."

"Back on?" He grinned at her. "What did you do? They didn't actually let you run loose, did they?" he snickered. "Cap said when they stopped it was your doing."

"Yep. I found the fuel room and shut all the valves, but they've got them back open now. Can they shake us off?"

"Only if they want to blow all their air—and people—out their damaged airlock. I hope to hell they're not that stupid, or desperate."

"You and me both," she prayed. "I didn't stop for details, who's along?"

"Cap, Paris, Peter, Ron and Steve."

"That's all!" she said, appalled. "Give me that pistol, I'd better get back there." He handed it over without comment. And she reversed out the door and up to the airlock.

The pirate's corridor was empty but for the floating bodies. With shock, she recognized Peter Franklin, a neatly charred spot on his forehead. Grimly, she turned to the control room, but it was inhabited only by a floating limp pirate. She headed down and back, toward engineering. Hearing voices, but no fighting she listened, then called out, "Cap?"

"Come ahead," he called back, and she swung around the corner. They were all there, all alive, although she quickly saw that Paris had his arms around his chest and appeared to be trying to breathe as shallowly as possible.

The engine room door was open. "All secure?" she asked.

"Other than the minor detail that we've now got two ships and one pilot, yes, mostly." Ron wiped water from his eyes. "Peter . . ." His voice trailed off as she nodded.

"I saw him." She hesitated. "Have you seen Dr. Zimmer?"

Caps eyes flashed. "We have not found him, yet."

Jenny glanced again at Paris. "Don't hurt him. Although I'm not actually sure he's a doctor, anymore."

Cap followed her gaze and nodded sharply. "Ron, Steve, finish searching down here. Jenny, let's check the crew's quarters. Paris, back to the ship, slowly and carefully."

Paris nodded, slowly and carefully, and shoved himself, slowly and carefully, toward the stairs. Jenny and Cap passed him by, taking a hard left at the top of the stairs and away from the control room. The rooms down this way were locked and didn't open to the same code...but the last one had a manual clip on it, enabling it to be locked from the outside. Jenny waved Cap over and unclipped the door. Zimmer was waiting apprehensively, but apparently after the pirates realized his hostage was responsible for the sabotage, they hadn't taken the time to do much more than shove him in here. His mouth dropped open in horror as he spotted Cap.

"Why doctor, what a pleasure to see you again," Jenny

purred. "I figured the pirates would have just shot you. You must be a big shot in the organization." She hesitated. "Are you actually a doctor, or is that just how you get onto ships?"

"I'm a doctor," he snapped. "It wasn't my fault, they . . ." He shut up abruptly.

"Good idea," Jenny told him. "Save the whining and excuses for the trial. Come on."

They herded him out to the airlock and into the cargo ship, and found Carl and Paris in the control room, peering worriedly at the grav meter.

"Another ship just jumped in, very close, by the strength of the tic," Carl reported. "But nothing is showing on the radar."

Zimmer smirked. "A lot of the pirates, the ones with no legitimate cover business, are stealthed. Do you feel up to fighting another pirate today?" His glance measured Paris's careful lack of movement, and his smile widened. "Would you care to surrender peacefully?" He smirked at Cap. "Jenny would live, that way. Not the rest of you, of course."

"I think I liked you better when you were acting like a sniveling coward," Jenny answered.

Then the speakers crackled to life and the comm image lit up. "Unidentified ships, this is JF Ticonderoga, identify yourselves." The stern man in the image was joined by an unmistakable Cinnab, who began (probably) repeating the message in his own language.

Wincing through a fast spreading grin, Paris reached out and flicked the transmit button. "Ticonderoga, I am Captain Neil Perris, JCI2746352221." He stopped to take a careful breath. "I haven't the faintest idea what the legal designations of either of these ships is, but we control them. I was undercover as a passenger on the 'Far Seeker' when it was hijacked. My volunteer militia." He waved over his shoulder, at the rest of them. "Is part passenger and part crew of the 'Far Seeker'. I would appreciate your taking over this situation, especially if you've got an astrogator to backtrack our course to the space station we have also captured, and where more of the 'Far Seeker' passengers are waiting, at this time."

Jenny leaned into pickup range. "Do you know if the 'Far Seeker' has made port? It left with about half the surviving passengers three weeks ago . . . ?" her voice trailed off as the Captain shook his head. "Also, we need a medic, and we have one live captive here and nine at the space station."

The Captain stepped out of pickup range for a moment, then returned. "Separate your ships and we will come aboard."

***

"From studying the comm recordings and questioning our prisoners, we put together profiles on eight pirate ships. I can't guarantee that there aren't more, but these are all that have come in over the last year or so." Paris sat stiffly and tried to keep his voice steady. Damn, even breathing hurt. The nanos would take care of that in another few days, but Captain Garrett wanted a report today.

He tapped the first on the list. "Miss Tannenbaum has tentatively identified the comm op of this ship as part of the crew that took the missing sixteen women. Unfortunately we didn't have any other crew members' pictures for cross checking."

"The 'Crazy Lady' we have in hand," put in the Ticonderoga's intelligence officer, reading down the list. "So these other six could come cruising in anytime." Lieutenant Fischer looked like he'd like to take on all six at once. The Cinnab first officer hissed a bit under his breath. The Captain was a bit more cautious.

"I wish we had more info on their armaments." He glanced from Paris to Fischer. "Do you think you could get more information out of the prisoners?"

Paris cleared his throat. "I . . . observed . . . the civilians questioning the prisoners, sir. They managed to intimidate them to the point of frankness.

"They did not," he hastened to add, "use any sort of drugs or torture. Captain Midnight can be quite frightening when he tries."

"I'll bet," Fischer sounded envious. "He's actually a Red Guard?"

"Yep, he's the real thing." Paris grinned. "I hadn't realized they enhanced the guards' sense of humor, but he's walking proof."

He bit his lip. "One of the prisoners appeared to have a position of authority, and gave us the least information. You might be able to get more out of him than we, than the civilians, did. And then there's Doctor Zimmer. If you can get him to talk. I have no way of telling how high up in the scheme of this mess he might be."

They nodded, but turned back to the comp without comment. "So when the 'Crazy Lady' came insystem, you suckered her into docking, and eight crew members exited the ship?"

"Right, they got far enough into the hub that when they realized that the 'station crew' were ringers we could pin them down and keep them away from the ship. We didn't want to actually kill the captain, figuring that as long as he was alive and in the station the ship wouldn't just start burning holes in the station." Paris frowned, *the Captain isn't going to like this bit!*

"Then our reinforcements came, and we found out the hard way that Doctor Zimmer, the physician from the 'Far Seeker', was with the hijackers. He knocked Poppenhusen out and using her for a shield and hostage got himself, D'alembert, and the two surviving crewers back onto the ship, which promptly undocked."

322

In the Rift

"Captain Perris," Garrett studied him coldly. "What was a eighteen-year-old girl doing in the middle of a firefight?"

Ouch! This is going to be embarrassing. . . well, no it isn't.

"Miss Poppenhusen had shown herself to be very versatile and inventive. We needed her on the spot for ideas if something went wrong."

"Like her being taken hostage and enabling the pirate ship to get away?" he asked mildly.

"As I will eventually find the time to write in my report, upon finding herself aboard the 'Crazy Lady', Miss Poppenhusen managed to escape observation, sabotage the ship's exterior laser, lock herself in the fuel room and turn off all the fuel valves."

Both officers stared at him. "That's why the station is not full of holes and we caught up to the pirate after only two jumps. They were still trying to burn into the fuel room when we docked." Paris shrugged. "The situation you find us in is entirely due to her efforts and Cap's. I have been scrambling to keep up with their liberation campaign, not leading the pack, in fact at times I felt like a clueless bystander as they grabbed the ball and ran with it."

"Well, Captain," Garrett said. "I'm going to send you and the rest of the 'Far Seeker' people straight to Eta on one of your captured freighters. We've moved Fifth Joint Fleet Operations there for the duration of the New Territories

Conference, so it will be handy to support this operation. The Ticonderoga will remain here in hopes of luring in another pirate or two before the word gets around about our taking the station."

Paris raised an eyebrow, and Garrett glowered a bit. "Your taking the station, then, if you prefer. Lieutenant Fischer will accompany you to report as well, and in fact I will place him in command of the ship."

Paris nodded in satisfaction. *Yes! Get us out of here and back to civilization!*

"While waiting for that ship to be readied, I would appreciate your writing a preliminary report, and we will no doubt be periodically asking you for clarification of some points."

"Yes, sir. May I recommend sending the other freighter with a minimal crew back to Beta Pegasi? I have a large number of questions I'd like CI there to look into as quickly as possible, plus we need to locate the 'Far Seeker'."

"Excellent idea. I'll send your Captain Portman back with them. Better medical facilities there than Autumn."

"Oh, and could you feed our cat while we're gone?"

Chapter Thirty-Eight
Really Safe

It was such a relief to be safe. Or at least it would be when her hindbrain accepted it and stopped twitching.

Paris was healing well enough to grumble about how few of them had been surprised that he was a cop and had sworn them to secrecy; Cheryl's sisters and brothers-in-law were comforting her, and the slightly larger of the two cargo vessels was just about ready to take them to Eta Pegasi. Barry, Carl and Terry had been relieved to have the JF intelligence officer take command of the freighter, and ecstatic over the addition of another pilot and two engineers. Not to mention the navigation database and extra air recyclers. The Ticonderoga was staying at the station, hoping to catch more pirates. Lieutenant Fischer and Captain Perris would report respectively to Joint Fleet Operations currently in Eta Pegasi system, and Joint Criminal Investigations on Autumn, the fourth planet of the smaller star of that system. It was the only CI office in the New Territories.

The pirate ship was being checked very carefully. It would be taken to Eta as well, but its passengers would be under lock and key.

Jenny rubbed her aching head. "I wish I knew where the

'Far Seeker' was," she complained.

Barry shook his head at her. "It isn't really overdue, from here, I mean, and in any case there's an information lag. If they had pushed the pace and headed for Eta, the Ticonderoga might just have heard about them. If they went to Beta Pegasi, or if the trip went slowly, they wouldn't have heard yet." He hesitated. "Juan was just the third pilot, you know? He doesn't have a lot of experience, and if he tried to push the jumps, he probably would have splatted."

"I hate that term," she told him. "It's not really dangerous though, is it?"

"No, it just trips every breaker switch on the ship and drains the capacitor." Barry smiled, at some memory perhaps. "It's embarrassing and time consuming and frustrating. Heck, they just may have made sure he was getting enough sleep, and taken it slow. He's only one man, after all."

"True." Jenny smiled back at him, relieved, then looked around at the cargo they were loading. "I think we've got everything we'll need. I'm going to make sure Paris is okay," she said, spotting him carefully and slowly maneuvering toward dock one.

Looking around, she caught Cap's eye and nodded toward the ship. She followed Paris into the ship, then passed him and solicitously opened doors for him until he was settled down in a bunk in one of the cargo pods the marines had hastily converted to passenger accommodations. Cap slipped through the door behind her.

He eyed them cautiously.

"Before the hijacking," Jenny got straight to the point. "You were asking a lot of questions about Michael Bornstein. When we get to Autumn, are we going to find that he has been ransomed and freed?"

"Possibly," Paris looked exasperated. "I can't imagine where I got the idea that a teenage girl would just gush and tell me everything without thinking about why I was asking."

Jenny smirked. "You don't spend much time around intelligent people, do you?"

"Bornstein's been a political troublemaker on Autumn and the rest of the New Territories for years. I suspect he'll be raving about the lack of protection given to shipping, playing up his frantic worries for Nicole for all the attention he can harvest, all the while lobbying for the New Territories' independence."

"I don't know if he has anything to do with the hijackers or the pirates, and if he does whether it's a loose agreement or if he's tight with them. Hell, he could be their leader for all I know." He flopped back with a sigh of exasperation. "Maybe one of the prisoners will talk."

"I see," said Jenny. "And if Zimmer, Descartes and the other prisoners say nothing?" she asked.

"We're screwed," Paris said flatly. "We won't even be able

to trace the ransom money; the banking system out here is unbelievable. *Occasionally* you'll see a letter of credit. Damn near everyone uses cash, except for large transactions, for half of those those they use gold. God knows why, it really is rather common."

"Force of history, I think," Cap offered. "It's almost as old a medium of exchange as salt."

Paris eyed him thoughtfully. "What are you planning on doing after we get to Autumn?"

"First I will inform the Red Dawn Revolutionary Council of the death of Chairman Wong. Then I will wait to see if there is anything I can do to aid in the destruction of the pirate and hijacker group that killed him." He shrugged. "After that, it will depend on the success or failure of our salvage claim."

"If it fails, will you return to Earth, to the Enclave?"

"I'll return to Earth, but only briefly to the Enclave. There is nothing there for me." His eyes flicked toward Jenny. "Before, I wasn't aware of the possibilities."

"Jenny, would you excuse us for a moment?" Paris gave her a totally false smile. She rolled her eyes, but stepped out the door and slid it closed, placing her ear firmly against it. Nothing. Damn. Was Cap being recruited? Or worse yet, lectured about her age? *Bloody stupid men.*

She stomped off to the cargo pod all the women and kids were sharing.

Chapter Thirty-Nine
Reunion

"The 'Far Seeker' docked at the outer system station six days ago." Carl's jubilant voice rang through the ship. "The Joint Fleet says the passengers and crew are already enroute to the planet, to Autumn. Everyone's safe." His voice flattened a bit halfway through that last statement.

Except for the dead. Except for the few who were taken off before the escape. Jenny thought, knowing that was what everyone was thinking. *We got almost everyone back. The authorities will have to do the rest.*

By the time they docked, the news of their arrival had spread, and apparently inflated itself. Jenny was nearly blinded by the lights, the crowd behind them a blur of vidcams and jostling bodies, with a background of shouted questions.

Where the heck did all the reporters come from . . . oh, they're here for the conference. Of course.

They were hustled off the ship and into an anonymous meeting room on the transfer station.

The Joint Fleet officers tried to look important, but it was already clear that the reporters knew they had rescued themselves, and apparently thought they'd captured or killed hijackers and pirates by the hundreds.

Opal and Paula, as the prettiest women, drew most of the vids. Paris (in outrageous stage makeup) and Obadiah did most of the talking. Everyone was introduced.

"The brave widow" Cheryl looked like she wanted to paste the officious station manager that was emoting all over them. The "brave children" either preened or hid behind their mothers.

Then they escaped. The fast courier was an insystem ship; with no heavy jump rings impeding it, the captain pushed its acceleration and cut the journey to eight days.

Jenny talked—so to speak, with a time delay measured in hours—then sent a hopefully reassuring message to their mother, to be sent off with the first ship heading back across the Rift, then handed off to a ship heading Earthward. No telling how long it would take to get there, or even if it would get there at all.

But at least I tried.

The planet Autumn, the fourth out from the F type star, had been settled for more than sixty years. Ancient by New Territories standards, although less than a fifth of the age of the first star colonies. It had a scattering of towns utilizing various natural resources, but most of the population was concentrated in the spaceport city of New Frisco.

The spaceport was a dozen kilometers outside of the city, but someone had laid on limo service for the trip.

In the Rift

It was spring locally, but the native groundcover had a yellowish tinge between the brilliant green fields of Terran grain. The taller plants were a dark reddish purple, their vaguely treelike appearance at a distance evolving as they got closer into something like very large mushrooms having perpetual bad hair days.

The center of New Frisco was dominated by two hotels facing each other across a park. The convention facilities, seemingly too large for such a modest planet, connected the hotels along the south side of the park. The government offices attempted to dominate the square on the north, but were overwhelmed by the tall hotels.

"Someone thinks this place is going to grow," Jenny commented. Paris kicked her ankle. *Ha! Dear old Michael, eh?* Then they were pulling up and Nicole was dashing out to hug her, tears in her eyes.

Chapter Forty
Autumn

"So, between checking everything eight times between every jump and making sure poor Juan got some sleep, it took us this long to get here. We were starting to run out of food, but they hadn't stripped the ship completely," Nicole told her audience, draped informally around the posh suite Paris had rented.

"And, well, you know how we eat. We mostly sat around having nervous breakdowns, trying to figure out how a proper support group ought to work, doing our nails and hair, and worrying over what they might do to everyone who was left behind." She glared at Jenny. "Especially about a certain little sister I thought was on board."

Jenny just grinned, she was sitting cross-legged on the end of the bed Paris lay flat on. Ethereal was alternately fussing over him and glaring at Nicole, whom she obviously suspected of trying to steal her sponsor.

When Nicole had whispered to Jenny that she ought to, Jenny had had a giggling fit and refused to explain. Nicole was beginning to suspect that Ethereal might just be jealous of the wrong sister. Hmm, maybe she should encourage a relationship. Musicians were eccentric, no accounting for their tastes, but a rich brother-in-law would be very handy. At least Jenny hadn't fixated on the Chinese bodyguard, who was currently sitting on the floor at her feet.

"Well," Obadiah drawled, from the couch where he cuddled with Aria. "I guess she just couldn't leave until she'd kicked some more hijacker butt." Most of the people there either laughed or grinned, but there was something a bit . . . awed? Or maybe proud, about the way they looked at Jenny.

Good grief! She's barely eighteen, and they're acting like she's a heroine.

Nicole thought back to the way Jenny'd instantly organized the 'Far Seekers' departure. Perhaps they knew her sister better than she did.

"So tell me what happened on the station afterwards? Were they angry?"

One of the pros giggled. "Honey, they was pissed." Her pink haired friend nodded. "They beat us up on general principles and tossed us in with the other gals, and searched everywhere."

"Like we could hide forty-six women in the lavs or something." One of the older women sniffed. "They left us alone for a day, then came back for some women to, to, well, that's when Cap struck." She nodded her gray head at the man.

"Jenny backed off and drew them into the perfect position for him to hit them," said another old woman.

334

In the Rift

I really need to learn which one is which!

"One of them got away, that hideous Maitre d'. My, he was fast!" said the third old lady. "But we had all the guns and Paris had found out the door codes, so we stormed their quarters and killed them, well most of them."

"Actually," Paris said, "Jenny gave me the door code. Cap, did you figure it out?"

"They were careless and used it were I could observe. I told Jenny."

Jenny took over. "So then, we waited to see who would show up first, the Joint Fleet or the pirates."

"And it was the pirates." One of the four, three now, ugly businessmen, chimed in. "We'd have had them if that damned doctor hadn't turned out to be one of them!"

"Well, maybe." Obadiah sounded dubious. "Once they realized we weren't the real station crew, things went downhill fast." He carefully fingered an ear with a notch in it, and Aria beamed at him proudly.

It was enough to make one nauseous. Nicole wished Michael was here to be fussed over. Not that he liked fuss, it would have to be subtle.

All the Farseeker people had been put on this floor, perhaps for the ease of controlling the press, and it was full to overflowing with the new additions. Paula and Jenny had been added to Nicole's reduced entourage. Stephanie Corey, Heidi Schmidt, and Corella Caruthers had been among the sixteen women taken off by the first pirates.

Will I ever see them again? Or at least find out what happened to them?

She had four interconnecting rooms, as did Ethereal, and Aria. Paris and Obadiah had added to their territories, but she didn't dare, just in case the Far Company decided it would be cheaper to declare bankruptcy than deal with the expenses of this debacle. The four sisters and their surviving husbands had connecting suites, and the families with kids, the two pros were together in a single room.

Only the bodyguard was by himself, and she'd better keep an eye on him and Jenny, really, he wasn't suitable. Even if he weren't Chinese, or whatever, and a bit dark for a chink, wasn't he, not that that really mattered to her, but he was unemployed. Unemployed wouldn't do at all.

Although if it comes to that, I want to see the Step Father's face when Jenny introduces him to her fiancé.

Maybe even more so, if it's Paris the Crash Rock star, instead. Wow. It's weird thinking of Jenny as the popular girl.

Another ex-passenger wandered through Paris's open door.

"Kids asleep?" Jenny asked the newcomer.

"Yes, finally." The woman looked tired, flopping into a chair Opal pushed in her direction. "Has anyone heard when they're going to get our luggage here?"

In the Rift

"So far we've only got what was in our cabins." Ethereal scowled. "They haven't unloaded the cargo pods, yet." She twisted her hands together nervously, then frowned at them and placed them elegantly displayed, on her lap. Nicole recognized the assertion of conscious control; a nervous gesture at the wrong time could lose this contest. Everything, and especially the hands, must express grace. Not nerves. She glanced at her own hands, but long ingrained habit still served. They were fine, she was sitting perfectly.

"They're having to inventory it for insurance and salvage purposes," Mac told her. "But they've rushed your personal belongings. They're enroute on a high G drone already. It should be here by tomorrow, I talked to the insurance representative a couple of hours ago."

"Good." Obadiah twinkled. "I know of three women who have not given up on the Miss Outer Space title who need their entire wardrobes."

Jenny rolled her eyes. "Normalcy returns. If you can call a beauty contest normal."

Nicole frowned, determinedly. "There are more than fifty other contestants here. We need our wardrobes now." Ethereal and Aria nodded in unison.

"I feel like a tramp, dragging around in the same old clothes," Aria lamented. The newcomers looked unimpressed, and Nicole had to guiltily agree. They probably didn't even have a change of undies left by now.

"Well," Jenny told them, "If it's just psychological advantages at this point in the contest, you should all stride around like Amazon warriors, any one of you is worth ten of those pampered wimps." Ethereal and Aria looked taken aback, like they were trying on a very different image and finding it a poor fit. Nicole couldn't help but smile, Jenny really did understand about psychological advantages, but Amazons? Well, she had kicked that pirate, even if she hadn't killed him, and the Fleet Officers had been so glad to get their hands on him. Hmm, yes, an Amazon. Full wardrobe or not, tomorrow she would stride through the world as if she owned it by right of personal conquest.

Chapter Forty-One
Reporting In

Paris stretched carefully, but for the first morning in a couple of weeks raised barely a twinge. *Safe from pirates and hijackers, now it's time to take on the politicians!* Then he heard Ethereal rustling through the door that connected 'his' room to the rest of her suite. *Err, first a Beauty Queen, then I'll tackle the politicians!*

"Are you all right, Neil?" Crumb, the first time she'd used his first name in months.

"Great, actually, good nanos those Fleet types use. What's up? Besides getting here barely in time for the pageant, instead of a month early?"

"Look, I wanted to say how sorry I am that I've been so nasty to you."

"Oh, geeze, Ethereal, I figured out real quick that trying to get back together was a bad idea." He ran his hands through his hair. "But I'd already agreed to help with the expenses and it seemed like an adventure to come way out here for, excuse me, such a silly thing."

She glared at him. "I was coming in here to seduce you."

He took a deep careful breath. "And then we'd go back to fighting? Umm, how about we average it out and just get along okay until after the contest?"

She laughed at him. "Now I remember why I used to be so madly in love with you at the same time you were driving me up the wall. You're going to regret turning me down!" She walked back out, still smiling.

"I already do." He muttered, trying to stuff memories of her in bed behind memories of her throwing plates *crash* at him for being so *crash* bloody *crash* practical *crash*. At least her aim had been bad, and he'd always kept a safe distance during temper tantrums. Ah, to be young and stupid again! To not be facing the start of an investigation into the hijacking, while attempting to pick up the pieces of his original assignment of tracking the political movers and shakers. Would Bornstein ever show up? Had CI taken his suggestions to heart, and put a watch on the Far Seeker passengers?

He needed to slide out of here and check in with the Joint Criminal Investigations office. He'd sent in an updated and more complete version of the preliminary report he'd given Captain Garrett, and with luck would get an updated brief on the political maneuverings in the Conference, and more importantly, out of the Conference. It would be a month before any reports from Beta Pegasi could reach him. Investigating with no idea how all the women had been maneuvered onto the right ship would be frustrating.

Was the political scene connected to the piracy out here,

or not? The more he looked at it, the fewer reasons he could see to be anti-petition. Pirates and hijackers seemed to be the only winners in the current situation. He ran his fingers through his hair and decided to assume that anyone who was anti-annexation was a pirate until proven otherwise.

He shook his head at the nonexistent contents of his closet. The girls weren't the only ones whose wardrobes were showing wear and tear, but men had the advantage when it came to shopping. He called up the in-hotel clothing store and placed an order for his size shirt, his size slacks, specified colors, even new socks and boxers. Voila, a new outfit in two minutes flat. It was at his door by the time he got out of the shower.

With no makeup—thank god he'd thought to grab some from the dump—and dressed conservatively, he attracted absolutely no attention in the lobby or on the street. He sauntered around the central park square and wandered into the government buildings like a tourist. At the JCI office, the door comp identified him and he was bustled straight into the chief's office.

"Took your time reporting in, didn't you?" General Christianson, despite his rank, had never been anything but a bureaucrat. The military ranks were used to avoid confusing the Cinnabs with parallel hierarchy nomenclature, and also helped clarify relations with the Fleet. Sometimes. Sometimes the ranks indicated competence, but all too often it was competence in internal politics. Paris had dealt with enough desk jockeys to know how to handle them.

He grimaced as if in distaste. "Still undercover, sir. Had to wait for the media to leave before I dared come here."

"Your report on Bornstein, MacGregor and the Wall Street Gang is very interesting. If we could tie that lot into the pirate network we could really clean house out here."

"If you noticed, sir, MacGregor was instrumental in the 'Far Seeker's' escape. What his political leanings are I don't know, but I don't believe he has anything to do with the hijackers. Nor, as you saw in my report is there any indication that the Wall Street Gang is anything but exactly what they appear to be. Bornstein, on the other hand . . . "

"Just got word from the Fleet, He's coming in system on a small freighter. Claims to have been ditched on a small station after his ransom was paid."

Paris leaned forward. "Now that is interesting. What did he have to say about the rest of the Far Seeker people?"

"His first contact with anyone was a broadcast message to the local authorities or the Joint Fleet, with the information that the 'Far Seeker' had been hijacked and that he had paid a ransom to be freed and that action needed to be taken immediately to save the women that had been taken further out to be sold as sex slaves."

"Anything about the rest of the passengers?" Paris asked.

"Just that he and sixteen women had been separated

342

from the rest, and that he did not know your fate."

Paris grinned nastily. "Nothing about a space station? How interesting!" he thought for a moment. "Any hope of keeping him ignorant of our return? Can we get him to say something that . . . "

The General was shaking his head. "He's already seen the public broadcasts, his second message was 'a detailed statement' and included the station. It's suggestive, but nothing that would stand up in court."

"Damn. Well, I'll be well placed to keep an eye on him, both in the hotel and during the contest, plenty of excuses to socialize." Paris scowled. "Maybe he'll say something incriminating."

"Keep an eye on MacGregor as well." The General directed. "And 'the Wall Street Gang', they're very active out here." He shook his head. "All this on top of the conference."

"More like, because of the conference, sir. If Bornstein is connected with the hijackers, he must have planned this hijacking as the best way to demonstrate how little protection the New Territories get for all the wealth they've poured into the zones and all the taxes they pay."

"They don't pay taxes."

"Everything they ship to or through zone four is taxed and they know it, sir. Just because the tax is collected later rather than directly from them doesn't make much difference. This hijacking, this particular group of passengers, so many women, is guaranteed to capture the attention of everyone in the New Territories."

"Because there are so few women out here." The General nodded.

"It could, however, boomerang on him. It could increase calls for UCP membership so that the Fleet can legally patrol out here, which is the whole problem." Paris studied the man across the desk. "If you have any influence with the representatives, you need to emphasize that the Fleet can't legally patrol out here unless the New Territories join. We need to explain that there won't really be any new taxes, just that they will pay them directly, rather than taking a lower price for their goods from a buyer who then pays the taxes."

"Hmph, you're quite the politician yourself. How did you end up in this position?" His expression failed to hide his opinion of Crash Rock Stars.

"It was a short term assignment that turned out to be quite useful. I haven't escaped it yet." Paris abbreviated the explanation.

"Well, we're getting some pressure from the Fleet to let them handle this situation, but planet-side it's our baby, although I can guarantee I'll be borrowing personnel from them." The General nodded. "For now keep your eyes open while I try to put even more security around the Miss Outer Space Contest than we've got around the political conference. If there's anything I need to know, contact me, otherwise concentrate on Bornstein and MacGregor."

"Yes, sir." Paris hesitated. "Can I borrow an office and get myself up to date? I'd also like to do as complete a minute by minute record as I can."

"Excellent idea." The General looked at him with approval for the first time. "I'll get you an office immediately."

Paris suppressed an obscenity and nodded formally back. *Now he's going to be bugging me for the minute-by-minute, when what I really want is to research all the questions I've been saving up. Oh, well, at least I'll have the net access.*

He winced at the size of the files as he called them up. *I hope most of this is irrelevant. If I have to read every word I'll be here all week.*

Mac was known to the locals, but not in any bad way. He'd been in-system once or twice a year over the last eight years. Always on the regular passenger ships. Mac and Bornstein were the only survivors that had passed through the local system.

Yeesh! Bornstein had a huge file. The appended note from a sympathetic fellow investigator simply summarized it as "has his nose in everything legal, never been caught in illegalities. Rabidly anti-petition."

It didn't have any background info on anyone else he'd requested, that would all have to come, well, probably from

Earth for the most part.

Paris decided to concentrate on the surveillance that had been set up since their arrival. Had any of the Far Seeker passengers met with anyone questionable in the five, now six days since they returned? Ha, finally, a short file.

Whoops, Frank Monico had rushed straight out and dropped by some odd spots and talked to some people of interest to the local police. Many of them known to be against annexation, reference to another report. Damn! Frank was practically invisible. Had he overlooked a major player?

Macgregor had made a few calls to people he dealt with regularly, reference another file.

The first group of women hadn't gone out much.

No clothes, he thought with a grin.

And then there was his group who hadn't even had a full day on planet yet.

The Wall Street Gang had called their usual business contacts here, with reference to yet another file, mention of overlap with Macgregor's contacts, special analysis thereof, see yet another file . . .

Kissy and Misty, he was relieved to see, hadn't talked to anyone, apparently not ready to start working yet.

Jenny, as he had expected, hadn't done anything beyond gawk at the sights and buy breakfast, ditto Cap, and in her company. He smirked a bit, imagining his poor overworked colleagues back on Earth trying to get background info on Red Guards at all, let alone a specific one.

But that sort of background he wouldn't receive for a couple of months, by which time any excitement would probably be history. With luck he'd get some results back from his Beta Pegasi inquiries before both the pageant and the annexation conference were over.

With a sigh, he looked at the first of the huge reference files. He had a feeling that it wasn't going to help a bit. He reached out decisively and shut down the comp, and headed out the door. He'd be better off out talking with the suspects, rather than reading about them.

Chapter Forty-Two
Reward

Jenny frowned at her image in the mirror. The current fashion of tight bodysuits with loose and filmy draperies really wasn't well suited to the ample figure.

FarCo had delivered not only their traveling luggage, but their stored luggage as well, mid-morning. So she had her whole wardrobe to choose from. Such as it was. Some of the women had been stressed out and barely able to eat over the last weeks, but she had gone the other way and calmed her nerves by stuffing her face. The draperies were still going to have to drape long enough to cover up thunder thighs.

At least the black body suit was stretchy enough that it still fit. She shook her head at herself. *There is no point in trying to impress anyone with my looks. Especially with all the beauty queens parading around.* She grabbed the more businesslike camel skirt and scarf. It would have to do.

Cap was hovering down the hallway, wearing another of the quilted gi-like jackets and loose black pants that were apparently the uniform of a Champion of the People. He approached to meet her.

"No red belt?" she asked.

"No. I have lost the right, by allowing my master to be

killed."

She eyed him, suddenly worried. "They won't punish you, will they?"

He shrugged. "I spoke to Quincy this morning, the 'Pegasus Rift Salvage Company' is now a legal entity and has filed for ownership by right of salvage of the space station, the two cargo ships and the pirate ship we captured, as well as the bounty on the pirates and hijackers we killed or captured and salvage on all the dead ships floating out there."

"That was quick!"

"Unfortunately, that may be the only quick part of it. Probably the decision of the salvage court will take at least four months." Cap frowned. "Salvage on this scale is unheard of, in space, and of course, is usually just a percentage of the value of the property. Trying to be awarded outright ownership is unusual. It will depend on whether the court can locate the owners of record."

"Maybe we can take at least a percentage ownership, instead of money. Back before the hijacking, Mac was talking about how badly a halfway station was needed."

Cap was nodding. "He spoke to Quincy, too, and was very excited. He said it would be very lucrative; with so small a gravity well it is easy to get back into the big waves for economical and fast travel."

"What about the 'Far Seeker?'" she asked. "Where does it

fall as salvage?"

"The Wall Streeters think that with Juan never leaving the ship, and returning it to port under its own power, it doesn't qualify as salvage, having never actually been abandoned. They suspect that the insurance company will try to settle out of court, paying for deaths and injuries, and perhaps five percent of the value of the ship as a reward split among those who actively helped retake the ship." He looked thoughtful. "That will probably just be Zuniga, Parker, Mac, Frank, Nicole and you."

"You should get a portion, too," Jenny remarked. "Although neither of us may, as we didn't return with the ship."

"And only I saw you tackle two armed hijackers to give them time to close the locks and leave."

"Oh, well." Jenny shrugged. "I guess we'll just have to be satisfied with a space station and three other ships."

"Quincy said he'd also filed a UCP New System Claim on the planet itself and also put a claim against it as salvage. It may not fly, it's obviously been known and used for decades, but our claims will prevent anyone from undercutting us by doing the same."

Jenny frowned. "I thought that New System Claims were done for star systems, but in this case I guess it's all that would fit."

As they exited the lift, Paris spotted them, met them

halfway and pulled them back toward a group that included two JF officers.

"Michael Bornstein has just turned up." His eyes were snapping. "He's on a freighter coming from a station called 'Nowhere'. He says he was released when his ransom was paid."

"The women?" Jenny asked, her stomach sinking.

"He says they were still aboard the ship when they dumped him, and bound for somewhere even further out," one of the officers growled. "We hope he has details."

"I see," she said, feeling a bit faint. She hadn't expected a fairy tale ending, after all, but this sounded very bleak. *How do you track down sixteen women scattered through a frontier stretching hundreds of light years?*

"However, Miss Poppenhusen, Mr. Er," his eyes slid to the pad in his hand as if reading, "Lian Zhang Wu Ye?" Apparently he was close enough; Cap nodded politely. "On a happier note, I was on the way to personally deliver these, when this news came in." The Commander extended the touch pad. "If I could have your fingerprint for receipt, I have your parts of the reward for the capture of the pirates. This isn't anything to do with the salvage claim," he added as they applied fingers to the pad. "Just the posted reward." He passed them each a chip.

Jenny blinked in startlement at the amount, looking up at the officer.

In the Rift

"We've wanted the 'Crazy Lady' very badly for a very long time. You should hear the suggestions going around the Fleet about what to do with D'alembert's body." He smiled grimly. "Unfortunately the Admiral won't let us."

"Well known, was he?" asked Mac.

"Yep. We have numerous recordings of him ordering ships to cease acceleration or be fired on," the Lieutenant answered. "Some from ships that got away, more sifted from debris fields that used to be ships. We wanted him very, very badly."

"What about the crew we described to you?" Misty had quietly drifted into the group, Kissy trailing her. "Do you know them?"

"From your descriptions, probably, and we're getting together some pictures to see if you can positively identify them." The Commander nodded to her. "You two and Bornstein are the only ones who've seen them. Maybe a firm ID will help us trace the missing passengers." His lips thinned, Jenny wondered if it was because of unvoiced suspicions of Michael, or the suspicion that tracing the missing was an exercise in futility.

Nicole came fluttering over, an apt description in view of the number of feathers among the netting and bangles on her whatever-that-sort-of-thing-was-called. It looked rather as if a collision between a fishing boat and an exotic bird farm had been turned into a skimpy bathrobe. "Michael's alive!"

There were tears in her eyes. "He's on a freighter and will be here the day after tomorrow."

Jenny's heart sank as she saw the tremulous smile on her sister's lips. "We just heard, Nicki. Great news!"

This is not good, it would be much better if Nicki thought of Michael as just a source of money. Nicole is just not cold blooded enough for the role she's chosen in life.

"He'll be here in plenty of time for the start of the pageant." Nicole was nearly radiating relief "I'm going to record and send a message, I'll see you later." She wafted away.

Jenny looked after her glumly, then perked up as she remembered the chip in her hand. "Is there an Earth-based bank in town?" She split her question between the two officers.

"Yep, there's a Bank of North America right here in the hotel." The Lieutenant pointed. "It's way down that corridor, so it could also have outside and Convention Center entrances."

She thanked them, and headed in the indicated direction.

Money! Enough to pay for all my college expenses, if I want to go back. If. An interesting concept.

Chapter Forty-Three
Now Back To Serious Stuff

Having recorded and sent her message, Nicole fairly skipped back to the Hotel Pegasi's Grand Ballroom.

The money's okay, I don't have to worry about the money.

She felt a twinge of guilt, but shoved it down ruthlessly. She had been upfront with Michael about the money and sex from the start. She had bought her next set of competition clothes from her prize money after winning the Miss Great Plains Crown, but the regional sponsors were cheap, with a regional recession and the unexpected expense of an interstellar voyage and had only ponied up for three tickets.

Michael had stepped in and paid for the rest of the transportation, housing and the publicity expected of the 'Great Plains Region Sponsor'. He'd been generous and encouraged her to bring all her friends, and yes, of course, her little sister was welcome.

But now I don't have to worry about the spacelines not honoring return tickets paid for by a dead man, nor about the hotel and restaurant bills here. Now it is time to forget all that and take this pageant by storm. Her deep blue skin suit and primitive mélange duster were overdue for an airing. *The hotel is keeping the Newsies out, so it is time for me to go to them.*

With that elegant stride possible only with long legs augmented by high heels and thousands of hours of practice, she swept through the lobby and out the front doors. The lighting was perfect! The high overcast lit everything but softened shadows, was bright enough to gleam off her loose golden hair, but wouldn't make her squint. She glided down the steps like a queen, and across the road to the public square like an Amazon warrior.

I fear nothing! I conquer all I see!

And the newsies had indeed spotted her and were converging, vidcams in hand. She scoped out a good 'native' interest, those ugly purpley plants would make a marvelously dramatic photo backdrop; she walked up to them and turned in just the right way to maneuver the newsies into the proper position for her best pictures. The slight breeze wafted her hair behind and to her left. She watched their astonished and admiring faces and smiled warmly at them at them. Piece of cake, getting good exposure from this lot.

"Miss Peace," an eager young man started. "We understand that you single-handedly captured a pirate aboard the 'Far Seeker' during your escape."

This is so easy it's almost sinful!

Chapter Forty-Four
And Politics

Jenny exited the bank with the Wall Streeters, whom she had found there also depositing their reward money. "Good God, Nicole didn't lose any time!" They looked where she pointed. Nicole was leading, while appearing to be led by, a group of vid-toting newsies; they seemed to be giving her a walking tour of the central plaza.

"Her picture's going to be on all the major channels tonight," chuckled Noreen. "She's even collecting the political reporters that ought to be interviewing the politicians over there."

'Over there' was the Hotel Eta, where Nicole had found a spot with good background, good lighting and apparently, Jenny squinted. "Good God! Did North America actually send the Secretary of State?" Obviously, since Nicole was now shaking his hand while the entire news corps recorded.

"Yep," confirmed Quincy. "It makes sense, too. Whatever relationship the New Territories negotiates with the United Countries and Planets will have a real impact on how all the Earth nations do or don't continue to relate to each other."

"North America, especially, would love to be able to trade independently with the Cinnab systems," said Cheryl.

"So would Zone One, for that matter."

"So," Jenny worked it out. "Now that the New Territories are large enough to have economic clout, and settled enough to not really be a frontier, if they reject UCP membership, they'll be the first independent human interstellar nation since Alpha Centauri joined the UCP. Setting a huge precedent for the old Zones?"

"Exactly." Quincy said. "Zone Three might decide to go it alone, if for no other reason than to get some attention on trade negotiations. The 'Equal Labor Costs' laws are just killing their industry. And it goes further than that. Beta Pegasi, for instance, might well want to be an independent single star system. It is self-supporting and makes most of its outside money through travel taxes, but rebates over half of that to the UCP."

"So, how many of these reps are on which side?" Jenny was baffled. "Does anyone want the New Territories to join?"

"Oh, yes," Oliver answered. "All the UCP power structure, and all the little countries that think North America would leave them in the dust to sink back into poverty if the UCP fell apart. All the Cinnab experts, and the Cinnabs themselves, that want the humans to police themselves and don't want to have to figure out which human government they need to talk to for every problem they have with humans. Zone Two has no room to spread, it's surrounded and the current status quo is economically

358

favorable for it." He shrugged. "And of course, lots of people here in the Territories feel that membership would be good."

"What do you think would be best?" she asked.

"Membership." He was definite. "The main problem out here is piracy and hijacking. We desperately need to expand both Joint Fleet and Joint Criminal Investigations out here. Destabilizing the UCP, even a bit, will just give the criminals more time to cripple trade and stymie growth. For the Territories, membership is a very, very good idea."

"How strange! On Earth, everyone was talking about how we had no right to 'force' the Territories into the Union, and force taxes on them." Jenny frowned, how much of that point of view had she gotten from Michael?

"Ha!" Steven snorted. "Maybe ten percent of the people out here feel that way, the vast majority is more than willing to pay to get the Fleet out here. Not to mention new colonists, companies and schools. Did you know that Autumn has the only accredited University in the entire Territories?"

"Aren't there a hundred or so settled planets out here?" Jenny asked.

"Oh, a lot more than that. Only twenty-three of them have more than ten thousand people on them, though. Autumn's the largest, with a total population just passing three million."

Ronald grinned. "There was a big fight over how to

determine if a planet was 'settled' or merely being exploited. They finally defined it as having a population of at least one thousand, that was at least ten percent female. One hundred and thirty nine planets qualified for settled status, with the rest classified as exploited. Which was defined as being claimed, registered and with some economic output. There're about five hundred of them, and four times that number that have been claimed and registered, but no one's doing anything with them."

"That was the census the Pegasi Congress finished two years ago, to go with the annexation petition," Laurie said. "I was surprised so many of the planets qualified. Even with all our trading interests out here, I hadn't realized how large it was or how fast it was growing."

"Mind you, a lot of the planets barely made it." Laurie laughed. "There was one planet, I can't remember the name, that sent its report in on the last day. They waited for a baby to be born. The little girl got them qualified as settled, a boy wouldn't have. She was their one thousandth citizen, and one hundredth girl."

"I think that has to be an urban legend," Cheryl protested. "The numbers are just too perfect."

Jenny spotted Cap, Paris and the Fleet Lieutenant on the stairs of the Hotel Pegasi, and started that way.

"Jenny," Paris was back in his makeup and inner mask. "And all," a mocking flourish of a bow to the Wall Streeters.

360

In the Rift

"The Fleet is so pleased with us, we've been given poor Lieutenant Bryson here as a flunkey."

The Lieutenant flushed a bit and glared at the musician. Jenny studied the Lieutenant. "I see."

The Fleet wants someone official and obvious near the group, to watch Michael when he shows up, and probably also divert attention from Paris.

"Actually, my commander wanted me on hand in case any of you spotted anyone that you recognized." The Lieutenant glanced reprovingly at Paris.

Quincy nodded. "I think we killed or captured all the ones we saw, but we didn't actually take an inventory."

Lieutenant Bryson nodded, a grin overtaking his face. "We're sending a crew out to the station to do just that; they're trying to find all the bodies that you threw out the airlocks. You have no idea how glad I was to be chosen to liaise here with you on the ground."

"Oh, dear," Noreen sounded dismayed. "That will be a very nasty job!"

"I suppose you have to try to determine which of the crew was killed by the hijackers, and which of the crew were hijackers," Jenny said. "For contact tracing and so forth, not to mention the insurance companies that won't want to pay out death benefits to the criminals instead of the victims."

The Lieutenant blinked at her, and Paris tried to hide a smile behind scratching his nose. "Yes, Miss, that pretty much sums it up."

"Not to mention the sheer unsavoryness of regularly encountering dead bodies when people go collecting ice and asteroids and so forth," Jenny added.

The Lieutenant looked relieved at this evidence of feminine sensibilities.

"Will you be joining us for the Miss Outer Space Contest, Lieutenant?" Cheryl asked politely. "We'll all be watching because of Aria, Etherea,l and Nicole, although I must say I never was attracted to such things myself."

"I was planning to, and was able to get tickets in the same area as your group."

"Should be a good view of the swimsuit competition." Paris smirked at him. "Unfortunately, it's rather close to the stage and we'll also get the full effect of the talent show, not to mention the evening gown contestants answering the judges' questions."

"I'm sure that will be very interesting." Laurie's voice was determined.

Undeterred, Paris batted his eyelashes and pitched his voice to a squeaky falsetto. "I hope to devote the rest of my life to Universal Peace and Love."

"Behave." Jenny poked him. "Even Nicole has better answers than that committed to memory. I can't speak for your girlfriend, however."

"My girlfriend is an accomplished flautist. She will ace

the talent competition." Paris stuck his nose in the air in an excess of snobbery. "I understand your sister does, umm, Free Form Dancing?" He didn't quite give a supercilious sniff, but the tone was spot on faintly incredulous disbelief.

"But of course!" Jenny elevated her nose in turn. "No one can beat Nicole at making a public spectacle of herself." In fact, Jenny quite liked Nicole's dancing, but wasn't about to admit it. She turned to the silent Cap. "Are you going to watch the contest?"

"Oh yes," he said. "Everyone will be there, so I will be as well."

"Good." Jenny had had quite enough of being taken hostage. *Being within reach of Michael Bornstein for the five days of the preliminaries and the final pageant is not a calming thought. Pity to survive and conquer so much and then get myself killed when there are finally cops around to handle things!*

Cap was being very quiet though. She wondered what Paris and the Lieutenant had spoken to him about, and whether he would pass anything on to her. *If I don't watch out, I'm going to be relegated to helpless female or even worse, child, and shut out of any action. Dammit, if Michael really is part of the hijacker/pirate ring, I'll be perfectly placed to observe him. They'd better not keep me ignorant, because I'm going to watch him like a hawk for Nicole's sake.*

Chapter Forty-Five
Bornstein's Back

Nicole was relieved that she had guessed right in her conservative dress today. Michael was angry, or projecting anger in any case, she really wasn't sure which this time.

He wanted an attractive concerned dewy-eyed near-victim as a backdrop, and the navy-and-white dress was perfect. While the neckline was deep enough to catch their attention without being an obvious sexual lure, the short puff sleeves brought up subconscious child-must-protect instincts in all the male viewers.

Michael's first embrace had been as fervent as she had hoped for, even if she suspected it was as much to please the vids as her. And now he was in full speech mode in front of the vidcams.

"They say they can protect us, I say why haven't they been doing so? They say we don't pay taxes. Excuse me? Half my business flows through Zone four and I most certainly do pay taxes. Either directly there or in lower prices to buyers who pay the tax. The passengers on board the 'Far Seeker' were certainly taxpayers, the crews likewise. FarCo itself is based in Zone four and pays taxes.

"I say it is time for the United Countries and Planets to

either show that they can and will provide protection by doing so, or stop holding their hands out for more money. We've paid and paid, and gotten nothing. Why should we pay more until they show us what we're buying?" He nodded angrily at the vidcams, and circling an arm protectively around her waist, steered her away, down some steps to where a private ground car awaited them.

Alone in the car, he sighed in exasperation. "Sorry about the rant, honey," He threw her his charming grin. "I'd say I've had a bad four months, but you've had worse."

"Oh, but you're absolutely right! If the UCP means to protect us, they should start by finding the girls those pirates took off with. Poor Stephanie! I feel so guilty being safe, when I have no idea where she is or what is happening to her."

"Yes . . . the girls." A calculating light gleamed momentarily in his eyes. "I don't hold any hopes of the Fleet finding them; do you realize that the 'Far Seeker' passengers have captured or killed more pirates than the entire Fleet in the last two years? Not to mention the space station! How did they miss finding that for fifty years?" He shook his head. "I'll put out feelers to all my contacts, and post a reward for information. News like this will get around and we'll hear all the rumors. I think it's about time that the New Territories had an armed space police fleet of their own."

Nicole murmured vague agreement but so much of what

he said sounded faintly . . . rehearsed. Had he spent all his time on the way back since his release writing speeches? The return of the 'Far Seeker' and especially Jenny's group's daring escapades must have surprised him.

The car whisked them through light traffic in silence for a long moment.

"Tell me what happened," Michael asked. "I don't understand how you got away in the 'Far Seeker' or how those women attacked the hijackers and killed nearly all of them."

Her rendition took up the time until the car pulled up to the side door of the Hotel.

Chapter Forty-Six
Future Plans

Jenny stayed completely out of everyone's way as the Miss Outer Space Contestants prepped, or should she say primped, for the parade. Today they were showing off for the crowds, not the judges, so flamboyant and sexy was the name of the game. Sliding out the front door of the hotel, she saw that there were already plenty of people loitering around, waiting for the parade which would both start and finish here in the central square. Most of the loiterers were men, and Jenny started keeping an informal survey in her head.

By the time she'd been wandering for an hour, she'd concluded that either the women were staying away in droves, or the population of Autumn was about seventy percent male. The eight offers of marriage made her tend to suspect the later. Winding up back at the hotel, she shed her most persistent admirers, three young men who were offering to marry her singly or en mass, at the door. She spotted Paris, Obadiah, Michael and Lieutenant Bryson, and maneuvered through the crowd in the lobby to them.

"Are you guys riding with the Ladies?" she asked, knowing full well they weren't.

"Darling Jenny!" Paris exclaimed, in full idiot mode. "We

aren't even allowed to touch today!"

"Or for the rest of the week," added Obadiah. "If it weren't that Aria expects me to be in the audience as her chief admirer, I'd rent a cabin in the woods, such as they are, and hide for the week."

"God," Paris closed his eyes as if in prayer. "That sounds so good."

"This week the contestants all pretend that they are pure as driven snow, and we're just good friends, helping out the advertising of our regions through this contest," Michael put in.

"One does rather wonder just what people think we grow on the Great Plains, if Nicole is what we're advertising." Jenny grinned. "At least the crowd waiting outside didn't seem to be discussing the wheat of Kansas from what I overheard!"

Lieutenant Bryson snorted at that. "No, I doubt that." He eyed her with a bit of irritation. "You probably shouldn't go out without an escort, you know."

"Lieutenant," she sighed, suspecting he wasn't going to understand. "I avoid obviously dangerous situations, but I don't curtail my activities from fear. I have recently dealt successfully with much worse than the eager and frustrated bachelors of Autumn."

Fortunately, before he could start the standard spiel about her 'not understanding the dangers out there', the

370

festivities started with the Grand Marshall of the parade, the Mayor of New Frisco, giving a brief history of the contest and the honor of being the host city the first time The Miss Outer Space Contest was held in the New Territories.

From inside the lobby, Jenny caught a few snatches about "expansion from the Miss America contest," "taking over the financially ailing Miss USA contest series" and "reviving the old Miss Universe contest in the twenty-second century," and "expanding it to include contestants from other planets, then from different planetary systems, then . . . ."

Jenny rather thought that the contest organizers should have purchased either the Miss Galaxy or the Miss Universe name, as a first move in any revitalization they had planned. *And now 'Miss Outer Space' has a century and a half of history all its own. Figure that, if you can.*

"I'll believe all that when they add Cinnabs to the contest," Paris whispered behind her, she could hear the other sponsors snickering, then Paris leaned in closer. "See if you can get this damned Lieutenant away from us," He breathed.

"Behave." She elbowed him, as if he had said something amusingly rude. "I can vouch for Nicole, but Ethereal . . . hard to say, what does she eat? I have noticed a close resemblance in the eating habits of anorexic beauty queens and polite Cinnabs barely nibbling for the sake of appearances. Perhaps you should be careful."

"Damn," Obadiah chimed in. "Aria eats like that, too, now I won't dare get a good night's sleep in her company." More chuckles; the Lieutenant smiled weakly.

Jenny slid back beside him. "Are you from here, Lieutenant?"

"Well, not here, but I was born in the outer part of Zone Four, so I've been out in this region a lot."

"Really?" Jenny stayed in place, blocking him as Paris and Michael shifted just a bit. "Then you probably have a pretty good idea of the practical difficulties the Fleet will face in trying to locate our missing friends."

"Well," he blinked, "that is going to be more the provenance of the Joint Criminal Investigations than the Fleet."

"Really? I thought the Fleet would be more independent and able to investigate; where the JCI has few facilities, the Fleet takes theirs with them."

"Actually . . . " The Lieutenant swung into PR mode and was explaining the difference in investigative responsibilities as Paris and Michael slipped quietly away. Obadiah stayed and argued; he felt responsible for the missing women from Aria's entourage. He'd paid their way out here, and he wasn't going back without them, and as he launched his determination in the poor Lieutenant's face, Jenny slipped away as well.

372

In the Rift

She spotted Cap at the rear of the lobby and worked her way backwards through the press to him. He was looking subdued.

"What's wrong?"

"I keep trying to think what I have to contribute to the station if we get ownership." He was quiet for a moment. "The station will need a steady supply of ice for the hydrogen refueling, if it is to become a regular stop. So we need to get a tug to move ice. And either more solar panels or a reactor, for power. I can drive or fly about any type of atmospheric vehicle, I could learn how to pilot a tug, and probably run the hydrolysis equipment. Plus do any translating needed, although most space travelers speak English."

"Do you speak Cinnaban?" she asked curiously.

"Yes, although I have had no practice with a native speaker, and may not be as fluent as with human languages."

"Okay, what else does a space station need?"

"Housing for the workers, a hotel for transients. Food Labs." His eyes narrowed. "Offices, storage inside and out. I wonder what the capacity of the hydrolyser is? Will it be enough for regular traffic?"

Jenny nodded. "I guess I'm in the same situation. I don't really know anything about space stations.

"Before the hijacking, my plans were pretty straightforward. I needed to get away from the stepfather. So I needed training for a job as quickly as possible. I've won scholarships barely sufficient to cover four years of college, and half a cheap dorm room.

"I'm good at math and sciences. Artificial Intelligence Engineers and Programmers have a huge job market with plenty of demand. Although there are other fields I'm more interested in, they offer more uncertain job prospects, so AI was what I was aiming for.

"Nicole offering me this trip was marvelous. I signed up for remote classes, enough credit for nearly a full year once I turn in the class recordings and test out. It was more expensive than regular tuition, but no dorm expenses so I'll come out way ahead, quite apart from the opportunity to see other places.

"Then the hijacking and everything else that has happened, happened. Now . . . now I have possible futures I had never dreamed of before. Before, I was looking forward to a job with computers, probably in a huge cubicle farm and a tiny apartment all my own. Now, I may soon own part of several spaceships, a space station and possibly even part of a planet. Now, I need to think again about what I want to learn. I like geology and planetary sciences and astronomy, any of those would be just as, if not more useful than a degree in AI.

"I'm not much of a gardener, but learning about hydroponics would be a good idea. And space station maintenance, air systems, water recycling. Accounting and business management. Hell, I could also sell out and do," she flung her arms out, "anything."

She looked at him and grinned. "The one thing I'm not going to do is go back to hoping for a cubicle and an apartment all my own. That is no longer on my list.

"Umm, sorry about the rant. I think we need to talk to Mac." She looked around to see if she could spot him.

"And the Wall Street Gang. We do not yet own the station."

To her surprise, Kissy and Misty were making a glum tableau at a table. "Hi, what's up?" she asked, trying for a cheerful tone.

"Absolutely nothing," Misty sighed. "All these single men everywhere, and we just flat don't want to anymore." She explained obliquely.

"Hmm," Jenny sat down in the third chair. "Cap and I have been talking about what we'd do if we did get the station. One of the things it will need is a hotel. Do you two know anything about hotels?"

Kissy giggled. "Oh we've worked plenty of hotels." She sobered a bit. "Actually, before I got desperate I worked in several motels, maid, front desk, that sort of thing. Hotels aren't that big a deal, or at least a small one wouldn't be."

"Space station hotels are usually pretty big, they're just either full or empty, depending on what ships are in or laying over and so forth," Misty said.

"The 'Far Seeker' was small, by most standards, because it was long range, it carried fuel instead of people," Jenny mused. "Once the station is operating, ships with a thousand passengers could pass through the rift easily. But most of them would just stop for fuel, most of the passengers wouldn't need rooms. Have you seen Mac anywhere around? He'd probably know this kind of stuff."

"And a restaurant," said Misty, looking over her shoulder at the hotel restaurant. "Maybe Georges would like his own restaurant?"

"There should be a spacecrete sprayer somewhere on the station, but I did not see it," Cap said. "There was a lot of that metal mesh, however. We could easily make lots of rooms like these." He pointed above them. "Add the plumbing."

"There were molds for the lavatory fixtures, I found them while grubbing around in the stacks," Kissy said, looking more and more interested.

"So we could make the hotel." He looked at Jenny. "What about the sewage?"

"I have no idea of the capacity of the water recycling system," she admitted. "That's certainly one of the things I need to find out."

Misty was doodling on a paper napkin. "Kissy, you remember that really pretty place on Zapata? All the tile roofs and stucco and those pretty gardens? We could do something like that, a series of courtyards, two or even three levels."

"Oh, that place was marvelous. Remember the fountains?" She bent over Misty's napkin. "We could start with just one or two courtyards and expand if..."

Chapter Forty-Seven
The First Day of the Miss Outer Space Contest

The Dreaded Interview. It was easily the most nerve-wracking part of the Miss Outer Space contest. Half a prepared sales pitch for her region, half a question and answer grilling. The only part of the judging to be done "in private," if seven judges, two vidcams with techs, two contest representatives, and the door warden could be called private. It was not so much a test of knowledge, as a test of grace and poise while being interviewed in front of vidcams.

Nicole walked up gracefully, radiating confidence, smiling. She sat gracefully, legs and hips turned slightly to the right, torso twisted back to the left to face the judges, hands clasped and resting lightly on her left thigh, upright, poised and graceful. At least it was supposed to look that way, it was actually a bit uncomfortable, but she would only be here for seven minutes.

The door warden finished introducing her and faded back, timer in hand, as the first judge asked her first question. Standard and predictable, asking about the Great Plains, she answered confidently and easily meeting the woman's eyes and then the other panel members, all the while talking warmly and glowingly about her much beloved home.

On a few of the questions she had to mix and match from several themes; she actually surprised one of the men with her firm stand on standing up to violence. Did he actually expect a soft platitude after what she'd been through the last two months? Then her time was up and flashing an even brighter smile, she rose gracefully and let the door dragon usher her away.

Nicole waited until the door was closed behind her before heaving an audible sigh of relief. She returned to her seat, almost collapsing with the realization that one of the main ordeals was over.

The contestants were split into three pools for the contests, labeled Alpha, Beta, and Gamma in the tradition of the old Miss America Pageant sorority type Greek letters, even though they were using different ones. Today and tomorrow they would all be interviewed, and the day after that the public portion of the contest would start with her Gamma group doing the evening gown portion, Wednesday they would do swimsuits, and Thursday the talent segment.

Ethereal and Aria were both in Alpha and would do Talent the first night. The lucky dogs, she'd have to do hers after at least two thirds of the others had already maxed out the judges' sensibilities. Not to mention that on just that day they would have already had to sit through twenty-five swimsuit contestants, and still had to judge the last twenty-five evening gown contestants after the talent segment.

Well, she'd lucked out with an early interview, and caught their attention. The judges would remember her. The next best thing would have been first day swimsuit. Oh well. It wasn't something she could control, and therefore not worth worrying about.

After the three days of the preliminaries, all the contestants would stew until Saturday evening, mentally dissecting their various performances while dieting like mad so as to still fit into their favorite dresses. Then they'd all troop on stage at the big arena where they'd announce the ten finalists, who would instantly fly into overdrive to do it all over again in one night for the celebrity judges and the public. And then the final announcement.

Had she done all right in this interview? Had she already blown it? Dammit, this was as bad as being hijacked. Her nerves were worse than when there were dead bodies on the floor and guns pointed at her. Why was she doing this to herself?

She could tell from the posture who had been in already, she'd been in about the middle of her group, and now the next tense girl was called through, a rather washed out child from some group of colony worlds, none large enough to qualify for a contestant of their own. The girl relaxed forcibly, and with a bright confident smile strolled through the door.

Good Luck keeping up the front, honey!

Nicole wondered how hard it would be to glowingly present a handful of backwater farming or mining planets.

She got her poise back and sat gracefully, but in a more comfortable position, until the entire group was done and they were released. They all looked wistfully at the bar as they strolled past, but there would be no public drinking this week, and probably no private drinking either. Not a one of them dared risk bloating on liquids, no matter what nanos they used. Back to slim and trim by tomorrow or the next day didn't cut it when you had to fit into an already tight swimsuit first thing in the morning. A girl didn't get this far without iron control of her appetite.

They stopped for a moment when a group of vid-toting newsies appeared, but they were allowed only official interviews now that the competition had officially started, so they just smiled at the questions and passed on.

She saw Michael across the room, sitting and talking with some men she didn't recognize, he didn't gesture her over, so she looked around, ah, there was the gang, even Jenny, waiting for her.

"How was it?" Barbara Pearson took the lead as they all swooped in to hear about it. Was that a newsie that had snuck in past hotel security in the background? Would he have a concealed vidcam?

"I think it went well, not nearly as frightening as being

382

hijacked." She smiled and led them all to the lifts. If that was a newsie, that little gem should be worth a sound bite this evening!

Now what she needed was to get out of sight so she could completely collapse and relax and chatter a bit. Wash off the makeup and slather on a skin restorer. She'd better relax while she could. There'd be rehearsals this afternoon and all day tomorrow for the group stage productions, and there was no way she'd be one of the klutzes standing around in the background, barely able to sway in time to the music!

Chapter Forty-Eight
Second Day of the Miss Outer Space Contest

"I haven't recognized anyone he talked to from the station recordings, or in person." Jenny flopped into the comfortable chair and put her feet up on the bed. "Nor anyone around town."

One quick glance at the frantic beauty pageant activity had driven them from Paris' suite to Cap's room.

"And he hasn't said a word out of place for a pissed off businessman about to dive into open politics," Paris groused. He sat down, then with a groan, laid flat on his back on the bed. Jenny frowned, wondering how much of his apparent recovery was just a front he put up in public.

"What about Descartes and Zimmer? Have they said anything?" she asked.

Paris glanced over at Lieutenant Bryson, and at his shrug, answered. "Fleet still has them, but from what they are sharing with us mere policemen, they aren't talking at all. The other ones have told their life story, but it doesn't do us a bit of good. Not one of them knew Zimmer was their inside man, so we can neither convict nor clear Bornstein as the same." He blew out his breath in something close to a laugh. "The Fleet people must be tearing their hair out and dreaming of pharmaceuticals."

"New pharmaceuticals," Bryson corrected. "I assure you they've tried all the old ones. They both have complete spectrum immunity. Even to a few we, ourselves, don't have vaccinations for. We've got lots of names of pirates from the small fry, but none of them show up as having passed through the local ports."

"I'd think any sensible pirate would avoid the place while the UCP conference is going on. Whatever his usual activities, Michael may be doing nothing but politicking now." Jenny frowned. She'd been informally keeping an eye on Michael, on top of the official surveillance. She eyed the Lieutenant. "What about his comm calls?"

Lieutenant Bryson radiated disapproval from every stiff inch as he sat in a straight chair at the small table. "We could not possibly discuss that with civilians." Bryson not only didn't approve of women trolling for pirates on the city streets, they weren't even allowed to help with the brainstorming. May be he just didn't approve of women doing anything. May be it was an effect of the low female population on the frontier? Overprotective males might be a natural result, she supposed, although the vids always showed strong independent women defending the homestead from hostile whatevers.

"I've overheard bits and pieces of his conversations," said Cap. "It was all politics; he sounded like he was trying to convert the locals."

"Not just locals." The Lieutenant scowled at him (obviously a worse security breach than a woman). "A lot of his contacts have been with men who've come in from the nearby systems for the conference. I think we'll see him trying for a withdrawal of the Petition before the conference delegates vote."

"Did you catch his interview today?" Jenny asked, then continued even though they nodded their heads. "He's challenging the Fleet to find the missing passengers to prove their concern and competence. He's putting up a reward and says the people of the New Territories can do a better job than the UCP."

"Could he know where they are?" Cap asked. "Is he keeping them somewhere, to produce dramatically at the proper moment?"

"Damn, I don't know whether to hope that's it or not!" Paris thumped the bed in frustration.

"I'd like to think they could be rescued," said Bryson, "but Bornstein pulling a stunt like that would stink of a deliberate setup. He couldn't possibly get away with it."

"If he gets the petition withdrawn, what might his future plans be?" Jenny asked. "Would he try to form a government, with of course himself in charge?"

"I don't think he's that well known." Paris hesitated. "Yet."

"He could go from offering rewards to forming a local 'Militia' to trace the women. He could get his pirate buddies to be the militia, and track down the women. After all, they know where they are. Hold elections, with periodic reports of his militia rescuing yet another of the 'Far Seeker' women, all through the campaign season." Jenny wrinkled her nose. "Please tell me that wouldn't work!"

Even the Lieutenant could only look sour.

Paris sighed. "Well, it would have to stretch through a constitutional convention and so forth as well, but it is broadly believable."

"The pirates could all wind up as the police and military of the Territories." Cap frowned. "So first we should ensure that the annexation petition is granted. What is Bornstein most likely to do?"

"Something dramatic during the Miss Outer Space Pageant?" wondered Jenny. "It's certainly getting a lot of vid time, and everyone important will be at the stadium for the final day."

"The stadium holds fifty thousand people and is sold out." Paris shoved himself up to a sitting position. "Mostly the same people who will be there the following week to witness the formal UCP vote on the petition. The movers and shakers of the New Territories."

"We shouldn't rule out the next three days. They'll all be broadcast, even if the live audience is only, what, five

388

thousand?" Jenny shrugged. "All the sponsors will be there, including Michael, and quite a few of the New Territories people have gotten tickets. Just not as many of the inner zone lobbyists and diplomats. So it might be just as good a venue for his purposes as the final day."

"Where are your seats?" Paris asked. "All the sponsors are displayed ringside, surrounding the judges."

"The friends and family reserved section is opposite you then," said Jenny. "I believe the FarCo bought seats for the 'Far Seeker' passengers that didn't already have tickets?" Cap nodded confirmation. "I don't know where though."

"There were only twenty three of us without tickets, and of course they didn't buy any for the crew," Cap put in. "But the children aren't very interested, so they've swapped them around quite a bit so the crew will all get into one session or another." He pulled a card from his pocket. "347B, for the finale, thirty-one in the gallery for the convention center auditorium."

"Damn." Paris scowled. "You're far away from anywhere you could be of help. Jeff," he turned to the Lieutenant. "See if you can bag a backstage pass or whatever they are called here."

"We will have people of our own," the Lieutenant was stiffer than ever, "all over the place. The Fleet does not require the assistance of either the Red Guards or the Girl Scouts."

Paris slapped his right hand over his mouth and reduced his laughter to snorts, wrapping his left arm around his ribs. After a moment he got it back under control. "Ouch! Don't say things like that!" He pressed a hand to his chest and breathed carefully.

"Lieutenant, have you read my report? Girl Scout, oh, ouch, ouch, ouch. Then read it again, for heaven's sake." He sat up taller, grimacing. "OK, Jenny are you as handy with a pistol as you are with a rifle? Good. I'll get you a concealable laser and holster and a pass for it. Cap, for the final night I want you either backstage or up close to the stage."

Paris glared at the Lieutenant. "If you can beat your way through the Fleet undercover security back there. Do you want any special weapons?"

"No, if I am that close, I'd rather throw things than rely on a gun."

"Things," muttered the Lieutenant, grumpy over being laughed at. "Chinese stars or knives?"

"Rocks will do nicely," said Cap. "I have been collecting." He rolled a two inch, spherical rock between his fingers for a moment, then disappeared it so quickly Jenny couldn't tell which pocket it had gone into. If it was in a pocket.

Bryson hunched his shoulders. "Rocks!" He glared at Paris. "May I have a word with you Captain?" He sounded sarcastic.

Paris rolled his eyes. "Jenny, Cap, would you mind
390

stepping out for a moment?"

"No problem." Jenny headed for the door, followed by Cap.

As the door closed behind them, Cap asked, "Which one of them is in charge, do you think?"

"Paris. Fortunately. The Lieutenant said himself that the Fleet is in charge in space and Criminal Investigations on planets. They battle it out on stations, but usually it's still CI. Here it's pretty clear."

"Good. What is a Girl Scout?"

She grinned. "An organization for female children; it teaches camping and first aid and so forth." She hesitated. "And so forth includes things like cooking and sewing, so he was both calling me a child and disparaging my competence at the rough stuff, because I'm a woman."

He leaned comfortably back against the wall to think this over. "There are women in the Joint Fleet, in police organizations, in the government, even the Red Dawn Revolutionary Council has two women members, and we are considered backward and repressive. Isn't that an odd attitude?"

"He's from the frontier, where women are scarce and I suppose tend to be overprotected. And some worlds were colonized by odd subsets of human society." She shrugged. "Or it could be an unfortunate personal experience, or something. Maybe he just doesn't like fat chicks."

The door opened, and Lieutenant Bryson stalked past with a glare.

"Bet you he's off to his superiors to try and go over your head," Jenny said as she walked back in.

"Probably," Paris admitted. "And he's probably right about not involving you two, but I don't trust the Fleet to have the same sensibilities to, umm, collateral damage that we CI types do."

"So given a pirate with a hostage, they start shooting instead of negotiating?"

"Exactly. There's a place for that," Paris added. "If they'd found the 'Crazy Lady' with you as a hostage, they would have been right to blow it to pieces, you can't let people like that get away and in space you have few alternatives. But you don't do that onstage before fifty thousand live spectators and millions in the vid audience. Especially not when you're trying to get those spectators to cozy up with you. With this vote coming up we have to demonstrate competence and restraint, all at once. It's, it's..."

"Politics?" Jenny offered.

"Exactly." Paris nodded, then looked at his watch. "Showtime! Nicole has Evening Gown first, doesn't she?" Jenny nodded. "Ethereal and Aria have Talent." He groaned as he levered himself off the bed. "I really need to get back to just plain old police stuff, undercover sucks," he added, as he examined his makeup in the mirror.

392

In the Rift

"How'd you wind up doing this, anyway?" Jenny asked curiously.

"It wasn't intended as a long-term covert operation." Paris shrugged. "At one time I was a plain old, well actually a raw newbie, narc. We were working with a crash rock star who was being blackmailed into smuggling zombie nanos around the world.

"As an excuse for traveling with him, we put together an opening act for his show using anyone in the force with the faintest flicker of musical ability and a bunch of showmanship. By the end of the tour, we'd spotted twelve local rings, bagged the source, closed the factory, and become a top ten crash rock group." He grinned in memory.

"It was pretty strange, but so useful they kept it up for a while, thinking the fad would fade and we could get back to work, but there's so much money and drugs floating around So Cal that I never stopped being useful."

"I could make some comments about faintest flicker, but I suppose it wouldn't be polite," Jenny remarked.

"I played the bassoon in High School, I'll have you know, young lady! I was first chair."

Even more dryly, she said, "Ah, a High School mentality. That would explain what you do with your bassoon on stage. It should be illegal."

Paris felt himself blushing. "Well, we figured outrageous showmanship would make up for lack of musical ability; we didn't think it would last."

"I still remember what my Dad said, the first time he watched one of your vids."

He eyed her warily. "I think I'm going to regret this. What did your Dad say?"

She deepened her voice to male mimicry. "If I saw my dog wiggling around like that, I'd take him to the vet and get him wormed."

Paris started snickering helplessly, waved wordlessly and left.

"I wish I had a gun already." Jenny chewed a fingernail.

"I wish I were closer to you." Cap frowned down at her. "You get into trouble too easily, and there will be half an auditorium in panic between us if something happens."

When they got to the auditorium, however, they found that the organizing committee had done some fast rearranging and PR work and gotten all the 'Far Seeker Heroes' seated together behind the judges and sponsors where the multitude of vidcams would be able to catch both the contestants, the judges and the Farseeker group. Cap looked vastly relieved, and they negotiated seats together at the forward end. They couldn't see all of the recessed stage, but could get there if something happened. They did have a good view of the runway and the entire audience.

The opening song and dance performance tried to include all the evening gown contestants equally, but

394

couldn't help but focus attention on the women with the best voices and dancing ability. Nicole was front and center with two other women, doing twice as much work as the next line of dancers, the third line managed a few simple steps pretty much at the same time. Two women carried the singing while five more hummed in the background.

Jenny leaned over to Cap and said, "A lot of these women are talented solo performers, and very good musicians, they're just klutzes when it comes to group dance, or don't have good singing voices."

Cap was scanning the audience, rather than watching what little they could see of the stage, and nodded absently. Then he looked at her curiously. "Can you sing?"

"Not well enough for something like this," She admitted reluctantly. "If I were insane enough to pursue something like this, I'd probably . . . well, I don't know. I like drawing and painting but the performing arts are not really my forte."

"I suppose a demonstration of language proficiency would not do for the male equivalent?" Laughter in his voice.

She snorted. "You obviously have not seen the male equivalent. It involves the massive over-development of every muscle of the body, and for its proper display, the men shave all their body hair and oil themselves up and go through a routine that is just a series of poses to show off their best muscle groups. It is, believe it or not, much worse than this."

Cap eyed her uncertainly.

"True story. 'Mr. Outer Space' is a lumpy androgynous caricature of humanity." She hesitated, then answered honestly. "When they're not greased up and posing, really muscular men are very attractive."

He settled back to consider this as the swim-suited beauties started their stroll. After the third one, he nodded. "Rather like the unsettling juxtaposition of famine starved bodies with incredibly large and apparently healthy breasts?"

"Exactly, although I believe the Mr. Outer Space contest bans implants."

His brows drew together, and over the wolf whistles of the enthusiastic mostly male crowd, asked uneasily. "What do they implant?"

"They used to clone their own muscle tissue and transplant it in parallel with their own. The results were even less aesthetically pleasing than the standard obsessive weightlifting musculature. Grotesque, in my opinion."

His lip twitched. "You seem very well informed, given your disinterest."

"Can't escape finding out about stuff like that growing up with a big sister like Nicole." She grinned.

A professional group of acrobats (imported for the occasion) tumbled down the runway to a sprightly tune from the live orchestra (imported for the occasion), while the stage was quickly reconfigured behind an opaque field.

He added, "Cloning and implanting muscle tissue does sound bad."

"Not as bad as some of the talent about to be displayed, I'm afraid."

But in fact, at this level all the contestants were reasonably good, and all professionally trained. Ethereal Savannah's flute solo was delightful, and got its deserved applause, some of the dance numbers were merely unmemorable, two quite good, three of the singers were good, including Aria Dune, whose medley of old favorites was well chosen to display a wonderful range. A few of the instrumentalists could easily have gone professional, including a pianist from the frontier of zone three who would no doubt be a star in a symphony orchestra in very short order.

Then the evening gowns. "The poor things are supposed to display their personality, poise and expression in less than one minute," Jenny whispered.

Nicole, in the middle of the group, took her tour, with no one but the judges knowing how she scored.

Then the Beta group took the stage having swapped swimsuits for matching costumes for the closing production, and the first night was over with no sign of disruption.

Chapter Forty-Nine
Reports and Investigations

Paris sucked down coffee and scanned the report
updates. It looked like CI had ears everywhere.

The Brown's, the Denver's, and the Ellis's hadn't known
each other prior to leaving Earth.

Herman Brown had bought into a new operation on
Confetti, one of the more settled planets of the territories.
His experience in the Earthside manufactories was much
needed, and would have helped Confetti shift from exporting
refined metals and importing machinery to manufacturing
their own heavy machinery, vehicles and so forth. Helen had
notified them of her husband's death, telling them that she
would be selling out, but had not yet heard back from them.

The Denvers had been planning to be pioneering dirt
farmers. Now Irene was wondering if she could get a job as a
school teacher here on Autumn, she'd taught everything
from Kindergarten to Junior High School English, back on
Earth.

Jackie Ellis had been a data entry clerk before she
married, she had already applied with the government offices
here. Her late husband John had been a mathematician, with
a position promised with the University here.

Obadiah Latham was totally focused on Aria and the beauty pageant. Paris snorted to see that the conversation he'd had with Latham over breakfast was referred to, and Latham's indifferent support of membership when Paris had asked him outright for an opinion on the annexation. CI literally had nothing else on him.

The tapntrace on Misty and Kissy's comm had revealed absolutely nothing. A watch of their contacts had been unedifying; they didn't appear to be working, and hung around mostly with the other Far Seeker passengers, especially Jenny, Cap and Georges. Apparently they were making plans for a hotel and restaurant if they gained ownership of the pirate station.

Georges' comm calls were equally uninteresting; when out around town he had been looking at restaurant equipment. He'd conferred quite often with Jenny about vat tech and hydroponics. A side note from an anonymous CI agent noted that neither of them had a clue about either subject and would most likely poison everyone on the station within a year. Paris snickered a bit over that, and made a mental note to say something to Jenny.

MacGregor had sent a flurry of messages off, as soon as they had arrived. Unfortunately, both Criminal Investigations and Fleet had dropped the ball. By accident or intent, Mac had sent the messages from a terminal that was outside of fleet monitoring, before CI had instituted complete coverage of the de-hijacked passengers. The messages he been sending since were all business related, and the CI cipher types hadn't been able to do more than speculate about code words. Their convoluted reasoning about what might or might not be a phrase with secret meaning was worse than the worst High School English assignment analysis of a short work Paris had ever seen.

Mac's actions were unexceptional, he'd talked only with a few politicians whom he knew personally, and seemed to favor annexation, although he'd mostly stuck to small talk and only spoke about the petition when others brought up the subject. Of course, just now there were only three things being talked about – the Petition, the Far Seeker Hijacking and the Beauty Pageant.

Cap baffled the CI. They had copied and translated his report to the Red Council. It had been brief and factual and hadn't even mentioned the Conference on the Annexation.

Paris stretched and flipped off the comp. What he really wanted was the dirt on Bornstein, but there didn't seem to be any. And now he was playing clean. Not a word that could be construed as in support of the hijackers. Lots against the UCP, but all in terms of outrage over the hijacking. Paris wasn't even certain of his position on the petition. "Do what's right or go to hell" seemed to be the gist of both his public and private pronouncements.

Paris shook his head at the comp. He wasn't going to get

the answers he really wanted until a ship got back from Beta Pegasi. If then. Perhaps he could dig up a few more answers himself. He signed himself out of the JCI office.

Strolling across the central plaza, he spotted a few of the Far Seeker group. They were still traveling in packs and not going far afield. He wondered how much of that was a defensive habit, and how much just being in a strange place with little money. The three families were out in force, the oldest boy breaking off what looked like a game of tag when he spotted Paris.

"Are you going to have a concert while you're here?"

Paris raised his eyebrows. "No, I'm just along to help Ethereal." He eyed the kid dubiously, he was a bit young. "Do you like my music?"

"Nah, it's stupid. All about girls." They'd been walking back toward the seated women as they talked, and Adam's mother shook her head reprovingly.

Paris grinned. "You'll look back fondly on this attitude, soon enough." He looked inclusively around the little group. "Have you decided what you're going to do yet?"

Helen Brown nodded. "The people from Confetti have been very nice. I talked last night to John Ribbons, who's at the conference representing the planet. They've suggested that we travel out and see Confetti before making up our minds where to settle. The company Herman had bought into said to go ahead and use the tickets, and they guaranteed our return all the way to Earth, if that was what we decided. Apparently the return is part of their life insurance policy, and Herman was covered. I can also use the money there, if I wanted to open a business or join a business partnership there. That's the way they've set up their whole economy, lots and lots of partnerships."

Adam nodded and his two brothers copied him. "Maybe we'll buy a ranch, and be cowboys."

"Mom, I want to be a cowboy, too!" Rena Denver started bouncing. "I want a horse! Daddy said I could have a horse!"

Irene rolled her eyes, and exchanged glances with Jackie Ellis as the entire child cohort decided as one to demand horses. "We'll see." She ran out the standard parents waffle, generating a doubling of equine demands.

Paris grinned. "Since you all get along so well, maybe you should all look into Confetti ranches." He waved a general goodbye and retreated from the increasing volume.

He hadn't managed to ask how they felt about the annexation, but did it matter? There just wasn't any way he could bend his brain around any of them being in league with the hijackers. He walked into the hotel and spotted Cap just exiting the lifts.

"I suppose it's a madhouse up there?" he asked.

"Yes. The entire floor is flooded with pre-show nerves. I would advise you avoid it."

"Good idea. Join me for lunch?"

"Certainly."

Paris led the way and snagged an-out-of-the-way table. "Are you going to attend the Conference on the Annexation?" He pretended to scan the menu, waiting for a response.

Cap seemed taken aback. "No." he frowned. "I was just an eavesdropping translator disguised as a bodyguard, I have no idea what the Red Council's position is, and certainly no authority."

Paris raised his eyebrows. "Don't you even want to observe?"

Cap shook his head thoughtfully. "I . . . have been thinking, the last few days. I do not want to reopen contact with them. I was never anything but a faceless nonentity to them. I have sent my report and I will never return. It is done."

Paris bit his lip. "Will they let you go that easily?"

Cap shrugged. "How not? I am gone, and will take care to stay that way."

Paris noticed for the first time that Cap, while still dressed in black, had bought new clothes. Cutting his ties with the past.

"And what of you? Have you found out anything?" Cap changed the subject.

"Nothing." Paris sighed. "Everyone that I thought was innocent is acting with perfect innocence, except," he suddenly recalled, "Frank Monico who seems to be putting out feelers to several local gambling casinos."

"Any connections with the pirates?" Cap's eyes had narrowed a bit.

"Not that we've found." Paris sighed. "Nor that we can rule out, but his conversations were all about financial backing for starting a casino on the pirate station."

"A casino?" Paris started as Jenny spoke from behind him. "Interesting concept, but not if it's going to bring in any sort of organized crime."

Paris twisted around to look at her. "Not helping your sister?" he kidded, wondering how much he could grill her in front of Cap.

"Nah. She's got more than enough experts picking on her as it is." She plonked down in the chair he shifted out toward her. "Anything interesting beyond the casino?"

"Nope. Still no word from Beta Pegasi." He eyed her. "How many of Nicole's entourage were hired by Bornstein?"

"If you mean, who were strangers that might be helping him, no one. We've known the Pear forever." Apparently he looked blank. "Sorry, Mrs. Barbara Pearson. She lived next door to us when we were growing up, she's, oh, eight years older than Nicole, maybe? She helped Nicole in a lot of her early contests, and if you knew what a backstabbing, well, I guess you do, venue the contests are, you know how unusual that is. Anyhow, as soon as Nicole had the money to hire anyone, the Pear was it. The others we knew fairly well, they organized a lot of the local contests, worked as volunteers in the regional and state contests, gave makeup and dress workshops and so forth. They're very good at what they do, and were all logical choices." She grimaced. "This trip was partly by way of a reward for lots of work done on the circuit."

"But they're not actually friends, like Stephanie, Gail, Heidi..." He trailed off the list as she nodded.

"Right, they're people Nicole knew from the shows; the others are Nicole's High School clique, like her they sort of attend college part time, work part time, and bar hop every weekend." She sighed. "You know, some of the women in these contests are quite bright; college graduates competing for money so they can go to grad school. Miss Avila just got her PhD in superconducting physics. Why does my sister insist on acting like some wild rockstar?" Her eyes twinkled at him.

"I don't know." Paris admitted. "Ethereal could easily get into a big city symphony, she's nearly got her PhD in Music, but she wants to be Miss Outer Space, and that's that. Part of it, I suppose is the desire to prove she's as good, as pretty, as any Earther." He shrugged. "Some Alphans are a bit insecure about our messed up gene pool."

"She's First Family isn't she? She denies it so fiercely I figured she had to be. Are you?"

"Heavens, yes! My great, great, great whatever was one

of Mata Hari's gang, he's the pilot that hijacked the Chamberlain, and you'd better believe he did not return to Earth after FTL was discovered." Paris grinned at her surprised expression. "Actually I've got a bunch of other firsters in my background, yes, including ichimps, but Mycroft Perris is the most famous one, not that you ignorant Earthers know any history but your own."

"Actually, our history lessons, for some odd reason, concentrate on the noble Space Marines that sort of almost un-hijacked the ship." She grinned back. "Got any of those in your background?"

"Well, yes, but we keep quiet about it." He grinned back. "I mean, without hijacking a spaceship, they're not hardly authentic Alphans. And don't make any comparisons to this lot we just dealt with." He mock frowned at her. "We didn't kill anybody." He cleared his throat. "Hardly."

She looked dubious, then grinned at him. "It's just about the only interesting bit of history they teach, anymore. Odd what three hundred years perspective can do."

Chapter Fifty
Third Day of the Miss Outer Space Contest

The Convention Center auditorium was again packed. In this overwhelmingly male frontier, they probably could have sold out the stadium every night. Nicole eeled out on cue in high heels and a swimsuit that skimmed the bare edges of 'modest'. Emphasis on bare.

"And another contestant from Earth, Miss Great Plains, Nicole Peace!"

She swept her smile around the auditorium, with extra attention for the judges. Especially the four men. *Oh, handsome, I do love you, I want to get private and even nakeder.* She thought, and tried to broadcast, *I'm beautiful, fit and healthy, and I exist just for you!* Down to the end of the runway and back. *I am the conqueror of all I survey, and you are next!*

And then she was back offstage, with the third of the four stages over, gone and irredeemable. She grabbed the robe Barbara held out, and hustled over to where she could peek out. She could see the contestants face-on just before they walked on, could see in their faces what wouldn't show in a second as they came into the view of the crowd. The nerves, the uncertainty, the fear. For some, the contempt for those that dared to judge them like livestock. Even anger on a few. And the probable winners of the swimsuit segment, the ones like her that got a total sexual thrill out of that many men drooling, and gave it right back at them.

Then it was time for the talent demonstrations. The first one was a dance number, and she watched jealously. Nancy Danger, Miss Europe, had a comedy dance routine, acting out an editorial role with an oversized red pencil that matched her hair. She was good enough to get a few laughs from the audience, and Nicole ground her teeth in frustration. Even though each performance was supposed to be rated on its own merit, the judges couldn't help but subconsciously compare them all. The next dancer, thank god, was slow and tedious.

She dashed back to the dressing room, where Barbara, Paula, and Irene had her outfit for the group production show laid out. She dressed quickly, then returned backstage to watch two more dances separated by an appalling singer. One of the dances was fast, flashing and athletic. Damn! Not good. She rushed back for a makeup refresh, then trooped out with her group for a lively little song and dance. She, and two other contestants, both gymnasts, were out front doing all the work and garnered most of the attention and applause. Excellent!

Then it was back into the dressing room as the evening gown contestants trooped out for their trip down the runway

410

'displaying Poise, Personality, Expression, Energy, and Attractiveness.' And from the best of them, that elusive attribute called 'Star Quality'.

For this first round of judging, the interview counted forty percent, with swimsuit, talent, and evening gown getting twenty percent each. But on the final night, an all-new panel of 'Celebrity' judges would decide among the top ten preliminary scorers. There would be no interview as such, but the evening gown section would include a question from the judges, and then the girls' intelligence, ability to communicate, and star quality would make or break them.

Nicole watched on the vid, studying the clothes, and the crowds' response to each one. The judges were not immune from subconscious herd behavior. What the crowd liked did influence them, whether they admitted it or not. She'd done well yesterday in evening gown, but perhaps a few adjustments to her other gown might be a good idea. If she made the final ten.

Ethereal swooped backstage with a gleeful smile, tossing off, "I maxed out the applause meters, dahhhhling," in the most irritating drawl imaginable. Her gown was cut simply, with green and blue sparkles on a deep blue background. She looked fantastic.

Goaded, Nicole raised her eyebrows. "Oh, was that your applause, I thought it was for Aria?" Bland smile.

Ethereal's smirk froze, and she stalked past without

saying more.

Nasty bitch, pity she's the prettiest of the three of them, and so good on that flute! The flash of niceness underneath it all that had surfaced during the hijacking and escape was well buried, now. Which was even more of a pity.

I will not be like that!

Nicole spotted Aria coming offstage and waited until Ethereal was out of sight. "I can't believe the crowd goes for the metallics. Bachelors!"

"Honestly, Nicole." Aria smiled wryly. "You know as well as I do that they're cheering our notoriety."

Nicole shook her head. "You need to lose the honesty, Aria, we're all primo egotists this week."

Aria stuck out her tongue. "I thought we were all back stabbing bitches? You shouldn't needle Ethereal, we're all uptight enough as it is." She grinned as she headed off to change, leaving Nicole frowning.

I am not a backstabbing . . . Ethereal deserved to have a bit of wind taken out of her sails . . . Oh, all right . . . I shouldn't have said that. And I shouldn't have harped on Aria's metal fetish.

Her brief flirt with shame was interrupted by the thunderous applause from the auditorium intermixed with the rumble of crowd movement and the second day was over.

Chapter Fifty-One
Stock Holders Meeting

Jenny squeezed into the packed room as Quincy called the meeting to order. Paris made as if to stand and offer his chair to her, she glared him down, and stood on tiptoe to see through the crowd. All twenty-nine owners of the Long Rift Salvage Company were packed into the biggest room in the Wall Street Gang's suite for their 'first annual' shareholders meeting.

"Okay, we've gotten the preliminary offers in and need to look them over. The two cargo ships have two different owners, but both have offered and sent to escrow the standard ten percent salvage award. I don't see any point in fighting for more, this is the standard."

Jenny could see Barry, Carl, and Terry all nodding glumly.

"Now, the space station was insured, and in the interim the legal ownership has fallen to the insurance company. Their offer is twenty percent of value, in the form of common stock in a new company owning the station. I recommend we make a counter offer," Quincy was in his element here, barely glancing at the notepad in his hand, "of sixty percent, in view of the fact that we not only freed the station from the hijackers, but also defended it from a subsequent pirate attack. If they compromise at forty percent, that will still be a big chunk of cash if we sell it, and not too difficult to obtain a controlling interest if we want to run it."

Steven broke in. "Mac is already making plans; if the insurance company sells its shares, which it sounds like it will, I'll bet he'll jump in and bag a sizable chunk."

Everyone nodded agreeably, Mac was nearly one of them, and it was rather reassuring to know that an established businessman wanted to buy in with them on this step into the unknown.

"Then there is the pirate ship 'Crazy Lady'." Quincy grinned at the spacers. "Being unable to determine any registry or form of identification that would indicate the legal ownership of that ship, it is declared forfeit to the court and our petition for ownership is approved."

Carl whooped. "That is one nice little ship! Fast as all get out!"

"What about cargo space?" Barry was grinning as he tried to pick holes.

"What kinds of engines?" Terry asked. "Dang, I never even looked at it!" He was grinning too.

"The other claims we filed are still pending," Quincy continued. "The Planet as Salvage and the New System Claim may have to be tested in court. The outcome is anybody's guess.

414

In the Rift

"We also filed for assisting party salvage of any other ships that are found derelict in the system. I would expect three to five percent if the ships are repairable. The fact that they were not fenced may mean that they are without value as anything but scrap. There may be rewards for some of them. The accumulation of junk in the station will take a while to inventory and trace, but we should get ten percent if it can be traced, and sole ownership if it can't." He sat back. "That's it, folks."

Jenny cleared her throat. "I move we accept the bids on the two cargo ships, accept ownership of the 'Crazy Lady', and negotiate as you recommend on the space station claim."

"I second the motion," Helen Brown stepped in quickly.

"Do I hear a motion to consider any of these matters separately?" Quincy asked, and was answered with silence and head shakes all around. "All in favor, raise your hands; all against? We have a unanimous approval of the motion."

In the back, Adam could be heard gloating to his brothers in a gleeful semi-whisper. "A pirate ship! We own a pirate ship!"

"I don't like the name." Seven-year-old Rena Denver stated. "It's nasty."

"We can change it, can't we?" Irene asked.

"Easily, in fact it doesn't have any official number or name at this point." Barry grinned at the kids. "Why don't you kids see what you can come up with for a new name."

"I know! I know!" Toni was jumping up and down waving her hand wildly. "Princess Power!"

"Oh barf!" yelled one of the boys.

Jenny ducked out of the room with Obadiah and Paris. "Barry's going to regret that idea."

"He probably already is," Obadiah glanced at his watch and ruefully told Paris, "Time for us to go." He added in an aside to Jenny, "We sponsors' representatives have to be seated early."

Paris sniffed. "I'm beginning to realize that you like all this!"

"Oh, I do!" Obadiah chuckled. "For all I claim otherwise, it's great fun for the gals, and even if they don't make the top ten, they get scholarships, and they've had a great experience." His face fell briefly. "Usually. This is my eighth year as the East Coast Sponsor's Rep, and I've loved every one of them." He hesitated. "Well, a few of the girls were tedious." He turned a stern gaze on Jenny. "And don't go thinking I slept with them all either! Aria's special. Aria's . . . Aria's a keeper, I think."

Jenny grinned. "And have you popped the question?"

"God no!" he exclaimed. "Not in the middle of this riot. Later, when everything has settled down, and," he ran a hand through his thinning hair, "Maybe after another round of rejuve." He looked embarrassed to have displayed this vanity. "Of course, if she wins, I wouldn't dare ask until next year. Miss Outer Space has Hell's own schedule, running everywhere for interviews and public appearances and fundraisers for every charity on or off Earth."

Dropping down the lift created a brief hiatus in the conversation.

"Huh," at the bottom, Paris was still boggled. "Eight times? You've done this eight times, and don't even usually sleep with the girl?"

"Umm, well actually, umm, never before," admitted Obadiah. "Most of the regions have tons of corporate sponsors and the girls don't need private backing. It's the girls from poor regions that get pressured into situations they'd rather avoid." He frowned down at Jenny. "I'd heard that the Great Plains Pageant and Scholarship fund is hurting this year, what with the downturn in petrochemicals and steel."

"Yes, but Nicole had already fastened onto Michael," Jenny said, surprised by Obadiah's protective tone. "Nicole's always been after the money, and not picky about who she climbed in bed with." She looked at Paris. "How did you get into this?"

"Zulu is the parent company of my usual recording company, and also the main sponsor of Miss Alpha Centauri." He shrugged. "I volunteered in a moment of insanity. I've known Ethereal, I went to University with her big brother, and, err, dated her, for quite a while. Mind you, if I'd had a clue what it would be like, even without the hijacking I'd never have done it. I thought I'd be getting a rest from my live concert schedule and resting my voice and so on." He shook his head in dismay. "Well, my voice is getting a break, but," he put his hand to his chest, "My wind is definitely going to suffer."

"You'll be back in shape in no time," Obadiah said, ruthlessly. "And it's no good pretending to be the big bad crash rock star, all the girls say you're not sleeping with Ethereal, the two of you just carry on in public to fend off all the other possible nuisances."

Paris actually blushed deeply enough for it to show through his makeup. "I can't claim any moral high ground, fact is we've been fighting like cats and dogs." He shrugged, clearly embarrassed to be seen as a nice guy. "Oh, this is for you, Jenny." He fished a small packet out of his coat pocket and handed it to her.

"Thanks, see you later." She waved casually and headed back upstairs. She didn't need to get to her seat early, and she thought she should figure out where to conceal this little surprise in private.

Cap was hovering with one eye on her room and one on the lifts. She grinned at him. "You really are worried about me, aren't you?" She headed for his room.

"Why should I worry? I've only had to rescue you three times in two months." He frowned. "You're overdue for your next crisis."

Behind doors, she opened the packet. "Oh, it's a beauty!" And tiny, it nearly disappeared in her hand. After some experimentation, she attached the holster under her left breast and rearranged her scarf wrap to cover it. The laser pistol was fully charged, set to short bursts; with the short muzzle, it probably wasn't very accurate, but being low-powered the beam would scatter fast and probably wouldn't be effective at ranges over ten meters. She nodded. Short range only. Any long range shooting would be up to Fleet Security or CI.

"So, you brave enough to see what passes for talent in my family?"

He made a show of bracing himself, then grinned and ushered her through the door.

The auditorium was once again packed solid. She wondered how on earth the judges could still be ranking yet another score of swimsuited bodies. It had to be mind-numbing. She cheered Ethereal and Aria on and listened to the roar of the enthusiastic crowd. Well, maybe the male judges weren't tired of this yet.

Cap frowned at one dappled contestant. "That isn't her natural skin color, is it?"

Opal, sitting behind them, giggled. "No, it's subdermal. Totally out of style."

Jenny grinned. "The first Miss Outer Space contest I

remember seeing was at the height of the skin pattern craze."
She glanced back at Opal. "Do you remember the woman
with the Escher type patterns?"

Opal snorted. "Are you kidding? She still won't answer
questions about whether or not she was completely nude for
the talent contest."

Cap bit his lip, and Jenny's grin widened. "All her clothes
blended right into her skin and the pattern. It was impossible
to tell where skin stopped and fabric started. If it did." She
snickered a bit at his expression. "Today's 'Nude Look' is so
boring, in contrast."

A professional trio of singers that hadn't even registered
on her finished their break-filling routine and gave way to
the Talent show.

Nicole was third up, following two lackluster
performances with instruments. She got her required
dramatic lighting and jazzed up classical music. Her flame
red sparkling body suit was more dramatic than sexy,
although it was certainly skin tight. Her dance routine took
the best qualities from her gymnastic athleticism, dramatic
drill team crisp precision and had a flavor of martial arts
kata to it as well. She flowed, snapped, leaped, spun, and
kicked for her allowed three minutes, then exited to
deafening applause.

Jenny realized she was holding her breath. "Good one,
Nicki! That should move her up in the standings."

In the Rift

"Yes." Cap seemed a bit stunned, and she stomped hard on a jealous twinge.

Silly. Nicki would be horrified if he showed any interest. And . . . dammit. He's so old. I guess I'd better stick to hero worship. Or being some weird combination of boss and sidekick.

The next performer was one of the better singers, then a dancer that couldn't hold a candle to Nicole. Jenny tried to scan the crowd as the rest of the group passed through, but the lighting was on the stage and the crowd was anything but still.

The swimsuit group, in new costumes of course, trooped on to provide entertainment while the judges toted up their numbers; a pity they weren't judged on it, Arial and Ethereal starred, with Ethereal's flute dancing around Ariel's huskiest tones. Then the evening gowns were gliding gracefully down the runway and the fourth night was over. If anything was going to happen, it would be tomorrow at the vast city stadium.

Chapter Fifty-Two

Final Day of the Miss Outer Space Contest

"Ladies and Gentlemen, live from the New Territories, it's the Miss Outer Space Pageant!" The Em Cee was onstage alone, but not for long. The women started parading up the east ramp in their preassigned, theoretically random, order.

"I'm Miss Nova Tejas, Marie Curie." Smile. "I'm Miss Andes, Julianna Vera." Smile. "I'm Miss Mars and Asteroids, Roxanne Marsh." Smile.

The amplified voices and applause bounced around in the stadium, part of the high energy of the crowd. From the conversations Nicole had overheard, a lot of the people here had attended at least one of the earlier sessions, and certainly the parade, and were here to cheer on their favorites.

Rumors of heavy betting on the results had engendered much speculation as to the favorites and the odds. The officials were trying to keep a lid on gossip and had stepped up their campaign against outside contact for the last three days. They were also beaming.

Third rank newsies had been replaced by the major networks' first line of faces as fast as they could be hustled away from the political conference. The 'Far Seeker' affair had put the Pageant back on the map in a big way.

Nicole swooped out and smiled. "I'm Miss Great Plains, Nicole Peace." She could barely hear herself over the cheers. Grin. She waltzed over to her assigned place on the slowly rotating tiered platform as more contestants trooped through. Aria and Ethereal both got huge cheers. The pageant organizers were probably wondering what they could do to top this next year.

Hopefully they wouldn't be able to come up with anything.

While the rest of the contestants paraded through to introduce themselves, Nicole studied the crowd. The setting sun was low enough to not shine in the crowd's eyes. The stadium lights were bright against the deep blue sky. It would be completely dark within another hour.

The Celebrity Judging Panel was pathetic, a bunch of has-beens and second raters stalled in their careers, suddenly catapulted into the limelight and hoping to turn this into a career revival. They were the only 'celebrities' the organizers had been able to persuade to come all the way out here, when they set this up last year.

She bet there were at least a dozen real stars back home that were now tearing their hair out wishing they had accepted.

Michael was behind them and a bit to one side, among the "Sponsoring Regions Representatives." Paris was in the row directly behind him. Her fellow "Far Seeker survivors" were displayed in the next three rows, and worth a mint to the organizers. She spotted Jenny, snuggled up with that Chinaman. And Heidi, Corella and Stephanie weren't there.

Please God, let them be found quickly, and the rest too.

And now the introductions were done and the Em Cee was stepping up with a big grin on his face.

"It is my pleasure to introduce to you Miss Outer Space on the last night of her reign, Miss Maribell Cantrell." Much applause and wolf whistles. Maribell had been introduced to them backstage and given some mostly unneeded advice, but every one of them, Nicole included, had watched and envied her last year.

"And now the moment these lovely ladies have been waiting for." Dramatic pause. "The Top Ten Finalists of the Miss Outer Space Contest." He kept on beaming as he slowly, to an off stage drum roll, opened the archaic paper envelope and removed the traditional list.

"Miss Cassiopeia." Good grief, that washed out looking child that had followed her in the interviews! Well, she was a very good gymnast, and had a great figure.

The Em Cee waited until the clapping had died down before announcing the next. "Miss Alpha Centauri." Well, Ethereal was in. There was a longer pause for applause, then "Miss Tau Ceti" was getting her round of applause.

Two more outer world girls, then "Miss East Coast." Aria

pranced radiantly up to the front. Three more announcements, one from Earth, two from elsewhere.

"And the last Finalist," drum roll. "Miss Great Plains!" Nicole started breathing again and slid up to the front, hoping her smile looked natural.

She barely registered the Em Cee's patter, then they were guided offstage and down the east ramp for costuming while the losers tried to put some enthusiasm into a stage dance.

They dressed, checked their makeup, and then waited at the base of the west ramp, where the techs and all their equipment lurked. Out-of-sight, but close at hand when needed. It was the long way around from the dressing rooms, but the fastest way to get the finalists back on stage, while the other women finished the dance and were guided down the other ramp.

Then they were striding back onstage in 'a modest swimsuit' otherwise known as whatever you can best project sex appeal in while staying within the modesty rules.

Of this group of seven judges, five were men.

Thank you Lord.

And thank you, you sexy old thing, yes you, I want you. And you and you and you. What a handsome devil, let's go have some fun!

In this oblong Arena, instead of the usual runway, a walk circled the main stage; she got to see and be seen by, the entire crowd.

426

In the Rift

I lust after every single one of you!

Then it was rush back to the dressing room and into her dance outfit, this one flame red and gold. And back to wait through Ethereal's mesmerizing flute performance.

Damn, she aced that one! Nicole thought, and the wild applause agreed.

Then she was swinging onstage, and freezing in the start position and the music swept her up into it and danced with her, a long concentrated four minutes of motion and then she was utterly still again for a beat, and then bowing herself off stage.

It was always over too quickly.

Except of course to hustle off and a quick spritz to cool off and into her evening gown and all new makeup and back to the stage.

"Why," the Em Cee relayed a question from the judges to Ethereal. "Would any of the settlers of the New Territories not want to join the United Countries and Planets?"

"I think it is basic to human nature to exist in small groups, and in modern society, that is reflected in our desire to have our government answerable to us. And for that, the government has to be available." She paused for a breath. "It is a great leap of faith to place yourself under a government two months away from your problems, and a daunting challenge for that government to not fail in the trust placed in it." The crowd loved it, clapping, stomping, and whistling.

Then Ethereal was taking a turn down—around—the walkway, glowing at everyone, judges and crowd alike.

Nicole experienced a sinking feeling.

She is very, very good at this.

Then the redhead from some stellar system with an unpronounceable name got flustered and her answer barely had anything to do with the question, the brunette from South America answered like she was brain dead, and then it was her turn.

"What do you think of the old saying 'Violence never solves anything'?"

"Between nations, or other groups of people, I think that old saying is useful only before any violence occurs. Once one side of a conflict has resorted to violence, only a violent response will make them back off and accept peace."

The Em Cee looked a bit shocked.

"For instance, the pirates that have been looting and murdering all over the New Territories are not going to suddenly decide to be respectable citizens. They are going to have to be hunted down and destroyed."

She took her stroll to massive applause. These people really wanted those pirates dead.

She collapsed offstage for a few precious minutes, barely hearing the onstage voices over the background music. The losers came through for another performance while the votes were tallied. And then they were being chivvied into line and

428

trotted back onstage.

After a bit of quipping and joking, yes we are nervous, no not one of us thinks we should draw straws, actually a card game might not be a bad idea . . . Then the judges handed up the written results.

"And now ladies and gentlemen, it is time for these lovely ladies to discover who will be the next Miss Outer Space." The Emcee's voice was dramatically deep, the off stage drum roll soft as he unfolded the paper. "Of these ten ladies, five will walk out of here with major prizes. So without more waiting..."

"The fifth place goes to Miss Andes." Julianna blinked, then walked, still smiling, to hug Maribell, shake hands with the Em Cee, lean down and shake hands with the judges, both the first panel and the celebrities, then walk back to the designated place.

"The fourth place goes to Miss Cassiopeia!" And the washed out girl lit up like a torch and glowed all through her round, leaving Nicole pondering the elusiveness of 'Star Quality'.

"The third place finisher is Miss East Coast!" Only Nicole heard Aria's sigh, then, smile in place, she trooped out for hugs and handshakes.

***

"Now the suspense builds!" Jenny's attention jerked

away from the announcer as Cap elbowed her. He was staring intently to the left, toward the ramp that led down into the dressing area from the stage.

"We have only two more awards for these seven ladies. Who will be the Runner Up and who will be the new Miss Outer Space?" The Em Cee's voice faded from her consciousness as she saw the stocking masked men advancing up the ramp, pausing in the shadows, apparently counting on the announcer's showmanship to keep them unnoticed.

Cap slid out of his seat at the end of the row, sliding under the rail and dropping smoothly into the pit between the audience and the stage. Jenny hesitated, her attention caught by the sound of her sister's name.

What? What did I just miss?

***

"Now the suspense builds!"

Em Cees should be driven extinct, Nicole thought.

"We have only two more awards for these seven ladies. Who will be the Runner Up and who will be the new Miss Outer Space?" At least there was no damn drum roll again while he made a show of examining the list.

"First Runner Up goes to Miss Great Plains! Nicole Peace!" Nicole kept the smile on her face, and in some sort of odd detached emotional state, walked out and hugged the reigning Miss Outer Space, shook the Em Cee's hand, and walked down to lean over and shake the judges' hands.

But they were frowning and looking behind her. As she straightened, she was grabbed from behind, an arm around her neck, a gun at her temple.

There were thuds and screams behind her. She couldn't see, but as the man holding her pulled her back, she carefully dropped off first one high-heeled shoe then the other.

"Like the Lady said." Someone had the Em Cee's mic. "You've got to answer violence with violence. So here's our answer to the Fleet for taking Pirate Station. These ladies are coming with us, and all of you are going to sit and watch us leave, or watch us kill them in front of you."

As soon as the masked men grabbed for the contestants, they broke from their frozen stances and bolted in all directions. They certainly weren't going to get all of them, and it looked like the entire audience was rising up to assault the stage. Where were all those military types they'd been tripping over for days?

***

Then as the men boiled up the ramp and ran toward the women on stage, Jenny climbed over the rail and dropped. She could hear screams, a few thumps, but the rise of the stage above her hid the action taking place up there until futilely kicking legs waved above her, one of the contestants

431

held like a shield before a masked and armed man.

"Like the Lady said," One of the attackers must have the Em Cee's mike; the words were being broadcast. "You've got to answer violence with violence. So here's our answer to the Fleet for taking Pirate Station. These ladies are coming with us, and all of you are going to sit and watch us leave, or watch us kill them in front of you."

Jenny pressed up against the stage, drawing her pistol. From this angle, from this close, she could fire behind the woman, into his ribcage from beneath and the side, a lot of protective vests didn't cover . . . from the corner of her eye she saw Cap flowing up over the edge a dozen meters to her left. She fired. The squirming woman bounced off the edge of the stage and hit the ground beside Jenny, scrambling desperately away as the man folded more slowly. He hit the ground lifelessly, his chest bulging and gory. Internal steam explosion.

Guess this little pistol is a rated higher than I thought.

Jenny stepped on him and peeked over the edge. The stage was a riot of fleeing women, except for a few still bodies, all of masked men she was relieved to see. She spotted Cap just as he threw something with a quick snap of his arm. A pirate at the head of the ramp spilled forward, and the pirates behind him released the women they were holding to bring up their laser rifles.

Jenny steadied her arm on the edge of the stage and

snapped off a shot. As she'd feared, she was out of range, and the man just flinched back from the sudden heat, turning in her direction. His companion collapsed into him and then he was collapsing in turn as Cap scooped up a rifle and swung it into his head, not even pausing in his run down the ramp. Jenny heaved herself over the edge and trotted toward the ramp. A quick glance behind showed half the audience trying to follow her.

I hope some of them have enough sense to get out and around to the maintenance tunnel entrances.

She dodged a moaning semiconscious attacker, then flattened against the wall as a mob of panicked women stampeded up the ramp.

She ran on, following the sounds of fighting.

***

"You won't get away with this!"

Michael, oh god!

Nicole could see him mounting the stage and advancing as she was pulled down the west ramp. Even in the shock of the circumstances, she boggled over the scene there. Dead men laid out over the back half of the room like a careful tableau. Joint Fleet troops and plainly dressed men, she recognized some of the techies who had been operating one vid or another all week. The other girls were out of sight, had they gotten away?

Then Michael charged down the ramp, scooped up a JF rifle and started shooting. Missing. And the return fire was missing. And the black clad pirates manhandled a techie out, put a rifle in his hands and shoved him forward as Michael shot him and then the men were 'fleeing' with Michael shooting 'at' them. She felt cold as ice, the obvious and unavoidable conclusion hitting her like an avalanche.

The man holding her no longer had the gun to her head. Nicole sidestepped and turned enough to get a knee where it would do the most good. As he folded, she snapped two more quick kicks to make sure he'd stay down. She picked up a rifle, and all the old lessons came back. She dropped a man that was reaching for her, and when Michael turned, Nicole put the bead on his leg and fired.

***

Jenny caught up with Cap in a confused melee of hand-to-hand fighting as the flimsy walls of the temporary dressing rooms crashed down on them. Two of the pirates were staying back, rifles raised, looking for a clear shot. Jenny dropped the closest immediately, then ducked behind a screen as the other swung toward her. Peeking out the far side, she saw the position he'd last been in was occupied by two flailing figures trying to pick themselves up. The center of the room was still, bodies lying haphazardly about, except the one flowing in on the scrambling pair.

434

In the Rift

She stopped for a long moment of pure esthetic appreciation as Cap dropped them both, nearly as an afterthought, as he headed down the corridor clearly marked Emergency Exit Only.

There were two pirates well down the corridor, lurking beside a stalled forklift, and looking away from them toward the posse of former spectators advancing down the tunnel from the outside. Their escape seemed thoroughly blocked, but one of them reached into the forklift and started it rolling toward the posse.

They shadowed the rolling blockade for a dozen feet, then dodged through a door on the left. Jenny and Cap ran down the hall. Cap threw himself through the doorway in a flat trajectory and lack of cover or care that had Jenny, panting along behind, cringing. But she heard nothing and followed with barely less caution.

The back wall had been holed, a ragged gap in the lower half. Cap was listening carefully and she tried to control her breathing.

"They're running," Cap glanced up at her. "Shall we follow?"

"They must have some sort of large transport close by, for kidnapped beauty queens." She hesitated. "Let's take a look, then call for help."

***

Other people, variously dressed, no masks, Good Guys, were charging down the ramp now.

Nicole yelled, "Find the other women!" as she walked toward Michael.

"Drop it!" she ordered him, ignoring the Fleet Lieutenant and Paris who suddenly saw what was happening and skidded to a halt. "I know you're one of them."

He swung the rifle toward her and she fired again. The gun spun away as he clutched his shoulder.

"Where are Stephanie and the others? What have you done with them?"

His eyes were wild, as he pushed himself away from her. "I don't know what you are talking about! I saved you!"

"No, you had this pretty scene all set up. You were pretending to save me." She was close now, and kicked his injured leg. He screamed again, curling up. "Where were you taking these women you've grabbed tonight?"

The Lieutenant was watching with his mouth hanging open, Paris nodded. "Glad to see you finally noticed what side Michael was on."

A uniformed soldier trotted in from backstage. "We got them all on the other side." He seemed to be splitting his report between Paris and the lieutenant. "We've got a couple more live ones captured. The girls are all fine."

"Excellent." Paris nodded like an officer taking a report. *Good grief, he couldn't be.*

436

In the Rift

They all looked back at Michael. Who was not moving.

"Oh, shit! I've killed him!" Nicole wailed, and kicked him. "Where are the rest of the women!" She yelled.

"Too late." Paris felt for a pulse. "Must have nicked an artery, or maybe he had a bad heart." He blew an exasperated breath, then turned back up the ramp.

She followed him back onstage. The stands were chaotic, with most of the men trying to get down to help. Paris scooped up the fallen microphone. She recognized the piece of paper on the floor beside it and grabbed it.

"Settle down. We've got them and all of the ladies are fine." The fast departing audience wavered, uncertain whether to go or stay.

Nicole glanced down at the paper in her hand, and decided there was no reason why not. She held her hand out for the microphone. Paris gave a startled look at what she was holding and started grinning as he handed the microphone to her.

"Ladies and gentlemen, it is my pleasure to announce the winner of the Miss Outer Space contest." Everyone left up in the stands froze, silence crashing down. She could hear the scampering of feet behind her, and hoped the right woman was there.

"The winner and new Miss Outer Space, Miss Alpha Centauri, Ethereal Savannah!"

Chapter Fifty-Three
The Getaway

Jenny dropped through the hole after Cap.

"Storm drain." She identified the large concrete pipe easily. "It must run out to the river, or close." Far off in the dimness, she could see a brighter area, although the only footsteps she could hear were her own, as she cast caution to the side and ran after Cap without trying to see the floor of the tunnel. If there was something there, she'd trip.

She tripped, and the something had a red readout of numbers, scrolling rapidly downward. She didn't bother cussing, just ran faster. Ahead she could see the light coming from the side, and a figure that suddenly collapsed in the entrance. A larger figure climbed over it and disappeared.

She followed, to see Cap closing in on another running figure. She paused a second to drag the unconscious pirate all the way out of the hole.

She surveyed the area, clipped lawns, the purple tree things, bulky round constructions and large angular buildings, a water or sewage treatment plant probably, sparsely lit by the floodlights scattered about, high on poles.

She flinched as a booming roar followed by an eruption of smoke and dust rolled from the hole behind her. Not that it should have been a surprise. She jogged over to Cap, stepping around the unconscious man on the ground.

"There's activity, but no lights in the first building, there." He gestured at a large metal-walled building.

"Let's get around back, see what we can hear."

They circled around the floodlit areas, keeping the purple things between them and the building as much as possible. "If they have night vision glasses, we're toast," she muttered.

"They're space pirates, not ground troops. And incompetent." Cap added, freezing behind a tree. Jenny went to one knee behind a low mushroomy thing, tracking multiple footfalls. Heavy ones. Jenny peeked out and saw two men, each with a figure over his shoulder pile through the door of the building unchallenged.

"Get us out of here!" the first one gasped, an officer apparently, as the sounds of movement doubled inside the building. "The fleet's all over the Arena."

The barely audible reply. " . . . vid . . . ", seemed to indicate that the pirates here had witnessed the debacle remotely.

Lights came up suddenly, shining through the windows and out the back of the building. Cap bolted up to the back corner of the building, peered around and waved her up. As her eyes adjusted, she realized the lights were actually quite dim, and the entire rear of the building was open, storage for large equipment perhaps. It was now being used as a jumpship hanger. It was the same small sleek type of ship as the Crazy Lady, crammed into the barely adequate space. Landing it must have been nerve racking, it looked as wide as the opening and the bulge of it stuck out the big bay doors.

"How many people were they planning on kidnapping?" Jenny whispered. "That ship isn't very large!" *For a jumpship,* she thought, eyeing its impressive bulk.

"I counted eleven pirates, there must have been at least a dozen more to grab even just the finalists. Five more visible here." Cap said.

Good night vision, Jenny concluded. "I suppose they could have this thing fitted up for passengers instead of cargo." She bit her lip. "Did they get two women, or were they carrying their wounded?"

"They were light enough to be carried easily," Cap admitted. "The next question before us is, where are they going?" Cap slid around the corner and knelt behind some boxes piled out of the way. Jenny joined him.

"What odds they're going to wherever the missing women were taken?" she murmured, looking around the warehouse. The ship loomed claustrophobically close over them, the ramp still down. Temptation. Irresistible. "Shall we?"

"Yes." Cap slid along behind more odds and ends that had been hastily shoved aside for the ship. Freezing periodically. Jenny copied him. The only pirates she could see had their backs to them, guarding the wrong side of their improvised hangar. Opposite the ramp, still no more pirates in sight. They traded glances, and walked quietly out and up the ramp.

The layout was the usual, they could hear murmured voices and electronic beeps coming from forward. They eased toward the stern of the ship; all was quiet. The cargo pods on the outboard side were open.

A quick glance inside one answered all her questions. Bunks and air recyclers. Doors that locked from the outside.

More voices came from behind them, steps on the ramp. Jenny hustled to the stairs and Cap followed on her heels, looking behind him. Apparently they'd been quick enough; the yelling voices carried only news of approaching forces and the need to quickly depart.

"Are we insane?" Jenny asked.

"Yes." Cap grinned. "We need to find out if the people being carried were pirates or beauty queens." She staggered a bit as the ship lurched backwards, biting her lip at the dragging crunch coming from the side. So much for the skill with which they landed.

Parked by feel, just like Mom. She grinned at the thought and looked around. "They won't be expecting anyone from the far side stairs, can we take them before they get off?" A metallic squeal as the ship scraped the building again set her teeth on edge. "We don't have much time."

Cap flattened to the floor and peered down the stairs. "Gun," he breathed, extending a hand. She offered him both the laser rifle she'd picked up and her little laser. He took the latter, and shot down the stairs like a sprinter out of the blocks.

Jenny hustled after him, but he was already out of sight. But leaving an easily followed trail. Two bound women lay on the deck inching away from the two messily dead pirates. She staggered again as the ship bounced off something a few times, then started rotating.

She dove for the pilot's compartment, dodging a body that came flying out. Another bloody mess was strapped into the pilot's seat. Cap hovered uncertainly. Jenny quickly reached out to the power controls and tapped the sensitive material just below the line showing the power level. Nothing noticeable happened. Lower.

One landing skid touched down and the ship started swiveling around it as it dragged. She shut down the power completely and the ship grounded with a thump. Looking out the viewport, she could see that they had just cleared the building.

There was movement out there. Not carrying lights, and barely visible even in the floodlights.

"I think the Marines have landed." She glanced at Cap. "Shall we let them deal with engineering and any other pirates around?"

***

Paris crawled out of the still smoking hole in the sewer pipe and nearly slipped as something rolled under his foot. He stooped and retrieved a nearly round two inch sphere of quartzite, and held it out for Lieutenant Bryson's perusal.

"Okay, I'll never bad mouth the Red Guards' rock throwing ability again, but where'd he go from here?" The lieutenant stepped over the still form of the pirate at his feet and advanced cautiously into the open.

Paris looked around uneasily. Another unconscious man lay on the ground ahead, and there was no sign of Cap or Jenny. "I suppose we can just follow the trail of bodies they're leaving behind."

"Who?"

Paris turned to find General Christianson coming up behind him. In his crisp dress uniform, he'd sensibly gone around instead of crawling through the damaged pipes. Figures in full ground combat gear were spreading out and moving toward the buildings ahead.

"Cap Midnight and Jenny Poppenhusen. They may have pursued the pirates this far," Paris replied.

"So long as they don't turn into hostages." The General scowled. "We're trying to do a headcount in that madhouse." He waved toward the stadium. "We may be missing some of

444

the young ladies."

Paris hesitated. "Everyone was running everywhere, it would be easy to lose a few."

"Yes, and we hope that's all there is to it, but until we find them all..." The General broke off as a subordinate galloped up behind him, waving some sort of scanner.

"We've got a ship powering up." His gesture toward the first warehouse was followed by a metallic scream and the entire structure quivered.

The barely visible figures of the marines were flowing toward the building. "Do they have anything that can bring down a ship?" Paris asked, a bit taken aback at the idea, trotting after the General who had apparently forgotten that he was unarmored.

"As slow moving as that is, yes." The General was quite certain. "We can hole one of the rings."

"The superconducting . . . umm, right." Paris hesitated. "If they've got hostages, should we . . . " He trailed off as the ship, two-thirds out of the building, ricocheted from one side of the opening to the other, and drifted the rest of the way out, starting to spin a bit.

"Haven't they got a pilot?" A landing skid hit the ground and started dragging along and acting like a pivot for the rotation. The ship thumped down, and settled. "That's pretty bad flying . . . " Paris's voice trailed off as he thought of what, or rather who, might have just happened to the pilot.

445

"Hey, Bryson," he called abruptly. "What do you want to bet the Girl Scout just captured another spaceship?"

The two uniformed officers glared at him, then turned back to the ship as the ramp lowered.

"Hello?"

Yep, Jenny.

"Don't shoot!"

He sauntered up to the ramp, marines closing in behind him, rifles at the ready. "Caught another one, have you?" Paris could feel the strain on his cheeks from his grin.

"Only halfway, your friends out there can clean out the engine room and so forth." She came down, grinning. Cap on her heels, supporting two staggering women, stepped out of the way as the marines climbed cautiously aboard.

Paris waffled between following the Marines and accompanying Jenny and Cap, but jerked around at the sound of cursing from General Christenson.

"Damn! But the ship they're in is local?" the General was apparently asking thin air, implant or ear rig no doubt. His gaze hit Paris and he scowled. "Descartes and Zimmer have escaped. They're in a racer, outrunning everything the Fleet has handy."

"They must have had plans to meet a jumpship," Jenny said, not budging as the General's glare hit her. "Could it have been that ship?" She gestured behind her.

The General frowned, but apparently in thought, not

disapproval. "It would take too long to get out there, I think." He turned though and flagged down another officer, who opined that being a jumpship it would take at least a week to get out far enough to meet the racer.

"They had hostages," Jenny pointed out. "They could take as long as they wanted, and split the fleet's ships between them."

Cap had left the two women somewhere and reappeared silently behind her.

"Yeah, but you know, this was a really stupid thing to do, any way you look at it." Paris bit his lip. "We need a pilot to check the Nav Comp on that ship."

The General leaned his head toward a skimmer that grounded, men hastily piling out, and into the captured jumpship. "There's one now." There was a long pause. "He reports that there was a plot for a least time course out to a reasonable jump distance."

"Is the course, or at any rate the general direction of the racer, toward that spot?" Jenny asked.

Paris wondered with resignation how long it would be before Jenny was back on board the ship and headed for a pirate rendezvous. From the way Cap was eyeing her, he was wondering also. General Christianson growled. "Civilians! Oughta shoot the lot of them. Or recruit them."

Might as well speed things up. "Sir, if you could get a crew together, we could take the ship . . . " Paris shut up at the General's glare.

"We'll have a complete crew here momentarily, then we," the General waved at the marines, "Will be off."

"Do you need a hostage to blubber and beg to the pursuing Fleet ships to not shoot and back off?" Jenny asked.

"Yes." Christianson smiled. "Fortunately the Fleet is a mixed service, and we won't be calling for volunteers."

"Drat." Jenny slumped again.

A larger skimmer grounded, crate and weapon toting uniformed men, and a single civilian clad woman scrambling out.

"Sir, I know both the perps . . . " Paris wondered if he really wanted to volunteer, but Christianson nodded decisively.

"Good idea. Can't let the Fleet hog all the glory." He turned to the officer approaching. "Captain Berrena, this is Captain Perris, CI. He will accompany you, he knows both of the escapees." He waved them both off. "Go as quickly as possible."

Paris trotted after the Fleet Captain, waving in Jenny's direction as he heard her call. "Sic 'em. And remember to duck!"

Paris felt out of place, but ran a quick inspection of the ship. It was an Earth manufactured ship, about the size of the Crazy Lady. The lower level had access to the cargo pods slotted in between the rings, fuel room and engineering that

448

took up most of the rest of the room inside the ring space. The bridge, well, more of a pilot's cubbyhole, was shoehorned into the front on the lower level.

A stairway on either side led to the upper level, which held four tiny bunkrooms and a single utilitarian bathroom tucked in wherever the engineering and fuel rooms allowed. Outboard of the upper circular corridor was mostly a blank wall, sporting only a few painted over hatches, presumably giving access to the upper engineering and fuel areas, or even the ring support structure. Forward against the jump rings was a combined food prep/dining/gym area. Tiny.

He wondered a bit why the upper level even had a ring corridor...but he already knew the answer: "That's how the Cinnabs build ships." Even human constructed ships tended to follow the same pattern, perhaps out of some uneasy feeling that with several thousand years of space travel behind them, the Cinnabs must have some reason for their basic layout.

A steep stairway led from there up to the "penthouse," the docking ring and airlock, that were only used for ship-to-station or ship-to-ship connections. He eyed it narrowly. There was no place to hide or set up an ambush, short of the mess area. The only positive note was that the stolen racer couldn't hold many people, and as far as they knew contained only the two escapees.

And a pilot, perhaps?

Returning to the lower level, he nodded to the ship's new Captain, and the Marine Captain. They all murmured polite "Captains" at each other, smiles twitching as they all refused to salute each other. Paris decided as the least useful officer to defer first.

"Since I'm CI, supposed to be undercover and haven't a uniform to my name closer than Earth, call me Perris. E not A, two Rs."

The Marine grinned. "So how much of your multi-million dollar singing income do you get to keep?" He stuck out a hand. "Ernie Helke."

Paris shook carefully, not wanting to get into a strength contest. "Not a penny more than is needed to keep up the façade, and forms to fill out like you wouldn't believe."

"Geeze." The marine shook his head in commiseration. "Call me Hell."

The Fleet Captain pulled his head out of the pilot's cubby long enough to tilt an ironic eyebrow at them. "Does this mean I get to be 'Captain'?"

"It is traditional for a ship's captain to be the only one actually addressed as such while onboard." Hell agreed.

"In that case, grab a hold, we're out of here."

The mass of the jump rings on an interstellar ship, even one designed for planetary landings, reduced their acceleration drastically. This ship was no exception, wallowing into the air and floating upward at what Paris

450

judged was barely one and a half gees.

Once the ship had dragged itself out of the atmosphere, their speed increased rapidly.

The speed of light communications kept them apprised of events from four hours ago as the fleet lost track of the escaping racer among the debris field of the system's wide-flung icy asteroid belt.

"Either they'll meet us, or they had someone standing by out there and they're gone already." Berrena opined, taking his turn at piloting the ship as the news played on the screens.

Captain Berrena, Hell, the female marine, Lieutenant Lisa Woods, and Paris each commandeered a room on the upper level, while the rest of the Marines claimed one of the converted cargo containers as their territory and the pilots and engineers grabbed another.

However nerve wracking the next week, they'd face it in comfort.

Chapter Fifty-Four
Worrying and Partying

Jenny surveyed the wreck of the Miss Outer Space Contest stage with some satisfaction. At least her part had come off well. Half of her attention was on the grim faced Criminal Investigation staff, as they in turn kept half their attention on news of things beyond their personal reach.

"What's happening?" Misty and Kissy had apparently ducked out of the impromptu parade and citywide party thrown, apparently, by the entire local audience. "Have they got the pirates?"

"Most of them, but simultaneous with the attack here, there was a breakout from Fleet headquarters out at the transfer station."

"Descartes and Zimmer?" Kissy hissed.

"Yep. Long gone." Jenny looked back at the CI officers circled around the comm. "Or at any rate, off the transfer station. They're in a ship, apparently an imported racer, that the fleet types keep saying they can catch eventually because it doesn't have jump rings."

"They must have had plans to meet a jumpship," Carl said. "Possibly the one from here that got away."

Barry flopped into a seat in the row behind Jenny and

opined that being a jumpship it would take at least a week to get out far enough to meet the racer.

"They may have hostages, we haven't finished the headcount," Jenny pointed out, suppressing guilt as she presented the cover story. "If they do, they could take as long as they wanted, and split the fleet's ships between them."

Frustrated by her inability to mention the subterfuge going on out there, Jenny stayed quiet as the news of events hours past caught up to them, reports on how the jail security was breached, how the little insystem racer had been overlooked because of its obvious lack of carrying capacity, an analysis of the "escaped" jump ship's probable power systems and probably limited range.

Finally the men around the communicator turned away. "They'll find it abandoned, eventually," opined one man about the racer. Jenny wasn't sure if he was aware of the capture of the ship here or not. "It doesn't have to go far, just far enough to meet a jumpship."

Jenny could hear the defeat in his voice.

"If they get away now, you can't chase them, can you?" Kissy asked quietly.

The officer, Jenny peered at his shirt tag, Lieutenant Garrigan, replied, "No. Even the Fleet presence here for the conference is a borderline violation of the Joint Agreement. Thank God the Cinnabs aren't sticklers for the rules. We'll only get crap from all the member countries about wasting their hard earned tax money on our expansionist schemes. Once we're not in 'hot pursuit' we're stopped cold."

"What's the time lag?" Jenny asked. "About four hours?"

"Just under." Garrigan glared at the comm unit. "Whatever is going to happen has already happened."

Jenny trotted a few feet down the ramp to the arena intercom system and punched the button marked media control and started talking to someone. "Scan the news channels, there's something going out at the Transfer Station. If the regular channels have anything, could you put it on this screen, without preempting anything the investigators need?" She paused. "Okay, thanks." As she stepped back, the huge replay screens lit. "The tech guy said the cops weren't needing any more replays, so he's . . ." she shut up as the speakers came up with the vid.

The scene was one of carnage, not unlike what surrounded them, but in a smaller area. " . . . Fleet is still in pursuit of the escaped pirates, but captured transmissions indicate that they have a hostage and are steadily putting more space between themselves and Joint Fleet pursuit."

"Captured transmissions!" Lieutenant Bryson stomped up behind them. "We can't code emergency transmissions deeply enough to stop their decrypting without slowing communications down even more." He scowled at the weedy talking head as if he were personally responsible for the problem.

Which could be true, Jenny mused. The kid had that nerdy look, and was definitely not one of the regular talking heads. Those dignitaries were all here, covering the contest and now the street party. The company may well have been reduced to throwing their in-house tech in front of the vidcams.

Bryson heaved a sigh. "It would be pure luck for the fleet to catch them now, and we used up all the luck up down here."

"Don't be superstitious. This was bravery, skill and daring."

He glared half-heartedly at her. "Amateur night. Pure luck none of the contestants got shot." He jammed his hands into his pockets, frowned and pulled out a round stone. "Okay," he muttered, tossing it up and catching it. "Maybe there was one professional around."

He looked back at his colleagues starting to drift away from the comm and back to the collecting of evidence. The stage was empty of the Beauty Queens and their entourages, and looked shabby in the merciless light of the floods.

He grinned suddenly, shedding his professional seriousness with a speed that had her blinking. "You know, if we slipped out now, they couldn't catch me to make me start writing reports until morning, and I believe I need at least a little partying first.

Jenny nodded agreement. The next week, waiting for

456

In the Rift

Paris's ship to make contact with the racer, was going to go slow. Might as well start with a party. She grabbed the dubious looking Cap and followed the Lieutenant.

Chapter Fifty-Five
Playing (the) Pirates

Paris found himself in charge of food, and was shocked to be complimented on his results. Apparently between the limited expectations of the Marines and a month of occasionally assisting Georges on the pirate station, he'd added a new talent to his repertoire.

Lisa Woods was delighted. "I may be female, but I burn water, trust me." She was slouching around the ship with disheveled hair and slightly ripped blouse, stage setting for her twice a day performance as a hostage begging the two 'pursuing' Joint Fleet ships to keep their distance. She and Paris had quickly ID each other as Alphans, partly from their original colonist family names, and partly recognition of subtle genetic engineering differences. They were in fact second cousins and had probably met at one of the big family reunions when children.

"Not that I remember you," Paris apologized. "At that age I thought girls had cooties."

She snorted. "The only boy I recall was Marlin Something-or-other. I developed a major crush on him."

"Marlin Riverside. I hate his guts, mostly because every woman that's ever met him has developed a major crush on him, and partly because he's so smug. He owns Zulu Recording, filthy rich, on his fifth wife last I heard."

"Oh, dear. Well, I wouldn't marry him myself, but mostly because I think the First Families are quite sufficiently inbred already." She twinkled a bit at him. "I'll bet genetically I'm closer to being your sister than a distant cousin."

Paris shook his head. "Nah, my family does lots of outbreeding. I'm one of the Terrible Mountain Perris's"

"Oh dear," Lisa leaned away from him in mock horror. "Them. You're not actually an ichimp, by my family's standards."

"I don't get that," Hell put in. "You both look like humans, and both your last names are from human colonists, aren't they? I don't think I've ever seen but a few actual ichimps."

Paris nodded. "The colony was basically started by two thousand ichimps and perhaps thirty humans. Not to mention the Huangs, Woods and Terribles, who were all variously genetically engineered and only mostly human. Actually, I haven't a clue as to what species to call Ivan D. Terrible.

"In any case, the early ichimp genetic engineering was unstable, it tended to not replicate properly. Anyone, male or female, who wanted to up their chances of a live, fairly normal baby used the frozen ova and sperm banks that were

460

onboard the Chamberlain. One hundred percent human ova and sperm.

"We hijacked the ship and had to take what we could get." He grinned as Hell scowled, catching the insult to purebreds that was an Alphan trademark.

"There were a large number of hybrids in the population already, and within a century we were all virtually human. Even after we went back to the old-fashioned methods of reproduction, babies with high percentages of spliced genes had a much higher rate of miscarriage, infant mortality, handicaps and infertility. It has gotten quite rare to see someone who actually looks like an ichimp."

Lisa added, "You left out the part about most of the original ichimps being male; slave labor, you know, just enough females to keep them happy. Most of the guys that wanted kids had to use the frozen human ova and artificial wombs."

She shrugged. "Everyone is pretty well resigned to the eventual elimination of the ichimp genes through natural selection, although some of them seem to have stabilized and become widespread."

"Which genes are those?" Hell asked.

"Strength is the most widespread one." Paris nodded at Lisa. "Lisa's general build, just a bit short, just a bit long armed." He held out his own hands. "Long hand bones. Very handy for a musician, but unless you know, you probably wouldn't think 'ichimp'. Don't ever arm wrestle someone with hands like mine."

"Go on!" The tall broad marine looked him over. Paris knew he was seeing a thin man, barely over average height.

Hell switched his inspection to the grinning Lisa dubiously. She propped her elbow on the table and held up her arm invitingly.

"Nope. I'm not gonna challenge you. I have my reputation to consider." His eyes twinkled. "It wouldn't be gentlemanly to beat you."

The Captain called up for Lisa, and the next performance of Hostage in Space. Everyone trailed after, sworn to silence as she had hysterics and burst into tears. Laughter was reserved for after the comm was definitely off. The effects of her performances on the civilians of Autumn were rehashed in every news show, as Lisa's pleas were broadcast rather than tight beamed, hoping to fool the escaped Descartes and Zimmer both directly and through the unscripted rage of the locals on the News every night.

Paris hoped they weren't all lynched by enraged mobs when they got back to Autumn and confessed to the subterfuge.

"Okay," Berrena called out to everyone. "Here's where the course starts getting interesting."

The Eta Pegasi system was a double star system. The G type Giant had inherited the old Earth name Matar, but it was the smaller main sequence F star that Autumn orbited. Autumn had been almost between the two in its orbit and the ship had been programmed to loop south and away from the Giant. They were far enough out now that small jumps, while still much more costly in fuel than normal acceleration, were large enough to be a useful tactic in losing pursuit.

"First jump." Paris grabbed a sensibly placed bar on the wall as the acceleration died and the queasy twist of a jump rippled through him. The thrust picked up immediately, dropping his feet back to the floor. Accelerating through a jump was a major energy hog, one this small ship couldn't afford. What it did have was a second capacitor.

"Calculated the jumps close, didn't they?" Ken Alban was off duty, but awake, craning for a look at the radar screen. "I think we'd lose the fleet even if they weren't trying to let us get away."

"Surely they can cut them as close as we can," Paris protested.

"Oh, sure, but they have to try to hit at the same phase and angle, or they'll come out wide and or short. By cutting the margin so close, if they try over jumping us, they'll probably splat." Paris could see the military ships on the visual screens between intervening heads. First one, then the other set of running lights cut out, but the barely seen reflections from the white hull of the first one stayed where they had been. The second vanished entirely.

Ken snickered. "The first one splatted." He looked around at the crowd and decided to lecture. "See, too close to the peak or trough of a gravity wave the angle of incidence is too steep and instead of folding through gravity space, you bounce, with large induced electrical currents in everything. They'll have to reset all their breakers and recharge their capacitor before they can go anywhere."

He looked back at the screen. "There's the second ship. She jumped slightly past the phase where we jumped, and didn't go as far. So we're even further ahead, and because we have a second capacitor..." He reached up and grabbed a bar, as they jumped again. "We jumped as soon as we hit the critical threshold of the next wave. We'll have to run straight until the capacitors are charged up again, but they'll never catch us now." He grinned. "It's so much fun being on this side of the chase, for a change!"

Two more preprogrammed jumps and they were in the ice belt. Some preprogrammed dodging and even knowing where they should be, they couldn't detect the fleet ships.

"Who programmed this thing?" Paris tackled Captain Berrena before his shift.

"Hard to say, but it appears to be a canned contingency program." He jerked his chin at the pilot's cubbyhole. "These pirates seem to have top of the line, AI level computers. The program uses input navigation, radar and gravmeter data to simultaneously lose any following ships and navigate to a particular spot."

"A regular contraband or supply rendezvous?" Paris hazarded. "Drug runners are like that, with drop spots so they never actually meet others in their chain."

"That could be. Makes more sense than having something so complex for a just-in-case-of-pursuit."

Paris thought back to the Far Seeker's hijacking . . . "You know, I don't think they have a lot of pilots, and probably fewer specialty navigators. When they hijacked the Far Seeker, they didn't kill the pilots or engineers. I think they were going to try to suborn them, or something less pleasant."

Berrena's eyes narrowed. "Which would make comps like this worth the money."

"When we're done here, I think perhaps some experts should dissect the comp. We might be able to trace its sale from the manufacturer..."

"Corundum Computers."

"Ah, that's the company that's using those natural rubies that are mined out here instead of artificial crystals. It's a subsidiary of the Mayde Company, that owns the system where they are found." Paris suppressed a smile. *Jenny strikes again!* "They're supposed to be really good—if they work at all."

"Well, this one really works. And someone who knew what they were doing programmed it." He showed his teeth.

"I'd like to meet him, because I really can't think of a legitimate use for this program."

"Contact!"

Berrena squeezed in close to peer at the screen. "Yep. That's the racer. Bet they're glad to see us." He backed out, teeth and eyes gleaming in anticipation.

"The computers are exchanging information." The pilot sounded surprised, and after a moment's thought, Paris caught the inference.

"Who owns that racer?" He murmured. "We really need to ask him how it happened that the escapees stole a ship that was programmed to share protocols with pirate vessels."

The 'normal' acceleration suddenly slacked to about a tenth.

"Protocols, nothing." Berrena had lost his humorous streak. "They're maneuvering to mate airlocks with us." He hustled out and headed for the marines' quarters.

Paris stuck his head far enough into the pilot's cubby to see the visuals of the racer closing in on their top hatch. "Why a tenth G?" he asked.

"As long as both ships are doing it, it's nearly as easy as no acceleration at all, and a lot more convenient for transferring people. It's standard to dock at about a tenth G." Ken assured him. "For little ships docking to jumpships," he hastened to add. "They have their docking rings on the bottom, so nobody's upside down. If it was another

466

jumpship, we'd probably do it in zero G." He waved at the overhead. "Not that the ship isn't built to go either way, but it's hell on the kitchen and quarters."

"Huh." He eyed the textured ceiling, which bore a strong resemblance to the deck, and the circular seal around the pilots' cubby, could it rotate?

Pulling his mind back to the present, he turned and trotted around the ring to the stairs to the upper deck and then forward again to the steep steps up to the top airlock. The Marines were assembling quickly, followed by Captain Berrena, buttoning his uniform jacket.

So formal, to welcome pirates aboard? Paris kept that thought to himself.

Hell and Lisa, both in civilian dress, were the only people in sight of the airlock, Hell behind the 'frightened' woman with a gun to her head. Lisa had a pistol in each of the hands she held behind her back. Paris hoped neither Descartes nor Zimmer, or anyone else with them, knew the crew of this ship. In theory they'd walk right out and into the uniformed Marines.

Paris hastily joined Captain Berrena well back out of the marines' way, feeling the ship jolt as the docking rings caught. He strained his ears and heard the airlock door open. After a long silence, he heard Hell's voice. "All right, c'mon down." He came backing down the stairs, pulling Lisa after him, but with his gun holstered now, as if satisfied that

467

Descartes and Zimmer weren't bringing in marines. A nice touch. Down from the stairway, he 'roughly' 'shoved' his hostage to the side, and stepped to the side himself. "Welcome aboard," he said, with a genial wave. Zimmer shuffled out, looking very much the worse for wear. Descartes was also a bit shabby, but still held himself confidently and sneering, hands in his jacket pockets. He was behind Zimmer but was still quicker to register the rest of the reception committee. The Marines in full uniform, a mix of stun guns and laser rifles aimed at him. He started, half turning his head back up the stairs as if to flee, but froze as Sergeant Hodges closed in on him. "Hands up, bring them out of the pockets slowly and empty."

Descartes slowly brought empty hands into sight. Zimmer's face went blank for a moment, then he slumped. All the way to the deck, hands over his ears . . . Paris had just enough time to throw himself around the corner and cover his own ears as the stun grenade's blast screamed through his bones, the vibration at just the correct frequency to scramble the brain's natural signals . . . Jagged flashes of light darting in his peripheral vision, ears ringing, he staggered to his feet and back around the corner.

Descartes was the only one moving. At point-blank range he should have been comatose for the better part of a day. In centuries of use, only a few genetically altered people had brain functions so different that stunners didn't affect them.

468

Only the very, very rare Speed gene rendered one immune to the effects.

Oh. Shit.

Paris belly flopped beside the nearest Marine, grabbing his laser rifle, wrapping the Marine's hand around it for the implant that would satisfy the weapon's safety program, and fired a long, wild, barely aimed burst over the prone bodies sprawled around the deck.

Descartes whipped around the far corner at inhuman speed, and Paris scurried over to the wall comm and triggered the panic button. "One intruder, with enhanced speed. Shoot on sight."

Gods! All the marines are here, out cold on the floor.

He grabbed the non-regulation laser pistol Hell had held to Lisa's head, and plastered himself against the forward wall to get a long distance look around the corner. Wisdom from training so long ago.

When facing an opponent with Speed, you must keep your distance so your reflexes have time to act before he is on you.

Squeezing along, with his back to the outer wall, trying to see in all directions at once, he slid around to where he could see down the stairs to the lower level. He launched himself down the stairs at a run. Either Descartes would be waiting for him, or he'd get down in time to regain a clear field of fire.

His right foot was grabbed before he was halfway down and he measured his length along the rest of the flight, trying to twist and fire as he went down. Even in the low acceleration, his ribs met the steps with painful force.

His foot released, he tumbled the rest of the way down and threw himself across the corridor against the outside wall, pistol sweeping the now empty curve. He slipped quickly to the left, checking the pilots' cubbyhole. Ken Alban was slumped over the controls, his head at an odd angle.

Paris had a second's warning, a flicker of movement out of the corner of his eye, but only enough to start to move, then his right arm was wrenched backwards. He threw himself back with it, ramming Descartes and grabbing a wrestling hold.

If in close quarters, hold on, don't let them get a full swing, or kick at you.

He wrapped himself around the man, trapping his arms, wrapping his legs around him, as much to get them away from any kicks as to accomplish anything, and squeezed. There were more people coming, the engineers, and as Descartes pounded him against the wall, he flipped the pistol toward one of them.

Descartes lunged for it but he held on, pinning Descartes' arms, and squeezed harder, trying to cut off his breath. Descartes tried to run, but Paris dropped a leg and dumped them in a tangled heap.

470

In the Rift

Mike Johnson snatched the pistol. Descartes tried to twist away from it, but he wasn't abnormally strong, and he couldn't move with Paris clinging leech-like to him.

"Head." Paris gasped, not daring relax his grip enough for a deep breath. "Kill him."

Descartes jerked futilely, trying to shift Paris into the line of fire, but Johnson stepped up, put the barrel against his head and pulled the trigger. Paris shoved the quivering body away, and climbed shakily to his feet.

"Thank you." He limped back to the pilot's cubby, to check Ken. No pulse. He looked over his shoulder at Johnson. "See if Remo's all right, and get him up here. Wait, give me the gun." He limped back up the stairs, where the Marines were still unconscious; Berrena, having been the most distant, was twitching. He pulled himself up into the airlock and through to the racer. A quick search showed that it was empty.

Mike was hunched over the Captain when he staggered back down. "Remo?"

"At the controls." Mike sat back "Why the hell did he kill Ken?"

"I suspect he was just in a hurry." Paris started rolling the marines over, checking pulses, loosening their collars and belts. They were all alive, but the ones closest to the grenade didn't have good color. The nearest air unit was standard Cinnab; he adjusted the oxygen levels up as high as they would go. Hell and Hodges had been the closest. They both looked bad. The other engineer came in then, with the med kit, Paris grabbed the blood monitor and checked that their blood oxygen levels were rising, then took the handcuffs from Hodges' limp hand and bound Zimmer.

He limped back down to the pilot's cubby. Ken's body had joined Descartes on the floor, he stepped past and hailed Remo, before coming into sight. As he'd suspected, Remo was armed and angry. "Have you radioed Joint Fleet?"

"Yeah, just got a reply, they'll be here in two hours." Remo waved at the controls. "Should I change anything? Get the acceleration back up?"

"No. I think this is probably best for the Marines." Catching a curious look, he amplified. "Stun grenade at point blank to maybe five meters. They're going to be out for a while, and hurting when they do wake up."

As the senior officer conscious, Paris prowled the ship, bouncing from checking the marines, all looking better, to hanging over Remo's shoulder waiting for the Joint Fleet ships, to resisting the urge to kick Zimmer. When the Fleet ships finally arrived, the shaky but conscious Berrena detached the racer, then Paris thankfully handed the ships to the Fleet and the marines to the doctors.

Done.

Chapter Fifty-Six
Homeward Bound

"What on Earth are you doing?" Nicole's voice interrupted Jenny's note taking. "Hiding in an obscure corner of the bar, watching a vid cooking show?"

"Taking notes, this Fancy Farmer person is quite good, even if she makes some Beauty Queens look like geniuses." Jenny straightened out a grin. "I used to watch this show every once in a while and laugh my head off at the blatant advertising."

Nicole sniffed, peering at her notes. "Interstellar brand Autocheeser, Starcher and, eww, Lactomatic? That's *disgusting*."

"Very practical, out here, to use all the tube cloned foods you can," Jenny pointed out. "If you can scrounge up the basic nutrients. Which are mostly the non-edible parts of the crops you grow the old-fashioned way. Protein's the hardest. You've got to supply all the necessary amino acids."

"Well, if you ask me, some of that stuff sounds like a disease, not something to eat." Nicole scowled at her. "I take it you're still thinking about living in that space station?"

"Yes. Quincy's got everyone's proxy authorizations and will finalize all the legal stuff. He says we can take possession in about three months, although the Joint Fleet will probably hang around longer than that." Jenny glanced sidelong at her sister. "So I'm going back to Earth next week to arrange things with the University, and buy all kinds of stuff, then come back to help start up the station. How about you?"

"I need to be back on Earth by the end of the year, according to my contract." Nicole looked more relaxed and happier than Jenny could ever remember. "It was so nice of Paris to look it over for me, I had no idea what the standard percentage was, and would never have had the nerve to ask for that large an advance. So what ship are you taking?"

"'The Queen of the Waves', the ship we should have been on for the trip out here. It's leaving next week."

"Maybe I'll book a cabin, too." Nicole eyed her. "What about that man?"

"Cap? He's in charge of collecting everything we think we'll need immediately to run a commercial refueling station and getting it out there. He's off now with Barry, Carl and Terry checking out 'The Loose Goose'."

"I can't believe you named a pirate ship that!"

"Ex-pirate ship. Neither can we," Jenny admitted. "It's the sort of thing that happens when you leave names up to kids. Apparently it's both a musical group that all the older kids like and a cartoon character that the little kids like."

She shrugged. "Anyway, Georges is going to start his own restaurant, Misty and Kissy are going to start a hotel.

474

In the Rift

"Opal and Paula are selling their shares to Mac, who'll probably buy more, as soon as the legalities are done, and open a new office of his import-export business. Frank is thinking about a casino, but Georges says he'd make more money working as a waiter for him. All the families are heading further out, they're going to stick together for now. And Paris and Obadiah are keeping their shares, even though they probably won't be back anytime soon."

"What will you be doing, once you get back, I mean?"

"I'm not really sure," Jenny admitted. "They'll probably have hired someone with actual training to maintain the air and water recycling machinery, and just about everything else." She dropped her gaze to the University catalogue she had up on her second screen. "I guess I'll just see what's needed and learn how to do it." She grinned at Nicole. "I've gotten good at being bossy, so maybe I'll just sit around giving orders, or something."

"Well, I suspect after all the pirates and hijackers, that you can easily deal with legitimate spacers," Nicole admitted, turning and standing then as the lead elements of the Miss Outer Space entourage poured into the lobby. Ethereal herself was nearly invisible in the mob until it opened up and displayed her for the worship of the vidcams and adoring bachelors of the New Territories.

"How many marriage proposals have you had, so far?" Jenny asked curiously.

"Three thousand nine hundred and twenty nine, as of yesterday." Nicole smirked. "I haven't checked my mail yet today."

"Three . . . " Jenny said admiringly. "That's the highest total I've heard so far." The majority of the staffs and friends of the seventy-five contestants had been single, and seemed to be inclined to stay in the New Territories and collect husbands. "The last time I checked, the score was running thirty-six weddings, four hundred forty-five betrothals, and five hundred and sixty-nine bachelorettes still being madly pursued by multiple suitors."

Nicole giggled. "Are you counting yourself in that?"

"But of course. Although," Jenny admitted, "My twenty-two puts me dead last in the competition for sheer volume of proposals."

"Ethereal's probably got that in the bag," said Nicole, smirking. "But she's under contract not to actually get married for her year as Miss Outer Space."

"Nope," Jenny said. "You're way ahead. I asked Ethereal's new secretary this morning. I think everyone knows she has to go back to Earth and spend the year doing publicity stuff. You don't seem the least bit inclined to accept any of yours."

"That's for sure." Nicole was firm. "I'll finish up my year as Miss Great Plains, and actually get some money for public appearances now. HighDHo Productions says they'll

476

schedule all the vid sessions around my appearance schedule; they know it'll be great publicity." She nodded happily. "The first vid should be released about the time of the next Miss Outer Space Pageant."

"My sister the adventure flick vid star!" Jenny laughed. "You're perfect for it, and the publicity from this will really jump start your career."

"So, what about you?" Nicole looked at her worriedly. "Are you going to accept any of your proposals?"

"No way."

"Well, I shouldn't comment. Look at what I've been sleeping with for the last six months. And speaking of stars," Nicole was staring over her head. "Here's Paris. You're looking very subdued, today."

Jenny grinned. "No makeup? No glitter? You're not giving up your musical career, are you?"

Paris made a rude noise. "I wish! I'm under orders to depart as unobtrusively as possible, in the hope that no one notices what I've been up to." He grimaced, then struck a heroic pose. "As long as the music scene is saturated with money, drugs and violence and politicians keep sticking their noses in with their hands out for donations, I'll be there, fighting for truth, justice and safe nanos."

"Looking like I need a visit to the vet." He grinned and flapped a loose wrist at them. "Nicole, daaaahling, if you ever have a problem, just come to me, and I will use it!"

"Isn't that supposed to be 'fix it'?" Nicole tried and failed for a censorious tone.

Paris just grinned. "I figured you knew me too well to believe that."

"So, is the Fleet, or CI, going to find the others?" Jenny asked.

"We know where they were probably going to go, the name of the station at any rate, and where it is supposed to be." Paris shrugged. "Apparently it's a bare bones trading post where the miners from a couple of dozen systems can sell to the buyers from the refineries closer in. It doesn't have that bad a reputation, no drug problems, more than a few business type complaints, but nothing actually illegal.

"We'll know in another four months whether the women were actually taken there, and what happened." He scowled. "It's a joint Fleet/CI operation, so there will be some actual criminal investigators onboard to hopefully ask the right questions and follow the right leads." He ran frustrated hands through his hair. "After the vote and if they hurry up and finalize all the paperwork, and submit the signed formal request for admission to the parliament. It seems to be taking forever, and legally the fleet can't operate out here until it's a done deal." He cleared his throat. "Of course it's purely a rumor, and you definitely didn't hear it from me, that a few ships just might have already quietly slipped off somewhere."

In the Rift

Nicole sighed. "I hope they find them." She gestured at the packed lobby around Ethereal. "Most of the men out here are decent; I keep hoping that however far away they've been taken, human nature will still be the same. Mostly good."

The crowd cheered as Ethereal finished her speech, then gradually oozed out the front doors as the new Miss Outer Space started her triumphal tour. She was scheduled to visit seven other planets in the New Territories, then work her way inward, arriving back on Earth in about five months. Nicole looked briefly envious, then a bit thoughtful.

"Starring in adventure vids will be a lot more interesting than the Miss Outer Space tour, and it doesn't automatically expire in a year." Jenny mentioned.

"I know." Nicole looked perplexed. "Why did I fixate on this stupid contest?"

"Because it was the first and easiest way out you could see," guessed Jenny. "Mother always took you to those child beauty contests, it was an easy step in a familiar direction for you."

Paris sniffed. "Because it gave you an excuse to dress up in the latest fashions and travel around showing them off?" He intercepted their glares, and smirked. "Hey, that's what Ethereal always said, it wasn't my idea." He sniffed. "I'm innocent." And glanced at his watch. "And I have a shuttle to catch. Adieu, ladies." He bowed himself out, angling away from the tail of Ethereal's audience.

Nicole watched him go. "He is rather cute, isn't he?"

"And you probably won't ever need to shoot him," Jenny pointed out. "Although I wouldn't rule out wanting to." She glanced up at her sister. "Nicole, do you think you could possibly go an entire month without a boyfriend?"

Nicole looked horrified. "A whole month?"

Laughing, Jenny followed her out.

About the Author

I was born and raised in California, and have lived more than half my life, now, in Texas.

Wonderful place. I caught almost the first bachelor I met here, and we're coming up on our thirty-ninth anniversary.

My degree's in Geology. After working for an oil company for almost ten years as a geophysicist, I "retired" to raise children. As they grew, I added oil painting, sculpting and throwing clay, breeding horses, volunteering in libraries and for the Boy Scouts, and treasurer for a friend's political campaign. Sometime in those busy years, I turned a love of science fiction into a part time job reading slush (Mom? Someone is *paying* you to read??!!)

I've always written, published a few short stories. But now that the kids have flown the nest, I'm calling writing a full time job.

In the Rift is my twenty-seventh novel, placed in the same universe as Fancy Free but otherwise unconnected.

Email pamuphoff@gmail.com to join the mailing list for notifications of new releases, or follow me on facebook at https://www.facebook.com/pam.uphoff

www.ingramcontent.com/pod-product-compliance
Lightning Source LLC
Chambersburg PA
CBHW051937020726
47501CB00001B/171